MANNER OF DEATH

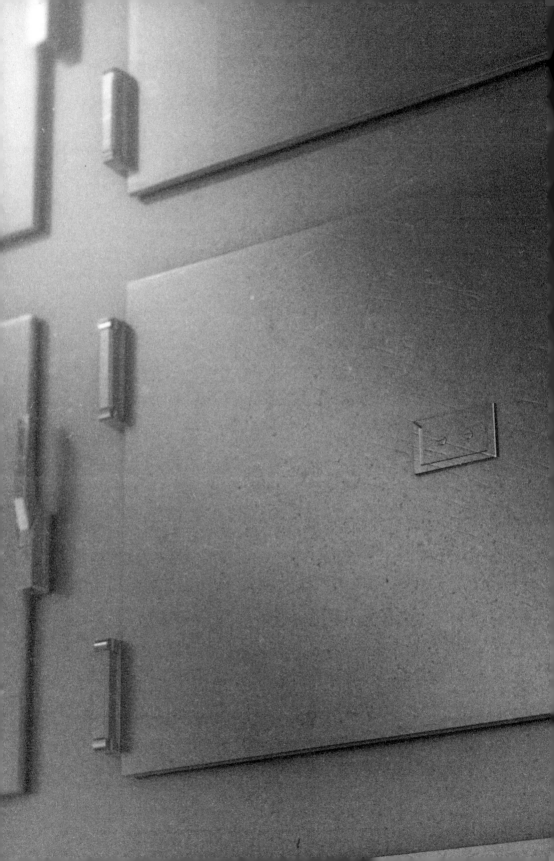

MANNER
OF DEATH

A NOVEL

ROBIN COOK

G. P. PUTNAM'S SONS
NEW YORK

PUTNAM
— EST. 1838 —

G. P. Putnam's Sons
Publishers Since 1838
An imprint of Penguin Random House LLC
penguinrandomhouse.com

Library of Congress Cataloging-in-Publication Data

Names: Cook, Robin, author.
Title: Manner of death : a novel / Robin Cook.
Identifiers: LCCN 2023040174 (print) | LCCN 2023040175 (ebook) |
ISBN 9780593713891 (hardcover) | ISBN 9780593713907 (ebook)
Subjects: LCGFT: Thrillers (Fiction) | Medical fiction. | Novels.
Classification: LCC PS3553.O5545 M36 2023 (print) |
LCC PS3553.O5545 (ebook) | DDC 813/.54—dc23/eng/20230905
LC record available at https://lccn.loc.gov/2023040174
LC ebook record available at https://lccn.loc.gov/2023040175
p.   cm.

Printed in the United States of America
1st Printing

Book design by Ashley Tucker

For Jean,
My partner

MANNER
OF
DEATH

PROLOGUE

Hank Roberts walked with a definite spring to his step and a whistle under his breath as he headed east on West 46th Street in New York's Hell's Kitchen neighborhood. Until the late '70s and early '80s it was an Irish American working-class neighborhood with a plethora of seedy bars among its warehouses and tenements and boasted an impressive crime rate. Calling it *gritty* back then was a euphemism despite it housing the acclaimed Actors Studio and serving as the temporary home to many ultimately famous actors and actresses. Hank was aware of the area's history because he'd been inappropriately brought there on a handful of occasions by his ne'er-do-well older brother from their home in Weehawken, New Jersey, when Hank was a skinny preteen in middle school and his brother was toying with the idea of an acting career.

To get to Hell's Kitchen, Hank had taken a rideshare from the Upper West Side where he was presently residing, and he'd had the driver drop him off on the corner of Twelfth Avenue and 46th Street in the literal shadow of the WWII aircraft carrier *Intrepid*, which was now a museum permanently anchored in one of the Hudson River berths. The weather was clear and seasonally chilly, which justified his dark peacoat and a wool Navy watch cap. Dangling from his shoulder by a leather strap was a Gucci satchel that contained a Glock 19 fitted with a silencer as well as a few other tools and cleaning materials he thought he might need, including a second, ghost Glock, which he planned to leave at the scene.

With a sense of excitement, Hank had to cool his heels while waiting for the traffic light to change so he could cross the busy avenue. Once he had, he found himself passing a collection of upscale bars, night-clubs, and multiethnic restaurants nestled between the few original businesses remaining in the rapidly gentrifying neighborhood. Despite it being a midweek Wednesday night, the area was hopping with smart-looking people and was generally far different from the place he'd visited as a youngster with his brother. Like the environment, he was a different person, no longer a seventy-five-pound slip of a boy, but a heavily mus-cled, six-foot-three, two-hundred-and-ten-pound, forty-eight-year-old ex–Navy SEAL who still worked out every day.

The reason Hank was feeling chipper yet anxious was because he was totally caught up, heart and soul, in a *mission*. He had been tasked by his current employer, Action Security, to carry out a job in a fashion that had required significant planning over the previous twenty-four hours, for which he was to be paid a sizable fee on top of his normal salary. As with his other Action Security missions, of which there had been almost a dozen, tonight's was going to require him to utilize his extensive military experience as well as all the hands-on instruction he'd had in Naval Special Warfare and SEAL Qualification Training.

What all that schooling had accomplished was to transform a twen-tysomething Hank Roberts from a relatively normal, empathetic, ath-letic, and competitive college graduate into a highly trained killer. That had been all well and good until his fourth mission, which took place in Idlib, Syria. That mission's goal was to take out Abu Rahim al-Afri, a deputy leader of the Islamic State of Iraq and the Levant. The goal had been achieved, but it also left a lasting effect on him. Six years later, he could recall details of that ill-fated operation as if it had happened the previous week. Back then, Hank had been a member of SEAL Team Five, deployed to Iraq, where he had participated in four successful operations against ISIL, all of which had gone off without a hitch thanks to superb intelligence gathering, extensive planning, full-scale mock-up rehearsals, and flawless execution.

Even now, as he neared the location of the evening's mission, he could remember as if it were yesterday, sitting in the Black Hawk helicopter with six of his fellow SEAL Team Five comrades in the blackness of the wee hours of the morning, closing in on their objective and experiencing the invariable rush of adrenaline. Because of the noise of the copter's engine and the characteristic thump of its rotors there'd been no conversation, nor was there any reason to think that this mission was going to be any different than the previous four, as they had made equivalent preparations, complete with exhaustive rehearsals.

Once over the target, which was a two-story concrete block structure with a flat roof, Hank had been the second on the Fast Rope, mere seconds behind Lieutenant Commander Miller as had been planned. As he slid down the rope, he was shocked to hear the characteristic *rat-a-tat-tat* of a Kalashnikov despite the copter's deafening racket and wind. For nearly a month of nightly surveillance of the terrorist leader's home, there had never been a rooftop guard, but it was painfully obvious to him that that wasn't the situation on this fateful night.

Reacting by instinct, Hank immediately let go of the Fast Rope and dropped the last four or five feet rather than waiting for his boots to touch the ground. As a consequence, he landed full force on Lieutenant

Commander Miller's corpse. Rolling off onto the concrete roof, he managed to extract his P266 sidearm because his M16A2 assault rifle was slung over his shoulder on a snug sling for the descent from the helicopter. In the next instant, Chief Petty Officer Nakayama landed on top of Miller and Hank. From his agonized breathing and reflexive twitching, he knew Nakayama, too, had taken some rounds from the ISIL guard, but the man's labored breathing ended when Hank felt him absorb several more rounds that were being sprayed in their direction.

With some effort, because Nakayama's body was partially on top of him, Hank rolled over onto his belly and looked over the top edge of Miller's torso. In the eerie green light of his night vision goggles, he sighted the ISIL fighter in the shadow of the building's bulkhead, which was slated to provide SEAL Team Five access to the building's interior. Holding his weapon upward at waist level, and lit up by muzzle flashes from the Kalashnikov's barrel, the terrorist was now firing at the armored belly of the Black Hawk. Without a second's hesitation, Hank used the laser night sight of his SIG Sauer pistol to pinpoint the guard and pulled off several rounds. He was rewarded by seeing the man drop his weapon, stagger a few steps backward, then fall to the roof's surface.

In the next instant, Hank was joined by three more of his teammates as they reached the roof unscathed while the Black Hawk peeled away to wait to be summoned for the extraction. All three SEALs already had their assault rifles in their hands. Hank faced Lieutenant D'Agostino and made a motion across his throat as he pointed to Miller and Nakayama. The lieutenant nodded and then waved for what was left of the team to rush over to the bulkhead, where they made short work of the door.

The rest of the ill-fated mission was equally as bad, although there was no more loss of any members of SEAL Team Five. The helicopter and firefight on the roof had alerted the building's occupants, particularly the target, whose response was to leave his bedroom on the second floor and find refuge among his mini harem on the ground floor.

Armed with an intricate knowledge of the sizable home's floor plans, the SEAL team had no trouble finding Abu Rahim al-Afri and dispatching him, but not before a number of other ISIL fighters had roused themselves from nearby homes to join what became a serious firefight. In sharp contrast to the other missions Hank had been on, this one resulted in a horrendous loss of life, even of women and children. On top of that, the extraction was delayed and rather difficult because an Airborne Tactical Extraction Platform had to be brought to the scene to get Miller's and Nakayama's bodies back to base. SEALs never left any of their comrades behind.

As Hank approached his current objective, now less than a half block away, he felt a welcome rush of adrenaline, wonderfully reminiscent of when he'd been on active duty. For him it was like an addict's fix, something he desperately needed. At the same time, on the flip side of the coin, the welcome euphoria also reminded him about how much that fateful Idlib mission had affected his life. Although he was lucky to have survived, what he didn't expect was that from that day on, he would progressively struggle in his private life. Even prior to Idlib, his calm and contented demeanor had been changing over the years to one characterized by sudden and confusing mood swings with mission flashbacks and difficulty sleeping, primarily when he was at home on leave and away from his team. He strenuously denied it when confronted by his wife. In contrast, she had no problem pointing out that his unpredictable behavior was negatively affecting the family, particularly their two young daughters. The problem was that as a SEAL he'd been conditioned, almost brainwashed, not to admit to such human weaknesses.

The result was that within six or seven months after the Idlib disaster, his private life quickly imploded, ultimately leading to a diagnosis of post-traumatic stress disorder. Despite his futile attempts to deny its reality, he found himself having to deal with a contentious divorce, discharge from the Navy, and loss of custody of and even visitation rights to his daughters.

What followed was a year's descent into hell of unsuccessful PTSD treatments involving various methods of psychotherapy and drug trials, all of which had minimal or no effect. Falling further into alcohol and drug abuse and near to giving up hope, Hank became desperate. Then, as if in answer to a prayer, he got a call a year and a half ago from Chuck Barton, a fellow ex–Navy SEAL, a bit older than he whom he'd met briefly when Hank was near the end of his SEAL training. Following his own discharge from the military, Chuck had started a highly successful company called Action Security, which was staffed largely by ex-military special forces personnel. After several meetings, during which Chuck scoffed at Hank's purported psychological issues, which Hank did not try to hide, Chuck offered Hank a job that he assured him would be perfect for his training and experience. Sensing manna from heaven, Hank accepted the position. What followed for him was an almost magical reboot of his self-esteem as well as some welcome relief of his incapacitating PTSD, especially after he had been sent on a few missions along with another Action Security employee, David Mach, an ex–Army Ranger. Those missions involved traveling to Mexico at the behest of a drug cartel to eliminate individuals who had fallen from favor either within their organization or in a rival's.

From then on, as long as he was kept somewhat busy with such missions, which he recognized as a kind of real immersion therapy in contrast to those psychological ones he'd tried, he continued to improve symptomatically. Soon he was back to sleeping reasonably well without horrific nightmares, able to focus, and even able to see his daughters again.

Then, six months later, things began to improve even more when Action Security signed on a new account called Oncology Diagnostics. This client became a particular boost to Hank. He wasn't sure exactly what the healthcare company did, but he didn't care or bother to find out. What he cared about was that they had already provided him with six missions right there in New York City, which obviated the need for international travel and avoided the associated complicated logistics. All of these missions Hank had carried out himself, although David Mach was available if he'd been needed. The current mission was for the same client, and Hank was confident he didn't need assistance, saving the client considerable expense.

As he got closer to his objective, he found himself once again wondering why a medical organization needed to eliminate people—and it mystified him. Yet as thankful as he was for rebooting his life, he was not about to look a gift horse in the mouth. What made these NYC missions particularly challenging was that the client insisted they be accomplished in a fashion that would avoid any potential homicide investigations. This demanded extra planning on Action Security and particularly Hank's part, and a solution that had been decided from the get-go was to make these hits appear as suicides. So far as Hank or Action Security knew, it had worked fine. The important thing was that the client was pleased. As for the current mission, a thirty-year-old male, Hank was planning on the same format, which was why he was packing a ghost gun.

He passed a Salvation Army thrift store, which was shuttered for the night, and several doors down, he stopped in front of a five-story brick building with a large decorative cornice. From all his preparation and research done over the last twenty-four hours, he knew that the mark, Sean O'Brien, lived alone on the third floor in the rear apartment. Sean had been living in Manhattan for three years and worked in the financial industry. He had a girlfriend, but conveniently only saw her on week-ends, meaning that the chances he was alone on a Monday night were near to a hundred percent. Although he had passed some revelers on the previous block, between Twelfth and Eleventh Avenue, where he was now standing was devoid of people despite Manhattan being home to more than a million and a half people. The circumstances were nearly perfect.

With a welcome upsurge of adrenaline, he pulled out an empty envelope from his satchel addressed to Sean O'Brien with a return address of Oncology Diagnostics. He then quickly mounted the three-stepped stoop to face the building's buzzer to the right of the front door. After pressing the button for apartment 3B, he waited, his body trained to project calm and ease. With consultation with the client and discussion with the Action Security operations team, Hank had already planned on what to say. Finally, with a bit of static he heard a questioning "Yes?" come out of the intercom.

"Mr. O'Brien," Hank said, leaning close to the microphone. "I have a letter for you from Oncology Diagnostics that they felt you would want to see immediately."

"Really?" Sean questioned.

"Really," Hank responded.

After a brief pause, which Hank expected, since it had happened on all six of his missions for Oncology Diagnostics, the door's buzzer loudly sounded. Quickly, he pushed open the door and entered the building. As with all those other missions, he thought with satisfaction, this one was progressing flawlessly.

CHAPTER 1

Laurie Montgomery woke up with a start at the sound of her smartphone's alarm. It was the default radar sound and wasn't terribly loud, but as if in a panic, she snatched the phone up from the bedside table to turn it off as if her life depended on it. Ever since she was a teenager, wake-up alarms had triggered a kind of fight-or-flight reaction that she'd never been able to control. Back then she'd been fearful that she'd be late to school and suffer the consequences even though she'd never been tardy. Eventually, when she had developed more insight into herself, she had an inkling the habit stemmed from conditioned fear of authority figures like the school principal and a concern of evoking their ire, which she attributed to her authoritarian and emotionally distant cardiac surgeon father.

After turning off the blasted alarm, she allowed herself to sink back under the covers for a few moments to calm down and prepare herself for the busy day ahead. She also glanced over at Jack to give him the first of several anticipated nudges. The result was the second shock of the young day: He was not there!

Sitting back up again in the early-morning darkness with just a hint of the coming dawn seeping through the two windows that overlooked 106th Street in Manhattan's Upper West Side, she strained her ears to pick up any unusual sounds in the morning stillness. As a mother her first thought was always about her children, Jack Jr.—JJ—who was thirteen, and Emma, seven, wondering if one of them had awakened and aroused Jack. The other possibility was that something was amiss with Dorothy, her mother, who was still living with them following the death of Laurie's father. With a bit of relief, she quickly became aware of the distant but reassuring sound of the shower. Obviously, Jack had just gotten up without disturbing her and was already showering.

Allowing herself to sink back once again into the warmth of the bed, Laurie vaguely wondered what had awakened Jack. Since his scary bike incident a year ago when he'd been targeted by a murderous driver, necessitating a lengthy recovery from the hip and fibula fractures of his right leg, she'd been the one to wake him in the morning rather than vice versa, despite her always having had trouble waking up in the morning. The reason was simple: She was a night person who liked to unwind by reading in bed—usually longer than she should—before turning out the light. Back in the good old days of college, medical school, and even after becoming a medical examiner, she'd usually read nineteenth-century British novels. But once she'd agreed to take on the role of chief medical examiner of the City of New York, all that changed.

Now Laurie's nighttime, in-bed reading was all work-related, as she felt there was always some additional details she desperately needed to review despite her having invariably spent ten and occasionally twelve busy hours in her office. When she'd accepted the chief's position five years ago, she'd had no idea it was going to require such a commitment of time and attention, and it had been a rude awakening. Now, when she thought about it, she was the first one to admit that she should have guessed. After all, she knew that the NYC Office of the Chief Medical Examiner, or OCME, had to oversee some seventy thousand deaths per year and do it twenty-four hours, seven days a week, 365 days a year. She also knew that to accomplish this Herculean task required more than six hundred dedicated city employees, including nearly forty board-certified medical examiners, an equivalent number of medical legal investigators, and a budget of more than seventy-five million dollars. Being the chief medical examiner of the City of New York, the largest such institution in the world, was the opposite of a sinecure.

When Jack had first come home from the hospital after his accident and resultant surgery, he'd been bedridden for almost a week, which meant Laurie had to use an alarm to wake up in the morning, as he was sleeping later than usual. Then, a month later, when he insisted on returning to work even though he wasn't all that mobile, she had finally agreed to accept a perk her position as chief provided, namely work-related transportation. But being painfully cognizant of budgetary pressures, Laurie chose not to requisition a new vehicle nor create a new job as her driver but rather to rely on the existing OCME Transport Department personnel and equipment to ferry her and Jack to and from the morgue. The only problem was that the team's change from the night shift to the morning shift occurred at 7:00, which meant that she and Jack had to be picked up well before the night-shift drivers' shift ended, meaning at 6:30, or 6:40 the latest. Since it took her a bit longer than him to get ready, she had to wake herself. Prior to Jack's incident, he'd get up way before Laurie and wake her before he left for work on his bike. Such had been their morning modus operandi for more than ten years.

With a sigh and the realization she couldn't delay any longer, Laurie reluctantly tossed back the covers, stood up, wiggled her toes into her slippers, and donned her robe. Thus prepared, she headed into the bathroom. The warm humidity was welcome. As she approached her sink—the bathroom had two, side by side—Jack was turning off the shower. He then stepped out of the spacious stall. The healed surgical incisions on his hip and calf were bright red from the hot water.

"Top of the morning to you," he said cheerfully, imitating a heavy, cultured English accent as he pulled his towel from the heated rack.

"Good morning yourself," she said as she looked at her image in the mirror to survey what she called *the damage* after a night's sleep. "What are you so chipper about?"

"Today's the day!" Jack exclaimed enthusiastically, covering his head with the towel to vigorously dry his hair. "I'm psyched!"

"What on earth are you talking about?" Laurie questioned. "What's so special about today?" Jack's usual morning levity never ceased to amaze her, yet his attitude on this particular morning seemed exceptionally effervescent.

"Today is the day I'm finally getting that new Trek bike that I had to order four freaking months ago," Jack said as he hung up his towel. He glanced in the mirror, and with a couple of simple pats nudged his Caesar hairstyle into position. He then headed for the door leading into what they called their changing room, which connected to the bedroom and the hallway. "I still can't believe it's taken so long to get the damn thing," he said over his shoulder before disappearing from view. Raising his voice to be heard, he added: "If I had had any inkling about how long it was going to take thanks to the pandemic-induced supply chain issues, I would have ordered the damn thing the moment I got out of the hospital."

"Good lord," Laurie managed softly. She continued to stare at her image in the mirror. She'd forgotten about the bike and had secretly hoped Jack had as well. She'd never liked that biking was his preferred mode of transportation in the city, and after his accident, she'd hoped that he'd gotten the message and finally come to share her position. Even though biking was becoming dramatically more popular with all the additional bike rental stations sprinkled about the city and all the new bike lanes, she still thought biking in NYC was only for people with a death wish. The OCME regularly saw thirty to forty bike deaths per year, and it was on the upswing, especially because people on the rental bikes rarely used helmets and electric bikes were available that went far too fast.

She leaned on the edge of the sink, recognizing she didn't want to get into a heated discussion of why she thought that, as a father and husband, Jack's biking and the risks involved was irresponsible, even selfish on his part. Laurie long ago had accepted she wasn't going to win the old argument, since his biking and even his intense pickup basketball on the neighborhood's outdoor court served a lot more than mere transportation or exercise for him. Both were a way for him to deal with his demons associated with the loss of his first family, which he still blamed on himself. From her perspective, it wasn't all bad. The suppressed anxiety involved was also responsible for the intensity he directed to being a medical examiner. At the OCME, he was by far the most productive of all the MEs, always looking for a forensic challenge to occupy his mind.

Laurie sighed. It was an ongoing battle, so to avoid conflict, she just changed the subject. "I'm looking forward to the day as well," she called out.

"Really?" Jack questioned with interest. He reappeared at the door to the changing room in the process of pulling on his undershirt. "What's up for you today?"

"It's Thursday," she said, trying to come up with something believable. A year ago she had instituted the rule that every Thursday she would do an autopsy with one of the forensic fellows who were training at the OCME to become eligible for board certification as a forensic pathologist or with one of the two New York University pathology residents who spent a month in their fourth year of pathology training. As a consequent, she truly looked forward to Thursdays as her favorite day of the week.

Besides the long hours and the frustrating politics of being the chief medical examiner, the other thing Laurie disliked about the position was that she seriously missed being a medical examiner and the challenge of doing the autopsies to determine the cause and manner of death. For her the field was a true calling to speak for the dead. Although she did make what she called chief rounds every morning, meaning she'd go down to the autopsy room and briefly go from table to table to listen to each case being presented and offer suggestions and advice based on her extensive knowledge and experience in the field, it wasn't the same as being personally involved in a case.

"Oh, right!" Jack called out even though he was again out of sight. "Are you doing an autopsy this morning?"

"Absolutely!" Laurie yelled. "I wouldn't miss it for the world. It's what keeps me sane."

"Who are you doing it with today?" Jack yelled back.

"Interesting that you should ask. I'm doing it with one of the new pathology residents who started on Friday. His name is Ryan Sullivan. Have you met him?"

Jack reappeared in the bathroom doorway. He was now buttoning one of his chambray shirts, which, along with his corduroy jacket, was his signature attire. "No, I haven't formally met him, but I've seen him and his fellow resident in the autopsy room. I haven't worked with either or spoken with them yet." Jack wasn't completely up to speed with the number of autopsies he normally did as he still found standing for long periods at the autopsy table bothersome for his hip, despite his being back to all other activities, including half-court basketball. Dr. Chet McGovern, who was responsible for the residents as the director of education, had avoided including either of the new residents on Jack's cases for fear doing so would extend how long the case took.

"Have you heard anything from any of the other MEs who have worked with him?"

Jack shook his head. "Not a word. Why do you ask?"

"Because Chet made it a point to ask me to work with him today. According to Chet, Ryan has a bad attitude. He's not a fan of forensic pathology and is resentful of having to spend a month here. As a result, he's been shirking some of his assigned autopsies, particularly in the afternoons when he sneaks back to the Hassenfeld Children's Hospital to go over the day's pediatric pathology cases."

"Uh-oh," Jack said. "That's starting to sound like a disturbing déjà vu."

"You got that right," she agreed. Several years ago there had been a similar problem with one of the NYU pathology residents, Aria Nichols, who also evaded some of her responsibilities during her OCME rotation. Back then, Chet had asked Laurie to do a case with the woman to see if Laurie could help the situation by fostering her interest in forensics, something Laurie had accomplished to great success with at least one other woman in the past. Unfortunately, although she again succeeded with Aria, there'd been a sad and tragic outcome. Awakening the woman's interest in forensics led to a series of events that ultimately resulted in her murder and Jack's having to sorrowfully autopsy the youthful resident. The case Laurie did with Aria was a suspected overdose that Aria ended up proving was a homicide, and as Aria closed in on discovering the perpetrator, he killed her.

"Don't tell me this Ryan Sullivan is another Aria Nichols," Jack said with a roll of his eyes.

"That fear occurred to me, too," Laurie said. "But without me even raising the issue, Chet put my mind to rest straight out by saying Ryan doesn't share Nichols's in-your-face antisocial aggressiveness. In fact, it sounds like Ryan is quite the contrary. Chet described him as passive-aggressive. On the plus side, he's reportedly just as smart as Ms. Nichols was. To prove it, according to Chet, he's already been offered a pediatric pathology fellowship at NYU. That's obviously a big feather in his cap, so he otherwise must be an exceptional pathology resident."

"Good grief! Having a second troublesome resident calls out that the OCME should be an elective, rather than a requirement for NYU anatomical pathology residency. Since that's not going to happen, it seems to me that we should at least be warned of a resident's negative mindset, so we can be prepared."

"I couldn't agree more," Laurie said. "That's an interesting suggestion. I've wanted an excuse to go over to the NYU Pathology Department to meet the new chief, and this could be it. Maybe early this afternoon I can find the time. If nothing else, it would be an opportunity for me to let the department know that after the Aria Nichols tragedy, we've encouraged our MEs to give the NYU residents more of a sense of participation, particularly after our general counsel put the kibosh on our giving them more actual responsibility."

"Uh-oh!" Jack voiced as he buckled his watch on his wrist and glanced at its dial. "You'd better get a move on and jump in the shower. It's already after six."

"Yikes!" Laurie said. In response, she peeled off her robe and kicked free of her slippers. Stepping into the shower she yelled: "Since you're already dressed, how about making us some coffee?"

"You got it," Jack said.

CHAPTER 2

Thursday, December 7, 7:00 am

The shrill sound of crickets coming from Isabella Lopez's phone jolted her awake. After turning off the alarm, the first thing she became aware of was that her mouth was bone dry. Luckily there was a nearly full glass of water on the bedside table. The second thing she noticed was a mild headache, undoubtedly from having had too much to drink the night before. As per usual she vowed to be more careful in the future even though she knew that the next time she was out on the town she'd most likely live in the moment, which was more her style.

Isabella was a highly motivated, career-oriented, twenty-eight-year-old second-generation Cuban American from Miami, Florida, who'd gone to the University of Florida as a graphic design major. To her credit, after lots of hard work, she'd managed to get a dream job in advertising in New York City and was having the time of her life in the Big Apple.

Turning around, she looked over at Ryan Sullivan, who surprisingly had not been bothered by the alarm. He was still fast asleep, lying on his back with his hands folded over his chest, breathing deeply. They were in his apartment in the Kips Bay neighborhood on East 25th Street. They'd only known each other for a bit over two months after having met online, but things were going well. This was the third night they'd spent together, and he'd given her a key to his apartment, so she could on occasion use his terrific Razer computer, which had a graphics card that was far better than her Mac's. Looking at him sleeping, she had to admit that he was as attractive in person as he had been in his photos: porcelain skin, dark hair, high cheekbones, a killer smile, and, most important of all, an upturned nose that made her jealous. It was the kind of nose she'd wished she had since she was a teenager.

What had turned out the most surprising for Isabella about Ryan was that he truly was a medical doctor. When he'd first offered that information online, she'd not given it much credence. In her experience, peoples' online personas and the real individual were often at odds. Such discrepancies never bothered her because her online banter with men was akin to a kind of game, and she rarely had any inclination to meet them in person, so she didn't care. Catching men in their online deceptions was what made the interactions fun, a challenge, and worth the time for Isabella to sift through hundreds of people on her favorite dating apps. With Ryan, it had been different, since he'd been entirely consistent with his details from day one despite her trying to uncover minor inconsistencies in his story.

The previous evenings they'd spent together had been at noisy clubs with loud music and, at least for Isabella, too much alcohol, both of which had made any real conversation all but impossible. In contrast, last night they had met at Via Carota in Greenwich Village for dinner, and although crowded, the restaurant had provided them an opportunity to talk, and they had talked a lot. Ryan had spent quite a bit of time complaining about his current circumstance, saying he was a pathology resident who was now on a month's rotation at the New York City morgue known by the acronym OCME. Instead of saving people, he was autopsying dead bodies, and it was a burden that he truly hated and couldn't wait to be over. She couldn't help but commiserate, as it did indeed sound awful to the point of evoking her mothering instinct, something rather new for her.

After looking back at her phone and noticing the time, Isabella recognized she had to get a move on, as it was important for her not to be late for work. The powers that be at her office viewed tardiness as disinterest. Glancing back at Ryan, she debated what to do. She could slip out of bed, dress, and leave. Yet, in deference to the previous evening's interaction, which included her also revealing more about herself than usual, she was reluctant to part with such seeming indifference. With that thought in mind, she propped herself up on an elbow and, with her other hand, reached out and gave his shoulder a mild shake. His hazel eyes popped open, and he rapidly sat up.

"What time is it?" he asked as if in a panic.

"It's early," Isabella said, holding the covers under her chin to keep from being exposed. "It's only a little after seven, but I've got to get back to my apartment to change before heading to work. I didn't want to just sneak out."

"I appreciate that," Ryan said as he collapsed back. Seemingly relieved he didn't have to jump up and start his day, he relaxed and put his hands behind his head. He even sighed, glad to have the reprieve.

"I had a nice time last night," Isabella said. She, too, relaxed back. Suddenly something occurred to her: Her apartment was within walking distance in neighboring Gramercy Park, meaning she had more time than she originally thought and didn't need to rush.

"I did, too," he said. "That is, provided I didn't talk your ear off."

"Not at all. And I could worry about having done the same to you."

19

"Not in the slightest. I enjoyed hearing about your job. Advertising is a world I know nothing about, and it was nice to hear your excitement about your work. Of course, it made me jealous, especially when I compare it to what I'm facing these days at the city morgue. It's a freaking nightmare."

"You did make it sound unpleasant."

"Repulsive is more accurate," Ryan said with a dismissive wave. "Especially with my strong sense of smell. Even with two masks, which I tried yesterday, I have trouble hacking it in the autopsy room, particularly when there's a body with any putrefaction or maggots." He grimaced and shivered. "Sorry! I don't want to gross you out, but it's disgusting."

"Yikes!" Isabella said, wrinkling her nose. "I can't imagine."

"Believe me, you'd hate it as much as I do. Any normal person would. To be honest, I truly don't know how I'm going to handle being there for the rest of the month. It's really a nightmare. I'm not joking. I mean, even the building is a disaster. It's got to be one of the ugliest ones in the city and slated for demolition, which couldn't happen soon enough as far as I'm concerned. And the inside is worse than the outside, particularly in and around the autopsy room. Without exaggeration, it's like a movie set for an old horror film. And we're just talking about the physical space. Last night, did I describe any of the inhabitants of this netherworld?"

"No, you didn't. Are they creepy?" During their dinner when she was listening to him rant about his current work situation, the question had passed through her mind exactly what kind of doctor would be attracted to working in such an environment. It was inconceivable to her how anybody would choose to deal with death all day, every day, year in and year out, after taking all the time and energy to go through medical school to learn how to cure people.

"*Creepy* isn't a strong enough word. *Weird* is better. Everyone I've met so far is on the strange side, particularly the medical examiner who oversees us pathology residents. I didn't mention it last night, but my fellow resident partner is an ass-kisser, which just makes me look worse. It's too bad I got paired with her for the rotation. Regardless, this medical examiner was all googly-eyed over her. On the first day, he took me aside to ask if she was married or had a serious boyfriend. It's so obvious he's a womanizer. And on top of that misogynist, the head honcho, or chief medical examiner, who we met briefly on our first day, is this holier-than-thou woman who's convinced that forensics and being a medical examiner is the end-all medical specialty. And, weirdly enough, her husband is also a medical examiner in the same office, who supposedly is a workaholic who can't get enough autopsies. I can't imagine what they talk about in bed. Anyway, it's a strange crew."

"Wow! It sounds bad."

"The worst," Ryan muttered. It depressed him to give voice to his feelings.

"My advice, for better or worse, is to just put your head down and try to make the best of it. It's only a month, meaning you are already nearly a quarter done." Isabella reached over and picked up her phone to check the time. She gritted her teeth. Time was now getting tight despite her apartment being nearby.

He chuckled humorlessly and shook his head. "Easier said than done. But thanks for the advice. You sound like the mother I never had."

Surprised by this comment coming out of the blue, Isabella looked back at him with a questioning expression. "What do you mean?"

"Sorry," Ryan said. "That was a slip of the tongue. My mother died of cancer when I was eight, so I had a mother for a while. It's just that I don't remember much before I was eight."

"Oh, gosh! I'm so sorry," she said, and meant it. Her mother was the most important person in her life, and Isabella couldn't conceive of growing up without her. "I hope your father was able to step up to the plate. Did he ever remarry? Did you have a stepmother?"

Ryan chuckled again derisively at the question. "Hardly! My alcoholic, abusive father, the prick, killed himself a little more than a month after my mother died."

"Good grief," Isabella managed. With her tight-knit large Cuban family, such a circumstance seemed inconceivable to her, and her heart went out to him. "You lost both parents! What happened to you? Were you an only child?"

"No, I had a brother who was three years older," he said. "But, look, I'm sorry for saying what I said. I apologize, but thinking about my work situation puts me in a bad mood. Can we talk about something a bit more upbeat, so that I can face my day? I really don't like to talk about my childhood because it was a mess. It will make me more depressed than I already am."

Isabella stared at him, feeling a burst of empathy, yet strangely tongue-tied at his unexpected revelations. She was at a loss for words, which wasn't like her. The idea of one's childhood being a mess and still succeeding as he apparently had was unimaginable.

"How about we plan to do something together this weekend if you're available?" Ryan suggested. "I wouldn't mind checking out the Christmas tree at Rockefeller Center Saturday or Sunday afternoon. Would you be up for that?"

She broke off from staring at him and to try to reboot and gather her thoughts. "I'll have to get back to you about the weekend," she managed, stumbling over her words. "I'll text you later this morning."

"Fair enough," Ryan said. He looked as if her response to his offer didn't sound very positive but what could he do? "Well," he continued. "I hope you can make it. Having something fun to look forward to would help."

"Your work situation sounds horrible," Isabella said, finding her voice. "I'll give you that. But becoming a doctor after losing both your parents at age eight is so extraordinary, I would think that dealing with being at the morgue for a month, as distasteful as it sounds, would be a comparative breeze."

"So you're saying I should just buck up."

"I guess I am, in a way. But I'm also giving you full credit for what you've already accomplished."

For a moment they just stared at each other across the relative expanse of the bed.

Isabella broke the silence. "But now I have to go!" With that, she slipped out of bed, snatched up her clothes from the floor, and ducked into his bathroom.

For a few minutes, Ryan stared at the closed bathroom door. He couldn't help but feel resentful of Isabella telling him he should buck up and then dashing off into the bathroom. It was patronizing! He'd expected more empathy, considering how open he'd been with her. If he never saw another autopsy, the happier he'd be, yet he was facing three more weeks of them. To be truthful, he'd never been much of a fan of anatomical autopsies, either, as there was some distasteful aspects even with them, but they were nothing like the forensic ones and their inevitable assault on the senses. He shuddered to think of the putrid cases he might face that day.

What Ryan liked about the specialty of pathology was its intellectual nature, particularly the microscopic and laboratory side of it. It was carried out in a clean environment and mostly without the messy realities of dealing directly with patients. What he liked the best was making the diagnosis of childhood illnesses, particularly childhood blood disorders like leukemias from bone marrow aspirations. During the last few days he'd taken it on his own to forsake several assigned afternoon autopsies, slip unseen out of the OCME, and head over to the Hassenfeld Children's Hospital to review the day's bone marrow slides. To his great satisfaction, yesterday, at an attending's request, he'd reviewed a case and had been able to pick up a significant finding that had been missed by those who had originally looked at the slides.

A few minutes later, completely put together, Isabella emerged from the bathroom. She came over to the side of the bed, gave him a peck on the cheek, and was gone. It all happened in a blink of the eye.

Ryan took in a deep breath of air, held it, and then let it out all at once. Thus fortified, he threw back the covers and got up to face the day.

CHAPTER 3

Thursday, December 7, 7:45 am

As per usual of late, she and Jack had arrived at the OCME building at the corner of First Avenue and 30th Street before 7:00. The ride had been rapid and uneventful thanks to the minimal traffic. Her only regret was having once again left the apartment before the children were awake. For her, the current biggest bane of being the chief medical examiner was having to leave before JJ and Emma were up, and despite her sincere efforts to the contrary, she occasionally did not get home before Emma had gone to bed. Such was her life, which all too often required making difficult trade-offs between family and career like many other workingwomen. On weekends, Laurie tried to make up for her workweek absences by spending as much time as possible with both children, especially Emma, who was doing remarkably well—since September she had been attending a school for autistic children located close to JJ's school.

When Laurie and Jack came through the front door at 520 First Avenue that morning, they were greeted by night security, as none of the day staff had arrived. After a quick goodbye with Jack, she headed into the administration area that led to her office, while he hustled off to the ID room to cherry-pick the cases that had come in overnight with the hopes of finding something forensically challenging.

Laurie turned on the overhead lights in admin before doing the same in her office. Her secretary, Cheryl Stanford, wouldn't arrive for another hour. After hanging up her coat, she sat down behind her massive, dark mahogany desk. Despite the daily agony of waking up to the alarm, she ultimately appreciated the time it gave her to be in her office with no one else around. This afforded her the opportunity to go over tasks that required her undivided attention, and that morning was no exception.

One of the most pressing problems for Laurie as the OCME chief was that the physical plant and its autopsy suite sorely needed to be replaced. When it had been built more than a half century ago, it had been state of the art, but that was no longer the case. In addition, the aging building belonged to New York University Medical Center, which had its own designs on the site.

For a number of years, Laurie had toiled under the understanding that a parking area just east of the new OCME high-rise at First Avenue and 26th Street—which housed the renowned Forensic Biology Laboratory and a host of other OCME functions—was slated for the site of the new OCME Forensic Pathology Center with a new autopsy room, ME offices, and toxicology laboratory. To that end, she had spent countless hours perfecting the architectural plans of a modest building to meet OCME needs and the budgetary concerns of the city council. Then, to her surprise, that plan was summarily discarded when Bellevue Hospital claimed the parking area for its own development needs and the governor and mayor announced the creation of a new 1.6-billion-dollar Kipps Bay health science center that would include space for the OCME.

This new health-related Science Park and Research Center, or

SPARC, was now slated to occupy an entire city block of Hunter College's Brookdale campus. It was conveniently located adjacent to the relatively new OCME Forensic Biology Laboratory, such that Laurie could envision a pedestrian bridge across 26th Street to connect it to the Forensic Pathology Center. Such a bridge would be an unbelievably positive step enabling the OCME to carry out its mission, yet for her it wasn't going to be a cakewalk. Instead, it was now her job to compete head-to-head for space inside SPARC with the other healthcare occupants, namely Hunter College, CUNY School of Public Health, Bellevue Hospital, and multiple private health and biotech companies. In some respects, it was going to be much more difficult and time-consuming than dealing with the city council. Later today, at 11:30, Laurie was scheduled to meet with the dean of the Hunter College School of Nursing and School of Health Sciences to discuss respective space requirements.

Suddenly, someone said, "Knock knock," while simultaneously knocking on her open office door. She looked up to see Dr. Chet McGovern standing in the doorway, holding two mugs of coffee with an autopsy folder under his arm. He was an athletic-appearing man who could have been Jack's brother, though unlike Jack he had a seriously receding hairline. To compensate, he'd grown a goatee, but had recently shaved it off to Laurie's silent appreciation. She was not a fan of facial hair, as she thought it looked unprofessional. Laurie knew him better than she knew most of the other medical examiners, because he and Jack had shared an office back when they joined the OCME, several years after Laurie, and over the years Jack had shared many stories of Chet's social quirks. Professionally, he was a highly competent medical examiner.

"Do you have a moment?" Chet asked.

"Absolutely," she said. "Come on in."

"I brought you a coffee, if you're interested," he said as he advanced into the room and put one of the mugs on Laurie's desk. "There's a touch of sugar and cream, just like you like it."

"Perfect! How thoughtful," she said appreciatively. "Thank you." She picked up the mug and, holding it in both hands, took a welcome sip. It was delightfully warm and delicious.

"I wanted to let you know that I have a case set up for you this morning, as promised, and have arranged for Marvin Fletcher to lend a hand." Chet extended the autopsy folder to Laurie. He knew she believed the more you knew about a case before you began, the less chance there'd be something missed. It was the opposite of Jack's technique. He preferred to do his cases relatively cold, believing that knowing too much detail risked making him biased and thereby possibly missing something important.

"Thank you," Laurie repeated. She took the folder. "I'm looking forward to it." Marvin was her preferred mortuary tech. Since they had worked so much together prior to her becoming chief, he knew her preferences. She glanced briefly at the name: Sean O'Brien. "What kind of case is it?"

"It's a gunshot wound," Chet said.

"Excellent," Laurie said. She had asked him to find a case that could highlight the powers of forensics to help make this reluctant resident appreciate what the OCME was tasked to do. The autopsy results and the applied forensics of gunshot wound cases often helped law enforcement apprehend the perpetrator and ultimately aided the district attorney to obtain a conviction. "Has there been an arrest?"

"No! No arrest. It's been determined a suicide."

"Oh," Laurie said simply. She was now mildly disappointed.

"It's not a completely straightforward suicide," Chet said, seeming to sense her reaction. "At least according to Janice Jaeger." Janice was one of the more experienced medical legal investigators, or MLIs, and had been working at the OCME longer than Laurie. Her opinions were particularly well respected, especially by Jack, who often sung her praise. "The police have called it a suicide and are treating it as such, but Janice's report nonetheless raises a potential red flag because of two things that caught her attention. The first was that the pistol was still in the victim's hand, who was found in a sitting position, a circumstance that she claims she's never seen before. The second was that by interviewing a number of the residents of the ten-unit building, she learned that no one heard a gunshot. Why this was particularly important to her was because she estimated the time of death to be right around ten in the evening, according to the state of rigor mortis and body temperature. The idea is that's when most everyone in the building would have been home and likely awake. She thought this fact was particularly significant because the building is relatively old and never renovated, suggesting sound insulation isn't top notch."

"Those are interesting facts, but hardly definitive," Laurie commented.

"Agreed," Chet said. "But they at least raise the question of whether the manner of death was indeed suicide or a staged suicide. My feeling is that the case can be a good example of how forensics can help answer that important question. Interestingly enough, we've seen a half dozen such cases over the last six months, as I brought up in the Thursday-afternoon conference last week. This makes seven, if it is indeed a suicide."

"You're right," Laurie said, seeing his point. What immediately came to her mind was that determining the path of the bullet as well as whether the barrel of the gun had been pressed against the skin were going to be critical. "Did Janice mention whether she thought it was a contact wound?"

"Oh, it was a contact wound, for sure," Chet said. "It's an intra-oral case."

"Oh, okay," she said. She knew that the vast number of gunshot suicides from a handgun involved the right temple, but that the mouth was a distant second followed by the forehead, the left temple, and a few under the chin. But putting all that aside, she found herself agreeing with his idea that it was a good case to illustrate the power of forensics and thereby hopefully pique Ryan Sullivan's interest in the field, which was the goal of the exercise.

"Does nine work for you?" Chet asked.

"As far as I know," Laurie said. "Provided no disaster occurs between now and then."

"And provided Dr. Sullivan shows up on time. He was told on his first day to be here at seven-thirty, but that's certainly not been the case, and I've yet to see him this morning. As I explained to you yesterday, he's acting rather passive-aggressive and being late is one symptom."

"Well, I'll see if I can help turn him around," she said.

"If anybody can do it, you can," Chet said. "See you in the pit." *The pit* was the nickname everyone at the OCME used for the autopsy suite. With a wave, he headed for the door.

"One other question," Laurie called out, bringing him to a halt. "Do you happen to know if Jack found himself an interesting case this morning?"

"He did," Chet said. "I was told that he'd found a chiropractic neck manipulation case, which he was excited about and immediately put dibs on."

"Oh, no!" she murmured. She knew that such a case would most likely require a vertebral artery dissection, which made for a difficult and time-consuming autopsy. Her concern was whether Jack would be up for it physically and try to tough it out and maybe do himself additional harm.

"I know what you're thinking," Chet said, "but I'll keep an eye on the situation, and if the case does drag on, I'll insist on stepping in to relieve him."

"Okay, terrific," Laurie said, flashing a thumbs-up.

"Actually, the chiropractic case has yet to start," Chet said. "When I arrived this morning, Jack was already down in the pit doing a case with Lou." Detective Lieutenant Commander Lou Soldano was an old friend, first of Laurie's and now of Jack's as well, who frequently came into the OCME to observe autopsies. As a homicide detective, he was particularly enthralled with the help the OCME provided to law enforcement.

"What kind of case is he doing with Lou?" she asked. This sounded as bad as a potential vertebral artery dissection.

"Multiple gunshot wounds of a suspect during a traffic stop," Chet said.

"Oh, no, not another one of those," Laurie said.

"Yeah, it's an important case. It turned out there'd been a warrant out for the guy's arrest, and when the officers pulled him over, he pulled out a gun, resulting in a shootout."

"How many shots in the corpse? Do you know?" Her concern for Jack returned in a rush. Multiple gunshot cases were notorious for requiring hours to trace and recover bullet fragments.

"I have no idea, but I could find out."

"Don't bother," Laurie said with a wave. "I'll check in on them when I go down for my case. Thank you, Chet."

"No problem," he answered. With a little wave, he hustled out of the office.

After gazing at the empty door while taking another mouthful of the coffee, Laurie returned her attention to her desk and then tipped forward in her executive chair. Although she knew she should go back to preparing for her meeting with the nursing school dean, the short conversation she'd had with Chet spurred her interest in her upcoming autopsy.

Picking up the autopsy folder, she slipped out the contents and located Janice's investigative report. Skimming through it to get the basics with the idea that she'd go over it more carefully before she did the case, she learned that Sean O'Brien had been a single, thirty-year-old man originally from Charlestown, Massachusetts, who worked for Morgan Stanley as a wealth management consultant. Suddenly her eyes stopped on a single sentence relating that the man had recently been diagnosed with cancer, and, more important, at least according to the girlfriend, who found the body, he had been significantly depressed about the diagnosis.

Laurie stopped reading and stared ahead. This information resonated with her because she was aware that a diagnosis of cancer was a devastating psychological blow that doubled the risk of suicide, particularly with certain types of cancers such as pancreatic and lung. Returning her attention to Janice's report, she tried to find out what type of cancer Mr. O'Brien had been facing, but it wasn't provided.

Slipping Janice's report back into the autopsy folder, Laurie again stared off into the distance as she couldn't help but recall that she herself had been faced with a cancer scare two years ago, which had caused her a lot of soul-searching. She'd never contemplated suicide, but there had been much decisional heartache, ultimately resulting in a double mastectomy and an oophorectomy. The experience gave her a special understanding of what Sean O'Brien had undoubtedly faced, possibly causing him to take his fate in his own hands.

CHAPTER 4

Despite being already twenty-five minutes late, Ryan paused outside of 520 First Avenue and looked up at the structure in front of him. It was just a six-story blank wall of light-colored brick without windows or architectural detail made worse by aging scaffolding that ran across the front and side of the building for no apparent reason. He had wondered about the scaffolding because the building certainly wasn't under renovation. After taking in his final breath of fresh air, he walked under the staging and entered.

Inside he flashed his temporary ID to the friendly OCME receptionist who buzzed him into the building's interior. His destination was the residents' office on the second floor, which wasn't much of an office. It was a small, windowless room off what was generously labeled the lunchroom. Inside there was barely enough space for two aged metal desks facing each other. Both supported monitors and keyboards and not much else. Sharon Hinkley, Ryan's fellow resident, was seated at one of the desks typing away. She looked up as he entered.

"You're late again," she said. Her tone was accusatory.

Ryan merely nodded. As he had explained to Isabella that morning, Sharon was reasonably attractive in his estimation, with a slim figure; a wide face; invitingly blue eyes; light brown, shoulder-length hair parted in the middle; and perhaps her most striking attribute, exceptionally white and straight teeth. She was also a particularly youthful-appearing senior pathology resident having been accepted into Princeton at sixteen and medical school at nineteen. What he didn't like about her was that she was such a suck-up with all of the attendings when she sure as hell didn't need to be, as smart as she clearly was.

"Dr. McGovern called twice looking for you," she added.

"That's nice," he said as he pulled off his coat and hung it over the back of his desk chair.

"He was clearly miffed you weren't here yet," she continued. "He said that we should meet up with him in the ID room as soon as you arrived. Are you ready?"

The ID room was where victims' families or acquaintances were brought to make the final identification of the deceased. Although in the past it had been required for people to view the dead, now it was normally done with digital imaging provided the identifiers didn't demand to see the body. Most people didn't. In the early morning, the ID room also served as a gathering place for the medical examiners to review and be assigned the autopsy cases that had come in during the night.

"I suppose it can't be avoided," Ryan said with resignation.

Sharon got to her feet. She was a tall woman, close to Ryan's five foot eleven. "I don't think it's serving either of our interests that you are late every day and so negative. Next time, I'm not going to wait for you."

"Suit yourself," he said. "I'm sorry, but I'm doing the best I can. I hate this place. It amazes me that you don't."

"I'm liking it better than I thought," Sharon said as she pulled on her short white medical coat that medical residents generally wore. "You should give it more of a chance. I was on an interesting case yesterday afternoon. It was a prolapse of a mitral valve that was initiated by a mugging. What's fascinating is now the mugger is going to be charged with murder, even though he didn't lay a hand on the victim, because the death certificate will say homicide."

"I might have been able to tolerate that autopsy," Ryan said as he followed her out of the tiny office and into the deserted lunchroom. "My last two cases were of bodies that hadn't been discovered for days."

"Yeah, that can be tough. You've got to allow the science involved to make it possible to deal with the distasteful aspects."

"Easier said than done."

They used the stairs to get down to the first floor and made their way to the ID area using the longer interior route to avoid going out into the reception area. They found Dr. Chet McGovern seated behind one of desks in the ID common area. Doors into multiple smaller rooms lined the walls. As they approached, Chet looked up. His state of mind was easy to access by his expression.

"Good afternoon, you two," he said irritably.

"Sorry," Ryan said. "It was my fault. I woke up later than I should have."

"Do you wake up later than you should have every morning?" Chet asked superciliously. "And what the hell happened to you yesterday afternoon? Dr. Blodgett said you never showed up for the floater case." A *floater* was a corpse found submerged in one of the bodies of water surrounding New York City for various amounts of time. Due to varying degrees of decomposition, floaters were notorious for being unpleasant autopsies, and having been forewarned, Ryan decided he couldn't take it.

"I went over to the Hassenfeld Children's Hospital to look at bone marrow aspiration," Ryan said, hoping the information might make his obvious lapse more forgivable. His sense was that the medical examiners whom he'd been scheduled to work with didn't care that much whether he was there and wouldn't tattle. "Dr. Sanger, one of the hospital's pathology attendings, was interested in my opinion."

For a moment Chet stared at Ryan while drumming his fingers on the surface of the desk. After a pause, he cleared his throat and added: "Your responsibility for this month is to be here to learn as much as you can about forensics. That does not mean disappearing back over to NYU Medical Center, regardless of the reason. I already warned you about this the first time you did it. Do I now make myself perfectly clear?"

"Yes," Ryan said.

"As head of OCME Education, it will be up to me to certify your performance here. If that doesn't happen, you might not get your pathology residency certification from NYU," Chet said.

Ryan seriously doubted that would happen, but he held his tongue.

"All right," Chet said. He picked up two brief case summaries that he'd put together. "Let's get on with this. I've assigned you each a case. Dr. Hinkley, you will be working with Dr. Mehta on a purported overdose. Dr. Sullivan, you will be working with the chief, Dr. Montgomery, on a purported suicide." He handed the appropriate summary to each of the residents.

Ryan was stunned as he glanced at the summary, especially seeing the case involved a thirty-year-old originally from Charlestown, Massachusetts. Chet continued talking, making the point that although such cases sounded routine, particularly the overdose, the OCME on occasion found the manner of death in both situations not to be what it seemed. But Ryan wasn't listening. Instead, he was recalling his faux pas with Isabella, mentioning his father's suicide. What he hadn't said was that suicide subsequently had played an even larger role in his life at age fifteen while imprisoned in reform school. When Ryan combined this fact with his intense dislike of feeling imprisoned in the OCME for a month immersed in death in all its hideous circumstances, he wasn't interested in autopsying a suicide victim the same age as he was who had grown up in a neighboring Massachusetts town a mere stone's throw away across the Mystic River. The identification was too immediate, too close, too easy, and brought back painful memories of despair and depression.

"I'm not doing this case!" Ryan declared suddenly, interrupting Chet in midsentence. Chet stared back at him in disbelief, as did Sharon. "It'd be better if I do the overdose," he added in a more normal tone, as he extended his summary toward Sharon and tried to take hers.

"Hold on!" Chet declared, finding his voice. "No! You two are not switching cases. No way! I've just come from Dr. Montgomery's office. She's set on doing the suicide case with you, Dr. Sullivan, and she is looking forward to it."

For ten seconds of silence that seemed to stretch out endlessly, the three people stared at one another. It was Ryan who recovered first, secretly castigating himself for losing control and making a scene. He felt he was caught in a trap, as there was no way in hell that he would be willing to explain to these two people why he didn't want to do the case. He had to take the suicide. There were no two ways about it.

"I don't care which case I do," Sharon said with a shrug. "It's all the same to me."

"No, I'll do it!" Ryan said. "I apologize. I don't know what came over me, just a moment of temporary insanity. This case is fine. I guess I was just hoping for something more challenging."

"Every autopsy can somehow be challenging," Chet said. "Really! I'm not exaggerating. Every case is unique, even the ones that seem to be mundane. It's just like people in general. Maybe more so."

Oh, sure! Ryan thought, dismissing his banality. But he stayed silent.

"Okay. Dr. Hinkley, you're first up," Chet said, flashing her a thumbs-up. "Dr. Mehta is already downstairs and probably eager to get going. Dr. Sullivan, you've got a bit of a breather, since Dr. Montgomery can't start until nine. Regardless, I suggest you also head down to the pit and familiarize yourself with the contents of the autopsy folder, which is already down there. I can assure you that Dr. Montgomery will be expecting you to be totally familiar with the case."

CHAPTER 5

Having already changed into her protective gear, including a mask, Laurie pushed into the autopsy room, which was in full swing with all eight tables in use. Inside there was a generalized low-level buzz of conversation mixing with the background whir of the powerful ventilation system and the sloshing sounds of the water that continuously ran down each autopsy table. Since it was still early in the day, the bone saws used to open the craniums to allow for the extraction of brains were silent. Laurie was thankful, since the high-pitched whine was one of the few things she didn't like about being in here.

On table #1, which she could immediately tell was reserved for her, she saw an intact young adult male corpse lying supine, the only outward evidence of trauma being a slight scorching of the lips. On the far side of the table stood Marvin Fletcher, one of the few African American mortuary technicians and, from her point of view, one of the best. Next to him he had arranged a tray of autopsy instruments, labels, and specimen jars, indicating he was prepared for the case to begin. On the near side stood Ryan Sullivan, whom she recognized despite having only met him briefly on Friday to welcome him to the OCME. Both were clad in protective gear like herself.

"I see you two are ready to begin," Laurie said brightly as she paused at the head of the table. With the body lying faceup, the exit wound was not visible.

"We're ready when you are," Marvin said. "I think I've thought of everything, but is there any special equipment you think you might want?" He was aware that she always extensively prepared for her autopsies and was able to anticipate particular needs.

"Can't think of anything," Laurie said. "It should be a straightforward case, as far as the autopsy goes. What about the X-ray?"

Marvin pointed off to the side, where there was a bank of X-ray viewing boxes. "I have it up. It's the first one on the left."

She turned to Ryan. "Have you checked the X-ray, Dr. Sullivan? Do you mind if I call you Ryan?"

"Ryan is fine," he responded. "And yes, I checked the X-ray."

"And?" Laurie questioned.

"There's rather extensive damage to the first cervical vertebrae," he said. To Laurie's sensitive ears, the tone of his voice sounded edgy or uptight, making her wonder how she could put him at ease. "And there are several opacities, which would appear to be bullet fragments," he added.

"Excellent," she said, making an effort to be complimentary. She remembered how nervous she'd been when she'd done her first case with Dr. Bingham, who was the chief when she was hired. At the time, she was already a medical examiner—Ryan Sullivan was still a pathology resident. "Now, I know you two are eager to begin, but unfortunately I need to check on Dr. Stapleton briefly. So will you excuse me for a moment?"

"Of course," Marvin said. Ryan merely nodded and didn't make eye contact.

Laurie moved down the line of tables rapidly, nodding to whoever interrupted their work to acknowledge her. But she didn't stop. On days other than Thursday when she wasn't scheduled to do a case herself, Laurie made it a point to visit the autopsy room at 9:00 a.m. or a little earlier to do her chief rounds, when she'd stop at each table. But that morning she wasn't going to take the time even though it was by far her favorite and most rewarding time of the day, and justified having to deal with all the frustrating politics of being the chief medical examiner.

Jack was busy at table #8 at the far wall. It was his preferred workstation since it suffered the fewest interruptions by being at the end of the line, because if fellow MEs were going to interrupt him, they had to go out of their way. Jack was usually able to claim it because he was invariably the first ME to start a case in the morning.

As Laurie approached, she could see that Jack was working deep in the victim's open and empty thoracic cavity. She also recognized Detective Lou Soldano, who was standing on a stool trying to catch a glimpse at what Jack was doing. Vinnie Amendola, the mortuary tech who usually worked with Jack, was the only one who saw her approach.

"Hello, Dr. Montgomery," Vinnie said. Both Jack's and Lou's heads popped up.

"How's the case going?" Laurie asked.

"Not bad," Jack said.

"I heard it's a multiple gunshot wound case," she said. "How many?"

"Eight," Jack said.

"Ay ay ay!" Laurie commented. "That's going to take time to trace all of them."

"Maybe so," Jack agreed, "but we're making good progress."

"That depends on who you ask," Vinnie corrected. He and Jack were known for teasing each other with belittling wordplay.

"We'd be doing better if we had some decent help," Jack said, volleying back. "Anyway, at the moment, I'm trying to locate the bullet that pierced the heart and was probably the coup de grâce."

"Which will be highly significant," Lou added. "I'm hoping ballistics will prove the fatal shot was self-inflicted, with obvious positive ramifications for the NYPD."

"Interesting," Laurie said. "And undoubtedly important, but I'm worried about how long it's going to drag on, considering Jack's limitations. You do know, Lou, that Jack continues to have issues with his injured hip when he's forced to stand for too long."

"I didn't know, but I do now."

"I'm feeling just fine," Jack responded.

"I'm glad, but I want reassurance you'll speak up if your hip starts acting up. Chet has agreed to step in for you if need be. Tell me you won't just suffer in silence and make yourself worse."

"Yes, Mother," Jack scoffed, rolling his eyes.

"Vinnie, I'm holding you responsible. Keep an eye on him," she said.

"My pleasure," Vinnie said.

Although hardly confident Jack would follow her suggestion, Laurie felt she'd done what she could and turned to head back to start her case. In doing so, she bumped into Marvin, who'd come up behind her.

"Oh, my goodness," Laurie said as she recoiled with surprise. "I'm sorry."

"My bad," Marvin said. "I just waiting to have a moment with you to tell you I'm a bit uneasy about Dr. Sullivan."

"In what regard?" Laurie questioned. She looked over Marvin's shoulder. She could see the resident still standing in the same position he'd been in earlier alongside table #1, his back to her, facing the exit.

"He's uptight," Marvin said.

"I sensed an uneasiness myself, but how do you mean? Anxious or angry?"

"More anxious."

"Do you have any idea why?"

"My only guess is that he's identifying with the dead guy. He did happen to mention that he was the same age and grew up in a neighboring town in Massachusetts. Anyway, whatever the cause, there is something weird going on with him, and I thought it best to say something."

"I appreciate your concern and letting me know. One thought: Did he say anything to suggest he was socially acquainted with the deceased?"

"No, and if he was, I think he would have said so right off the bat."

"Well, thanks for the heads-up. Let's see if we can't put him at ease, and in the process turn him into a fan of forensics. According to Dr. McGovern, he currently has zero interest in the field. Unfortunately, the situation is reminding me of Dr. Aria Nichols. You remember her, I'm sure."

"Who could forget that woman?" Marvin said. "It was a sad deal, but she was so high and mighty with us techs."

"The only reason I bring her up is because you and I were at least able to turn her into a forensic fan during that overdose we all did together. My hope here is that we will be able to do the same with Dr. Sullivan."

"Why not," Marvin said as a statement, not a question.

With Laurie in the lead, they made their way back to table #1. Ryan hadn't moved. Nor had his blank expression changed, even as he acknowledged their arrival with a nod.

"Okay, Ryan," Laurie said brightly. "Time to get going here. What I suggest is that you do the case, and Marvin and I will assist. What do you say?"

As if momentarily confused, he looked back and forth between Laurie and Marvin.

"Are you up for that?" she asked, to help break the ice.

"I suppose," Ryan said at length but without the enthusiasm Laurie had expected.

"Let me explain something," she said. "Affording pathology residents like yourself more responsibility during your rotations here has been an issue that my team and I have grappled with, trying to make your time here more interesting and rewarding. Unfortunately, due to legal restraints, we haven't been able to do that. But despite that limitation, I'd like you to do this case. I will still be the medical examiner on record, and it will be my signature on the death certificate, but otherwise you are in charge. Are you game?"

"I suppose," he said.

"That's not quite the response I was hoping for," Laurie said, trying to control her exasperation. "Do you feel disinterested or unqualified?"

"Neither," Ryan said. "It's emotional."

"Emotional?" she questioned. "I don't understand. Can you explain?"

"It's a case of suicide by someone my age who is from a town next to where I grew up."

Laurie was taken aback. It seemed that Marvin had been correct. There was obviously some element of identification going on here. "Look," she said after a moment of gathering her thoughts. "We're forced to deal with suicide here daily, as there is a suicide in New York City every sixteen hours on average, sadly enough, meaning about five hundred cases a year. The rate fell off about three percent at the beginning of the pandemic for unknown reasons but has now ticked up considerably. It's an unfortunate fact of life. Let me ask you this: Did you happen to know Sean O'Brien or anyone in his family?"

"No, that's not the reason," Ryan said. "I recognize my response seems unprofessional, so I'm sorry about that. The situation took me by more of a surprise than I thought it would, but I've recovered. It just took a few minutes. Yes, I'll do the case, and I agree with you. My being an active participant will be much more interesting than merely watching, which is what I expected."

"Would you like to be excused for a few minutes?" Laurie questioned. "Or, if you would like, we can talk more about why you are having an emotional response."

"No, I'm fine, thank you," Ryan said, gaining composure. "Let's get on with it."

"Fair enough," Laurie said. "But before we do, let's talk about the role of forensics and why we are required by law to autopsy all suicides. After all, the reason you are here for the month is to get an appreciation of forensics, which is why this case is particularly appropriate. Are you following me?"

"Of course," Ryan said. "A suicide can be either a true suicide or a homicide staged to look like a suicide."

"Exactly! Or even a suicide can be staged to look like an accident. We've seen all the permutations here at the OCME. One of the things an autopsy is supposed to provide is the cause and mechanism of death, which is usually rather easy to provide. In this case it's a gunshot wound with brain and spinal cord destruction. But, perhaps more important, the autopsy provides evidence to determine the manner of death, which can be more difficult to determine but equally as important, and in some cases more so. As I'm sure you're aware, a gunshot wound can look the same whether self-inflicted or the result of an execution."

"Obviously," Ryan responded. He switched his weight from one foot to the other. Now that he'd regained his emotional bearings, he wanted to get the autopsy over, so he could get the hell out of the autopsy room. There was no putrefaction smell now, but he knew it could change in a heartbeat and make him miserable.

"What I really want to emphasize is that the manner of death is ultimately a rationally reached opinion based on the preponderance of evidence from a combination of sources, namely the autopsy, the scene investigation, social and medical background knowledge, and toxicology. This is all part of the field called forensics."

He nodded. "I get it," he said. "It's not rocket science. How about we start?"

For a moment Laurie stared at the resident while struggling with a building sense of exasperation. Chet had said that Ryan was passive-aggressive, but his tone sounded pretty aggressive. To give her time to organize her thoughts and tame any negative ones, she changed the subject by asking: "Have you read the medical legal investigator's report?"

"Yes, I did."

"Then you are aware that the MLI on this case, who is one of our more experienced, raised several issues that she thought might be red flags in determining the manner of death. Namely, the victim was found in a sitting position yet still had the pistol in his hand, which she had never seen before, and, second, that no one that she interviewed in the building heard the shot, which she estimated to have occurred around ten last night. What does this mean to you as you begin the autopsy?"

Ryan rolled his eyes as he again shifted his weight. "We have to keep open the idea that this might be a homicide and not a suicide."

"Exactly," Laurie said, choosing to ignore Ryan's impatience. "But on the opposite side of the coin, what in the MLI's report strongly argues that we are indeed dealing with a suicide?"

"The girlfriend who discovered the body said that the victim had been depressed and agitated about having been diagnosed with cancer."

"Precisely," she said. "It has been established that people with a diagnosis of cancer have somewhere around an eighty-five percent higher suicide rate than the general public, particularly when there is associated depression. Another question: What about there being no suicide note? Does that influence your thinking?"

"I don't know," Ryan responded. "Should it?"

"No, it shouldn't," Laurie said. "The preponderance of suicides don't have notes, contrary to conventional wisdom. If there is a note, provided it is real, it can be helpful in deciding the manner of death, but the fact that there isn't one doesn't carry much weight. So, as we begin this autopsy, we are leaning in the direction of believing it is indeed a suicide with the facts we have at the moment."

She cleared her throat and continued: "As a matter of interest, we have of late seen a number of cases, six in fact, where the question of a suicide being a homicide had been raised by some red flag as with this case, but in each it was decided all were self-inflicted deaths. Dr. McGovern had brought the issue up in our last all-borough weekly conference, since there were six different medical examiners involved. Since it is only six out of around two hundred and fifty suicide cases we've autopsied in this time, it's only a small percentage. This might be the seventh."

"Can we begin?" Ryan questioned with a sigh.

"Yes, of course," Laurie managed. She mentally counted to ten to calm herself. Getting this resident to share her appreciation of forensics wasn't going to be as easy as she hoped. "But before you begin the autopsy, I'd like you to examine and photograph the exit wound and swab the hands for gunpowder residue."

CHAPTER 6

Thursday, December 7, 9:35 am

As the autopsy progressed, Laurie again found herself reluctantly thinking about Aria Nichols since Ryan Sullivan clearly was as good and rapid a prosector. But Laurie didn't dwell on the troublesome remembrance. Instead, she concentrated on reminding him periodically that there had been a diagnosis of cancer without the specific type defined, so she wanted him to be particularly careful and methodical as he inspected and removed each of the internal organs, particularly the lungs, liver, kidneys, and gut. Later, when no gross evidence of cancer had been found, she encouraged him to remove even the pancreas, which wasn't done on all autopsies, as it could be palpated and sampled without dissecting. But to be certain that pancreatic cancer wasn't the cancer involved, she had him remove it. It, too, was seemingly not cancerous.

"I'm a bit surprised we haven't found any obvious cancer," she said a few minutes later, following the removal of the adrenal glands, which also appeared normal.

"There is still the head and neck," Ryan said as he moved up along the side of the autopsy table.

"True," Laurie said. "And we shouldn't forget the bone marrow. Perhaps the cancer involved was a bone marrow and blood cancer instead of a solid tumor."

"It could be," Ryan agreed. "But diagnosing the cancer might have to wait for Histology to tell us."

"Possibly," Laurie said, but she wasn't convinced. She was wondering how the original diagnosis could have been made when they couldn't find it at autopsy, but she didn't dwell on the issue. Instead, she said: "I have to compliment you on the impressive dissecting speed you've demonstrated so far. But now that you are about to move to the head, neck, and mouth, I'd like you to slow down. Obviously with an oral gunshot wound, this is where all the pathology will be. You are going to have to expose carefully and photograph the bullet's pathway plus retrieve all the bullet fragments. But first, I recommend you do an anterior neck dissection, so we can rule out thyroid or laryngeal cancer."

Ryan's speed didn't change despite Laurie's words, but she didn't complain as she was further impressed by his prosecting ability. Within minutes he had the skin reflected, the straited neck muscles severed, and the thyroid and larynx completely exposed. In contrast, Laurie had always found anterior neck dissection tedious and time-consuming.

"The thyroid appears to be normal," he said while running an index finger back and forth over the gland's surface. "No nodules. Want to feel?"

"No, I believe you," Laurie said. "Take your samples. Next up is the mouth."

"I need a new scalpel blade," Ryan said after he'd taken several thyroid samples. He handed the instrument to Marvin, who ducked away from the table to get another blade. Ryan had already gone through the two that Marvin had initially put out.

"I recommend you open the buccal cavity on both sides," Laurie said. As she spoke she looked over Ryan's shoulder and could see all the way down to table #8. Both Jack and Lou appeared to be in the same position as earlier, making Laurie wonder how much progress Jack was making with eight bullets to track. She'd not seen Chet come by, despite his promise to keep an eye on Jack.

"That's exactly what I had in mind," Ryan said, pulling Laurie's attention back. Earlier during the external examination, it hadn't been possible to see into the mouth due to the extent of the rigor mortis, meaning the entrance wound had yet to be visualized.

Marvin returned in a flash and carefully handed Ryan the scalpel fitted with a fresh blade. Ryan set to work and soon had the entire buccal cavity exposed bilaterally to show the extensive burns from the combustible gases expelled from the gun's muzzle when it was fired inside the mouth. It was also now possible to appreciate that the entrance wound was straight back in the rear wall of the nasopharynx after having pierced the soft palate but missing the hard palate.

"Okay, hold on," Laurie said as Ryan was about to disarticulate the mandible to get a better view and facilitate tracing the bullet's pathway. "Before you go any further, you need to take photos. Several additional red flags are right in front of our noses."

"What kind of red flags?" Ryan questioned. He hated to slow down. If anything, he wanted to speed up. A body that could euphemistically be called *on the ripe side* had come in and been wheeled down to table #4. Although he had only gotten a whiff and, so far, the ventilation system seemed to be handling the reek, he was worried what the odor was going to be like when the body was opened. It amazed him that everyone else seemed immune.

"Look at the tongue," Laurie said. "What do you see?"

"It looks like the tip was shot off," Ryan said.

"Exactly," Laurie said. "And forensics tells us that's a rare finding in an oral suicide gunshot case. Damage to the tongue is not unheard of, mind you, just not usual. And forensics tells us something else unusual, now that we can see the entrance wound and mentally connect it with the exit wound."

Ryan straightened up. "What else is forensics telling us?" Despite his dislike of autopsies and their associated assault on the senses, he was becomingly progressively interested in what Dr. Montgomery was saying. Up until that moment, he was intent on finishing the autopsy as rapidly as he could, believing it was a straightforward suicide case despite the potential red flags.

"Step back from the table and look at the head," Laurie suggested. "And when you do, mentally connect the entrance wound in the back of the mouth to the exit wound on the back of the neck. When you have the bullet's pathway visualized, how would you classify the pathway in relation to the long axis of the autopsy table?"

"What do you mean, classify it?" he asked.

"Would you say the bullet's track was almost perpendicular or at a definite angle, and if at an angle, is it angled up toward the head or down toward the feet?"

Ryan took the suggested step back and mentally did what she suggested. "I'd say close to perpendicular," he said straightaway.

"I would as well," Laurie said. "Since we know that the victim was in a sitting position when he was found, the path of the bullet was almost flat instead of being angled upward, which forensics tells us is the usual situation. Imagine yourself if you put the muzzle of a gun in your mouth while you are sitting in a chair with the intention of ending your life, how would it most likely be positioned?"

"You know something?" Ryan said, trying not to think about doing it but imagining someone else trying. "I see what you mean, it would be angled upward."

Laurie laughed. "Yes, and the exit wound should be in the occipital region, not at the level of the first cervical vertebrae, as we have here. Also, since eighty-five to ninety percent of the general population is right-handed, forensics also tells us that the bullet's pathway in an oral suicide is usually angled, by the same percentages, not only upward but slightly to the victim's left rather than slightly to the victim's right, as we see here by looking at the right-sided, off-center damage to the soft palate."

"Fascinating," Ryan said. He was impressed, which was hardly his anticipated state of mind. "Wow!" he added for emphasis. "Are you thinking we're dealing with a homicide here?"

"No," Laurie said. "We're not forming a conclusion yet. What we are doing, particularly you as the prosecutor, is gathering forensic evidence to put it in the balance so that ultimately a rational conclusion can be reached. Remember, when we started this case, I talked about the manner of death being determined by a preponderance of evidence, of which the autopsy is only one part. Although forensics tells us that we are indeed seeing some oddities here, these factors have to be measured against evidence that's coming from the scene investigation, the victim's social and medical history, and what can be gleaned from the pistol after it is analyzed by our new DNA Gun Crimes Unit. So far, the information that a significant other in the victim's life has already revealed that the victim was depressed and had a recent diagnosis of cancer outweighs these suggestive autopsy facts we are uncovering. But it is an ongoing process until ultimately the death certificate is signed. And even then it can be changed if new information is uncovered that alters the preponderance of evidence equation. Do you understand what I'm saying? The forensics that we practice here is a lot more nuanced than most people realize."

"You are absolutely right!" Ryan said with a conviction that surprised him. Suddenly he realized with a bit of embarrassment that he hadn't been giving the month's rotation the attention it deserved; he'd let his revulsion dominate. "Thank you for taking the time to explain it to me."

"You're welcome," Laurie said with a bit of satisfaction. She suddenly was gaining the impression that her goal of stimulating the resident's interest was succeeding, at least for the moment. "Now, let's get on with this case. I'm afraid I have a full day ahead of me."

"Of course," Ryan said. With renewed vigor and interest, he fell to work and soon had the bullet's pathway exposed and photographed. He also managed to carefully extract the bullet fragments that remained after the projectile had collided with the dense cervical vertebrae.

When it was time to turn attention to the brain and assess the damage, particularly to the brain stem, Laurie and Ryan stepped away from the table. This gave Marvin the room to use the bone saw.

"You mentioned earlier six other cases where the question of suicide versus homicide arose," Ryan said. He had to speak louder than usual to be heard over the whine of the bone saw.

"I did," Laurie answered.

"Were they all oral gunshot suicides like this one?"

"No. If I remember correctly, of the four gunshot cases, there was one temporal gunshot and the other three had oral entrance wounds, which is not as expected, as temporal are more typical than oral. As I recall, the other two non-gunshot suicides were a hanging and an exsanguination from the wrists, but I wouldn't bet my life on it. I didn't hear the whole discussion because I was summoned out of the conference for a phone call. Besides, it wasn't a long discussion. The issue was brought up more to let everyone know the phenomena was occurring, so that an eye can be kept out for additional cases. One of our important functions here at the OCME is to call attention to emerging trends, particularly involving infectious diseases, but other causes of death as well."

"Well, this case of ours might be counted among those."

"True."

"Do you know if the red flags that suggested homicide on the oral gunshot cases were similar to what we have here?"

"I couldn't tell you, except I assume the guns weren't discovered in the victims' hands. I know how thorough the MLI on this case happens to be. But why are you asking?"

"I'm not sure," Ryan admitted. "It seems to me that it would be interesting to know what each of the red flags were and if there were any similarities among the cases, particularly if there was one similarity in all the cases."

"What do you have in mind?" Laurie questioned.

"I don't know," Ryan said. "Anything at all. Similar sex, age, race, histories. Any similarity that related them or, if not all of them, most of them."

"No, I don't think so, at least not that I remember. But . . . I'm not the one you should ask. Dr. McGovern would be a better source, as he was the one who brought the issue up and made the announcement and moderated the discussion. I do remember for certain it was six different MEs involved. Suicide is an important issue here at the OCME. During the height of the pandemic, the suicide rate in the city dropped. It didn't drop much but enough to be noticed. And now we are seeing an uptick."

"Why do you think it dropped during the pandemic?"

"No one has any idea other than thinking that when people were isolating and confined to their homes, they related more to each other. But that's just a guess. Anyway, It's an interesting social question."

"You said that these six cases you mentioned happened over the previous six months, and that during that time the OCME saw some two hundred and fifty suicides. That's about two-point-five percent. Do you know if that is a consistent figure over other six-month intervals?"

"I have no idea," Laurie said. She was impressed anew. She admired people capable of arithmetic calculations in their heads since she couldn't do it. She always needed a pencil and paper.

"I have an idea," Ryan said.

"What is it?"

"Before I make the proposal I have in mind, I'd like to say that you allowing me to do this case with you has truly sparked my interest in forensics. To be honest, now that I think about it, I have a sneaking suspicion that was your goal."

"It was," Laurie admitted. "Dr. McGovern let me know that your attitude was lacking and that you'd skipped some afternoon autopsies to head back over to the medical center."

"Well, you have succeeded in changing my attitude, at least about forensics, as it has pretty much done a one-hundred-eighty-degree switcheroo. I have resented having to spend a month here, particularly because, to be honest, I find autopsies extremely distasteful, which as a medical examiner you probably find incomprehensible. I won't go into the details, but take my word that observing autopsies is extremely un-pleasant and stressful for me. That said, the forensic issues you've raised here this morning I find truly interesting. What I'd like to do is spend some serious time and effort looking into this case in conjunction with the six previous cases you've mentioned. I'd like to see if there are any commonalities that might have been missed."

"How do you plan to look into them?"

"You mentioned there were six different medical examiners involved. What I propose to do is to talk to all six to do a detailed study and be able to compare them to look for any unappreciated commonalities."

"You would need to talk to the MLIs as well to get the full picture," Laurie said.

"Good point. Yes, I'll talk with the MLIs, too."

"I'm happy to have stimulated your interest," Laurie said. "And, sure, go ahead and look into the issue. I can assure you that no one is going to try to stop you. And I'm certain that Dr. McGovern would be happy to give you some time at one of the afternoon conferences *to enable you* to present any significant findings you might uncover."

"All right, he's all yours," Marvin called out to Laurie and Ryan as he gestured toward O'Brien's supine corpse whose head, propped up on a wooden block, was now missing the top of the skull, exposing the brain. His scalp had been pulled over his face to allow Marvin to saw through and remove the bony cranial cap.

As Laurie was about to step forward, Ryan put up his hand, motioning he had more to say. "I'd like to propose a deal," he said.

"What kind of deal?" Laurie questioned. Having seemingly accomplished her goal with Ryan, her mind was already shifting to her morning's packed schedule, particularly the upcoming meeting with the Hunter College dean.

"Tomorrow I will have been here for a week, and I have already participated in eight total autopsies including this one. I now have a good understanding of the autopsy process, which is reflected in my prosecting skill. What I'd like to ask is if I can be excused from observing autopsies at least while I concentrate on investigating these seven suicides." Ryan held his breath, as this was his real motivation.

For a few moments, Laurie stared at him while her mind processed his request. She was taken aback. No pathology resident had ever asked to be relieved of observing autopsies. The autopsy was the main pillar of forensic medicine. Even Aria Nichols hadn't asked to be excused from autopsies.

"It's not that I want to shirk responsibilities," Ryan added. "Except for this case, I'm only an observer, so my being relieved for a time from observing won't add to anyone else's burden. And as I have said, I find the autopsy experience extremely distasteful. Perhaps it is a failing on my part, but it is what it is."

"I'm not sure how Dr. McGovern would feel about this," Laurie said. She was reluctant to interfere with Chet's handling of the OCME's educational efforts, as he was doing a superb job as its director.

"Let's not bring in Dr. McGovern," Ryan said. "He and I have had our differences. I find his misogyny an anachronism in today's woke culture and hard to bear."

For Laurie, his statement was like an unexpected splash of cold water. Chet's attitude toward women and what to do about it was something she'd been struggling with. Also, the issue of administrative sexual harassment was another unwelcome reminder of Aria Nichols, because she had claimed that she'd personally experienced Chet's misogyny.

"I don't mean to find fault with Dr. McGovern," Ryan added quickly. "I know he's sincere about his educational role. Instead, I'd rather emphasize that I will make constructive use of the time."

"Okay, I'll give you a green light for this research idea," Laurie said, while also deciding not to get into a discussion about Chet's social failings with a pathology resident. "But you must keep me informed of your progress, and I don't want to hear you are dragging it out just to stay out of the autopsy room. There's so much more to learn in here than you can imagine, despite the drawbacks. I'm guessing this study of yours shouldn't take that many days since Dr. McGovern can supply you with the names of the victims, accession numbers, and the name of the medical examiner and MLI on each case, so you won't have to search for them on your own. If you have any trouble getting the original MLI workups, Bart Arnold, who is head of the department, can help. I'll let

Dr. McGovern and Mr. Arnold know your intentions. Otherwise, I'd like this agreement between us to remain private, particularly from other residents who have yet to rotate here. I'm sure you understand that I don't want to set a precedent."

What Laurie didn't mention was that Aria, too, had asked to do a bit of research, which ultimately led to her death. But this negative association was replaced by another much more positive one. Ryan's request to research a group of suicides with questions about their manner of death reminded her of one of her own similar investigations. It had been a series of suspected overdoses whose manner of death she ultimately proved were homicides. It had happened way back when she'd first joined the OCME, and crack cocaine was the illegal drug of choice. Most significant, the investigation had been one of her personal triumphs.

"I'll be happy to keep you informed," Ryan said. He was ecstatic but careful to suppress his response for fear of making her reconsider. Her eyes had briefly glazed over as if she were reconsidering, and he'd not expected she would acquiesce so quickly. "When will you let Dr. Mc-Govern know? I'd like to begin right away." He was hoping to avoid being assigned another autopsy that afternoon.

"As soon as we finish here," Laurie said. "Now let's get the brain out and complete this case so you can get started."

CHAPTER 7

The rest of the Sean O'Brien case went rapidly once the brain was out of the skull. The pathology was visually apparent with the lower half of the brain stem destroyed by bullet fragments after traversing the first cervical vertebrae. After photos were taken, since the brain damage was in essence the mechanism of death, Ryan sewed up the corpse with commendable speed.

"Well done!" Laurie said as she removed her gloves. "You've handled this autopsy with finesse despite your saying how much you dislike the process."

"It's been a comparative pleasure," Ryan said.

"Now, I have to get a move on," Laurie said, "but I trust you will help Marvin clean up here and get the body in the cooler. Also, I expect you to dictate the case and make sure all the samples are delivered to the proper departments."

"Of course," Ryan said.

She nodded appreciatively. Ryan's immediate willingness to pitch in with post-autopsy duties, particularly helping with the body, was a sharp contrast with Aria Nichols's attitude. Laurie was pleased. Although there were some similarities between the two residents, which had initially been disturbing, there were obvious major differences. The last thing Laurie wanted was a repeat of the debacle Aria Nichols's untimely and mournful death had ultimately caused.

Leaving Ryan and Marvin, she walked the length of the autopsy room, again nodding to those people who acknowledged her. She was intent on finding out how Jack was holding up and then getting to her office. As she neared table #8 she could see Jack and Lou were in essentially the same positions they'd been the whole time she'd been involved in the O'Brien case.

"How's it going?" Laurie asked as she stepped up to the table's head. At that moment Jack had both hands deep in the victim's pelvic area. Lou was still standing on the stool trying to see over his shoulder. Vinnie was holding a retractor to increase Jack's exposure.

All three men looked up at her.

"Terrible," Vinnie said. "We're going to be here until next Tuesday."

"You might be, but I'm going to be done with my part within the hour," Jack interjected.

"Dreamer," Vinnie said.

"It's going fine," Lou said.

"Of the eight gunshot wounds, how many have you traced so far?" Laurie asked.

"Six," Jack said. "And they were the difficult ones." He put his hands straight up over his head and stretched. "The last one is a thigh wound, which should be relatively quick."

"The important thing is that we've recovered the bullet that was the coup de grâce," Lou said with evident satisfaction. "And we don't have to wait for ballistics! It's obviously a full metal jacket, which exonerates the NYPD since we exclusively use hollow points. This perp died from a self-inflicted wound."

"Okay," Laurie said. "But how are you managing, Jack? How is your hip?"

"The hip's fine," Jack said with a wave of dismissal. "No problem at all."

"Are you sure?" she questioned. In the past, Jack was always one to minimize physical symptoms.

"Hundred percent," Jack said. "No discomfort at all."

"Chet was supposed to come by to check on you," Laurie said. "Has he been here?"

"Nope, not yet," Jack responded. His attention drifted back into the depths of the pelvic area. It was obvious he wanted to get back to work.

"All right," Laurie said, recognizing there wasn't more she could do. "Good luck!"

"Good luck to you, too," Jack said without looking up.

She headed back toward the exit. Again, she didn't stop. She knew time was closing in on her upcoming meeting with the Hunter College dean and, as per usual, she felt unprepared. As she passed table #1 Marvin and Ryan were busily moving Sean O'Brien's corpse onto a gurney and didn't look in her direction. A moment later she was about to exit through the double doors when they burst open, forcing her to reel back to avoid being hit.

"Oh, sorry!" Chet said as he saw what had happened. Neither he nor Laurie had looked through the small wire-enclosed windows in both doors, which were there for that very reason.

"Not a problem," Laurie said as she quickly recovered.

"How did the case go?" Chet inquired as he glanced over her shoulder toward table #1, where Marvin and Ryan were in the process of maneu-vering the gurney away from the table.

"Let's chat in the hall," Laurie suggested.

He nodded and followed her back out into the hallway, where they both removed their masks.

"It went better than I could have expected," Laurie said.

"Really?" Chet questioned with an expression of disbelief.

"Yes, really! Why the surprise?"

At that moment the autopsy doors reopened, and with Marvin guid-ing and Ryan pushing, the gurney emerged. All four people acknowl-edged each other with a nod as they passed, but no one spoke. A moment later the gurney disappeared around the corner, heading for the walk-in cooler.

"Only because he's a strange bird," Chet said. "I didn't have high hopes. When I told him he was doing a suicide case with you this morn-ing, he flatly refused, saying he wasn't going to do it."

"Did he tell you why?" Laurie asked.

"No, he didn't," Chet said. "He even tried to exchange his case for a run-of-the-mill overdose that I had assigned to his fellow resident. It made no sense because the overdose was ostensibly routine whereas the suicide at least had a forensic issue. The only thing that passed through my mind was that it was a suicide."

"Meaning he was making some personal identification?"

"Something like that," Chet said, spreading his hands and shrugging his shoulders in a questioning fashion.

"Actually," Laurie said, "both Marvin and I felt he was acting anx-ious before the case began. When asked, he admitted to feeling some identification because the patient was the same age and from a neigh-boring town where he grew up."

"That's curious," Chet said. "When he acted weird with me he'd hardly had time to read my case summary."

"Well, whatever," Laurie said. "The important thing is that it ended up being perfect for what I had in mind to showcase forensics, and he got caught up into it quickly."

"Wow! Great!" Chet, effused with some self-satisfaction from having made the arrangements.

"Anyway, it was a terrific case for you to find for us, so thank you," Laurie said. "The important point is that Dr. Sullivan has suddenly, and I believe genuinely, become interested in forensic pathology."

"Your persuasion abilities are legendary," he said with a laugh. Everyone knew that Dr. Jennifer Hernandez had chosen the field just because of Laurie's influence.

"I think his sudden interest was more due to this specific case you set up for us than anything I did," Laurie responded with a wave of dismissal. She found compliments mildly embarrassing and usually brushed them off. "In fact, thanks to this case, Dr. Sullivan has asked permission to investigate the issue you raised about the half dozen somewhat similar suicide cases that have been seen over the past six months. He wants to see if there are any unappreciated commonalities. I've given him the go-ahead to bolster his sudden interest in forensics. I hope that is all right with you. I don't want to interfere if you are in the process of doing it yourself."

"No, I'm not," Chet said. "I raised the issue at the conference with the hopes someone might do it, especially if an uptick of such suggestive cases continues along with the uptick in suicides in general."

"Good point," Laurie said. "Anyway, I told Dr. Sullivan that you would provide him with the names and accession numbers of those six cases you presented."

"I'll do it this morning," Chet said.

"There's one other thing," Laurie said. "He also asked to be excused from observing autopsies while he is busy with this project, and I agreed, provided he doesn't obviously drag the timeline out. As director of education, are you okay with that?"

"I suppose," Chet said with an almost imperceptible shake of his head.

"I can tell you're not excited about the idea."

"Observing autopsies is what the pathology residents are supposed to do. It's why they're here."

"True, but Dr. Sullivan seems to find them particularly unpleasant, which is a little surprising for a pathology resident. Be that as it may, my idea is that if we can get him truly interested in forensics by doing this research project, he will be able to handle autopsies better and hopefully make your job easier."

"Fair enough," Chet said. "I see your point. And it will be a relief not to have to worry about where he is and what he's up to for a few days."

"I also asked him to keep our arrangement private so as not to set a precedent for future residents."

"Good idea," he said.

Laurie debated bringing up Dr. Sullivan's surprising comment about Chet's misogyny, but she quickly changed her mind. Her plate was already overflowing, and she thought she'd bring the subject up again with Dr. Sullivan when the two of them got together to discuss the results of his investigatory efforts. She was mildly concerned it somehow involved Dr. Sullivan's fellow resident, Dr. Sharon Hinkley, who Laurie noticed was a strikingly youthful-appearing woman. From Jack's previous descriptions of Chet's social immaturity and his female preferences, she worried the young resident might be too tempting a target.

Leaving him, Laurie hustled into the locker room, peeling off her protective gear as she went. She felt wonderfully pleased with herself. Not only had she enjoyed an engaging autopsy, but she'd also seemingly accomplished her goal of upping the troublesome resident's interest in forensics. As an added benefit, she appreciated the idea that someone would be looking into the curious series of suicide cases Chet had put together, as it reminded her of when she'd been a medical examiner tyro.

CHAPTER 8

Thursday, December 7, 11:15 am

D r. Jerome Pappas had a bad feeling about the next patient he was to see at Oncology Diagnostics, a clinic he and his partner, Dr. Malik Williams, had started a year earlier on Park Avenue in the Upper East Side of New York City near the Lenox Hill Hospital. His scheduling clerk, Beverly Aronson, had warned him the appointment was for an indignant thirty-four-year-old woman by the name of Marsha Levi who was demanding to be reimbursed for her out-of-pocket expenses for a negative full-body scan that had been done the week before. Beverly had added that the patient insisted that the test had not been indicated nor needed.

What upset Jerome the most was that such occurrences had been happening all too often over the last six months or so, possibly at a quickening pace. It had only been a week ago that he'd been hounded by another patient, Sean O'Brien, with the same complaint.

Although in both cases the patients claimed they wanted their money back, what they were the angriest about was believing they'd suffered high-dose, unnecessary radiation from the computerized to-mography at Full Body Scan, another company Jerome and Malik had founded almost ten years ago. There was nothing to be done about the radiation issue, since it was true and couldn't be reversed, so the patients put all their frustrations on getting reimbursed. Unfortunately, this cre-ated a potentially serious problem because Full Body Scan was in major financial difficulties, which had required Jerome and Malik to prop up the business by mortgaging all their personal real estate in the short term, including their weekend homes in the Hamptons. The reality was that every PET/CT study currently done at Full Body Scan was important for the company's survival, and any rash of people demanding their money back could be a death knell not only for the business but for Jerome's and Malik's lifestyles.

Jerome took his glasses off and set them on his desk to take a mo-ment to rub his eyes and calm down to face Marsha Levi. As a doctor he knew that the anxiety he was feeling was not good for him, especially considering his atrial fibrillation, for which he was taking a beta-blocker and a blood thinner. Although his cardiologist didn't agree, Jerome was certain his heart rhythm problem had been caused by the anxiety he'd been struggling with over the last year, when Full Body Scan had first gotten into financial difficulties. When they'd started the business it had been a moneymaker as it had anticipated the demand for a cancer screening test by major corporations who were in competition with each other to offer the best executives yearly physicals, irrespective of their actual efficacy.

As radiologists by training, Jerome and Malik knew that the chances of a full-body scan finding a nascent cancer were minimal, far less than something truly efficacious like a colonoscopy, but that didn't matter. What mattered was that both entrepreneurs had gotten combined MD and MBA degrees and had an inkling that major corporations and their health insurers would be enormously interested in cancer screening—even if in name only—ergo, the founding of their company.

The initial profits had been so stupendous that Jerome and Malik were encouraged to invest heavily, with borrowed money, in a lot more of the hugely expensive equipment. What they hadn't anticipated was that science was going to provide a truly efficacious cancer-screen ability by blood analysis, which had come to market about a year prior, causing a catastrophic drop in demand for full-body scanning. Recently, though, Jerome and Malik had figured out a way to utilize this new blood-based cancer-screen technology to their advantage to prop up Full Body Scanning, by forming Oncology Diagnostics.

His attempt at calming himself wasn't working. Replacing his glasses, he pushed back from his desk and walked over to a built-in cabinet that concealed a small wet bar. With the door open he quickly poured himself a finger of single malt scotch, took it in a gulp, and then stared at his image in the bar's mirror. What he saw wasn't encouraging. He was a big man with a full face that reflected his financial worries by appearing puffy, particularly his eyes. He knew he had to get a grip on himself. In his agitated state, he was concerned he'd botch the meeting with Marsha Levi and make a bad situation worse. What he was hoping to do was to contain the problem, provided he could bully the patient.

Gradually, but thankfully, the alcohol began to calm him to a degree. To bolster its effect, he took a deep breath, held it, then let it out. Feeling progressively better, he popped a peppermint into his mouth. In the mirror, he adjusted the knot of his tie and smoothed the lapels of his white doctor's coat. Thus prepared, and holding Marsha Levi's chart, he walked down the hallway and entered the nearest examination room. The exam rooms were mostly used by Dr. Alexa Murphy and Dr. Jonathan Morgan, oncologists they employed on a part-time basis. It was they who did the lion's share of examinations.

Marsha Levi was perched on the end of the paper-covered exam table. She was a small woman with dark bobbed hair in moderate disarray. She had her legs crossed and was sitting up ruler straight with her hands tightly clasped in her lap. The most obvious indication of her state of mind was that her mouth was pressed shut in a tight line. Dolores Sanchez, one of the two nurses employed by Oncology Diagnostics, was standing to the side.

"Good morning, Mrs. Levi," Jerome said as brightly as he could manage. Inwardly he winced; Marsha being married was a potential complication of how she was to be handled. At least the other patients who had been a threat had been single and living alone. At first Jerome had strenuously argued that such a selection process of professional, single people should be adhered to for all the patients chosen to help Full Body Scan's bottom line, but there just hadn't been an adequate number, and at Malik's insistence, they'd expanded the qualifications. Now that decision seemed to be coming home to haunt them.

"Have you been told why I'm here?" she challenged. Her voice was taut and her question to the point.

"I've been informed that you would like to be reimbursed for your full-body study."

"That's the least you can do," Marsha snapped.

"We were pleased with the negative result," Jerome said.

"There was a negative result because there was no indication," Marsha said.

"But as you know, your initial OncoDx test was positive, meaning you are harboring incipient cancer somewhere in your body's GI system. What we are committed to doing is finding the source to give us the opportunity to eliminate it at this early juncture, offering you a total cure. We don't want you to wait until this hidden early cancer grows to become symptomatic and has a chance to metastasize."

"Listen!" she said harshly. "My husband, Nathan, happens to have earned a science degree before going into wealth management, specializing in healthcare investments. He's not a doctor, but one of the things he's learned from all the doctors he's had to deal with is that if a medical test is positive, the first thing to do is repeat it. False positives happen. Well, he insisted I do just that with our physician. And you know what? The test came back negative."

"What kind of test?" Jerome asked, despite already fearing the answer. He cringed because hearing Marsha's story confirmed his worst concerns. Her situation was identical to Sean O'Brien's and the others'. They, too, had had their OncoDx test repeated by their own doctors, and they, too, had come back negative, making them resentful of having endured a full-body PET/CT scan as well as other screening tests Oncology Diagnostics offered.

"It was the same as the test you offer here," Marsha said, to Jerome's chagrin. "So then we tried one of the other new cancer tests that my doctor recommended, which I can't remember the name of, and it was also negative. Obviously, your goddamn OncoDx test was a false positive, meaning I don't have cancer, and I certainly didn't need the full-body PET/CT scan, which I sincerely regret being talked into."

"I recommend we try OncoDx for a third time," Jerome said, despite knowing Marsha wouldn't agree. "We've never experienced a false positive." He secretly cringed again at such a falsehood because claiming tests were positive was saving Full Body Scan from bankruptcy.

"I think I have had quite enough cancer testing," she said. "What I'm here for, at the very least, is to get back the fifty-nine hundred bucks we shelled out for your goddamn worthless scan."

"We ordered the scan believing it was in your best interests," Jerome said, even though he knew the chances Marsha would relent on her reimbursement demand were minimal. "Oncology Diagnostics already paid Full Body Scan for your scan. Perhaps under the circumstances we could negotiate a settlement." Although it wasn't a secret, it wasn't common knowledge that both companies were owned by the same people.

"If you could take back the radiation I received, which I've been told is about the same as those innocent observers who were out in the desert watching the atomic bomb explode, we might consider a settlement. But, unfortunately, I know that is not possible. This is not a negotiation. We want our money back or you will hear from our attorneys."

"I will have to discuss this with my business partner and get back to you," Jerome said, wanting to buy time.

"You do that," Marsha said as she picked up her winter coat from the side chair. "We'll expect to hear something positive from you by the middle of next week. And to tell you the truth, I think someone should look into your business plan—and that someone might just be me. I'm an investigative reporter for CNN. From what my husband said, you should have been the one to repeat the test to rule out a false positive right away." She then nodded irritably at Dolores Sanchez before forcibly swinging open the door to the hallway and causing its hardware to bang against the wall before disappearing.

Jerome stood riveted in place while staring at Dolores, wondering what she was thinking. Although he was tempted to ask her in hopes of tamping down inevitable in-house employee gossip, he decided he was too riled up. What he needed to do was talk to his partner.

Leaving the exam room, Jerome hustled down to Malik's closed office door. Before knocking, he shot a glance at Beverly, their shared private secretary. She made a motion with her hand positioned like a phone next to the side of her face, suggesting Malik was on a call. Regardless, Jerome cracked open the door and leaned inside.

Malik was indeed on the phone, and he looked over at Jerome questioningly. Jerome silently mouthed, *Come to my office when you are done!*

Malik nodded to indicate he understood and held up two fingers.

Satisfied he'd be seeing his partner in two minutes, Jerome hustled back to his office, leaving his door ajar. Inside, he headed directly to the built-in bar. On this occasion he poured himself two fingers of scotch before polishing it off in several gulps. He then sat at his desk drumming his fingers as he waited impatiently for the alcohol to take effect and Malik to appear.

To Jerome's annoyance, it was more like ten minutes before Malik walked in, closing the door behind him. He was a gangly, tall yet nimble Black man, his stature reflective of his athletic past and in sharp contrast to Jerome's blocky silhouette. Their personalities were equally as contrasting. In the face of Jerome's inevitable pessimism and bleak outlook, Malik was always positive and upbeat, which was one of the reasons they got along so well and had been good business partners. They had met during their radiology residency at Weill Cornell and became fast friends when they learned that both had gotten combined MD-MBA degrees and had entrepreneurial inclinations.

"All right," Malik said. "What is it now?" He sat down into Jerome's low, deep leather couch. His knees stuck up into the air like stumps of trees.

"We have another acute disaster," Jerome said. His voice reflected his anxiety. "It's as bad as Sean O'Brien and probably worse. She's married, and she's a freaking investigative journalist at CNN threatening to look into our business plan! I hope I don't need to explain why that could be the worst possible situation."

"Okay, calm down!" Malik advised. "We'll deal with it. Tell me more."

"Her name is Marsha Levi," Jerome said. "She's a pistol, and I wouldn't put anything past her. Unfortunately, she had her doctor repeat the OncoDx, and of course it came back negative. A few minutes ago, she came in here demanding reimbursement for her full-body scan, threatening to get lawyers involved if we don't. This whole situation is serious and getting worse. Something must be done immediately. And dealing with this harpy is not going to be easy because she's married. I warned you that we shouldn't include any married people, but you wouldn't listen. So here we are. This is a disaster in the making."

"First of all, this is only the seventh case out of literally hundreds, so it's not getting worse. These last two might be close together, but the previous one was more than a month ago. Calm down. We're prepared for this."

"I don't see how you can possibly say that," Jerome stated, raising his voice. "We're not prepared."

"I disagree," Malik said soothingly. "Need I remind you that when this first happened and you thought it was the end of the world, we spent significant time and effort to find a clandestine organization that had the wherewithal and inclination to deal specifically with this kind of situation. And we succeeded. Right?"

Jerome stared back at Malik, feeling his anger ebb. After all, Malik was correct.

"This is the exact reason why we found Action Security," Malik said. "Do you want to call Chuck Barton, or do you want me to do it? Obviously it's something that can't wait."

"Okay, I'll do it, since I'm already familiar with the patient," Jerome said.

"Excellent!" Malik said. He slapped the tops of his knees and then stood. "Let me know what Chuck says. I'm sure that the Marsha Levi situation will be handled straightaway with the kind of military precision we've come to expect."

"Let's hope so," Jerome said. "But what about the woman being married? Aren't you worried that's going to be a major problem? The last thing we want is an investigation of any kind by anyone."

"I'm sure they'll know how to handle it," Malik said. He had already opened the door to the hall. "Remember, they're professionals, which is why we pay them what we do."

As soon as Malik left, Jerome's anxiety came back in an unwelcome rush. He reached for one of the burner phones they kept to contact Action Security, his hand shook as he dialed, and when he spoke, his voice came out in a higher register than he could control.

CHAPTER 9

Thursday, December 7, 12:35 pm

With a folder tucked under his arm, Chet traversed the second-floor lunchroom, which was a more generous term than the room deserved: It was just an open space with painted cement block walls and a linoleum floor filled with a bunch of aging Formica tables and mismatched plastic seating. The lighting was harsh; its recessed fluorescents made everyone look anemic. The few windows were high on the wall, not that it mattered: The NYU Medical Center building was less than six feet away. As for food, the only choice was a line of vending machines.

Although Chet rarely used the room, preferring to eat lunch in his office, a lot of employees did, and as he snaked his way across the space he nodded and smiled at a number of acquaintances, many from maintenance and janitorial services. In contrast with some of the other medical examiners, Chet got along fine with everyone, as he felt everyone was on the same team. On this visit, his destination was the residents' room.

As he knocked and walked in, he was pleased to find Dr. Ryan Sullivan seated at one of the ancient metal desks behind a monitor. In the week the resident had been there, he'd often been difficult to find and wouldn't always respond to texts. "I'm glad I caught you," Chet said. He grabbed the empty wheeled desk chair from the second desk in the room, pulled it over toward Ryan, and sat down. "I heard your case this morning with Dr. Montgomery went well."

"It did go well for a change," Ryan said, but his tone belied his words. There was a mildly hostile, blaming edge to his voice.

Chet eyed the resident. From the moment he'd met him a week ago he'd had the sense they weren't going to get along due to the man's attitude. Chet had made an effort to gain at least a male connection by asking about Ryan's resident partner's social status, but it had fallen flat. He was again making an effort now by coming to talk with him instead of summoning Ryan to his office.

After clearing his throat to give him a moment to gain a more positive mindset, Chet opened the folder he was carrying and pulled out a sheet of paper, which he held aloft. "Dr. Montgomery asked me to provide you with a list of the six cases I had drawn up a couple of weeks ago to present at our conference. From what she told me, they're similar to the case you just did with her where there was at least a suspicion raised about the manner of death for various subtle reasons. Ultimately they have all been signed out as suicides, just as Dr. Montgomery said she believed would be with the case this morning."

Chet reached over and handed the list to Ryan. Ryan took it and glanced at it. It was a list of six individuals with their ages, OCME accession numbers, the names of the medical examiners, MLIs, and dates of the autopsies. That was it. No other information was provided.

"This is all?" Ryan questioned with obvious disappointment. He had hoped for a lot more information than bare bones.

"Yes, that's it," Chet said.

"Okay, thanks," Ryan said simply. He was already looking on the bright side. With so little initial information, maybe he would be able to drag out the project for a few additional days.

"How do you propose to look into these cases?"

"I don't know," Ryan admitted. He hadn't given the issue much thought, since his real motivation was to get out of observing as many autopsies as possible over the remainder of the month.

"Perhaps I can give you a suggestion of how to start by telling you how the issue was brought to my attention," Chet said. "Provided you are interested."

"I'm interested," Ryan said in a tired voice. He had little patience with foible-laden authority figures like Dr. McGovern.

For another moment Chet just stared back at this young, irritating resident. Chet had half a mind to just get up and walk out. But then he remembered Laurie's obvious interest in his circumstance, and he reconsidered.

"Okay," Chet said. He closed his eyes for a moment to organize his thoughts. "As you can see, the medical examiner in each of these cases was different. But that's not the case with the medical legal investigators. Have you met any of the MLIs?

"No, I haven't," Ryan said.

"I sincerely recommend that you make an effort to change that. Our MLIs are well trained and have an abundance of experience, and they can teach you a lot while you are here. They are the OCME's first line of defense in dealing with the onslaught of the roughly hundred and fifty daily deaths in New York City."

"I'll take your word for it," Ryan responded.

Chet paused and once more considered walking out, but, again, respect for Laurie kept him in his seat.

"Case numbers one and three were investigated by David Goldberg," Chet continued, his voice now sounding tired. "It was he who initially brought the issue to my attention, as he knew we are interested in picking up trends. So I had Bart Arnold, who heads up the department, ask his team if there had been any others. Well, it turns out there had been. Kevin Strauss, another MLI on the evening shift, had seen cases five and six, while Janice Jaeger, one of the night shift MLIs, had seen case number two as well as the case you did this morning, and Darlene Franklin, also on the night shift, had done case number four. So, my advice is to start with the MLIs, get their take, and then move on to the MEs. That will give you a clear picture of the whole group, and you can let us all know if you uncover anything interesting."

"Dr. Montgomery said she was going to talk with Bart Arnold," Ryan said.

"Good! That will smooth your way. She also told me that you have asked to be relieved of your duties vis-à-vis observing autopsies while you are busy with this research project."

"Yes, to my relief," Ryan admitted. "I'm sensing you don't approve."

"Of course I don't approve," Chet said, giving vent to his irritation at having to pander to this passive-aggressive parvenu. "Observing a wide range of autopsies is why you are here."

"I'm here to get an appreciation of forensic pathology," Ryan corrected as he held up the list and waved it in the air. "Looking into these possibly stagged suicides will accomplish that far more effectively and without the torture. As far as I'm concerned, I've already seen more than enough autopsies. I wouldn't shed a tear if I never saw another."

"One can never see enough autopsies, considering their importance in forensic pathology."

Ryan rolled his eyes without trying to hide it. He found this man to be insufferable. Ryan had to deal with too many similarly flawed, self-absorbed people in positions of power in his difficult life and had mistakenly thought he'd finally reached a point nearing the end of medical specialty training where that would no longer be necessary.

"Let me give you some advice," Chet offered. "Medicine is a team endeavor, which requires pulling your weight along with making a serious effort to get along with your colleagues. Furthermore . . ."

Ryan didn't respond. He glanced back down at the list Chet provided and was momentarily transfixed. Although this current endeavor was more a ruse than a legitimate project, he was surprised that he was already looking at a commonality. The ages of the cases, including the one he'd just done with Dr. Montgomery, were strikingly similar, all within five years of each other, meaning the entire lot were a close cohort of millennials. The significance if any was a mystery to him. "Could this be a mere coincidence?" he questioned aloud. After a pause he added: "Why do you think the ages are so similar?"

"What the hell are you talking about?" Chet questioned. He was stunned to have been interrupted in midsentence while trying to provide some professional advice as well as talk some social sense into this irritating individual. "Weren't you listening to what I was just saying?"

"I'm talking about the ages of these random suicide victims," Ryan said. He turned the paper around and held it up in front of Chet's nose and pointed with an index finger. "They're all millennials within five years of each other. What are the odds that could happen by chance? I'd say pretty darn slim. I know it's only seven cases, but still?" Ryan left the question hanging in the air.

Chet got to his feet, suddenly deciding that trying to give the benefit of the doubt to this flawed man was a fool's errand, and he had better things to do. "I see I'm not making a lot of progress here," he said. "To your point, in the United States, adults ages twenty-five to thirty-five have one of the highest rates of suicide, only bested by the seventy-five to eighty-five age range. So the chances that all seven of these suicide cases are in that first category are not at all slim.

"Listen, Dr. Montgomery told me that she's excused you from observing autopsies while you work on this little project of yours. That's fine for the short term. As head of OCME Education, I'll honor it until Monday, at which time you can show me whatever progress you are making, if any. At that point your reprieve will be up for review. Are we clear?" Chet glared down at the resident.

"I'll take what I can get," Ryan said simply. He wasn't going to be intimated and forced to kowtow to this blowhard, as he'd had to do often in his younger life.

Chet turned around and stalked out of the room, obviously frustrated.

Ryan, still sitting behind his monitor, shrugged. Within seconds his mind reverted to the paper in his hand. The statistics Dr. McGovern had quoted made sense from Ryan's experience, yet he still couldn't help but feel amazed that all seven of these people were within five years of each other. He took a deep breath and let it out slowly. He was wondering whether he might by any chance be looking at yet another red flag that put the manner of death in question. Suddenly, he felt his interest heighten about this project despite it involving the emotional issue of suicide. In some ways, looking on the bright side, as a kind of immersion therapy, it might even make it possible to come to terms with the role suicide had played in his life.

CHAPTER 10

Thursday, December 7, 1:40 pm

The day was clear but cold, auguring the coming winter as Laurie entered the relatively new building that housed the NYU Department of Pathology as well as the Perlmutter Cancer Center. She had a 1:45 meeting with Dr. Camille Duchamp, who had been recruited to take over as chief of the department, replacing the disgraced Carl Henderson, who was now in prison as a convicted murderer. Laurie could have walked since the department's location on 34th Street was only four blocks north and two and a half blocks west from her office, but she elected to make use of one of the Transport Department drivers who was available. Her afternoon schedule was much too tight to indulge herself with a bit of outdoor exercise, although, if she had the time, she planned on walking back.

She felt a twinge of embarrassment at not having taken the stairs, as she was the only person to get off the crowded elevator on the second floor. As she entered the Pathology Department's administrative area, she couldn't help but compare the posh surroundings to her own in the

OCME's obsolescent building. Dr. Duchamp's secretary took Laurie's coat and directed her into the chief's office, the door of which was ajar in anticipation.

"Welcome," Camille said, getting to her feet as Laurie entered. They had met briefly at several departmental receptions, but this was their first private meeting. She was a thin woman whom Laurie estimated to be about two inches taller than her own five foot five. Her features were as sculpted as Laurie's but with a thinner, more aquiline nose. Her eyes were dark and piercing but her demeanor was welcoming. Although obviously confident, as reflected by her posture and the way she held Laurie's gaze, there was a warmth to her smile. Similar to Laurie's role as the first female chief medical examiner, Camille was the first woman to take on the reins of NYU's Pathology Department. Also like Laurie, she favored dresses beneath her white doctor's coat.

"Please," Camille said after a handshake across her desk. She pointed to one of several armchairs, and Laurie sat down. "I was happy when my secretary told me you called asking to get together. I've wanted to do it for some time and thankful there was this opportunity."

"Same with me," Laurie said. "It's a function of location, with us forensic people separated from clinical pathology literally and figuratively. Unfortunately, the physical aspect is going to get worse when we move the morgue four blocks farther south to Twenty-Sixth Street."

"But as I understand it, that is going to be big boon to your mission."

"Without a doubt," Laurie agreed. "Not only will we regain a state-of-the-art autopsy facility, but we'll be reunited to a large extent with our Forensic Biology Department."

After a bit of additional small talk about the realities of their separate missions, Camille asked Laurie what sparked her wish for a tête-à-tête.

"I wanted to chat with you about the anatomical residents' monthlong forensic rotation with us," Laurie began. "Since it has been recently decided it will remain a requirement and not an elective, we would like to ask that a mechanism be in place for us to be informed in advance if a resident sees the rotation as a waste of their time, are put off by the autopsy procedure, or there's anything about the individual's personality that we should be aware of."

"Has something happened we should know about?" Camille questioned with surprise.

"It has indeed," Laurie said. "I assume you've heard the sorry tale about Dr. Aria Nichols."

"Of course," Camille said momentarily, glancing skyward as if for aid. "That sad story has unfortunately become legendary around here. She proved to be a troubled individual."

"She was definitely a challenge for us, as she could not have been more resentful of her time at the OCME, and she didn't hide her disdain. We regretted we didn't have a warning about her attitude and her social difficulties. Perhaps there could have been a different outcome if we had. Unfortunately, we currently have somewhat of a similar problem with a new resident named Dr. Ryan Sullivan, although his personality isn't as confrontational."

"Really?" Camille questioned. "That's a surprise. I've heard nothing other than praise about Dr. Sullivan. He's one of our top residents, and he's already been offered one of our pediatric pathology fellowships."

"We'd heard the same and it speaks to his credit," Laurie said. "And he's not as disruptive as Dr. Nichols was, but he has skipped some autopsies, and he has not hidden his dislike of the procedure itself. I made a point of doing a case with him this morning to see if I could build his appreciation of forensic pathology and smooth things over, and it seems I had some success. He's now volunteered to look into a series of cases questioning the manner of death."

"That sounds encouraging."

"I couldn't agree more," Laurie said. "The case I did with him this morning was a suicide. At the beginning, Dr. Sullivan seemed hesitant and anxious, and he admitted to feeling emotional about the patient being his same age and hailing from a neighboring Massachusetts town. Is that kind of response anything you might know something about?"

"I'm sorry, but no," Camille admitted. "As a relative newbie to the department, the only residents I have any intimate knowledge of are those we're hoping to welcome in July. As for all our current residents, I've been introduced to them only as a group, not individually. But the person who knows them well is Dr. Philip Zubin, the director of our residency program, who also runs our residency acceptance committee. His office is two doors away. I could see if he is free to chat, since you're here already."

"I'd appreciate that very much," Laurie said.

While Camille got up to lean out her door and ask her secretary to check on Dr. Zubin's availability, Laurie pulled out her phone to look for any urgent texts. There were none. She also checked the time. Her next obligation wasn't until 3:15 with Twyla Robinson, her chief of staff, and Bart Arnold, director of the Medical Legal Investigator Department, so she was still in the clear.

"Good news! He'll be here in two minutes," Camille said, returning to her seat. "We caught him between meetings."

While they waited, Laurie gave Camille the latest on how the OCME was trying to give the pathology residents more of a sense of responsibility, even though they weren't able to sign the death certificates. Before they finished the conversation, Dr. Philip Zubin walked in.

Laurie had met Phil, as he preferred to be called, on numerous occasions. He was a tall, slender man who appeared even taller thanks to his long white doctor's coat. In many respects he could have passed for a relative of Camille's with the same thin, French facial features and coloring. He also reflected the same sense of confidence with his ramrod posture and unwavering, direct gaze. He greeted Laurie cordially with her first name as he took the seat next to hers.

Camille explained why Laurie was there, making specific reference to Ryan's negative attitude and the man's possible identification issues with an autopsy case he'd participated in that morning.

"I wasn't aware of his feelings about forensic pathology," Phil said as he leaned back in his chair and intertwined his fingers in his lap. "Why do you suspect identification issues?"

"The mortuary tech and I thought he was so hesitant and anxious before the case began, as if he wanted to flee, and he even said as much. I'm not exaggerating. I even asked him if he wanted to be excused."

"What kind of case was it?" Phil asked.

"It was a suicide of an equivalent aged male from a town near to where Dr. Sullivan grew up."

"Ah!" Phil said with immediate understanding, nodding his head several times. "Dr. Sullivan has an unfortunate personal history involving suicide."

"Such a thought passed through my mind," Laurie said. "Is this something we should have known about?"

"That's a good point," Phil said. "Perhaps so. He is a complex character having experienced a difficult childhood. We on the acceptance committee were torn between his obvious promise and his rather dark history. To help us, I put together some notes about information he willingly and spontaneously provided during my interview with him, which I circulated to all the committee members. I could offer you a copy if you are interested."

"I'd be very interested," Laurie said. She was becoming more and more intrigued.

"I'll be right back," Phil said. He got to his feet and left the office.

"This is all news to me," Camille admitted. "I'd only heard good things about Dr. Sullivan's performance as a resident, including his being highly recommended by the clinical staff for a fellowship."

Phil returned within minutes. He extended a sheaf of four stapled pages. Laurie took it as he sat back down. The first page had Ryan Sullivan's name followed by NEW YORK UNIVERSITY DEPARTMENT OF PATHOLOGY ACCEPTANCE COMMITTEE. Below that was a date from five years earlier. Laurie turned the cover and began to scan the pages. One of the things she'd had to relearn when she became chief was how to read. In medical school it had been a plodding word-for-word effort in hopes of committing every fact to memory. Now it was speed-reading to get the gist so that she could get through the barrage of memoranda she faced daily.

"You can keep those," Phil said. "But to give you a summary, Ryan Sullivan had a difficult childhood by any stretch of the imagination, starting out living below the poverty line in the hardscrabble town of Chelsea, Massachusetts. As if that wasn't enough, his mother died of untreated breast cancer when he was a mere eight years old, and his physically abusive, alcoholic father died by suicide within a month. When no one in the family was willing or able to take in Ryan and his older brother, Connor, the duo was remanded to the custody of the Massachusetts foster care system."

"Good grief," Laurie commented. It was a heartbreaking story. It also reminded her again of Aria Nichols, since her father had also died by suicide.

"Unfortunately, the foster care system did not serve the boys well," Phil continued. "As preteens with not the greatest behavioral histories, they were not adopted but rather sent to a series of short, inappropriate placements. As a result, both experienced recurrent incarcerations in juvenile correctional institutions."

"Good God!" Laurie commented. She was glancing at the last page. "And I see suicide came back and played more of a role."

Phil laughed hollowly. "Indeed it did. Connor shot himself when he aged out of foster care at eighteen, and Ryan attempted it himself shortly thereafter by slicing his wrists while incarcerated. Ryan has the scars, which he showed me."

"I hadn't noticed them," Laurie said.

"He doesn't try to hide them," Phil said. "He was very open with me and the other committee members he met with about his life's exceptional story, which is the origin of these notes. As I've said, he offered all this material voluntarily. Understandably enough, at this point he's appropriately proud of his accomplishments."

"The remarkable thing is that he somehow succeeded in beating the odds," Laurie said. "How on earth with such a history did he end up going to medical school, of all things? It seems too miraculous to be true."

"The knight in shining armor turned out to be an unlikely source," Phil said. "His name is Robert Matson, MD, a fifth-generation scion of the Matson family and currently a radiologist at Weill Cornell Hospital. The Matsons are a celebrated New York family that hobnobbed with the Vanderbilts, Astors, and Rockefellers back in the Gilded Age. Dr. Matson's main philanthropic interest with the fortune he inherited, which I was fascinated to learn, is to seek out intellectually gifted children caught up in the juvenile detention system, often adopting them, if possible, and sending them to elite boarding schools while at the same time exposing them to concentrated cognitive behavior therapy. Ryan Sullivan might be his best success story yet, since the boy truly excelled once he was removed from his environment."

"Ryan Sullivan was adopted by Dr. Robert Matson?" Laurie asked with astonishment. Like most New Yorkers, she'd heard of the Matson family.

"Yes, at age sixteen," Phil said. "And then the boy did well enough in Choate Academy to get into Yale college and then medical school at NYU, where he also excelled. He then applied here for a residency position and was obviously accepted."

"I wish I'd known," Laurie said. "In the future, we'd like to be informed of this kind of information. It's critical to dealing with these unique personalities."

"Well said," Phil agreed. "Since we have so many clinical Pathology Department heads on our committee, we were all aware of his unique backstory. As time went on, and he performed so admirably, it was more or less forgotten. I'm sorry. I should have made you aware. I'll try not to allow it to happen again."

"Thank you," Laurie said simply, feeling her mission had been accomplished.

Twenty minutes later, after a pleasant, brisk walk passing all the newly constructed Langone Medical Center buildings, Laurie approached the OCME and couldn't help but feel embarrassed. Her home away from home looked forlorn and forgotten with its blank façade, and she found herself wishing she could speed up the process of building the proposed billion-dollar-plus Science Park and Research Campus four blocks south.

Ducking under the scaffolding that protected visitors from any falling debris from the aged and crumbling structure, she entered and tried not to think about all the time and effort she was going to have to spend designing and negotiating space for the new autopsy suite, almost forty medical examiner offices, and a new toxicology laboratory. And worst of all was how all that effort would keep her away from what she liked to do the most, namely forensic pathology.

CHAPTER 11

With a final grunt and considerable effort, Hank Roberts managed to get the barbell, with its two-hundred-forty-five-pound weights, up and onto the bench press rack after only eight repetitions. He'd planned on doing ten but had cut it short when his phone rang. Although it was in the depths of his zipped-up gym bag, he'd heard the faint classical ringtone as he'd become sensitized to it with the ever-present hope it might be a call from Chuck Barton.

After a glance at the incoming number, he balled his right hand into a fist, contracted all his arm muscles, and made a series of pounding motions in midair. *Yes!* he mouthed. He excitedly accepted the call. Knowing Chuck Barton wouldn't just call to make small talk, Hank trusted the call very likely heralded another mission, despite his having executed one just last night. Hank lived from mission to mission to keep his demons at bay.

"What's up?" Hank said simply, suppressing his excitement and trying to sound nonchalant.

"The weather looks good in the immediate future," Chuck said. Except when using a burner phone, communication with Action Security was usually short and carried out in a kind of code. The phrase *the weather looks good* meant that Hank was needed for another mission, while *the immediate future* implied a certain urgency. In response, he repeated the celebratory pounding motion in the air with his fist. "Would it be possible for you to come to the office straightaway?" Chuck added.

"Absolutely!" Hank said with alacrity. "I'm close by, working out. I can be there in fifteen minutes."

With that short exchange, the call was ended. Hank snatched up his bag and headed for the locker room. He was at the Equinox gym at Columbus Circle, where he worked out daily. When the call came in he was at the beginning of his routine and had yet to work up a sweat, so he planned to skip the shower, just throw on his clothes, and head directly over to the Bloomberg Building at 731 Lexington Avenue where Action Security had its office.

Within five minutes of receiving the call, he was outside, dressed in sweatpants and a sweatshirt, jogging across Columbus Circle to enter the southern end of Central Park. From there, he ran east to the park's opposite corner, passing the Plaza Hotel in the process. At that point his destination was a mere three blocks over on Lexington Avenue.

In slightly more than the fifteen minutes he'd estimated, Hank was on the proper floor ringing Action Security's buzzer. Chuck Barton opened the door and greeted Hank.

"Good timing," Chuck commented. He, like Hank, looked the part of an ex–Navy SEAL with a fit physique and sharply masculine facial features. He was heavily muscled but not as toned as Hank, as he was a bit older and didn't work out every day like Hank. He also was several inches shorter. As for hairstyles, both maintained a military style, no-fuss buzz cut.

With a hand gesture, Chuck directed Hank toward his private domain. The spacious outer office was occupied by a group of IT specialists sitting behind impressive multiscreened computer terminals, which were manned 24/7. Critical information gathering and monitoring was a mainstay of Action Security's business model. It was difficult to protect clients unless the threats they were facing were known in detail, and agents in the field were always in close contact with new requests for critical information. As clandestine as the work was, there were no receptionists or secretaries. Most of Action Security employees, the ex–special forces personnel, were out in the field protecting clients. Hank's role was unique, as he and two others, including David Mach, were held in reserve for various individual missions, a role Chuck had not envisioned when he started the business.

As he walked, Hank glanced back over at Chuck and asked if he was facing another international trip.

"Nope, it's another New York operation," Chuck said.

Hank was pleasantly surprised. Coming so soon after his mission last night, he was convinced he was facing another Mexico trip. As he passed through the door into Chuck's office he was even more surprised to see David Mach, since he'd just heard Mexico wasn't in the offing.

In size, grooming, and body type, David Mach resembled Hank and Chuck, only he was a Black man with a close-cropped beard. Hank and David got along fine and had become comfortable working together thanks to their Mexico operations, all of which had gone off without a hitch. They also facetiously shared an ongoing and unresolved but friendly debate about which special forces training was the more arduous, Army Ranger or Navy SEAL, each believing theirs was superior by far. Both also had suffered significantly from PTSD, and Action Security had been their savior. Although they both lived in New York City, they were advised not to be social with each other for security reasons.

After a handshake and greeting, Hank and David sat down to face Chuck, who had retreated behind his desk.

"Okay, listen up!" Chuck said. With his elbows on the desk, he made a teepee with his fingers. "Thank you both for coming in on such short notice. We have an urgent job from Oncology Diagnostics. This time it's a thirty-four-year-old woman named Marsha Levi from the Upper East Side. So . . ."

"I thought Oncology Diagnostics was *my* bailiwick," Hank blurted out, interrupting Chuck. He felt possessive, even dependent on the Oncology Diagnostics missions and didn't want to share with anyone, lest he possibly be denied what had become his lifeline.

"Relax! It's your purview," Chuck assured him. "And you've been doing a bang-up job worthy of chest candy. Don't worry—no one's going to take it away. The reason I wanted to include David on this mission is because there's a complication. In contrast with the others you've handled, Marsha Levi is married and living with her husband. Dealing with her and her husband and avoiding a homicide investigation, as the client demands, is going to be more difficult."

"Roger that," Hank said. He felt immediate relief. Staging a murder/suicide, which he assumed Chuck was implying, would undoubtedly require more than one person to pull off. Trying to do it singly would be much too risky.

"Unfortunately, the client wants it done yesterday," Chuck said with a disdainful chuckle. "To that end I've asked the team to do a stat comprehensive report on the couple, and as soon as that is available, I'll pass it on to you two so you can decide when and how to handle it. So, stay tuned. It shouldn't be more than a few hours."

"Is that it?" Hank asked.

"That's it, unless either of you have any questions," Chuck said.

Hank and David exchanged a glance and a shrug.

"I'm good," Hank said.

"Me, too," David echoed.

"Then I'll be in touch," Chuck said. He got to his feet. "Be available!"

Hank and David stood up as well and acknowledged Chuck's order. Five minutes later Hank was jogging in the reverse direction, heading back toward Columbus Circle. With the prospect of a new mission, he felt energized and wanted to get back to the gym to finish his workout. With a bit of luck, he and David would be busy that evening.

CHAPTER 12

Thursday, December 7, 3:45 pm

Ryan returned the wave and smile to the congenial and impecca-
bly dressed receptionist, Marlene Wilson, who sat behind a
chest-high desk in the OCME lobby. Her elegance stood out
dramatically in the otherwise seedy room with its mismatched furniture
and invariable grieving visitors unhappily there to identify their departed
family members. For Ryan, she'd been the only bright spot when he and
Sharon had first arrived to start their month's rotation.

With a sense of relief, he emerged out into the fresh air on busy First
Avenue and began walking south to the relatively new high-rise building
that had been built four blocks away and housed, among other things,
the OCME Forensic Biology Department, which included the largest
DNA crime laboratory in the world. It was also the location of the
OCME Medical Legal Investigator Department, which was his destination. Following up on Dr. Montgomery's suggestion, Ryan had called the
MLI Department head, Bart Arnold, who had been friendly and accom-
modating, inviting him to come for a visit.

Entering the building on 26th Street, the contrast with the OCME forensic pathology building at 520 First Avenue couldn't have been more striking. The high-rise was modern and clean and certainly didn't look like the setting for an old horror movie. And, most important of all, there was no autopsy room and certainly no offensive odors. On the first day of his rotation, Ryan had been given a tour of the impressive facility, so he had a good idea of where he was headed.

"Can I help you?" asked a uniformed guard manning a desk next to a turnstile.

"I'm here to see Bart Arnold," he said as he flashed the OCME ID card.

"Floor five," the guard said while he released the restraining arm in the turnstile.

A few minutes later Ryan exited the modern elevator on floor five and went through a glass door defining the elevator lobby to enter a long hallway that stretched eastward toward the East River. Twenty feet away along this hall was a heavyset man in a short white laboratory coat holding open another glass door. This door led into a large office with a sea of small cubicles defined by shoulder-height partitions. Ryan assumed this was Bart Arnold. As Ryan approached he noticed the man was eyeing him in return. His face was full and lax, and he was mostly bald save for a semicircle of short, grayish hair that ran around the back of his head from temple to temple. In contrast his eyes were bright, and he was smiling welcomingly.

"I'm Bart Arnold," he said, extending his hand.

"Ryan Sullivan," he responded, shaking Bart's hand. He then followed Bart through the door and into the MLI office.

"As you requested, I've alerted David Goldberg that you wanted to talk with him, and he's waiting for you," Bart said, speaking over his shoulder and waving for Ryan to follow him. "David has a busy evening ahead of him and is eager to get started. So I want you to chat with him first and then you and I can talk later, if needed. Also Kevin Strauss was out on a call when you phoned but should be back rather soon unless there's a problem."

"I appreciate your help," Ryan said.

"Dr. Montgomery told me you were looking into that group of six suicides where there had been a question raised about the manner of death."

"Seven," Ryan corrected.

"Seven? I thought it was just six."

"There was a seventh case today," Ryan said.

"That's resourceful of you," Bart said as he headed down a long aisle between cubicles devoid of personnel. "Most of the three-to-eleven in-vestigators are already out on calls," he added, as if sensing Ryan was questioning why the office looked empty. "I asked David to hold up starting his site visits so you could talk with him."

"I appreciate it," Ryan said. He liked and was impressed by this man. Compared with the condescending Dr. McGovern, Bart Arnold was a breath of fresh air and genuinely congenial and helpful. Ryan also had a heightened appreciation of what the MLIs did. Before coming over for this visit, he'd taken a few moments to google the role and the extensive training requirements. Many MLIs had first become physician assis-tants or nurse practitioners before their dedicated forensic education and on-the-job training. It was they who handled the daily onslaught of deaths in New York City, sorting through them, deciding which cases needed to be investigated with a site visit and then which cases needed to be sent in to the OCME and potentially autopsied. As bad as autop-sies were, Ryan had the sense that being an MLI might be worse. He couldn't imagine having to deal face-to-face with death in all its varied circumstances out in the rough-and-tumble city, particularly murders and traumatic events, and doing it day in and day out, 365 days a year.

"What is it you're hoping to learn from David and Kevin? And I assume you are going to meet up with Darlene and Janice as well."

"Yes, I will meet with all four of them. I live in the neighborhood, and I plan to be back here at eleven tonight when Darlene and Janice come on shift. As to what I hope to learn, I haven't any idea. To be honest, I'm on kind of a fishing expedition. When I looked up each of the six initial cases on the computer to see what information was available, I was disappointed. All I found were condensed case histories and the death certificates. I'd like to ask about their site visits and get their original MLI reports. Once I have all that, I plan to interview each of the medical examiners and possibly obtain their original autopsy dictations.

"Beyond that," Ryan continued, "I'd like to ask the MLIs if there's anything else they might remember as being out of the ordinary. What's stimulated my interest is that all seven people were millennials with their ages spanning only five years. Could that be a coincidence? And could there be any other unrecognized commonalities?"

"Like what?"

"I truly don't know. Maybe something unexpected, like, they were all connected on social media or even something really far out, like being into mushrooms. The only thing I've noticed so far is they were close to the same ages."

Bart chuckled and shrugged his shoulders as he drew to a stop at one of the cubicles. "You raise some interesting questions, but I certainly doubt the mushroom idea. Something like that would have shown up in toxicology. But I get your point. I mean, it *is* the reason the list was created." Then he gestured into the cubical toward a boyish-appearing man who'd gotten to his feet. "Dr. Sullivan, meet David Goldberg. David, meet Dr. Sullivan."

Ryan entered the cubicle, which was in mild disarray with forensic books, articles, and autopsy folders stacked on the desk, hardly leaving room for the monitor and keyboard. Behind the desk was a cork tack-board filled with scribbled reminders as well as a few photos of children. Like Ryan and Bart, David was wearing a short white doctor's coat over a wrinkled white shirt and loosened tie. He was considerably shorter in height than Ryan, with rounded facial features and sleepy eyes. On the back of his head was a yarmulke held in place by a hairclip.

"I'll leave you two to talk," Bart said. "My desk is near to the door to the hall, so stop in when you are finished here, and I'll be able to tell you if Kevin has returned."

"Got it, thank you!" Ryan said.

"Oh, gosh, sorry," David said when he noticed his side chair was piled high with books and papers like his desk. He hastily picked it all up and then glanced around for where to put it. When it was apparent there wasn't space on the desk, he put the stack on the floor. He then gestured toward the seat.

"Thank you for seeing me," Ryan said. He took off his winter coat and draped it over the back of the chair before sitting down.

"My pleasure," David said. He'd retaken his desk chair. "I must warn you, I've got a number of site calls to make, so let's jump in. But first let me say that I'm pleased someone is looking into this. I was disappointed that Dr. McGovern didn't seem interested when I raised the issue with him almost a month ago. It caught my attention when Kevin happened to mention he'd had two similar cases that he'd seen just a week and a half apart. The two cases I'd seen were months apart, and to tell you the truth, I'd more or less forgotten about them. You have to understand, we're busy twenty-four-seven, year in and year out. You wouldn't believe how many site visits I make in a week."

"I'm learning to appreciate what you guys do," Ryan said. "I have to confess, I'd never given much thought to how deaths are handled, prob-ably like the rest of the general public."

"Yeah, no one wants to think about the nuts and bolts of death particularly in a city the size of New York," David said. "And no one wants to hear about it because it can be godawful. But I'm proud of what we do, and along with the medical examiners, we provide a real service to this community; there's no two ways about it. So, how can I help, Dr. Sullivan?"

"First, you can call me Ryan." Contrary to many of his fellow physicians, Ryan wasn't a stickler on titles, especially in a circumstance like he was now in where he was more beholden to David than vice versa. Ryan was hoping to get the MLI's thoughts and hunches no matter what they might be, and that was more likely to happen between equals.

"Fair enough," David said with a nod. He also used his hand to brush his lank, rather long hair out of his face. "I'm assuming that Dr. McGovern gave you the list I gave him."

"He did. In fact, I have it right here." Ryan got out the list, unfolded it, and put it on the only spot on the desk available, facing David.

"Good," David said after glancing at the list to be certain it was the correct one. "So, what do you want from me?"

"First off, just to confirm, you were involved with case number one, Stephen Gallagher, and case number three, Daniela Alberich. Is that correct?"

"It is. And I can see that you have correctly labeled Kevin Strauss to case number five, Sofia Ferrara, and case number six, Lily Berg, as well as Janice Jaeger to case number two, Cynthia Evers, and Darlene Franklin to case number four, Norman Colbert. With all that confirmed, how can I help?"

"I'd like to get your original workups on your two cases. Also, maybe any notes you might have made for yourself about any questionable aspect. What I'm interested in is anything at all that might have affected how you felt at the time. In all six of these suicide cases the preponderance of evidence ultimately pointed toward self-inflicted harm, yet I'd like to know of anything that might have suggested otherwise. Dr. Montgomery called them red flags in the case we did this morning. I don't know what you guys call them."

"I call it a bug in my ear," David said. "It's when something bothers me, but the significance is not definitive. Sometimes these bugs in my ear end up influencing my diagnosis and sometimes not, but they all stay there in the back of my mind like an itch I can't scratch, making me wonder if I might be missing something important."

Ryan laughed at the phrase *an itch I can't scratch*. He liked it. It seemed so apropos. It was the way he felt since the autopsy that morning.

"Give me your email," David said. "I'll send you my original workups, and all my notes on both cases."

"Perfect," Ryan said. "But now let's talk about the first case, Stephen Gallagher. What were the bugs in your ear that made you add the case to the list?" As he spoke, Ryan wrote his email address on a pad he brought with him, tore off the first page, and handed it to David.

"There were a few things," David said. He leaned back, tossing his hair out of his face in the process. "First was that he'd ordered a pizza and hadn't finished it. At the kitchen counter there was a half-eaten piece on a plate with an open bottle of beer, as if he was in the middle of a meal."

"I don't understand. Why did that make you question if it was a true suicide?"

"In my experience people who die by suicide usually aren't engaged in doing something else and then suddenly decide to do themselves in. Arguably, it's not a hard-and-fast rule, but it's something I've noticed over the years I've been an MLI and have come to expect."

Ryan nodded. It made a certain amount of sense to him and was consistent with his own understanding. His father hadn't been doing anything else when he'd shot himself, nor had his brother. Nor had he, when he'd tried to slit his wrists. Ryan made a note of the concept. "Was that the main issue that made you question whether you were dealing with a suicide?"

"No, that was just the first. The second was looking at the entrance wound. It was a temple gunshot, but it wasn't a contact wound, which is what is seen in maybe ninety-eight percent of such suicides. Instead, I guesstimated from the stellate appearance of the entrance wound and the amount of scorching and obvious stippling that the muzzle of the gun had been about two inches away from his head when it was fired."

"By stellate, you mean jagged edges?"

"Exactly. The closer the muzzle is to the skin, the more jagged the entrance wound from the explosive gases that come out of the gun's barrel along with the bullet. More than two inches away on out, the more circular the entrance wound becomes."

"Interesting. It makes sense. Anything else?"

"Yeah, there was no blood spatter on the gun, which is something I expected to see. But then I noticed the exit wound was more posterior than usual, meaning that maybe the victim had turned his head toward the gun as he pulled the trigger for some reason. That could explain no blood spatter on the gun. Anyway, it put a bug in my ear."

"Okay," Ryan said as he wrote all this down. "Is that it?"

"No, there was one more thing. From the state of the body, particularly its temperature, I determined the time of death to be somewhere around six p.m., but when I interviewed the immediate neighbors, no one had heard a gunshot. I thought that, too, was a bit strange until I realized the building had been recently renovated, meaning maybe there was significant sound insulation between apartments. Still, it bothered me."

"Okay," Ryan said as he wrote down *No gunshot heard* and followed it with an exclamation point because he recalled that no one in Sean O'Brien's building had heard a gunshot, either. "Is that it for bugs in the ear for Stephen Gallagher?"

"Pretty much," David said.

"That's four things that you noticed that made you question the manner of death, but still you called the death a suicide. Can you tell me why exactly?"

"Sure," David said. "Everything else pointed in that direction, the most important of which was the scene itself, which I look at in its entirety. There was absolutely no sign of a struggle or evidence of any staging or efforts at cleanup. That is very significant. I've dealt with a few staged suicides and there is always something about the scene that is telltale and jumps out at you. With Stephen there was nothing at all out of place. Also, there's something else you must keep in mind in a situation like this. As the investigating MLI, I'm under real pressure from the responding police officers who had been called on a reported suicide to hurry up and confirm the case as being just that: a suicide. Sometimes I have to argue just to get them out of the room since they may not be careful about the scene. The whole time they are constantly haranguing me to 'Hurry up, Doc!' If I don't confirm it as a suicide and instead raise the issue of a possible homicide, they have to *report* it as a potential homicide, which means calling in the detectives and crime scene people, all of which makes for a huge amount of busywork for everyone, and I mean huge. So, I'm reluctant to raise the issue of a possible homicide unless the facts overwhelmingly point to it. I tell you this so you might understand what the circumstances are. I mean, I'm not trying to make excuses. It's just reality because I deal with the police on just about every case I investigate. Later, when I get back here, I go over my findings and have an opportunity to change my mind since, in any case, the body is coming here to be autopsied."

"I appreciate what you're saying," Ryan responded. It made a lot of sense. He'd had more than his share of dealing with the police having their own agenda when he was a teenager. "I assume you spoke with someone at the scene to get the background on the victim."

"Of course," David said. "That's key. With Stephen Gallagher, it was his younger brother, Harold, who found him. He was there when I arrived. The two of them were supposed to go out later that evening, and when Stephen failed to call or answer his phone, the brother went over to his apartment."

"Was his brother's suicide a great shock to him?"

"Yes and no," David said. "I got the impression that the brothers weren't particularly close and were just trying to rekindle their relationship. But he did mention that Stephen had recently been broken up with by a long-term girlfriend."

"Did the brother say that Stephen was depressed?"

"He specifically said *disturbed*, not depressed, but to be honest, I don't know when one becomes the other."

"Do you have contact information for Harold, if I wanted to chat with him?"

"I'm sure I do in my notes. I'll send it along."

"Okay, let's move on to your second case: Daniela Alberich."

"That case is not as complicated as Stephen Gallagher's."

"Why not?"

"Fewer bugs in my ear. Mainly, there didn't seem to be as much blood in the bathtub as I'd seen on other such slit-wrist suicides. But then again, it might have merely been a dilution factor, as she'd filled the bathtub so full that when she got in, a lot of the water spilled out. That's how she was eventually discovered. The tenants who lived below saw water dripping into *their* bathroom from the ceiling. They called the building's super, who then used a passkey to discover the body."

"Anything else make you question whether her wounds might not be self-inflicted?"

"Yes, her coloring. She didn't appear as pale as other exsanguination cases I'd seen. In fact, her face, if anything, appeared a bit cyanotic and congested, which made me wonder how hot the water was when she got into it. I put it all in my write-up, as you will see. Out of interest's sake, I followed up to see if Toxicology had found anything like fentanyl. At the time, I wondered if she had taken something before getting into the tub and cutting her wrists, but the toxicology was negative."

"Interesting," Ryan said. Slashing one's wrist was getting a little too close to home, and he wanted to move on. "Who was your source for background information in this case?"

"It was a friend and coworker of Ms. Alberich. They were both respected and apparently well-compensated analysts for McKinsey & Company and lived in the same building. She appeared when the police arrived, curious as to what the commotion was all about. She was heartbroken and shocked."

"What was her name?"

"To tell you the truth, I don't remember. But I'll include it with my original workup and whatever contact information I have. She was very helpful and knew the deceased well."

"Was there any talk about depression?"

"There was. According to the friend, Ms. Alberich had also recently had a relationship end with a significant other and was depressed. The holiday season can play havoc on some couples and we see a spike in suicides around that time of year. It's sad when you think about it."

"Excuse me," a voice said. Both Ryan and David looked up to see a youngish man with broad shoulders and thick neck of a serious body-builder. His dark hair was cut in a fade that made his ears stand out. He, too, was dressed in a white doctor's coat, which was soiled from being out on a site visit. "I don't mean to interrupt. I'm Kevin Strauss. Bart told me you were here, Dr. Sullivan, and I wanted to let you know I was back and available when you are."

"Step in, Kevin!" David said with a wave. "Meet Dr. Sullivan, who prefers to be called Ryan."

Ryan stood up and shook hands with Kevin.

"Good timing," David said. "We're almost done here, and I have to get a move on, but why don't you join us?"

"Fine by me," Kevin said. He looked around for a chair in the crowded cubicle.

"Borrow a seat from Karen's cubicle across the way," David suggested. With Ryan and Kevin standing in the small space, he was trapped.

"Sure," Kevin said. He disappeared for a moment and then returned with a chair. Ryan made room by moving over as much as the space allowed.

"Ryan is looking into that list of six cases I put together for Dr. Mc-Govern," David said. "The group of possibly staged suicides."

"I know," Kevin said. "Bart filled me in. I'm glad someone is doing it. It struck me as unusual for us to see six in six months. Prior to that I hadn't seen one in several years, and then I had two within almost a week."

"I had one last year," David said. "And that one was really weird, but it was the other way around. When I first got there and saw the disarray, I thought for sure it was a homicide, especially since the victim had been shot twice, once in the stomach and then in the temple. Multiple gun-shot wounds almost invariably mean homicide."

"I remember that one," Kevin said. "It was, as you say, really far-out weird."

"What was so weird about it?" Ryan asked. He was impressed by these two men and confused at the same time. They were obviously knowledgeable and good at what they did, but he couldn't understand why they seemed to enjoy doing a demanding job that he thought was as bad or worse than doing the autopsies.

"Because ultimately it turned out to be a suicide staged to look like a homicide," David explained.

"Holy shit!" Ryan said with the shake of his head. There was more to this issue than he'd realized.

"The biggest part of this job is keeping an open mind," Kevin said. Then, turning to Ryan, he asked, "Is looking into suicides that are possible homicides a particular interest of yours?"

"Only since this morning," Ryan said. "I did a case with Dr. Montgomery that had some red flags, which is what got me interested in the issue."

"Janice Jaeger did the site visit just last night," David explained for Kevin's benefit. "That's why we haven't heard about it."

"Okay, interesting," Kevin said. "So now there's seven."

"I'm not a medical examiner, which I guess you know," Ryan said. "I'm just a pathology resident who's spending a month here as a requirement."

"We won't take that away from you," Kevin said with a chuckle. "But if you're interested in the issue, I can recommend a good paper on the rather esoteric subject written by a couple of Aussie medical examiner doctors. It's called 'Getting Away with Murder.' You should google it. It gives the details of 115 staged suicides over a number of years from multiple countries. They did a good job reviewing the literature."

Ryan wrote the suggestion down on his pad.

"What Ryan is interested in getting are our full workups on the six cases," David explained. "He also wants the contact info on the people who gave us the details of the victim and what it was in each of our cases that made us at least question if it was a suicide."

"Happy to give you all my notes, scribbled and unintelligible as they may be," Kevin said.

"I'd appreciate it," Ryan said as he looked back at the list. "What can you tell me about Sofia Ferrara?"

"Hey," David said, interrupting Kevin, who had been about to speak. "Sorry to butt in, but I have to get a move on here. You guys can continue without me." He stood up and grabbed his coat.

"Of course," Kevin said. He motioned for Ryan to follow him as he picked up his chair.

"Thank you for your help," Ryan said to David.

"No problem," David said. "I'll email the material when I get back. Just call if you have any more questions."

Ryan flashed David a thumbs-up and then caught up to Kevin.

Kevin's cubicle was nearby but a separate world. Instead of David's clutter it was orderly and immaculate.

"Please sit," Kevin said. He motioned to a side chair while he sat in his desk chair.

"I see you are a little more organized than David."

Kevin laughed with true hilarity. "We MLIs have our eccentricities. I think it comes with the job. I can't work in David's environment, and he can't work in mine. So, you're interested in hearing why my two cases were included on the list."

"I am, but first off, what were the causes of death?"

"They were both gunshot suicides," Kevin said.

"Okay," Ryan said as he made a notation on the list, which was getting filled up with them. He realized he would need to make a kind of matrix with the names of the individuals on the horizontal and then various descriptive points on the verticals like cause of death, age, and any other defining characteristics. If he was going to find commonalities besides the ages, that would be the way to do it. "Was it a temporal wound like David's first case?"

"No, both of mine were oral, which surprised me in retrospect."

"Oh! And why was that?"

"In my experience and in what's reported in the literature, most handgun suicides are temporal. These two were both oral, as was Darlene Franklin's, which is number four on the list. Despite that unusual circumstance, I was convinced both were legitimate suicides."

"And why was that?"

"First and foremost, both scenes showed no signs of a struggle of any sort, which I'd seen in the two previous staged suicides I'd handled and which I'd read is invariably present. Also, I found out that both had been known to have been depressed from the individuals who discovered the bodies."

"Interesting point about temporal versus oral," Ryan said as he added that information to his list. He remembered Dr. Montgomery saying the same, and he knew his father's and brother's suicides were temporal. "Is that the reason you added both these women to the list?"

"Heavens, no. As I said, that was a realization I made in retrospect. The reason I added both to the list was the same in both cases. Neither one had a lip laceration."

"Why is that important?" Ryan questioned. He remembered that there had been no lip laceration on Sean O'Brien that morning, so here was another potential similarity.

"On every other oral gunshot suicide I've seen, as well as the ones I've read about, there's always a lip laceration."

"And why is that?" Ryan questioned.

"It's from the recoil of the gun and the head snapping back, both of which cause the pistol to be forcibly yanked out of the mouth with the gunsight tearing the upper lip in the process. It's the same if the victim is sitting up or lying down, although a bit more so sitting up."

"Good grief," Ryan voiced as he wrote down this disturbing fact. Such details were excruciating for him to hear. The whole idea of a gun going off in a person's mouth and the destruction it would cause was hard enough to contemplate, but the idea of an individual's upper lip being torn was somehow particularly unsettling.

"And maybe the most important reason I added these two cases to the list was that both women were engaged in an activity. Ms. Ferrara's TV was on, whereas Ms. Berg had laundry in the washing machine."

"Okay," Ryan said as he added these new facts. "David brought up the issue of the victim's activity, too. You specifically said 'Ms.' with both your cases. Were they both single women?"

"Yes, they were."

"That's interesting."

"How so?"

"Both of David's cases were single and living alone, as was the case I did this morning."

"That's not surprising. Single and divorced people, particularly recently divorced, have a higher rate of suicide than married people."

"Okay," Ryan said while he thought about the issue. To him, it was another commonality along with the similarity in their ages, and he made a note on his pad to be sure to check on the marital status of the remaining two cases on the list. Then he looked up at Kevin. "So, let's get back to your cases. Is that it, as far as your red flags are concerned?"

"Pretty much, except for one other point: No one heard a gunshot in either case, at least according to the people I got to interview in the respective apartment buildings. Since it was early evening when I guess-timated the shootings took place, I expected someone to have heard something, but nada."

"Ah!" Ryan responded. "David mentioned the same thing with his case. Same with the case I did this morning. That's a bit strange, wouldn't you say?"

"Well, I don't know. Maybe it's not that rare, I suppose. Especially in newer, upscale buildings where a distinct effort had been made to soundproof the apartments. I don't know about David's case, but both of mine were in fancy digs. It was obvious both women were doing well for themselves, career-wise."

"What did they do?"

"You mean what jobs they had?"

"Yes."

"They were both bankers. Ms. Ferrara was a rising executive at JP-Morgan Chase and Ms. Berg was the same at TD Bank."

"That's interesting," Ryan said. "David's case, Ms. Alberich, was an analyst for McKinsey."

"Why is that interesting?"

"I'm looking for commonalities. All three of these victims are what I'd call executives working for major corporations."

Kevin shrugged. "I guess that's true."

"And they're all single, and nearly the same age."

Kevin nodded. "I guess that's true, too. But don't get too excited. It's a small group. It's hard to draw any conclusions from seven cases."

"One other thing before I go," Ryan said. "Just so I know, what are the names of the people you got most of the information from for each of your cases, and were they the same people who found the body?"

"With Ms. Ferrara, it was her mother, which was why I got so much material. With Ms. Berg, it was a boyfriend."

Ryan jotted that information down. Then he looked up at Kevin. "Okay, that's all my questions for now. Thank you for your time. Let me give you my email, so you can send me your workups and anything else you might think appropriate, including, of course, the contact information for the mother and boyfriend."

"Consider it done," Kevin said. "But just to warn you, it might not be for a few hours as I've another site visit to do, which I put off coming back here, and there will undoubtedly be more this evening. Death never stops in New York City."

Ryan got to his feet, as did Kevin. They shook hands.

"If you have any questions at all, don't hesitate to call me or David," Kevin said.

"You can count on it," Ryan replied. A moment later he was on his way back toward the elevator lobby. He was pleased with what he had accomplished by this visit with the MLIs. On top of becoming progressively intrigued by the issue of questioning the manner of death in the suicide cases, he was feeling increasingly optimistic about the amount of time he might be able to stretch out his little project. After all, he'd already seemingly uncovered some additional commonalities. First, no gunshots heard in four out of five cases; second, most victims were single and living alone; and third, three were career-minded professionals working for major corporations. What all this meant was that he had a lot of work to do, namely, getting the thoughts of the medical examiners. After all, they were the ones who ultimately had confirmed the manners of death.

CHAPTER 13

Thursday, December 7, 4:35 pm

F irst off," Chuck Barton said. "Let me apologize for ruining your afternoon by calling you back here so quickly." He was again at his utilitarian metal desk. Behind him were more than a dozen framed photos of him posing with various Navy bigwigs, mostly in dress uniforms. Hank and David had returned and were sitting in front of him. "The good news is that the team has completed the comprehensive background and status report on the Levi couple." He stood up, leaned across his desk, and extended a copy to each of them.

Hank and David raised up out of their chairs far enough to accept the sizable memorandums. Each settled back and opened the title page. This was common procedure. For all their missions either together or separately, the first step was gathering as much information as possible. The report's first page was a detailed summary, which was almost always adequate for carrying out the operation. The rest was useful if complications arose.

Chuck settled back in his chair and gave his two special ops personnel an opportunity to at least read the first-page summary. He didn't have long to wait. Within minutes, Hank closed the report and looked up. A moment later David did the same.

"There are several things that jump out at me when I read the report," Chuck said, "and I wonder if you share my concerns. First, they are obviously a well-off couple, socially and politically connected. He's a founding member of a highly successful private equity group and she's a journalist with CNN. What that means to me is that they are most likely more security-minded than the average couple, which is confirmed by the security arrangements they have made in their house in Greenwich as is spelled out later in the report."

"I see they have live-in help," David said. "That's a major complication."

"True," Chuck said. "But only at their Connecticut manse—not here at their New York pied-à-terre."

"That's the apartment at Eighty-second and Park," Hank said.

"Exactly," Chuck said. "And I imagine you saw that the team found out they have a dinner reservation tonight at Le Bernardin."

"Which means they'll most likely be staying in the city tonight," Hank said with a nod of understanding and approval.

"That's the near certain speculation," Chuck said. "And the nice part about that is that the client, as I said earlier, is more than eager to get this done sooner rather than later. They even called me again to emphasize the point, ergo they'd love us to take care of business tonight."

"That's not going to be easy," David said. "Security-minded people are not going to have an apartment in just any old building. We'll have to contend with doormen and maybe elevator operators. Dealing with those issues is going to take some time to arrange. I don't see how we can pull this off tonight."

"That's where we've lucked out," Chuck said with a sense of

satisfaction. He leaned back in his chair. "As it says in the summary, their pied-à-terre is a maisonette."

"What the hell is a maisonette?" David asked.

"I get it," Hank said, looked over at David. "It's an apartment in a large apartment building, which has its own entrance, which is obviously on the ground floor. Maisonettes are rare but very popular and in great demand."

"I'm impressed you know about maisonettes," Chuck said.

"When I was in high school, my brother dated a girl who lived in one. It was also on Park Avenue."

"Well, it can serve our purposes," Chuck said. "You guys can avoid having to deal with any doormen, as the entrance is around the corner on Eighty-Second Street."

"I'm not sure it will make much difference," David said. "The Levis are going to be reluctant to open the door under any pretense since it will be reasonably late by the time they return from dinner."

"That's why it is serendipitous to know where they're dining," Chuck said. "That way you can announce that you are from Le Bernardin, and you are there to return something they left behind."

"That might work," Hank said. "But what if they don't open the door but rather just call through it and ask what it is that they left?"

"The IT team suggests saying it's their credit card, which they've researched," Chuck responded. "It's a black Centurian American Express card and you will even have the number. I'm sure it will work. They're not going to make you stand outside at the door while they check if their card is missing, or at least I seriously doubt they will. If they do, then you'll have to switch to doing something in Greenwich over the weekend. But that will be a hell of a lot more challenging."

"I'm good with the credit card ruse," David said. He looked over at Hank.

"I am, too," Hank agreed. "If they don't let us in, they don't let us in, and we go to plan B over the weekend."

"Okay, let's talk nuts and bolts," Chuck said. "Let's hash out how you're going to pull this off and limit any NYPD investigation."

"I assume we're going to stage a murder/suicide," Hank said. "Staged suicides are what the clients requested for the previous seven missions. The only alternative would be a staged overdose with some fentanyl-laced drug, but I think the staged murder/suicide is a better idea. After our meeting this afternoon, I looked up the facts. There's an expected five to six hundred domestic murder/suicides cases in the US every year, so I don't think it will raise too many eyebrows, unless David and I screw up somehow. With two of us and a bit of planning, which is what we've been trained for, it should be a snap and result in very limited NYPD investigation once the suicide is confirmed. After all, with a murder/suicide they already have the perpetrator, so no need for a homicide investigation."

"Do you agree, David?" Chuck asked.

"No question."

"The key will be to separate the two people," Hank said. "With the vast majority of murder/suicides, the male is the murderer and the female the victim. The female is usually shot in the bedroom either in the head or the chest, so we can do that. I'll do the staged suicide since I've got the process down pat."

"I'll do the wife," David said. "No never mind to me."

"Okay! Sounds good," Chuck said. "How do you envision the timeline?"

"We'll stake out the entrance while they're having their fancy dinner," Hank said. "If we can, we'll deal with any outdoor lighting and eliminate and any obvious video devices. Once the marks arrive, we'll make our move quickly, as it would be best to catch them together, taking off their coats. If they're not together when they open the door, the first thing will be to find the missing spouse. If they *are* together, we'll confiscate their phones, separate them, and then do what we came to do. After that, we'll check the scene and withdraw."

"Sounds like a plan," Chuck said. "I assume you guys will get together beforehand and hash it all out to take care of any surprises."

"Absolutely," David said. He'd been nodding as Hank had been talking. "If we learned nothing else in the special forces, it was the importance of planning."

"Okay, that's it," Chuck said as he patted his desktop with both palms, fingers spread. He stood up. "I expect you to call in after the fact and debrief me."

"Of course," David said.

Hank also got to his feet. He was tempted to ask why Oncology Diagnostics was making such requests, but he didn't. He realized he didn't really want to know, lest he kill the goose laying the golden egg. The Action Security missions had in a very real way saved his life, and he wasn't about to cut off his nose to spite his face.

CHAPTER 14

I n contrast with the basement where the autopsy room was located and the first and second floors of the old OCME building, the third floor was not quite as depressing. Along with the fourth floor, it had been renovated in the not-too-distant past, creating the private offices of the thirty-some-odd Manhattan-based medical examiners. Besides Dr. Mc-Govern, Ryan had only met a half dozen of them to date and only those whose autopsies he'd been forced to observe. As a group, he found them somewhat eccentric, which he attributed to their field, but in general, rather friendly, including the doctor he was on the way to see. Her name was Dr. Riva Mehta. Three days ago, he'd watched her perform an autopsy on an overdose victim who, unfortunately for all concerned, had not been found for several days, making the experience particularly trying for him. To her credit, Dr. Mehta had performed the autopsy with considerable dispatch.

When Ryan had first returned from his visit to the MLI Department, he'd gone to his desk in the residents' office, where he took the time to transcribe and organize the scribblings made while talking with David Goldberg and Kevin Strauss. It seemed critical to do it with the conversations fresh in his mind. Although he was still planning on organizing himself further by making a matrix, he couldn't take the time currently because late afternoon was generally an opportune time to catch medical examiners in their offices. To that end, he'd called Dr. Mehta about Stephen Gallagher and Dr. Paul Blodgett about Daniela Alberich. Both had agreed to see him. He'd also tried calling Dr. Fontworth, who'd autopsied Sofia Ferrara, and even Dr. McGovern, who'd done Lily Berg, but both were unavailable.

The door to Dr. Mehta's office was open, but still he knocked on it to announce himself. Dr. Mehta had her back to the hallway, using her microscope. She responded by twirling around to face Ryan, then waving him inside.

"Thank you for agreeing to see me," Ryan said. He took the chair Dr. Mehta gestured toward. She was a tastefully attired, petite, slender woman with a dark complexion, dark hair, and dark eyes, which appeared to be all pupil and no iris. Most important, she had a kind face and a welcoming smile.

"Of course," Dr. Mehta said. "I'm glad to help and I applaud your obvious enthusiasm for forensic pathology. Most of the residents we see aren't as inquisitive."

He diplomatically didn't take issue with the mistaken compliment, and said, "I wanted to ask you a couple of questions about the manner of death of Stephen Gallagher."

"So you said on the phone," Dr. Mehta responded. "Since it was six months ago, I got out the folder and reviewed it."

"I appreciate that," Ryan said. "I'd also be appreciative if you would email me a copy of your full report." He handed her a piece of paper with his email address.

"I'll be happy to." She took the note, put it on her desk, and smoothed it out.

"I just got back from talking with David Goldberg, who was the MLI on the case," Ryan said. "Although I have not read his report, as I have yet to get a copy, he told me there were a number of details that made him question whether he was dealing with a suicide or a staged homicide. Do remember the specifics?"

"I do after rereading his report," Dr. Mehta said. "I also remember that despite these red flags, it was his opinion that it was indeed a self-inflicted wound."

"And you agreed after doing the autopsy?"

"Yes, because there was no telling-point to suggest the opposite. My fellow MEs and I have learned to respect the knowledge and experience of the MLIs. They're the ones at the scene, who take all the variables into consideration. The autopsy is just one aspect of forensics and occasionally not the most important."

"What about the issue of no blood spatter on the gun?"

"Mr. Goldberg mentioned that in his write-up, but he also suggested that the victim was seemingly turning his head toward the gun the moment he pulled the trigger. For me that seemed to be confirmed by the entrance wound being mildly asymmetric and the bullet's trajectory being more posterior than expected."

"Okay, thank you," Ryan said as he got to his feet. The other issues David Goldberg raised about the victim, involving the half-eaten pizza in the kitchen and the issue of no shots heard, clearly had nothing to do with the autopsy.

Dr. Mehta stood up, too. "Well, that was fast. I'll send you the autopsy report right away. If you have any further questions after reading it, I'm certainly available."

With an appreciative nod, Ryan walked out of the small office. He was now on his way to see Dr. Blodgett, who was on the fourth floor, one floor up. He took the stairs, as the aged elevators in the building were agonizingly slow. As he mounted the steps, he found himself wondering whether the medical examiner should be the one to make the call about the manner of death as was now the case. In many respects, he thought the MLI might be more qualified by being able to take many more significant elements into consideration. He wondered if the question had ever come up, because it made a lot of sense to him. There was no doubt the medical examiner should determine the cause of death, thanks to their extensive anatomical and physiological training. At the same time, determining the manner of death might be better done by the MLI, with their specialized and specific death-oriented training, combined with their firsthand knowledge of the scene and the information they gathered from the person who found the body, family members, and acquaintances. It seemed to him that it was the MLIs who could best put it all together once they were briefed on the autopsy results.

As Ryan reached the door to the fourth-floor hallway, he shrugged his shoulders and smiled at his musing. He could only imagine the blowback, particularly from the likes of Dr. McGovern, if he were to raise the issue.

Dr. Paul Blodgett's office was the mirror image of Dr. Mehta's but on the other side of the building and, instead of an expansive view of the remaining old Bellevue Hospital buildings across 30th Street, it faced a neighboring and taller NYU Medical Center structure a mere arm's length away. Although their offices were similar, their personal appearances couldn't have been more different. In contrast to Dr. Mehta's delicate refinement and exotic femininity, it was painfully obvious that Dr. Blodgett had allowed his health to suffer as reflected by his weight and sallow complexion. Ryan couldn't help but think that Dr. Blodgett reflected his environment, as his appearance was in perfect keeping with the forensic pathology building itself. Even his attire suggested serious neglect. On top of that, he was hardly welcoming like Dr. Mehta had been.

"I hope this isn't going to take long," he said immediately after Ryan introduced himself. He didn't invite Ryan to sit down. "I leave at five sharp."

"I'm certain it won't," Ryan responded, knowing it was already a little after five. He handed the man a copy of his email address. "I would appreciate it if you would send me a copy of your autopsy report on Daniela Alberich. Have you looked it over since I called?"

"Yes, I did. I remember the case perfectly well. It was a straightforward suicide, as far as I was concerned."

"I spoke with the MLI, David Goldberg, who had noted a few things that caught his attention. The first was that there didn't seem to be as much blood in the bathtub as he'd expected."

"He also said the tub was full to the brim."

"Let me rephrase the question. Was the autopsy consistent with an exsanguination?"

"As far as I was concerned, yes. What I was more concerned about was just getting enough blood from the heart for toxicology needs, which there was. To summarize, this was an unremarkable autopsy on a twenty-six-year-old healthy female with bilateral deep lacerations across both wrists."

"Okay," Ryan said. He was getting the impression that Dr. Blodgett wasn't particularly interested in the conversation and was taking mild offense that his judgment was possibly being questioned. "What about Mr. Goldberg's impression that there was some congestion evident in the victim's face and perhaps some cyanosis, neither of which is usually seen in an exsanguination?"

"There was a bit of congestion visible on the face and a few petechiae in the sclera, but it wasn't a lot."

"Did that raise any questions in your mind?"

"Of course, but the MLI also suggested the water in the tub had been scorching hot, perhaps eliciting a strong Valsalva maneuver. That's what he said in his report."

"When I just spoke to him a few minutes ago, he didn't say it was hot, he just suggested it might have been."

"Whatever," Dr. Blodgett said with a wave of dismissal. "If you'd like, we can discuss it more tomorrow when I have some time. Right now, it's already after five." He switched off the objective light on his microscope, which he had been using when Ryan walked in, and stood up.

"One more question," Ryan said, refusing to be put off quite so easily. "This case had been added to a list of cases where the MLI questioned the manner of death. Although the MLI on this case didn't say this specifically, I believe it passed through his mind that perhaps the patient was already dead when her wrists were cut, staging it as a suicide."

"Maybe it had passed through his mind," Dr. Blodgett said. "All sorts of things pass through someone's mind when they are doing their job. But the fact of the matter is that ultimately he decided it was indeed a suicide and that's how he wrote it up."

"You are correct," Ryan said, managing a smile. He made the snap decision it wasn't worth getting into an argument with Dr. Blodgett and possibly alienating him, as it would accomplish nothing and might even get back to Dr. McGovern. "Thanks for your time and thank you in advance for sending me your autopsy report."

"You are welcome," Dr. Blodgett said. "Call me tomorrow afternoon, and we can meet again if you have any more questions."

"I'll do that," Ryan said. With a slight nod of his head, he turned and left the room.

On his way down the hallway to the elevator, Ryan marveled that he'd learned less than he'd expected by talking with the respective medical examiners. He found that surprising. When he'd started his little project, he'd envisioned that it would be they who would be the source of the most important information. Instead, it seemed like it was going to be the medical legal investigators.

On the second floor, he passed through the now-deserted lunchroom and entered the residents' room. Turning on the overhead lights and sitting at his desk, he got out a ruler and a sheet of paper from a fresh pad and began making his matrix. On the left side of the page, he listed all seven names. Once he had that done, he began making columns for age, marital status, type of work, cause of death, and autopsy findings. Most of the page he left blank for future categories. He liked his handiwork and thought the creation of the matrix would look good as evidence of his progress and might even buy him a few more days of autopsy freedom.

Using the same pad of paper, Ryan started a kind of diary of his activities and wrote up his meetings with David Goldberg, Kevin Strauss, Dr. Mehta, and Dr. Blodgett. Not only did he write what they had said but also what he thought about what they said, including the issue about whether the medical examiners or the medical legal investigators were better equipped to determine the manner of death. His thinking was the more stuff he had, the more Dr. McGovern would be inclined to let him continue.

"My word, look who is still here after five," a familiar voice said. "Will wonders never cease?"

Ryan looked up to see Sharon, dressed in scrubs, breeze into the room. He rolled his eyes. "Don't tell me you've been in the pit at this hour."

"Yup," she said, taking the seat at her desk. She leaned back and stretched her legs out as if exhausted. "I just finished an interesting case with Dr. McGovern. Commotio cordis in a fifteen-year-old boy playing basketball. Really tragic because the autopsy was totally normal with no pathology whatsoever, particularly with the heart. The kid was the picture of health."

"No wonder I couldn't reach McGovern."

"You were trying to get ahold of him?"

"I was," he admitted. "He did the autopsy on one of the cases I'm looking into."

"Oh, that's right," Sharon said. "He mentioned you were doing a research project. As a heads-up, I have to tell you he's not happy that you've managed to get yourself temporarily excused from autopsies. My sense is that he takes it personally."

"That's his problem," Ryan said.

"What is it you're researching, if I might ask?"

"I'm looking into a group of suicide cases where there was some initial suggestion they might be staged homicides. Seven cases over the last half year."

"Cool! How's it going?"

"Better than I thought it might," Ryan said. "I've started getting drawn into it. I'm also learning the medical legal investigators carry a lot of weight around here in terms of the OCME's mission, maybe even as much or more than the medical examiners. So far with the two cases I've gotten to talk to both the MLI and ME, it was the MLI who called the shot about the manner of death, and the ME rubber-stamped it. It seems the MLI are like NFL referees—when they make a call, their call stands unless there is incontrovertible evidence to the contrary on the replay. In this case, instead of watching a replay, the medical examiner does the autopsy."

"I never watch football," Sharon said with an indifferent wave. She sat up, got out her autopsy log, and began compulsively adding the com-motio cordis case to her growing list.

"Do you know where Dr. McGovern is now?"

"I imagine he's in his office," Sharon said.

Ryan picked up the phone and dialed Dr. McGovern's office.

"Why are you calling him? I think you should let sleeping dogs lie. I can assure you that he's not a fan."

"Unfortunately I've got to talk with him because, as I said, he's one of the MEs on my list." As he waited for the call to go through, he added: "I've already talked with the MLI on the case and now it's time to chat with our fearless leader."

When Dr. McGovern picked up, he asked if it was convenient to come up and speak with him for a few minutes about the Lily Berg case. When he got a yes, he hung up the phone and grabbed his notes. At the door he hesitated.

"I have a question for you," Ryan said, looking back at Sharon. "You don't have to answer if you don't want to."

"What?"

"Did Dr. McGovern ask you to have a drink with him, like, some-time over the weekend?"

"He did. How did you know?"

"If I have to explain, you're worse off than I thought." With that, he disappeared into the empty lunchroom.

CHAPTER 15

Jack Stapleton was exhausted but thrilled. His last shot, a jumper from just beyond the foul line, didn't even touch the rim when it sailed through the hoop to win the game. He'd not had such a thrill for what seemed like years thanks to his extended recovery from his bike accident. Trying to catch his breath, he bent over with his hands on his knees, chest heaving. The next thing he knew, he was being thumped on the back by Warren and Flash, two of his four teammates.

"Hell of a shot!" Flash cried.

"It was even a better move to get yourself in the clear," Warren added with equal admiration, referring to the way Jack had confused the player trying to guard him. Flash and Warren were both impressed, which was a high compliment, since they were recognized as two of the best players in the neighborhood.

Jack nodded instead of speaking, as he was concentrating on breathing. He'd planned on only playing half-court that evening just as he'd been doing for the last month, but Warren and Flash had talked him into joining them for a full-court game. With a solid team, one win had led to two and then three. Jack was now paying for it, as he wasn't in his usual superb physical shape.

"Let's run again," Warren suggested enthusiastically. He could see their next five victims were warming up at the far basket. It was a rule that the winning team stayed on the court. If a team kept winning, they could remain on the court the entire evening.

"Not for me," Jack managed between breaths. "Pick up somebody! Sorry. I'm winded."

"Are you sure?" Warren questioned. "This next five are going to be a pushover."

"I'm sure," Jack said. He straightened up and with slightly wobbly legs started heading for his water bottle. After he'd had a drink, he waved a goodbye at Warren and Flash, who had already found a replacement. After pulling on his sweatshirt against the winter chill, he started for home, which was no more than a hundred yards away. It was a six-story brownstone on the opposite side of West 106th Street, in sight of the court. As his breathing improved, he upped his pace, feeling a bit guilty. It was after seven now, and when he'd left, Laurie was still not home from work, meaning their children, JJ and Emma, were being watched by their live-in nanny, Caitlin O'Connell, who took time off during the day when the kids were at school, and Laurie's mother, Dorothy. Originally Jack had thought he'd play for only forty-five minutes or so, but since he was having such a great time, it had turned into more like an hour and forty-five minutes.

As he waited for a few cars to go by before crossing 106th Street, he looked up. He could see a light on in their bedroom on the sixth floor, which was encouraging, since it meant that Laurie had arrived. Her usual routine was to immediately go upstairs to take a shower to wash off the remnants of being at the OCME all day before she hung out with the children. When Jack had arrived home almost two hours ago, JJ was still at basketball practice and Emma was closeted with her speech therapist despite having spent all day at her school.

His legs felt heavy as he mounted the stairs. Although he and Laurie owned the building, they only occupied half. They rented out six apartments on floors one through three, leaving floors four through six for their unit. Almost every day Jack thanked his lucky stars that they had bought the building, as the rents helped pay the hefty mortgage, meaning they lived in relative luxury at a reasonable cost, the nanny's salary being one of the highest. This was important because MEs' salaries were relatively modest, even the chief's.

"Hi, everyone," Jack called out as he came up the stairs leading into the expansive family room/kitchen. Laurie and Caitlin were the only ones who returned the greeting, as Dorothy was parked behind the TV watching *PBS NewsHour* while JJ and Emma were at the dining table engrossed in JJ's laptop. Caitlin was cleaning up from the kids' dinner, and Laurie was putting a salad together for herself and Jack. It was apparent from her muted response that she was less than thrilled Jack had been out on the basketball court as late as he had.

Despite being sweaty, he kissed both kids on the tops of their heads even though they tried to evade the gesture. They were both absorbed in a game JJ was playing. Jack was particularly impressed by the attention Emma was paying. As an autistic child, she was making impressive strides with her concentration.

"I'll be down in two shakes," Jack called out, but got no response. With a shrug, he dashed up the final flight of stairs, took a quick shower, put on a fresh sweatshirt and pants, and then returned to the family room. Although Dorothy was still watching the TV, the kids had left the dining table. JJ was at the kitchen desk doing homework while Caitlin and Emma were on the couch. It was a new evening routine that they would read a book together.

He went to the dining table where Laurie was sitting and eating a large salad while reading some office memoranda. A place was set for him, and he sat down. Laurie pushed her reading material to the side.

"My new Trek bike is terrific," he said with enthusiasm as he dug into his salad.

"Oh?" she questioned, with contrasting indifference.

"It has an electronic shifter," Jack said. "I didn't know whether it was worth the extra price, but the dealer talked me into it, and I'm glad he did. It's so easy to use. The bike also has disc brakes. I love it, and I can't tell you how much I enjoyed my ride home this afternoon."

"I'm happy for you," Laurie said unconvincingly.

"Okay," Jack said. "I can tell you're irritated with how long I was out on the court tonight. I'm sorry. I know it won't mean that much to you, but I got into my first full-court game tonight since my accident with a team that included Warren and Flash, and we were unstoppable. It was kind of a milestone. I was loving it and playing well. It also showed me how out of shape I am, same with riding my bike home from the dealership."

Laurie stared at him for a beat. He could tell she was thinking but didn't know what to expect.

"You know how I feel about your commuting on your bike, especially after you had a near-death accident. But I also realize how important it is to you and why, so I'm resigned to it. I also feel the same about your basketball playing. I just don't want you to get hurt."

"I'm aware of the dangers," Jack said. "I also got a new and safer helmet if that makes you feel any better. It's pretty obvious that my helmet saved the day on my last misfortune. But that unfortunate scenario occurred by my being targeted by a deranged individual, which isn't likely to repeat itself."

"I don't know how you can say that. There are thousands of deranged drivers here in the city."

"Yeah, but very few of them are out specifically to get me, and the one who was is no longer with us."

"You're right. What set me off tonight was coming home and having to face our children being denied parental attention and companionship when I thought you were here. I suppose a good part is my own guilty conscience. I was home later than I should have been as well, which I regretted as soon as I arrived, particularly since we left this morning before they were even awake."

Jack glanced over at JJ, who seemed to be intently engaged, and then over to Emma, who was equally committed to listening to Caitlin. "Luckily they seem to be doing remarkably well despite our parental lapses."

"At least that's true," Laurie agreed.

"Let's talk about our days," Jack suggested, to change the subject. "How was yours?"

"It was a mixed bag like always," she admitted. "At least I got to do an autopsy, which was the high point."

"Oh, right!" he said. "How did it go with the new resident?"

"It went quite well, strangely enough. He started with a negative opinion about forensic pathology, but that changed dramatically as the case went on."

"I'm not surprised," Jack remarked. "You have a talent when it comes to promoting someone's interest in forensics. What kind of case was it?"

Laurie gave him the details.

"Bravo," Jack said. "Sounds like a great teaching case. Where did it ultimately fall, self-inflicted or homicidal?"

"Actually, it could have gone either way, but what clinched it for me was Janice Jaeger had managed to learn that the victim had a recent cancer diagnosis and was depressed. After my personal experience with breast cancer two years ago, that information was decisive as far as I was concerned, especially knowing the statistics about cancer and suicide."

"But you never struck me as being depressed when your breast cancer screen was positive."

"I was certainly distressed if not depressed," Laurie said. "Anyway, on the case today none of the red flags suggesting homicide were nearly as definitive."

"The important thing is that it grabbed his interest."

"It did indeed. In fact, when I told him about the six similar cases Chet had put together, he decided to do a review of all of them since they were all done by different medical examiners. I encouraged it."

"Where was the cancer?"

"We didn't find it grossly, but we took more than the usual samples. I suppose Histology will have to answer that question for us."

"So, Janice didn't include the type of cancer in her workup?"

"She didn't. She'd gotten the information from the girlfriend, who'd discovered the body. Knowing how thorough Janice is, I'm assuming the girlfriend didn't know what type of cancer was involved. That's something Ryan Sullivan can follow up on as part of his study."

"I remember you saying this morning that Chet felt the resident was passive-aggressive. Was that your take on his personality?"

"I didn't see him as passive-aggressive, quite the opposite, and certainly not antisocial. What I noticed more was his sensitivity. Before we started the case he was momentarily shell shocked because it was a suicide by a man the same age and from a neighboring town from where he grew up in Massachusetts."

"Sounds like he was making an identification."

"That's exactly right, and he admitted it. Later I found out why. I met with the new Pathology head today. She's an impressive woman, I have to say. As new as she is, she didn't have much information about Ryan Sullivan. To get the real lowdown, she had me talk to Phil Zubin, the Residency Program director. What he told me about Ryan was astonishing."

"I'm all ears!" Jack said. He put down his fork and stared at Laurie. As well as he knew her, he could tell she was truly moved.

"Suicide played an oversized role in his life," she explained. "His father killed himself months after his mother died when he was eight years old. He and his brother were relegated to foster care that didn't work out well, which is an understatement as the brother also died by suicide after aging out. Not long after that, when Ryan was a teenager, he himself attempted suicide by slashing his wrists."

"Good grief," Jack mumbled. Then he added: "With that history, how in god's name did he end up in medical school?"

"It's a remarkable success story," Laurie said. She then went on to tell what she had learned about Robert Matson.

"I'm flabbergasted," he said when she fell silent. "I'm impressed but concerned at the same time."

"Why are you concerned?" Laurie questioned with obvious confusion. After recounting the story, she'd been again marveling at how much of a feel-good narrative it was.

"He's reminding me again of Aria Nichols," Jack said. "He might not be as antisocial as she was, but there are some similarities, and I'm questioning the idea of you encouraging him to look into a series of cases where there is even a hint of possible malfeasance. Aria was looking into a case thought to be an overdose, and it turned out to be a homicide. She got herself killed in the process. What if even just one of the six cases Ryan Sullivan will be looking into turns out to be a homicide?

That could potentially be big trouble if he uncovers something unexpected and incriminating for whoever is responsible."

"But it's all internal activity—he's not talking to anyone outside our department."

"I suppose you're right. It would be difficult to get in trouble doing that kind of research. You said the day was a mixed bag. Okay, the autopsy was your high point. What was your low point, unless you don't want to talk about it?"

"It was the meetings I had with the Hunter College Nursing School dean. When I heard that the city would be finding room for a Forensic Pathology Center in the Kips Bay Science Park and Research Campus with a million and a half square feet up for grabs, I thought the OCME had finally lucked out. But Ms. Walters set me straight. The site is, after all, Hunter College's property. So it isn't going to be the walk in the park I was counting on. Instead I'm going to be fighting for every square inch with City College and even with some of the biotech firms, who will be helping financially with the project. Getting adequate space in an appropriate part of the complex as near as possible to our high-rise is going to be a struggle."

"Yikes," Jack said. He was thankful he wasn't the one facing such a burden. Diplomacy and the ability to suffer fools weren't among his strong points.

"Enough of my day. How's your leg doing? It must be feeling okay if you were up to playing full-court."

"My leg is terrific," he said.

"Did it bother you at all during your two cases? It's been standing in one place that's been the bigger problem for you."

"There was a bit of discomfort. Ironically it does seem that standing is more difficult than exercise, which seems backward to me."

"I know your first case came out well, and Lou was happy, but what about your second case of the chiropractic neck adjustment?"

"Tragic," Jack said. "A perfectly healthy twenty-eight-year-old man with both vertebral arteries having dissections. It's rare, but people should know that it does happen. Tomorrow, I'll let Mrs. Donatello in public relations know. It's worth seeing if any news outlets are interested in the story to get the message out to the general public."

"Good idea," Laurie said. "Are you done with dinner? If so, let's try to spend some family time with the children before they have to be in bed."

CHAPTER 16

Thursday, December 7, 8:00 pm

Ryan's eyes drifted up from the computer screen and looked over at Isabella, who was sitting opposite him. They were both at his four-seater kitchen table. Since she was using his computer because of its superior graphics card, he was using her MacBook Air to read emails from David Goldberg, Kevin Strauss, Riva Mehta, and Chet McGovern. The only person who had yet to respond was Paul Blodgett.

For a moment, he was transfixed. Although he could only see her face from the middle of her nose up, he could still appreciate her radiant beauty. Her skin that he could see glowed as if she'd just been in the sun, and her dark brown hair was so shiny with gold highlights that it appeared molten.

Ryan had had a few but only brief, shallow relationships with women throughout his college and medical school years for a variety of reasons. Probably the most important was because he'd been reluctant to reveal his true self and history. As a result, he didn't quite know what to make of Isabella Lopez's easy and relaxed convivial sociability despite the brevity of their affair. She'd called him that afternoon while he was still at work to tell him that she wanted to take him up on his offer to use his Razer computer to continue working on a presentation project she needed to get done for tomorrow. "Is that okay?" she'd asked at the end as a kind of afterthought.

Taken by surprise, Ryan had immediately agreed, at which she'd added the idea for him to pick up some takeout food, preferably Thai or Chinese, on his way home so they could eat together. Cowed by her forwardness, he'd also agreed on the spot. So, not only did he find her waiting outside his apartment when he arrived home, they had eaten together and now were silently working across from each other as if they'd had a long relationship.

With a shrug of confusion, he returned his concentration to what he had been doing, fleshing out his matrix and the diary of his progress. Presently he had three more columns in the matrix: one for evidence of activity before suicide, another for living style—since all the victims so far were living in upscale apartments—and one more for the person who discovered the body and/or was the source of personal history, with their contact info.

Ryan was impressed with his handiwork. He couldn't help but think that his matrix and even the diary were looking better and better now as they were expanding. He then glanced at his watch. He wondered if it was too late to start calling the people who had found the bodies and whether they would even be willing to talk to him. It wasn't difficult to imagine how upsetting it might be getting a call out of the blue by a stranger on such an emotionally charged subject, especially after they had already been interviewed at length by the MLIs and maybe even the police. With the question in mind, particularly about the appropriateness of the timing, he again looked over at Isabella. "Hey," he said, breaking the sustained but surprisingly comfortable silence. "Sorry to bother you, but can I ask you a question?"

She responded by straightening up in her seat, so he could see her entire face and giving him her full attention. "Of course. By all means. What's up?"

"I have a need to talk to a series of people about a sensitive subject. Since it is after eight o'clock in the evening, do you think it's too late to call?"

"What kind of subject?"

"The suicide of a family member or friend."

"Whoa! That's a bit heavy."

"I know, but that's why I'm asking."

"Is it related to your month at the city morgue?"

"It is."

"I was afraid to ask how your day was since you were so negative this morning, but I have been curious since your mood seems totally different. What are you doing, if I might ask?"

"I've figured out a way to avoid autopsies, at least for a period of time."

"Good for you!" Isabella said. "Sounds like you took my advice."

"Maybe to a degree," Ryan said evasively. "The day didn't start out well. I was assigned an autopsy on a suicide victim my age."

"Ouch!" she voiced. "I guess that brought back bad memories."

"You got that right," Ryan admitted. "It did initially, but at least the case turned out to be intellectually interesting, and, most importantly, it gave me an idea to do a bit of research, which I've engineered to keep me out of the autopsy room for as long as I can stretch it out."

Ryan went on to describe the study he was doing. As he did so, he progressively got into it, as the process of explaining was giving him an opportunity of oversight. Although the entire exercise was supposed to be a ruse, there was no doubt he was surprisingly finding commonalities among the cases. Isabella listened intently, her face reflecting a mixture of curiosity and revulsion as he spoke, especially at the gory details of the gunshot cases. He even proudly showed her the matrix he was making and the study diary he was keeping.

"So that's it," Ryan said when he was finished. "The next step is to talk with the people who provided the personal information, often the one who found the bodies, in case there was a question they weren't asked, which I kinda doubt because the medical legal investigators are an impressive group, at least the two I interviewed today. The difference is that I have the benefit of knowing the autopsy results of three of the cases, whereas the MLIs didn't. I just don't know when the best time would be to call them."

She shrugged her shoulders. "It might be hard for these people to be reminded about their loss, but that's going to happen whatever time of day you contact them. At least now you have a good chance of getting people at home. If you try during the day, you'd most likely have to leave voicemail and hope for a call back. And it's only a little after eight. That's probably a good time as it's after most people's dinnertime but well before bedtime. I'd say, go for it."

"Good points," Ryan said. "Okay, I'll give it a try." He went back to his matrix to find the contact information for Harold Gallagher, the brother of Stephen Gallagher. He then picked up his phone and made the call. As it went through, he looked over at Isabella, who was gazing back at him. To make it possible for her to hear, if she was inclined, he activated the speakerphone and placed the phone on the table.

The electronic ring sounded a number of times, making Ryan pessimistic. Just as he was composing a voicemail in his mind, the line was picked up and a male voice said "Hello" in a not-too-friendly tone.

"Good evening," he said as he switched gears. "I'm Dr. Ryan Sullivan from the Office of the Chief Medical Examiner. I'm involved in a retrospective study of some of our cases over the last year, including the death of your brother." Self-consciously, he looked back over at Isabella. He'd not planned on exactly what to say and was just ad-libbing. She responded by giving him a lopsided smile and a shrug to show support.

"Would you mind speaking with me for a few minutes?" Ryan continued. "I'd like to ask you a few questions."

"I suppose," Harold said without a lot of enthusiasm. The audio of a TV in the background suggested he was watching *Thursday Night Football*.

"The medical legal investigator who spoke with you that evening mentioned that you told him that Stephen and his girlfriend had recently broken up and Stephen was distressed, but you didn't say depressed." Ryan made a point of speaking loud enough to be heard over the TV audio.

"Yeah, well, there's not a lot of difference in my mind."

"The reason I ask the question is that depression plays a large role in suicidality."

"I said 'distressed' because he was mad at the woman involved, but I guess maybe he was depressed, too. I don't know. I remember telling the investigator that he and I were not close by any stretch of the imagination. We were supposed to go out for a late dinner that night, and maybe he would have told me more about the way he felt, but who knows?"

"Is there anything else about your brother that you think might be important relating to his death that you have thought of now, since so much time has passed?"

"No, to be truthful, I don't think about it all that much."

"I understand," Ryan said as he glanced down at his matrix to see if he had any more questions when he noticed the category of profession. "Just another question or two. What was your brother's career?"

"He was a banker. He was a bigwig at Bank of America."

"My goodness!" Ryan said without thinking, feeling eager to find out the profession of the remaining three victims.

"Why is that surprising?" Harold asked.

"It's not surprising at all," Ryan said. "Thank you very much for talking with me. If I have any more questions, would it be all right for me to call you back?"

"Yeah, sure. Whatever." Then the line went dead.

"Well, that seemed to go well," Isabella said with another shrug.

"I suppose," Ryan said. Encouraged that he had at least gotten to talk with the man, he added the information to his matrix and diary, then got the number for Nancy Beardsley, the friend who'd found Daniela Alberich. Although David Goldberg couldn't remember her name when Ryan spoke to him, he'd sent it in his email along with her contact information.

"You did sound surprised the victim was a banker," Isabella said.

Ryan explained why as he tapped in Ms. Beardsley's phone number.

"Well, it sounds like you're making progress. Good for you!"

"Thank you. And thank you for encouraging me to call. But tell me this: Do you want me to go into the bedroom while I make these three more calls, so you can get some work done in peace?"

"No, it's not necessary, but thanks, I'm fine. I can work while you make your calls. No big deal."

The phone calls to Nancy Beardsley and Helen Ferrara, Sofia's mother, were markedly different than his conversation with Harold Gallagher. In contrast to Harold's seeming indifference, both Nancy and Helen expressed escalating emotion as the calls proceeded. When they were over, Ryan felt a twinge of guilt about having reawakened their sadness from having lost a good friend in one case and a daughter in the other, especially since neither call had added any significant information to what he already knew. The only possible positive addition was Mrs. Ferrara saying that her daughter may have been depressed because she'd been denied a promotion she'd been counting on at the bank.

The last person he wanted to call was Tyrell Friss, the boyfriend of Lily Berg. Before he called, he again checked the time. It was now nearing 8:30, but he still thought it was okay, arbitrarily deciding 9:00 was a reasonable cutoff point. As the call went through, he looked back at Isabella, who'd returned to her work. He marveled at how she could concentrate on whatever it was that she was doing despite his continuing his calls. He knew that if the roles were reversed, he'd not be able to do it, as he was unaccustomed to having someone in his apartment. At least he wasn't now using the speakerphone, which he thought would help to a degree.

"Ja," a voice said with a distinctive Scandinavian accent. In the background was the same football game Ryan had heard when talking with Harold Gallagher, but at a significantly higher volume.

Ryan went through the same spiel he'd honed from having talked to the first three people. When he got to the end, he expected Tyrell to respond, but all he heard was the roar of the TV crowd.

"Mr. Friss?" Ryan questioned, raising his voice.

"Oh, ja. Sorry. I'm just watching the game. Give me a second."

Ryan continued to hold the phone to his ear. He heard the soundtrack of the game reduced to a minimum, and then Tyrell came back on the line.

"Sorry," Tyrell repeated. "Certainly you can ask me questions about Lily. What a tragedy. What do you want to know?"

"You told the medical legal investigator that she was depressed."

"Yes she was," Tyrell admitted. "She was very depressed."

"Did you have any idea of the cause of her depression?"

"Unfortunately, I do," Tyrell said, his voice changing with a catch.

"I'm probably responsible for some of it. I'd recently told her that I'd met someone else, but I still wanted us to be friends."

"I see," Ryan said, feeling even more guilt than he'd felt with the last two calls.

"I was worried about her," Tyrell explained. "When I couldn't get her on the phone that night, I went over to her place and found her. It was a nightmare. You have no idea. It was the last thing I expected."

"It must have been a shock," Ryan said and meant it, as he did have an idea. At age eight, he had been the one to find his father with a bloody hole in his head after hearing the telltale sound of the gunshot coming from his parents' bedroom.

For several beats, neither Ryan nor Tyrell spoke, each waiting for the other. After an uncomfortable pause, both tried to talk at the same moment, causing yet another awkward hesitation. Ryan broke the logjam by saying, "You mentioned that you blame yourself for part of Lily's depression, but was there something else?"

"She was already struggling with a serious medical issue," Tyrell said. "She'd been diagnosed with cancer. I was just adding insult to injury. Before you judge me too harshly, she didn't tell me about it until I broke up with her."

"I see," Ryan said. This revelation reminded him of Dr. Montgomery's comment about cancer and suicide in reference to the case they'd done together that morning. "What kind of cancer did she have?" Chet had not mentioned cancer being found at the autopsy, and Ryan hadn't seen any mention of a cancer in the autopsy report Chet had sent. Ryan was quite sure about that, but he certainly was going to go back and check.

"The type of cancer had not yet been determined," Tyrell said. "A cancer screening test had been done as part of her required yearly physical by her employer. It was at a clinic called Oncology Diagnostics, and it came back positive, requiring a battery of more tests. It stressed her out because both her mother and grandmother died of cancer."

"It must have been very difficult for her dealing with two emotional issues simultaneously," Ryan said, feeling the urge to respond after another pause.

"Obviously," Tyrell said.

"I appreciate your willingness to have spoken with me about all this, so thank you. I . . ."

"You're welcome," Tyrell interjected. "Thanks for calling."

Ryan found himself holding a dead phone to his ear as Tyrell had apparently thought the conversation was over or had had enough of it. Ryan shrugged with acceptance despite having a few more questions to ask. Instead of calling back, he brought up Dr. McGovern's full autopsy report on the computer and quickly reread it to be absolutely sure there had been no mention of cancer. As he'd remembered, there hadn't been, which he considered at least curious. It now seemed that there had been two cases out of seven in which the patient had been dealing with a diagnosis of cancer and yet no cancer was found, at least at autopsy. He knew that could change with today's case if Histology were to find an early, microscopic cancer, which he thought was probably going to be the case.

"Listen to this," Ryan said when he finished rereading the autopsy report.

"What's up?" she asked, lifting her head.

"On the last call I learned the victim had been diagnosed with cancer."

"That's too bad," Isabella said. "Was that the reason for the suicide?"

"That's certainly a possibility because it is well known that people with cancer have an elevated suicide risk. It's curious because one other person out of my seven cases also had a recent diagnosis of cancer. That's almost fifteen percent."

"Is that surprising?"

"To be honest, I don't know that, either," Ryan said. "But it's at least interesting," Turning his attention back to his matrix, he added two new columns, one for known depression and another for cancer diagnosis, which he labeled CaDx for short. Then on the horizontal lines under KNOWN DEPRESSION he added what he had learned from Harold Gallagher and Mrs. Ferrara. On the horizontal of the CaDx column, he added a positive sign for both Lily Berg and Sean O'Brien and included *Oncology Diagnostics* in parentheses for Lily. Even if it was just two cases out of seven, the striking cancer commonality was another boost to the matrix's growing size and appearance and also to his confidence that the matrix would pass muster when Dr. McGovern demanded to be shown progress on Monday.

CHAPTER 17

A black Chevy Suburban with livery license plates turned right from Park Avenue onto 82nd Street and immediately pulled over to the curb. Simultaneously, both back doors opened, and a woman got out on the sidewalk side and a man got out into the street.

"David," Hank called out while giving his partner's shoulder a tap. "I think we're good to go."

Hank was sitting in the driver's seat of a plain white van while David was in the passenger seat. David had fallen asleep as he would often do when forced to wait for an operation to start. The first time it had happened on one of their Mexican missions, Hank had been surprised and impressed as there was no way he could do the same with the adrenaline he felt prior to action. When asked his secret, David explained he used meditation to rest his mind and body so that when the action started he could be at full tilt.

They had arrived in the area an hour earlier and had waited for an appropriate parking place that gave them a full view of the Levis' front door through the windshield. Wearing painters' coveralls and using a stepladder, they had removed a video device above the door while concealing their faces behind pandemic-inspired N95 masks. Later, when they made their entrance attempt, they didn't want it to be recorded. No one questioned their presence or activity as they did this. The building's main entrance with a doorman was around the corner.

"Looking very positive," David said as the couple headed toward the maisonette's door and paused, keying the lock. A moment later the door opened, spilling interior light out onto the sidewalk.

Earlier, when Hank and David were in the Action Security office, they'd spent considerable time along with Chuck going over every possible element of the upcoming home invasion. They had decided that they would try the credit card ruse to gain entry as had been suggested. There was no way they would use a forced entry as it would defeat the whole goal of staging a murder/suicide. If the credit card trick didn't work, they were all in agreement that the evening's operation would have to be canceled. Thinking about after the door had been breached, they had gone through all the different possible scenarios after gaining entry, all of which emphasized that both victims had to be secured within seconds and phones confiscated. Then the husband and wife would be separated, with David handling the female in the bedroom, and Hank doing the same with the male, preferably in the study. To make such planning easier, the IT team had obtained a detailed floor plan of the apartment.

"Go, go!" Hank barked the moment the couple disappeared from view and the apartment door began to close. Both men pulled up their N95 masks and grabbed their shoulder bags with their guns and other supplies before leaping from the van and sprinting across the street. Speed was important, as they were hoping to catch both people in the foyer, removing their coats. Just like last night, Hank also had a ghost gun that was going to be left behind.

As had been planned, David arrived first and rang the bell, whereas Hank merely made sure he was out of the line of vision from the living room window that looked out onto 82nd Street.

Although it was less than a minute before there was a response, it seemed interminable as they waited, holding their breaths. Finally, there was a bit of static before a male voice came through a small microphone and said simply: "Yes?"

"Good evening, Mr. Levi. It's Art Sinclair from Le Bernardin. I've been sent by the manager to return your credit card."

"I don't think I left my card?" Nathan said questioningly, now speaking directly through the door.

"The name on the card is Nathan Ariel Levi," David said. The team had determined the name on his American Express Centurion card.

"Really? Okay! Well, drop it through the mail slot, if you would," Nathan said.

"Sorry, I've been told I have to check your ID and give it to you directly," David said.

"Oh, for goodness' sake," Nathan complained.

Next the characteristic sound of a chain lock being disengaged could be heard, followed by a dead bolt being released, causing the two commandos to tense for action. Making sure they were not being observed by any passersby, both David and Hank had their respective handguns at the ready. The moment the door began to open, David burst through, followed by Hank. Totally shocked, Nathan took two steps back. In the next instant, with his right hand Hank had his gun's suppressor against Nathan's forehead and his left index finger against his lips to convey the message for the shocked Nathan to be silent. As a shorter-than-average man, Nathan appeared even smaller next to Hank's brawny six-foot-three.

While Hank silently engaged Nathan, David closed the front door and set out to find Marsha Levi. Since it had only been a moment since the couple arrived, he knew she was most likely on the first floor of the apartment. As he had guessed, he found her in the kitchen/family room that looked out into the apartment building's courtyard. She was standing at the refrigerator with the door ajar, holding a half-full bottle of wine that she'd brought home from the restaurant. She also still had on her fur coat.

"Just be silent and no one will get hurt," David said calmly and softly while holding his gun at arm's length, pointing it directly into Marsha's face. He took the bottle of wine and pushed the refrigerator door closed. Marsha acted shell shocked. "May I please have your phone?" he asked in the same calm voice. He even smiled.

Terrified, Marsha pulled her phone from her coat pocket and handed it to David, who pocketed it. Meanwhile he got his phone out and pressed send on a text to Hank, indicating he had the woman secured.

"Maybe you'd like to take your coat off and leave it here," David suggested with another reassuring smile. He pointed toward the door to the back stairway. "Then you and I are going upstairs to the master bedroom where the safe is located. We're going to open it, empty it, and then I and my partner will leave you two alone." The operations team had obtained renovation plans showing a safe in the wall of one of the primary bedroom closets.

Marsha dutifully slipped out of her mink coat. David took it and draped it over the back of one of the kitchen island barstools. He again gestured toward the stairs but kept his gun pointed at her.

"Where is my husband?" Marsha questioned in a quavering voice.

"He's safe with my partner," David said cajolingly to keep her calm.

The ops team had also researched murder/suicide cases that indicated the majority were males killing intimate partner females with the females shot either in the head or chest in the bedroom, whereas the suicide occurred with the same gun in the home office if there was one or living room if there wasn't.

On shaky legs, Marsha started for the stairs.

Meanwhile, as per the plan, Hank had pocketed Nathan's phone and directed Nathan into the study off the living room. After turning on the light, Hank had Nathan close the window blinds and then sit at his desk all the while keeping his gun pointed directly into Nathan's eyes.

After a few minutes of silence, Nathan found his voice. "What is going on here? Please take whatever you want and leave."

"Thank you for your cooperation," Hank said in a calm voice similar to David's with Marsha. "It's a simple robbery. Once we have what we want, which my partner is getting from your safe, we'll be on our way."

"What is it that you people expect in the safe?" Nathan repeated as anger began to overcome his terror. "There's no cash in it, if that is what you're hoping for. But, listen! I can arrange to have you sent some money right now."

Before Hank could respond, a faint, dull thud was heard that was more a mild concussive force than a sound.

"What the hell was that?" Nathan said as he started to stand up.

"Stay seated!" Hank commanded, moving the gun closer to Nathan's face by leaning across the desk. He knew instantly that the sound was David's gun, and that the mission was going to plan.

Reluctantly Nathan sat back.

"It must have been a backfire out in the street," Hank said calmly.

"If you give me a bank account and routing number, money can be sent," Nathan said. "It's as simple as that."

"We'll be content with what's in your safe," Hank said.

Before Nathan could respond, David appeared in the doorway and stepped into the room. He nodded, and they exchanged guns.

Hank leaned across the desk, bringing the gun he'd gotten from David closer to Nathan's face, and said: "Please open your mouth."

"What do you mean?" Nathan questioned, his terror on full display.

"It's a very clear order," Hank said, while he opened his mouth to demonstrate.

Nathan glanced at David, as if David might provide an answer to his terrified confusion. David responded by also opening his mouth widely.

Looking back up at Hank, who was towering over him, Nathan slowly complied, imitating the two people towering over him, both of whom had their mouths wide open.

Hank responding by forcibly shoving the end of the suppressor into Nathan's mouth and immediately pulling the trigger.

Nathan's head kicked back violently, and a spray of blood spattered against the bookcase behind him while his arms fell to the sides. A moment later a river of blood flowed out of his gaping mouth and from the lacerated and torn philtrum. After a few gurgling breath sounds and a few twitches of his legs, his body went limp, slouched in his desk chair.

"That was a bit more violent than usual," Hank remarked.

"What are you talking about?" David asked.

"The way the head kicked back," Hank explained. "I usually make a point of keeping the end of the silencer inside the mouth."

"Is that a problem?"

"I can't imagine," Hank said with a shrug.

David left the room as his role at this point of the operation was to make a sweep of the apartment to be certain there was no evidence of their presence while Hank attended to the suicide scene. First Hank put his gun away inside his satchel and picked up the ghost gun, which had been prepared by removing two bullets from its magazine. Stepping around the desk, he wiped his gloved hand against the victim's hand to transfer any possible gunpowder residue. He then inserted the gun's barrel into the man's bloody mouth before putting it into the victim's hand with the victim's index finger placed against the trigger. Then, lifting up the hand holding the gun to about the height of the victim's head while sitting, he let go. The hand and arm fell limply to dangle over the desk chair's arm while the gun fell with a clatter to the floor.

Hank then made one last look around the study to make sure his presence would not be suspected. He stepped out of the office into the living room just as David appeared, carrying the woman's mink coat.

"I'm going to hang this up in the front hall closet," David said as an explanation. "I'm sure that's what she would have done." Hank responded with a nod.

A few minutes later, after making sure the coast was clear through the door's peephole, they stepped out into the night, closed the door behind them, and calmly walked across the street to climb into the van. Once inside, with the doors closed, they removed their masks, latex surgical gloves, and high-fived.

"That could not have gone any smoother," David said with an expression of total satisfaction. "Do you want to call Chuck to debrief or should I?"

"You do it," Hank said as he started the van and pulled out into the street. It was only after he'd made the turn onto Park Avenue and was heading uptown for several blocks that he began to calm down. It had been as satisfying a mission as any he'd recently done, and his only concern was that he shouldn't get used to so many missions so close together, such that when the pace went back to normal, which was bound to happen, his PTSD symptoms might return.

CHAPTER 18

Thursday, December 7, 10:50 pm

Before heading over to the OCME building on 26th Street, Ryan had accompanied Isabella back to her apartment on 22nd Street. He had encouraged her to stay in his, but when he admitted he didn't know how long his visit to the OCME would take and she had finished her project, she thought it best to head home, as she needed to be in her office particularly early the next morning to meet with her production teammates. Although her decision had disappointed him, especially after she'd told him she had plans for Friday and Saturday nights, she did say that she'd love to have breakfast with him Sunday morning and then take in the Rockefeller Center Christmas tree afterward, provided he was still up for it. Ryan had agreed immediately, eager for something to look forward to. She'd also encouraged him to text when he got back from work and that they could chat if she was still awake, as she'd like to hear if his visit had been helpful.

After passing the postage stamp–sized playground and patch of grass in front of the modern high-rise building, Ryan stopped to look at the structure's façade. Just to the right of the main entrance was the name CHARLES S. HIRSCH CENTER FOR FORENSIC SCIENCE, making him wonder why he hadn't noticed the signage before and who Charles S. Hirsh was.

After flashing his ID to the guard just as he'd done that afternoon, he took the elevator up to the fifth floor.

Although all the overhead lights were on in the massive MLI office, there were now even fewer people in evidence, and Bart Arnold's desk, front and center, was vacant. For a few moments of indecision, he stood just inside the glass door. He briefly thought about seeing if David Goldberg or Kevin Strauss were in their cubicles, but then behind him he heard an elevator door open and a sudden cacophony of voices. Turning around, he saw a troop of people heading along the hallway with a sizable number coming into the MLI office.

"Excuse me," Ryan called out as a group approached. "I'm looking for Janice Jaeger and Darlene Franklin."

"And who might you be?" one of the women asked in a pleasant, sweet voice.

"I'm Dr. Ryan Sullivan."

"I'm Janice," the woman said. She was an older, petite, grandmotherly appearing woman with dark, gray-streaked wavy hair who was mostly hidden within a red, puffy down coat. Although Ryan hadn't imagined what she'd look like, hearing of her vaunted reputation as a medical legal investigator and now appreciating the role as a particularly demanding job, he'd expected someone more commanding.

"And I'm Darlene," another woman said in a deeper, almost masculine voice. She was considerably younger-appearing than Janice but larger and athletic, closer to what he'd anticipated.

The other woman and three men said their goodbyes and headed on into the forest of cubicles.

"I got a text you wanted to speak with me about the Cynthia Evers case," Janice said.

"As I did about Norman Colbert," Darlene said.

"Do you have a preference who you'd like to speak with first?" Janice asked.

"No, not at all," Ryan responded. "It's up to you people."

"Okay," Janice voiced. "Why don't you start with me, if that's okay with you, Darlene?"

"No problem," Darlene said, and she headed off.

Janice waved Ryan to follow as she led him over to her cubicle, which was adjacent to Bart Arnold's desk in deference to her seniority. It was a slightly larger space than David's and Kevin's with room for an upright file cabinet, a coatrack, and several extra chairs. Appearance-wise, it was less messy than David's but more cluttered than Kevin's. While she removed her coat and hat, Ryan did the same.

"Well then," she said once they were seated. "First let me say I'm glad someone from the medical forensics side is looking into this issue that David has highlighted. Six suicides with lingering suspicion about the manner of death over six months is six too many as far as I am concerned."

"It's seven now," Ryan said. "Another was autopsied this morning, and you were the MLI."

"Gosh, you're right!" Janice said. "That just shows how busy we've been. That hadn't yet occurred to me. Yes, the O'Brien case last night certainly falls in the same category."

"Let's first talk about Cynthia Evers, if you don't mind."

"Fine with me," Janice said. "I presume you've read what is available."

"I have, but the material I was able to get online is rather meager," Ryan said. "I do know it was a suicide of a thirty-four-year-old woman who was found partially hanging from a shower head by an electrical extension cord. It also stated that she had been known to be depressed prior to the event and had a history of attempting suicide by overdose when she'd been a teenager." As he spoke, he had to mentally block thinking about his own suicide attempt.

"Well, I have a lot more material than that, but you are correct, there was a history of depression and a previous suicide attempt, which is always highly significant."

"I'd love to get whatever you have," Ryan said. "If I give you my email address, will you send me your full report and any other notes you might find about the case? I'd also like the contact information for whoever it was that found the woman or who was the source of most of the information about her."

"I'll be happy to do so," she said. "As I recall it was a boyfriend who discovered the body and provided the information I needed, but when I got there I think the police had somehow managed to alienate him, which they can do sometimes, and he initially wasn't as cooperative as he could have been by the time I got to talk with him. But he came around eventually. Offhand, I don't remember his name, but I have it and will send it to you."

"David Goldberg explained to me how the police are, should we say, eager for MLIs to declare a suicide in such a circumstance, because it's less work for them."

"You have no idea," Janice said. "They can be very insistent, especially when they tower over me, which is always the situation, urging me to confirm it a suicide and get rid of the body. It's always a struggle, yet I don't allow myself to be cowed. But to be truthful with you, for me to talk about the case intelligently and in more detail, I'd need to review it as it was four months ago, and I've done a lot of cases since then."

"I understand," Ryan said. "I will look forward to reading what you send me." He wrote down his email address on the pad he'd brought with him, tore off the first page, and handed it to her. She glanced at it and then put it front and center on her desk. "I'll find time to gather the material together and send it tonight, I give you my word."

"Thank you, but let me ask you this: Do you at least recall any of the reasons you thought the manner of death might not be suicide?"

"I believe I do," Janice said. She paused and stared up at the ceiling, deep in thought. She then looked back at Ryan and said: "First off, it was obvious that at some point in the evening prior to the suicide that the woman had been cleaning the bathroom. There were all sorts of bathroom-cleaning paraphernalia on the sink and floor. That kind of activity, anticipating the future, is not typical of a suicide scene of a depressed individual, although I admit the cleaning materials could have been there for days. Who's to know, but it got my attention. Also, I noticed there were some vertical scratch marks on her neck two or three inches below the electrical cord, way up under her chin. And now that I'm thinking about it, there were also some evidence of congestion in terms of the color of her face along with a few petechiae on the whites of her eyes, both of which made me at least think of a strangulation, not a hanging. She certainly wasn't quite as pale as I expect to see in a hanging in my experience."

"I suppose that's important because signs of strangulation suggest homicide rather than suicide?"

"Yes," Janice said, looking askance at Ryan and shaking her head. "I'm getting the impression you are a babe in the woods when it comes to forensics!"

Ryan raised his hands as if in surrender. "I apologize. Guilty as charged! I'm just an anatomical pathologist. This is my first exposure to forensics."

"Apology accepted," Janice said with a smile. "From a forensic stand-point, there are differences between strangulation and hanging, al-though the signs of both merge at some point. With strangulation, and also burking, the pathological process is primarily cutting off the wind-pipe so the individual essentially suffocates, whereas with hanging, par-ticularly partial hanging, which is what is seen mostly in suicidal circumstances, the pathology is mostly cutting off the circulation of the carotid arteries and sometimes even the vertebral arteries. Unfortu-nately, in the real world, it's kind of a continuum with mixtures of each, which often requires a bit of interpretation, ergo why experience makes a difference in what we do."

"I'm learning that in a very real way by just trying to keep up with you all," Ryan said. "What does *burking* mean?"

"You've never heard the term *burking*?" Janice questioned with an-other smile.

"I don't believe so," Ryan admitted guiltily.

"The term comes from two nineteenth-century Scottish rogues, Wil-liam Burke and William Hare, who dug up corpses for anatomists to dissect. When they ran out of fresh corpses to dig up, they created their own by murdering people. The term *burking* comes from the way they killed their victims, sitting on their chests and occluding their mouths so they couldn't breathe."

"Good grief," Ryan uttered. He hadn't expected to hear anything quite so colorfully lurid. "So, at the time you were entertaining the thought that perhaps Cynthia Evers could have been burked?"

"Perhaps I thought so, but only briefly," she said. "Listen, as an MLI you have to keep everything in your mind as you survey the entire scene and circumstance."

"All the while with the police breathing down your neck."

"Precisely," Janice said with a nod. "You are getting the picture."

"But after taking all this in, you still decided that you were facing a suicide?"

"Indeed I did."

"And was that it?" Ryan asked after she went silent, seemingly lost in thought.

"Now that I'm thinking about it, there was one other thing that bothered me. The toilet seat was down."

"Why did that bother you?"

"It's hard to explain, but it just did, especially with the bathroom-cleaning paraphernalia, including a toilet brush. The bathtub had very wide, flat edges as I recall, so I didn't know why the toilet seat would be down because Ms. Evers could have stood on the edge of the tub to reach up to the shower head. I mentioned it to one of the officers who, of course, was hounding me to finish up, so they could move on to their next call. When I asked how long it might take for a crime scene specialist to come and dust the toilet seat for any footprints, he laughed at me, saying I reminded him of his mother, who couldn't make a decision about anything even when the answer was staring her in the face. Ultimately, with the preponderance of evidence pointing in the direction of a suicide, I called it as such, but it turned out to be one of those calls that bothered me after the fact."

"Like a bug in the ear."

Janice laughed heartily. "I guess you have been talking with David. Yes, it was a bug in the ear, along with the petechiae and the cleaning paraphernalia. But be that as it may, the overall evidence still pointed to a suicide, which was my ultimate call."

"Let's see," Ryan said, looking down at his notes to key his memory. "Oh, yeah. I presume Cynthia Evers was single."

"She was."

"Do you remember what kind of work she did?"

"Strangely enough, I do. The boyfriend offered that information because they worked at the same company, just in different departments. They were both in management with Citibank."

"So they were bank executives," Ryan said, writing this information down. "And would you classify Cynthia's apartment as upscale?"

"Reasonably so, but certainly not over the top."

"Okay," Ryan said. "Let's move on to Sean O'Brien. This situation is different. With this case, I read your full report. Compared with some of the other reports I've read from your colleagues, it was much more detailed."

"Thank you," Janice said with a smile. "I try to do my best on every case. What would you like to ask me? My memory's still fresh from last night."

"As I recall there were two things that bothered you, namely that the victim was still holding the gun and that no one heard a shot. Can you elaborate on both those points?"

"Of course," Janice said. "I've been involved with quite a few gunshot suicides, and in my twenty-five years of experience I'd never come across a situation where a sitting individual still had the gun in their hand after dying. On all other occasions, the gun ended up on the floor with the arm dangling over the side of the chair. In this situation, the hand apparently fell into the individual's lap with the finger still against the trigger and the barrel pressing against the left inner thigh, which I guess is what kept the gun in his hand. It just struck me as unusual. As for no one hearing the shot, because of the state of rigor mortis and the body temperature, I estimated the time of death to have been around ten p.m., at which time most people in the building would have been preparing for the night and sensitive to hearing sounds like a gunshot. Yet no one did, and I was able to ask the question to a good portion of the building's occupants. The commotion of the police's arrival had awakened most everyone."

"Sounds reasonable," Ryan commented when she paused. "What was the apartment like? Would you consider it upscale?"

"Most definitely," Janice said. "Even more than Cynthia Evers's. Why do you ask about the apartments?"

"What I'm trying to do with these seven cases is discover any commonalities. For instance, I've noticed they are all around the same age. With those whom I have been able to research so far, they are all what I would call professionals living in somewhat upscale apartments. If nothing else it seems curious.."

"He was a wealth management consultant for Morgan Stanley," Janice said. "Is that what you mean by professional?"

"Yes, but maybe it is more accurate to say they have all been executive-types working for major companies, like Cynthia Evers at Citibank."

"Interesting," Janice commented. It was apparent she was integrating this information into her vast repertoire of death investigations. If she had any ideas about the commonalities, she didn't let on, but he had the feeling she was thinking about it and that very little escaped her attention.

"Was there any indication that Mr. O'Brien had been engaged in any activity before he shot himself?" Ryan asked.

"The television was on in the kitchen."

"You didn't mention that."

"I didn't. It's so commonplace that I didn't consider it relevant."

"And otherwise the scene looked completely normal?"

"It did. There were absolutely no signs of a struggle of any sort. In my experience investigating suicides, there are never any hints of a struggle as there always is in a staged suicide."

Ryan said, "Let's go on to what Dr. Montgomery thought was perhaps the most decisive part of your report, namely that the patient was depressed about having a diagnosis of cancer. I'm finding this particularly interesting because we found no cancer at autopsy, at least not grossly. Histology might change that, but otherwise no cancer. I know you didn't name the cancer in your report, but did you know the type?"

"The girlfriend who found the body told me he'd been very upset and depressed about having been diagnosed by one of those new methods of detecting cancer before any symptoms occur. She said he'd become obsessed about it because his father had died of cancer at a relatively young age."

Ryan, who had been taking notes while Janice was talking, stopped and looked up at her. What she had just said brought back the conversation he'd had with Tyrell Friss just a few hours earlier. The similarities were surprising, to say the least. "What was the girlfriend's name?"

"Chloé Makris."

"Will you email her contact information, too, when you send me Cynthia Evers's report?"

"Of course."

"Did Chloé say anything else about the cancer screening test Mr. O'Brien had gotten? Did she say it had been part of a yearly physical?"

"I believe she did, actually, but let me look at my notes." Janice got up and opened the top drawer of her file cabinet. Pulling out a folder, she sat back down and opened it. After a brief scan of a page, she looked over at him and said: "Yes, it was part of his company's required annual physical. It was done at a clinic called Oncology Diagnostics. She said she knew the name because he had mentioned in on several occasions. He wasn't happy with the company for some reason, and he'd been complaining to her about his treatment."

Ryan wrote down *Oncology Diagnostics* and underlined it twice. He was certain it was the same clinic Tyrell Friss said had diagnosed Lily Berg, and he thought it was a rather amazing coincidence.

"Anything else about this cancer diagnosis that you have in your notes?" he asked.

"Yes, Mr. O'Brien's father died of pancreatic cancer, which Sean was particularly worried about having."

"Okay," Ryan said as he wrote that information down. He recalled dissecting out Sean's pancreas that morning and finding nothing even slightly suspicious. Perhaps Histology would say something different, but he doubted it.

"Is that it, then?" Janice asked. "I'm going to have to get a move on here because I've got a handful of calls to make."

"I think that's it for now," Ryan said. He stood up. "Thank you very much for your time, and I have to say I'm admiring and appreciating the work you MLIs do more and more. I could never in a million years do what you guys do daily."

"Thank you, but I'm sure you could be a terrific MLI considering all the effort you've had to expend to get where you are as a senior pathology resident. As for the material I've promised, I'll email it sometime tonight. I want to encourage you in what you are doing, so let me give you my mobile number. I'm aware my working the night shift makes getting ahold of me difficult, so this way you will be able to call me if you have any additional questions." She handed over one of her business cards on which she'd written her mobile number.

Ryan took the card, glanced at it but said: "I'd be afraid to bother you not knowing if you were asleep or not."

"No need to worry. I always put my phone on 'do not disturb' when I'm sleeping. And I don't sleep that much anymore. Five or six hours is about all I can manage."

"Many thanks," he said. "Now, if you can just steer me in the right direction for Darlene, I'd appreciate it."

Finding Darlene turned out to be easy. Janice merely called out her name, and Darlene stood up in her nearby cubicle to wave at Ryan. Literally within minutes he was sitting alongside her desk, again appreciating the striking difference between the two women. He could certainly imagine that Darlene was more capable of standing up to bullying policemen, in contrast with the more seasoned but diminutive Janice. She exuded the kind of commanding presence he had expected Janice to have.

"I've got to run out to make a site visit," Darlene said at the outset. "Meaning, we must make this fast. Since the Norman Colbert case was months ago, I got out my notes and read through them. What is it that you want to know?"

Ryan went through his now-rehearsed pitch and what he needed, then asked her directly to tell him why she had added the case to David Goldberg's list.

"There were a couple of red flags for me despite being told he'd been dealing with some depression," she said. "First there was evidence the man had been cooking dinner, which mildly suggested to me he couldn't have been all that imminently suicidal. It takes effort and a sense of future planning, which in my experience people who are about to kill themselves don't have, to prepare the food and put it in the oven where I found the charred remains of his dinner. Second was that the upper lip had not been lacerated. For me, the second reason was more salient than the first. I've handled my share of oral suicide cases and the upper lip has always been torn by the gunsight."

"Right," Ryan said. "Those issues have been explained to me. What was it that made you ignore them?"

"I didn't ignore them; it was just that the preponderance of evidence, including the history of depression, pointed toward suicide. We MLIs are forced to make that kind of judgment on lots of our cases, and it is not always easy. Concerning the upper lip situation, it's incredible how much kickback a nine-millimeter pistol has, especially when someone is holding it essentially backward while shooting themselves."

"I can imagine," he agreed while he thought of two new columns for his matrix, namely the caliber of the bullet used in the gunshot suicides and the type of weapon. He imagined trying to get that information from the NYPD, which would probably be difficult and maybe impossible, might gain him an extra day or two of avoiding autopsies.

"Is that it then?" Darlene asked, clearly needing to get to her site visit.

"A couple of quick questions in case the information isn't in your report. What kind of work did Norman Colbert do?"

"You're right. That didn't get in the report because it didn't seem relevant to me. He was an executive for AIG."

"Okay," Ryan commented as he wrote the information down. It seemed more and more that managerial-level employment with a major company was a distinct commonality. "What about the man's apartment?"

"What do you mean?" she asked, glancing at her watch.

"Would you have called it upscale, middle-of-the-road, or low-end."

"Upscale," Darlene said.

"Last question: Was there any evidence of struggle?"

"Hell no!" she said. "If that had been the case, I would have insisted the police bring in detectives and the crime scene people."

"Okay, that's it," Ryan said. He stood up. "Thanks for your help and thanks in advance for sending me the material you've offered. And I'm sorry to have held you up."

"You're welcome," Darlene said. "Sorry to have to rush out. Thursday nights are always busy for us. Not as busy as Friday and Saturday nights, but nearly so."

As he walked toward the elevators, Ryan pulled on his coat. He was pleased he'd made the effort to come over that evening, as he'd made some significant progress. When he emerged from the building it felt more like winter than when he had arrived. Thrusting his hands into his jacket pockets, he started off, thankful he lived in the neighborhood and only had a few blocks to walk. As he headed west on 30th Street with his shoulders hunched up against the nighttime chill, he found himself reminiscing about Isabella and, to his surprise, feeling acute disappointment that she had insisted on leaving. He had been enjoying her presence more than he realized, just being in the same room with her while they were both occupied doing their own thing. On top of that he would have liked to be able to share his sense of accomplishment his nighttime OCME visit had provided.

Although it felt good to be back inside his warm apartment, he did feel a touch lonely. As he put his notepad on his kitchen-table-cum-desk and pulled off his coat, he couldn't help but notice his Razer laptop with its screen up was still where Isabella had been using it. Thinking of her, he checked the time. It was only 11:37, meaning he'd been remarkably efficient with his visit. More important, it made him optimistic he still might catch her before she got into bed and turned out the light, as it had been less than an hour since he'd left her. With that hopeful thought in mind, he texted her to ask if she was still awake. For a few minutes he remained where he was standing in the doorway to his kitchen, keeping his eyes glued to his phone's screen with hope for a return text. As seconds turned to minutes, his optimism faded. But then, instead of a return text, his phone startled him by raucously ringing. With fumbling urgency, he accepted the call. To his delight it was Isabella.

"You caught me brushing my teeth," Isabella said. "How was your visit?"

"It went really well, and I have to admit that I'm learning to really admire these medical legal investigators. What they do is truly important but unrecognized and unappreciated by all of us. I tell you, it's an incredible, demanding job twenty-four/seven, plain awful but necessary."

"Interesting, but did you learn anything significant?"

"Without doubt, yes, and I've gotten more fodder for the matrix I showed you."

"Fantastic! Good for you. I'm glad to hear it."

"When I got back to the apartment I wished you were still here working on your project."

"That's nice of you to say."

"I just want you to know you can come use my computer any time you want, tomorrow night even."

Isabella laughed. "Thank you. That's sweet of you, but with my current project done I've got a bit of a breather."

"Too bad."

"I'll see you Sunday morning."

"Yes, see you Sunday morning."

After the call was over, Ryan stood where he was for a few minutes, thinking about his feelings for Isabella. He recognized he was in unfamiliar territory, floundering in deep water without knowing how to swim.

CHAPTER 19

Friday, December 8, 6:45 am

A quarter hour before sunrise it was already a glorious early-winter morning in New York City with a pastel, peach-colored sky directly above that gradually tended toward apple red in the east, where the sun was soon to appear, and blueberry silver in the west, where night was receding. From Jack's point of view, riding south on Central Park's West Drive perched upright on his brand-new Trek, the scene couldn't have been more beautiful and idyllic, except perhaps for the wintery-morning chill. But thanks to his dark-brown, wide-wale corduroy jacket, a wool scarf around his neck, gloves, and the sheer amount of physical effort he was expending, he was okay temperature-wise and could entirely enjoy the sunrise. He preferred a sunrise to a sunset because it heralded the promise of a new day rather than the ending of an old one.

Since it was exactly one year ago that Jack had last commuted on his bike, he was hardly in the same physical shape he'd been then. Still, with motor vehicle traffic now banned on West Drive, he averaged nearly twenty miles per hour, such that by the time he neared the south-western corner of the park where he planned to exit onto Columbus Circle, he was admittedly somewhat out of breath, with aching thigh muscles. Consequently, he didn't mind having to wait several minutes for a traffic light, which in the past always made him feel impatient. From that point on, he had to cycle considerably slower because he now had to deal with pedestrians and motor vehicles even though there was a dedicated bike lane all the rest of the way to work.

It was just a little past 7:00 when Jack pulled to a stop at the OC-ME's loading dock, where bodies came and went. Lifting his bike onto his shoulder, he carried it inside, nodding hello to the security people and then the mortuary techs as he made his way to where the Hart Island coffins were stored for unclaimed bodies. There he locked his bike and helmet to the usual standpipe. For a moment he stood there admiring the bike's design, its fire-engine red color, and its lack of the old-fashioned caliper rim brakes that gave it a particularly sleek design. It also had newer, slightly wider tires than older road bikes, giving it a smoother ride.

With a pleasant sense of contentment, Jack climbed the back stairs to the first floor and after passing by the Sudden Infant Death office, entered the ID room where the OCME day began. Here was where the on-call medical examiner, one of the newer forensic pathologists, was required to come in early to go over all the cases that had arrived overnight, make a final decision as to whether an autopsy was needed, assign cases to the various doctors, and schedule who was to be first up and who was to follow. That week, the on-call medical examiner was Dr. Nala Washington, a striking, outgoing Black woman who wore her hair in stylish cornrows. She and several of the other new hires, the majority of whom were women, made him feel ancient.

To Jack's pleasant surprise, Lieutenant Commander Detective Lou

Soldano was seated in one of two unmatched, aged leather easy chairs with his face hidden behind the morning's *New York Times*. Jack could tell it was him by the baggy, lived-in, creaseless dark blue pants sticking out below the newspaper. They were recognizably the same pants he'd had on the day before and probably the day before that, a fact that loudly proclaimed him to be the hopeless workaholic he was. Everyone who knew the detective knew he didn't have a life.

Along with being a workaholic, Lou was also a lifelong, committed fan of forensic pathology. From experience, he was intimately aware of its contribution to solving murders and often would follow bodies to the morgue about once a month to view the autopsies, preferably those done by Laurie or Jack. For that reason, all three had become friends, occasionally seeing each other socially. But the fact that Lou was there two days in a row was highly unusual, and it piqued his curiosity. Something serious had to be in the offing.

Behind Nala was a counter with a small refrigerator and the MEs' and mortuary techs' communal coffee machine. Standing in front and busily making the coffee was Vinnie Amendola, one of the more senior technicians. He was dressed in his signature gray hooded sweatshirt. Over the years they had become essentially a team, as they both were the first to arrive and Jack was always eager to get underway. The other MEs generally drifted in between 7:30 and 8:00. Often when they started their first autopsy, Jack was nearly at the end of his.

When Jack glanced in Nala's direction, she waved. Like all the newly hired, she quickly got acclimated to his early-morning routine. He was always happy to share his wide experience if Nala had any questions and needed a second opinion about whether to autopsy a specific case. She certainly didn't mind his interest in picking through the night's cases to find what he considered the most challenging, as he invariably was willing to do more autopsies than anyone else. Jack waved back but didn't go over to glance through the pile of new cases as per usual. Instead he peered over the top of the detective's newspaper at his seriously stubbled face.

"And to what do we owe the pleasure of your company two days in a row?" Jack questioned loud enough for everyone to hear. "I hope not another one of these police shootings."

As he looked up, Lou said, "No, but it's two deaths, not one, and chances are the case is going to become one hell of a pain in the ass. I'm sure I'm going to be hearing from the police commissioner on this one, and I better be prepared."

"Are the two deaths related?"

"Yeah, they're related," Lou said with a humorless laugh. "It's a homicide/suicide. The problem is the homicide victim, the suicide's thirty-four-year-old wife, is an investigative journalist for CNN, which undoubtedly is going to make the situation a media event. Just when we are trying our darndest to make a dent in the public's concern about crime in the city, this is going to be a field day for cable news and the tabloids. That means the mayor's going to be livid, and he's going to let the police commissioner know exactly how he feels, and the police commissioner is going to come down on us homicide guys, me in particular. Mark my word!"

"But there's not much you guys can do about a murder/suicide, much less suicide in general. That's a mental health issue, not a law enforcement issue."

"I doubt very much that's the way the public and hence the mayor are going to see this," Lou said. "One way or the other, it's a grisly crime. Anyway, will you do at least one of the cases, if not both? I want to know of any surprises before they happen, so I can be prepared."

"What kind of surprise are you anticipating?"

"I haven't the faintest idea," Lou said. "You are the one who's good at that."

"Did it involve a gun like usual in murder/suicide?"

"Yes, a Glock 19 nine-millimeter."

"Are they both head wounds?"

"Yes. Hers in the back of the head, and his was in the mouth."

"Back of the head? That's a bit unusual."

"See!" Lou exclaimed, spreading his hands widely, palms up. "That's exactly what I mean. I wouldn't have known that was unusual. What does it suggest to you?"

Jack shook his head. "It doesn't suggest anything necessarily other than they weren't facing each other when she was shot. In all of the cases of murder/suicide I've done, the woman was shot in the chest, sometimes multiple times if she was up and about. If she'd been sleeping, it was always in the temple."

"Okay," Lou said. "If you only do one of the cases, would you do the homicide, as a favor to me? My sixth sense is telling me that if there are surprises, they'll be with the woman and not with her almost twenty years older husband."

"I suppose," Jack said. Jack turned and called over to Nala. "Did you hear? I'd like to do the thirty-four-year-old homicide victim, provided it is all right with you." He started toward the desk where she was sitting.

"Yes, I heard," Nala said. She had already found Marsha Levi's folder and had it ready to hand to him. "As if I'd mind?" she questioned with a laugh and a smirk. Jack knew there was no way she'd mind.

"Looks like we're on deck, Vinnie," he called out to the mortuary tech who'd finished with his coffee making and had claimed the second leather easy chair. Sticking to Vinne's daily routine, he was now hidden behind his *New York Post*, pretending not to hear Jack. It was part of a near daily charade they played with each other. Jack didn't take the bait but after accepting the folder from Nala, he got himself a cup of coffee and settled at one of the other desks in the room.

Pulling out the MLI report from the folder, Jack was pleased to see that it had been done by Janice Jaeger. Although he didn't like to know too much about a case for fear it would make him biased and thereby possibly miss some crucial detail, he liked to have a general idea. To get it, he usually liked to speed-read through the MLI workup. As usual, Janice's was typically thorough. When he finished, he was still ninety-nine-point-nine percent certain there would not be any surprises, despite Lou's fears. It was going to be a routine autopsy of a relatively young, probably healthy woman who'd been shot in the back of the head. Jack sympathized with a life being prematurely lost, but at the very least, he imagined, she hadn't suffered.

CHAPTER 20

As Ryan walked under the scaffolding and into the old OCME building, he felt significantly better than he had since his forensic rotation had started, and the reason was simple: He was fairly confident he wasn't going to be subjected that day to the sensory torture of yet another autopsy. Instead, his plan was to remain either in the residents' room or, if that was too depressing, in the small but comfortable periodical library on the fourth floor. In both locations, he intended to appear to be busy and engaged. Since he had become rather absorbed in the project, it wasn't totally going to be an act.

He said a happy hello to the perennially welcoming Marlene Wilson guarding the interior entrance from the public waiting room. Passing the administration area, he used the front elevator to get up to the second floor. There he passed through the completely deserted lunchroom and entered the residents' room. Inside he found the lights on, meaning Sharon had already been there and was now most likely down in the dungeon being tortured. It truly amazed him that she seemed to be enjoying the rotation. *To each his own,* he thought vaguely.

After removing his coat, Ryan made himself comfortable at his desk before setting out the notes he'd made following the visit with Janice Jaeger and Darlene Franklin. He also got out his matrix, now in its expanded form, which was looking quite convincing with the curious commonalities of age, career, marriage status, and living arrangements. He then turned on his computer. Checking his email, he was pleased to see messages from Blodgett and the two MLIs. He opened Blodgett's first and read through it rapidly. No surprises there.

Next he turned to Janice's email and read through her report on Cynthia Evers, which was as detailed as he expected. Not only was it up to her standards, but he was impressed with what details she had been able to remember when he spoke with her last night. With all the cases she'd certainly done since the middle of August when she'd written the Evers report, it was amazing what she'd been able to recall without having done any reviewing. Just as she had explained, the report documented the presence of bathroom-cleaning paraphernalia, the evidence of some facial congestion, the scratch marks on the neck well below the electrical-cord noose, and even the concern about the toilet seat being down with the toilet brush standing right next to the bowl as if it was about to be used.

The email also contained the name *Robert Frank* with a mobile number. Although there was no explanation, Ryan presumed Robert was Cynthia Evers's boyfriend. Picking up his phone, he glanced at the time. It was almost 8:45. For a few moments of indecision, he debated calling. Believing that Isabella with her innate conviviality would most likely encourage him, he dialed. It was answered after two rings.

"Hello," a half-shouted voice called out. In the background was a constant roaring sound with a high-pitched screech.

Ryan had to shout to explain he was from the Office of the Chief Medical Examiner and wanted to talk with him about Cynthia Evers.

"I'm on the subway," Robert yelled back. "I'll have to call you back later."

"You can't win all the time," Ryan said to himself as he put down his phone. He wasn't discouraged. So far he'd been rather lucky getting the people he wanted to talk with. Going back to the monitor and Janice Jaeger's email, he found Chloé Makris's contact information. Hoping he wouldn't get her commuting, too, he placed the call. It took longer for her to answer than Robert Frank, but at least there was no background noise when she did. After exchanging hellos, Ryan went through his now-established explanation of who he was and why he was calling. When he finished, there was no immediate response. After several seconds of silence, he pulled the phone away from his ear to check to see if he was still connected. He was. "Hello, Ms. Makris?" he questioned after putting the phone back to his ear. "Are you still there?"

"Yes, I'm here," Chloé managed. Her voice sounded anguished.

As involved as he was in all the sundry details of the seven cases he was researching, Ryan acknowledged that up until that second he'd failed to give appropriate consideration of the emotional side of the stories he was hearing, and he felt a sudden acute embarrassment. He, of all people, should have been more sensitive.

"I apologize for calling you out of the blue," he said with a sense of true guilt and compassion as he suddenly realized how close the event was time-wise. "I'm sorry to impose on you so soon. I can call back in a few days to give you more time."

"No, that's okay. I want to help. I'm just so devastated. It was just such a shock finding him."

Ryan was momentarily tempted to explain that he understood just how much of a shock it was but held himself in check.

"What else can I tell you?" Chloé asked. "I think I told the investigator everything I knew the other night."

"I wanted to ask more about Oncology Diagnostics," Ryan said. "You mentioned to the investigator that Mr. O'Brien wasn't happy with the clinic. Can you be more specific?"

"I can't be very specific," she said. "Sean really didn't want to talk about it much because whenever he did, it angered him, and I certainly didn't want to add to his irritation. If I were to guess, I'd say it had something to do with his own doctor questioning the need for some of the continued and expensive tests that Sean was being subjected to by Oncology Diagnostics."

"Do you know by any chance the name of Sean's doctor?"

"Yes. It's Dr. Herbert Stein at Weill Cornell."

"I appreciate that information," he said. "I'll get in touch with Dr. Stein to see if he can add anything. In the meantime, if you think of anything else you'd like to tell me, let me give you my phone number."

"I have it if it is the number you are calling from," Chloé said.

"Yes. Thank you for talking with me, and I'm sorry to have bothered you."

"It's okay," she said graciously.

Ryan disconnected and stared into the middle distance for a few minutes, again berating himself for not having been more sensitive. He should have remembered that Sean O'Brien had just killed himself the evening before last and that Chloé Makris was undoubtedly still in a state of shock.

When he had recovered to a degree, Ryan turned his attention back to his monitor and did a Google search of Oncology Diagnostics. In a few seconds, he was on the clinic's website, which was rather impressive. It was clear to him that considerable money and effort had been spent for its construction and layout. On its General Information page, he learned that Oncology Diagnostics was a relatively new clinic located near Lenox Hill Hospital on Park Avenue between 82nd and 83rd Streets that specialized in cancer screening and cancer diagnosis in close association with another company called Full Body Scan. It also stated that the clinic did not provide treatment. For cancer treatment once cancer had been diagnosed and the organ system involved had been determined, it said it maintained close referral connections with numerous, nationally known cancer centers like Sloan Kettering in New York, Dana-Faber in Boston, and MD Anderson in Houston. It went on to explain that the company offered its corporate subscription clients free of charge one of the latest and most accurate cancer screening tests, called OncoDx, for all their executives as part of their required executive yearly physicals. It concluded with the explanation that OncoDx utilized newly discovered technologies involving extracellular vesicles circulating in the blood.

Returning to the home page, Ryan hovered over the menu options: Management, OncoDx page, and Contact. Although he was curious to read more, particularly about the technology, which he recalled reading something about in one of the major pathology laboratory journals, he decided he'd put that off until the weekend, as he had more pressing issues to pursue. But the idea that two out of the seven cases he was researching were involved with the same small clinic did seem curious to say the least.

Instead, Ryan googled *Dr. Herbert Stein* to find out the man was a general internist with an office at Weill Cornell Hospital. Although he doubted he'd be able to reach Dr. Stein directly, he put in a call to the office and left a message. With that out of the way, he closed Janice Jaeger's email and went on to Darlene Franklin's.

In keeping with the marked differences between the two women's appearances and personalities, Darlene's report was much less detailed than Janice's, and Ryan read through it quickly. It didn't add any information he didn't already know. He scrolled to the end of Darlene's email, where he found the name *Mia Parker* along with a number plus the note that the woman was a critical care nurse. Although he'd not been as successful at getting people as he'd been last night, he still tried the number. After the fifth ring, he left a voicemail. Although Norman Colbert's passing was more than two months ago, he imagined it might still be very painful for the woman to talk about it and he wasn't certain he would get a call back.

Next he turned his attention to the three medical examiners he'd not spoken with or, more important, gotten their full autopsy reports, Dr. Jennifer Hernandez for Cynthia Evers, Dr. Nala Washington for Norman Colbert, and Dr. George Fontworth for Sofia Ferrara. Of the three, he knew Fontworth was the most problematic, as he was the deputy chief medical examiner with ongoing administration duties. Consequently, he called his office first using the OCME switchboard. As expected, he didn't get to talk with the man directly but was able to arrange an appointment to see him that afternoon at 1:30.

Next he tried Dr. Jennifer Hernandez and was happily surprised when she picked up. He'd assumed she'd be down in the autopsy room because it was its busiest around this time. After he'd introduced himself and explained what he was doing, he asked if he could stop by and get a copy of her full autopsy report on Cynthia Evers. She agreed and invited him to come up directly to her office on the fourth floor.

Eschewing the slow elevator, Ryan used the stairs. When he passed the library on the fourth floor, he looked in to see if there was anyone using it. There wasn't, and he thought he might very well take advantage of the space that afternoon as it was a hundred times more pleasant than the residents' room. Dr. Hernandez's office was two doors down on the same side of the building as the library facing out toward the few remaining old redbrick Bellevue Hospital buildings on the opposite side of 30th Street. Her door was open, and Ryan knocked on it to announce himself. Jennifer was busy at her microscope with her back to the hallway.

"Please come in," she said, pointing to a spare chair by her desk. The moment he was sitting, she handed him a copy of Cynthia's autopsy report.

"Fantastic," Ryan said, glancing at it.

"I know this is just your first full week with us," Jennifer said. "I have to ask: How are you enjoying your rotation so far?"

Ryan looked up and hesitated answering. To him, she was a particularly youthful-appearing woman despite the years of training she'd had to be a board-certified forensic pathologist at one of the premier medical examiner establishments in the world. Her wide, oval Latina face framed by dark hair and full lips projected both cheerfulness and intelligence and reminded him of Isabella. Instead of responding in a socially expected fashion, he felt obligated to be truthful, recognizing he was talking more with a contemporary than an authority figure. "I probably shouldn't admit this," he began hesitantly, "but I'm afraid I'm not enjoying myself in the slightest. Quite the contrary. To be completely honest, I believe the rotation should be an elective rather than a requirement for anatomical pathology residents."

"Oh?" she questioned, showing immediate empathy. She swiveled around to face him directly. "I'm so sorry to hear. What's the problem, if I might ask?" What had propelled her to go into medicine and become a doctor was an innate sense of empathy combined with reflex urge to fix whatever was broken.

Ryan shrugged, not sure if he wanted to get into this discussion yet again, and wished he'd not been quite so up front, yet he knew he couldn't leave it without some explanation. "Let's just say I find autopsies an assault on my senses. I know it sounds rather contradictory for a pathology resident, but that's the way it is."

"And yet you are spontaneously researching this interesting series of suicide cases. That seems contradictory."

"I guess it does to some degree, but apart from my reaction to the autopsy, I'm finding the science of forensics an interesting challenge, especially regarding the manner of death."

"I agree with you there," Jennifer said. "But the autopsy is the foundation of medical forensics. It's what everything else in the field is built on."

"I understand, but it's just not for me. Can we leave it at that, at least for now? Instead, let's talk about Cynthia Evers's case." Ryan waved the autopsy report in the air. "Last night I talked with Janice Jaeger about it, and she noted a few things she initially thought were red flags."

"I remember. Sure, let's talk about it."

"Were there any surprises as far as you were concerned when you did the case?" Ryan asked. He went back to speed-reading through the report, a talent he'd perfected in boarding school to catch up to his contemporaries.

"Not really," she said. "Since it was almost four months ago, I read it over quickly while you were on your way up here. The one thing that isn't in that report is the results of the DNA analysis of some material I found under the fingernails of her right hand. I know Janice had made a point of describing scratch marks on her neck."

Ryan looked up. "What did the DNA analysis show?"

"It was her DNA. Obviously she scratched herself, perhaps in her last agonizing moments before death."

He inwardly winced as his mind conjured up the scene, wondering if the woman had possibly changed her mind at the last minute but couldn't get free. "So you considered the scratch marks consistent with the manner of death being suicide?"

"I did," Jennifer said. "In all the staged suicides by hanging that I've read about—and there is considerable literature—there had been evidence of a struggle. Had the DNA been someone else's, I then would have thought more highly of the possibility of a homicide staged as a suicide."

"Interesting," Ryan said. It made inherent sense to him. "What about the fact that the woman seemingly had been engaged in cleaning the bathroom? Did that influence your thinking?"

"That's Janice Jaeger's area of expertise," she said. "She was the one weighing that information because she was at the scene and I wasn't. So, no, that didn't influence my thinking."

"What about the signs of congestion in the face?"

"Yes, there was some congestion and there were a few petechiae on the sclera of the eyes," Jennifer said. "But it wasn't marked, and I've seen as much on suicide victims in the past. And there were a few other anatomical findings that pointed more toward what is seen with a hanging than a strangulation."

"Like what?"

"There was a small fracture of the hyoid bone."

"Yes, I see that here. What does that mean?"

"Well, it is seen more common with hanging, not definitive, but it is suggestive. Same with the internal damage I found with the left carotid artery. That's very rare with strangulation. Anyway, in a nutshell, particularly including the typical inverted V pattern of the ligature mark, the preponderance of evidence from the autopsy and the scene investigation pointed toward a self-inflicted mortality. Ultimately it is a judgment call."

"Wait a sec," Ryan said suddenly. He'd gone back to speed-reading the autopsy report and he came across a minor surprise. She had described a broken sixth rib on the victim's left lateral chest. "What's this about a broken bone?"

"Yes, that was somewhat of a surprise," Jennifer said. "It was picked up by the initial X-ray. We X-ray all corpses here, not just gunshot wounds. And this is a good example why. It might have been totally missed had an X-ray not been done, as there were no external signs of trauma like bruising."

"How did you explain it?" Ryan asked while his mind conjured up the memory of Janice Jaeger describing the exploits of Burk and Hare in the nineteenth century, killing people by sitting on their chests and occluding their mouths.

"I couldn't explain it until I dissected the area to look at the fracture. Once I did, I had a pretty good idea of its cause."

"And what was it?"

"Some sort of a screwup," Jennifer explained, making a questioning expression. "The key fact, as far as I was concerned, was almost no blood at the site of the fracture, suggesting to me that it had occurred after death and not before, specifically after the heart had stopped beating."

"I see," Ryan responded. He immediately got the implication, meaning that the break had most likely happened during the transit of the body out of the apartment and to the OCME, or possibly at the OCME. One way or the other, it suggested possible negligence.

"Bodies have been known to get dropped," she added as a kind of admission, but she didn't elaborate nor make any accusations.

"I'm sure," he said. He motioned to give the autopsy report back to Jennifer.

"You can keep the report. I have another in the folder."

Ryan stood up. "Thank you. And thank you for seeing me." For a moment, he considered asking Jennifer what she thought about the MLI being more suited to making the ultimate determination of the manner of death than the medical examiner, but quickly changed his mind. There was nothing to gain and possibly something to lose, and he could see with this case she had given the decision a lot of thought and hadn't merely rubber-stamped the MLI's finding.

"My pleasure," Jennifer responded. "And if I can help with your study in any way, don't hesitate to ask."

CHAPTER 21

Friday, December 8, 9:45 am

A s Ryan descended the stairs he thought about the conversation he'd just had, as it was the first time talking with the medical examiner that they'd added something unexpected, namely the broken rib. Vaguely he wondered how the Evers family would respond to the knowledge and whether it would cause a ruckus. He'd heard other stories of mortuary mishaps as part of medical school black humor, but they were much more lurid than merely dropping a body.

When he arrived on the second floor and was about to exit the stairway, he had two thoughts that caused him to hesitate, holding on to the door's handle. One was how Janice Jaeger might respond to hearing about the broken rib and what she might think about it. It made sense to Ryan that if there was little or no bleeding that the trauma had been a postmortem event, but still . . . it was another itch he couldn't scratch. Could it be yet another red flag? And even thinking about the issue made him wonder if there was an institutional mechanism for the MLIs to learn about the autopsy results of the cases they had investigated or if it was just up to them to ask.

The other completely unassociated thought that occurred to him was that Dr. Nala Washington, the medical examiner who had done the autopsy on Norman Colbert, was currently the medical examiner on call, meaning at that moment she was probably still in the ID room trying to finish doling out the day's autopsies. Rather than going back to the residents' room to call her and be forced to leave a message, it seemed a better idea to head over to the ID room and try to catch her in person.

Descending another floor and passing the Sudden Infant Death office, he walked into the ID room. The atmosphere at nearly ten o'clock was completely different than the previous days when he'd appeared along with Sharon Hinkley two hours earlier to meet with Dr. McGovern. On those occasions there had always been a number of MEs milling about, waiting to get their autopsy assignments and helping themselves to the communal coffee. By now, at almost ten o'clock, the MEs were either down in the pit autopsying or back in their offices working while awaiting their turn to do their cases for the day as there were only eight autopsy tables and thirty-some-odd MEs. But as Ryan hoped, Dr. Washington was still at the scheduling desk.

"Well, well," she said in her usual chipper style as she caught sight of him approaching. "If it isn't the man of the hour."

"Man of the hour?" Ryan questioned, confused. He hardly felt like the man of the hour as he was trying to fade into the background.

"I heard you volunteered to research that series of suicides. We all think that shows quite a bit more initiative than usual for a pathology resident. Bravo."

"Thank you," he said, not knowing how else to respond to what sounded like a backhanded compliment. "Actually, it's the reason why I wanted to talk with you for a few minutes, if you have the time."

"I'll make the time for a good cause. What's up?"

Ryan handed over his email address. "First off, I'd like to ask you to send me a copy of your full autopsy report on Norman Colbert. I'm assuming you knew one of your cases is on the McGovern list."

"I'll be happy to email you my report. As for whether I knew one of my cases was on the list, I did indeed."

"And do you remember why the MLIs added your patient's name to the group?"

"I do, especially since I went back and reviewed the case after Dr. McGovern's presentation. The MLI had made a point of the victim cooking dinner as being out of the ordinary with suicides. That was probably the biggest reason she initially questioned the manner of death. The second reason was a lack of laceration of the upper lip, which she had seen in all oral gunshot suicide cases she'd investigated in the past."

"What about your findings during the autopsy? Was there anything that made you question if it was a true suicide?"

"Not really, apart from there being significant direct tongue involvement and the bullet's trajectory being relatively flat rather than with the expected upward tilt. Since the case was my first oral suicide case, I made a point of looking up the literature, which describes both circumstances as rare. So it made me wonder."

"But you still determined suicide."

"Yes, I did, as did the MLI, and I'll tell you why, because it's something that's been on my mind. Not that many years ago the most common handgun was a .38 caliber revolver, whereas now it is by far a semiautomatic nine-milllimeter pistol. I think that makes significant difference."

"Why do you believe that makes a difference?" He remembered that his brother and his father had both used a .38 Smith & Wesson.

"Because of the diameter of the barrel. The older weapon had a comparatively narrow, round barrel and a sizable front sight, all of which fit somewhat easily in a mouth, invariably causing a laceration of the upper lip with the gun's recoil. The newer pistols, like the Glock 19, have wide, blunt rectangular ends to their barrels that are much more diffi-cult for someone to wrap their mouth around, and when they do, their tongues probably get pushed back into the path of the bullet. The MLI said that the Norman Colbert case involved a Glock 19."

"Interesting," Ryan said, and meant it. He could well imagine she was correct, and maybe the forensic literature in relation to oral gunshot suicides needed to be updated. With that in mind, he decided he would make it a point over the weekend to investigate the issue and possibly make it part of any presentation he might be required to make about his research project. "Did you ever bring this idea up with Darlene Franklin?"

"I didn't and maybe I should have. It's one of the problems with all of us being so damn busy. And it's also a problem that there is a physical separation between the MEs and MLIs with us stuck here in this be-draggled place and them in the new high-rise."

Ryan nodded in agreement and once again was tempted to bring up his idea that perhaps the MEs should be tasked to determine the cause of death and the MLIs the manner of death, essentially splitting the responsibility of completing the all-important death certificate. It would certainly force them to work together more than they did. But again, he held himself in check. He didn't want to do anything that would irritate anyone or cause upset and thereby attract attention. He was lucky to be doing what he was doing to keep himself out of the autopsy room for as long as possible, and he certainly didn't want to jeopardize the situation. Instead of potentially ruffling anyone's feathers, he merely thanked Dr. Washington for speaking with him and for being willing to send him her full autopsy report.

CHAPTER 22

Friday, December 8, 10:35 am

Feeling content about what he'd accomplished, Ryan returned to the residents' room. The depressing décor no longer bothered him as much as it had. On the contrary, its shabbiness made him feel secure, like he could essentially hide out, since the only person he'd seen in here had been Dr. McGovern, twice.

Sitting back down at the battered metal desk, he added what he could to his matrix. He also thought more about the broken rib, eager to mention it to Janice Jaeger. He put his phone on the desktop as he was still waiting for return calls from Robert Frank about Cynthia Evers, Dr. Stein about Sean O'Brien, and Mia Parker about Norman Colbert.

While he waited for return calls, he went online and googled *oral gunshot suicides*. As he glanced down the long list of articles, he came across one that seemed particularly relevant, as it dealt specifically with the forensic issues involved in the differentiation of suicidal and homicidal gunshot wounds, but all he could read was an abstract. To get the full article, he had to join an online research organization and prove he was an academic. While he was in the process of doing so, the door burst open and Sharon Hinkley suddenly swept into the room as was her fashion. She was dressed in scrubs, including a surgical cap that hid her voluminous, shoulder-length hair.

"Hey, Ryan!" she called out as she slammed the door, noisily threw herself into her desk chair, and switched on her computer in one continuous rapid motion before adding: "How's it going?"

It took him a few moments to calm himself. The shock and the frenzied commotion of her entry had caught him completely off guard and had evoked a strong fight-or-flight reaction. Oblivious to the effect her arrival had caused, Sharon was busily using her keyboard.

"What on earth are you doing?" Ryan asked with mild irritation as he watched her frantically type away.

"I'm keeping track of the details of the autopsies I've been observing," Sharon said. "This morning's was particularly interesting, and I wanted to write it up and add it to my list while it's still fresh in my mind."

The typing went on for an extended period.

"Well?" Ryan questioned at length. "Are you going to tell me, or do I have to ask what kind of case it was that made it so interesting?"

"In a second," she said without stopping.

He tried to go back to what he had been doing but couldn't concentrate. The idea that Sharon was enjoying, and not just tolerating what he vehemently disliked, was an ongoing mystery to him. At first he'd thought her enjoyment of autopsies was an act on her part, related to her reflex urge to suck up to her superiors, but now he could tell she was truly engaged.

Sharon finished typing, saved the document, and then wrote by hand an entry into her autopsy log. When she was finished, she spun around in her chair and looked directly over at Ryan, her cornflower blue eyes ablaze. Her excitement was palpable. "I'm glad you're here," she began. "I was going to make it a point to find you. I just did a case that I found fascinating and I enjoyed, and I'm certain you would have, too."

"That's highly unlikely," Ryan said. "But your excitement intrigues me, so tell me more."

"It's another case that can be added to your list."

"You mean it was a suicide, and there was a question of the manner of death?"

"Exactly."

"What was the cause of death?"

"Gunshot wound to the head."

"Was it temporal or oral?"

"Oral."

"Man or woman?"

"Man. The name was Nathan Levi."

Some of Sharon's enthusiasm was spreading to him; an additional case would certainly enhance the importance of what he was doing. Whatever significance two cases being only a day apart might have, he had no idea, but it didn't matter. Going from seven cases to eight added substantially to his study. "Who was the ME on the case?"

"Dr. McGovern, and I have to say despite what you think of him, he's a terrific teacher."

"I'm certain he is," Ryan said, rolling his eyes. "I'm sure he is a par-ticularly attentive teacher with an appreciative, attractive, and eager student like you, especially one who gives the right answers."

"What is that supposed to mean?"

"Who was the MLI?" he asked, avoiding her question.

"I didn't notice," Sharon said, "but the report was well done and de-tailed if that's your question."

"Could it have been Janice Jaeger?" Ryan said, knowing for certain she had been on duty last night.

"I really don't know," she said with a shrug.

"If it was a very detailed report, it could have been her," Ryan said. If she had been, he knew he could count on the investigation being thorough. "What was found at the autopsy that raised the question of the manner of death?"

"Two things," Sharon said, excited to show off what she had learned. "First was that the tongue was severely damaged, which Dr. McGovern explained isn't expected with an oral gunshot suicide. The whole end of the tongue was gone. And second: the path of the bullet was flat, with an exit wound at the level of the first vertebrae. He told me that wasn't expected, either."

"Well, calm down a bit," he said. "All this sounds familiar. Three of my seven cases were oral gunshot suicides, each with similar flat trajectories. So it's obviously not so unusual. Interestingly enough, I just had a conversation about this very issue with one of the medical examiners, Dr. Washington, who has a theory about it."

"I know her," Sharon said. "She's the one who's been assigning the autopsies to the other medical examiners this week."

"Correct. She also happened to autopsy one of my seven cases, one of the oral gunshot suicides. Her take is that the accepted forensics associated with such suicides needs to be updated because the most common handgun has changed. Today, the most common gun is a semiautomatic pistol, like a Glock 19, which has a completely different design than the previously commonly used revolver with a much blunter and bigger barrel. Just think about it! A Glock's barrel is probably too big to fit easily into the roof of the mouth of most people, which means the trajectory of the bullet is going to be flatter and invariably involve the tongue." Ryan inwardly cringed just thinking about someone pushing a semiautomatic's barrel into their mouth.

"I get it. Yeah, it makes sense. Hmmm. I can't wait to bring it up with Dr. McGovern. But now I have to get a move on. I've got another autopsy right now." She leaped up and stretched.

"You are observing another autopsy this morning? Yikes, you are really making me look bad."

"It's your choice. I'm finding these autopsies fascinating. The next case is a thirty-two-year-old flight attendant found in her hotel room who had been in perfect health. I can't wait to see if we can figure it out."

"We? Does that mean you are doing another case with our fearless leader?"

"Yes, indeed! Dr. McGovern and I work well together."

"No doubt," Ryan said sarcastically. "Good luck. I hope you find out the cause and manner of death. I might even find that autopsy tolerable, provided there weren't any other nearby ripe cases going on. But listen, I would appreciate it if you don't mention about the difference between handguns to Dr. McGovern yet. I'd like to do it myself and share the credit with Dr. Washington. It's a kind of justification for my study, if you know what I'm saying. I'm trying to stretch this research out for as long as possible, and I'd like to have something like this to present to him as a sign of progress."

"Okay, I understand," Sharon said. "But I can't promise anything if he asks my opinion about the manner of death on that previous case because of the bullet's flat trajectory. But he probably won't. At this point, I know he thinks, like the MLI, that it was a self-inflicted wound."

"That's all I can ask. But tell me this: Do you have any idea where the Nathan Levi autopsy folder is? I'd like to read the full MLI report to add the case to my cohort."

"No clue, but I imagine Dr. McGovern took it with him. He left the autopsy room while I was helping the mortuary tech get the body into the cooler."

"So he probably took it up to his office."

Sharon shrugged. "I have no idea. But now I have to get myself back down to the autopsy room. Good luck to you, too!"

"Yeah, thanks," Ryan said. He watched her eargerly hustle out of the room, closing the door behind her with a hurried bang. Raising his eyes to the ceiling, he went through his options. Without a doubt, he wanted to add this new case to his matrix, and to do so, he needed the MLI report. To get it, he had to interact with McGovern. Reluctantly, he knew what he had to do: follow Sharon down to the hated autopsy room.

CHAPTER 23

The irony wasn't lost on Ryan as he headed down in the elevator: His project to avoid the autopsy room was now necessitating a visit. Once down on the basement level, he passed the mortuary tech's office and pushed into the empty men's locker room. There he pulled a clean surgical gown on over his street clothes. He also grabbed two masks. Although the double-mask ruse hadn't worked terribly well when he tried it previously, his hope was that it would at minimum mitigate the unique smell of the autopsy room, especially poignant with all eight tables in use at once, which invariably was the case at that time in the morning. All he could hope for was that there wouldn't be any multi-day-old corpses.

Just outside the pair of swinging doors that led into the pit, he paused to put on his masks. While he did so, he peered through one of the wire-embedded glass windows. Since most of the tables had just two people, an ME and a mortuary tech, he looked for one that had three people. Table #3 looked promising, especially since he thought he recognized Sharon. Hoping for the best, and taking a last full breath of hallway air, he pushed inside.

A few people in the room looked up as he entered, but most didn't. A low-level buzz of conversation could be heard over the sound of the ventilation system. As he approached table #3, he could see that Dr. McGovern was about to start, holding a fresh scalpel in his right hand over the naked body of a youthful-appearing woman. With his left hand he was creating some tension on the skin of the chest in preparation for the first cut.

"Excuse me, Dr. McGovern," Ryan said.

Chet looked up and then straightened up. "Oh, my goodness. It's Prince Ryan. What have we done to deserve this honor?"

Ryan held himself in check rather than respond in kind. Instead, he said: "Sorry to bother, but Dr. Hinkley told me that you and she autopsied a case that might be appropriately added to the list of suicides you gave me yesterday."

"That's correct, and it's a shame you weren't here to participate in person. You might have learned something."

"Perhaps," Ryan said, struggling to control himself. He kept being reminded that he couldn't abide this individual. "I understand that the involvement of the tongue and the bullet's trajectory made you at least question the manner of death. Was there anything else that you found during the autopsy that in any way suggested it wasn't a suicide?"

"What do you think, Dr. Hinkley?" Chet said. "Was there anything else?"

"Nothing," Sharon said. "The only other pathology was what appeared to be mild cirrhosis of the liver."

"So, I guess not," Chet said smugly, returning his attention to Ryan.

"Who was the MLI involved?" Ryan asked.

"Janice Jaeger," Chet said.

"That's encouraging," Ryan said. "At least we know that was done well. For me to add the case to my study, I need to read and make a copy of her report. Where might I find the autopsy folder?"

"It's on my desk," Chet said, clearly losing interest in Ryan's presence and turning his attention back to the corpse in front of him by repositioning his left hand to provide tension on the skin.

"Would it be okay for me to go up and get it and make a copy?"

"I suppose," Chet said without looking up as he made a deep slice from each shoulder, meeting at the sternum before being extended all the way down the abdomen to the pubis.

"Thank you," Ryan said. With relief to be leaving, he quickly headed for the exit. Once outside in the hallway, he pulled off his masks and took a satisfyingly deep breath. The short visit hadn't been as bad as he feared, but he was still glad to be out.

After disposing of his gown and masks in the locker room, he took the back elevator to the third floor. Although the front elevators were faster, the back elevator rested on the basement level, and he didn't have to wait for it to arrive.

Befitting his seniority, Dr. McGovern's office was in the preferred location near the front elevators adjacent to Dr. Mehta's. Ryan had noticed it the day before when he visited Dr. Mehta. When he arrived, he found the door ajar, and he saw the Nathan Levi autopsy folder front and center on the man's desk.

Before picking up the report, he took a glance around the room. What struck him immediately was the lack of family photos or even of any memorabilia or personal items of any kind, in sharp contrast to the other medical examiners' offices he'd visited, particularly Dr. Mehta's. In a moment of empathy, Ryan wondered whether such a lack of connection explained anything about Dr. McGovern's character.

With a shrug of indifference, he redirected his attention to the autopsy folder and extracted Janice Jaeger's two-page report. Although he was tempted to speed-read it on the spot, he didn't. Instead, he walked out of the office and took the front elevators down to the first floor, where he knew there was a copy machine. With the copy in hand, he returned to Dr. McGovern's office, replaced the original report back in the autopsy folder, and then used the front stairs to get down to the second floor. There he retreated back through the now busy lunchroom to the empty residents' room, being sure to close the door behind him to shield himself from the buzz of conversation.

The first thing he did was add Nathan Levi to his matrix. The addition of another name made it look significantly more impressive, so he was initially pleased. Then, with his feet up on the corner of his desk, he began reading Janice's report. Almost immediately his attitude changed to disappointment. In the first sentence he noted that Nathan Levi was born in 1976, meaning he was forty-seven years old! This, of course, was in sharp contrast to everyone else on the list, who was considerably younger. Then, after learning Janice had gotten most of her information from the man's sister-in-law, Ryan read that Nathan Levi was married, lived with his wife, Marsha, and was a hedge fund founder and manager, meaning he wasn't employed by a major corporation, either.

Continuing with the report, he finally came across one similarity, namely that the victim resided in a truly upscale apartment complete with a study, where the corpse was found, but it was hardly compensation to make up for why this new name was a poor addition to his study list. Nathan Levi's situation was casting into doubt most all the interesting commonalities he was discovering with the other cases, yet he couldn't justify merely eliminating him, especially with Dr. McGovern knowing Ryan had intended to include him.

When Janice summed up her report, she called it a suicide despite the location of the exit wound indicating the bullet's trajectory was flatter than she would have expected. Then, to Ryan's bewilderment, she added that the only surprise she encountered was that there was no evidence in the entire apartment of a struggle or any disarray, which she described as being curious.

For a few minutes, he stared off into the middle distance. Why did Janice find no signs of a struggle curious since she had already made it clear to him that in her extensive experience, there was never signs of a struggle with a suicide? To Ryan it seemed contradictory, to say the least, and it suggested to him that he needed to question her directly. He had the distinct sense that there was something crucial missing but had no idea what it could be.

Letting his feet drop to the floor, he pulled out from his back pocket Janice Jaeger's business card with its handwritten mobile number, recalling her specific and what seemed like genuine encouragement to call her if he had any questions. He glanced at his phone to check the time. It was just a little after noon, which under any normal circumstance would be entirely too early to call someone whose night shift had ended only five hours earlier. Yet he distinctly remembered her saying she didn't sleep that much and when she did, she put her phone on "do not disturb." Feeling relatively confident he wouldn't be bothering her and believing he could at least leave a voice message, he placed the call. It rang four times, and he got her voicemail. He identified himself, thanked her for the time she'd given him the evening before, and asked her to call back whenever convenient.

With that done, he put his phone down and looked at his list of expected calls. Isabella had certainly been right when she encouraged him to call people in the evening rather than the daytime, as his score of getting ahold of people that morning was hardly encouraging. He had not heard from Robert Frank, Dr. Stein, or the critical care nurse, Mia

Parker, with whom he hoped to talk about Norman Colbert. As busy as such nurses were these days, he doubted he would hear from her until her shift was over, if then.

With all those calls pending, Ryan felt becalmed. He looked over his material and realized that for the moment he had nothing to do, at least prior to the meeting with Dr. Fontworth at 1:30. He considered sneaking back to the Hassenfeld Children's Hospital and checking out what was brewing in the pathology lab, but nixed the idea. He was already on thin ice with Dr. McGovern and didn't want to risk being seen leaving the premises. He even thought about going out and finding a food truck for a bite of lunch but dropped that idea for the same reason.

Pulling himself to the desk, Ryan turned his monitor on and went online. He googled the article Kevin Strauss had recommended, "Getting Away with Murder: An Examination of Detected Homicides Staged as Suicides," to see if he could now download it. Pleased that it was now possible, he clicked on the link, and was immediately engrossed.

CHAPTER 24

Friday, December 8, 2:45 pm

The jangle of the ringtone on his phone jarred Ryan out of his intense concentration. After reading the article Kevin Strauss had recommended written by the two Aussie pathologists, he'd googled *homicides staged as suicides* and had discovered a rich vein of information. The forensic literature on the issue was far more extensive than he had imagined, and rather captivating.

Ryan's early afternoon had passed relatively uneventfully. He'd spent the entire time reading online. Sharon had breezed in again to add to her growing list of observed autopsies but then had immediately dashed out for yet another, making him rue anew his being paired with her for the rotation. Her enthusiasm couldn't help but make his lack thereof more striking.

At 1:30 sharp, Ryan had presented himself to the secretary for Dr. George Fontworth, deputy chief medical examiner, for their meeting. Although he had to wait ten minutes, he got to see the doctor and request a copy of Sofia Ferrara's autopsy report. Other than that, he didn't learn anything new.

Of the return phone calls he was expecting, the only one he'd gotten was from Dr. Herbert Stein's office and it was not as he'd hoped. First off, it wasn't the doctor returning the call, but rather a member of his staff. When Ryan had conveyed his need to talk with the doctor about Sean O'Brien's medical history, in particular about his cancer diagnosis, he was duly informed by the staff member that Dr. Stein was restricted by HIPAA rules in revealing such information without the patient's release. When Ryan told the individual that he was calling from the OCME because the patient was deceased, the staff member told him that the patient's death did not absolve the doctor's responsibility concerning the patient's health information. She went on to explain that the OCME would have to obtain a warrant from the court for them to release it.

Now, as Ryan picked up his phone, he hoped this call would be more successful, and he immediately sensed it would, because the caller was Janice Jaeger.

"Sorry to not call back sooner," Janice said. "How are you making out with your study?"

"It's progressing," Ryan said, wanting to sound optimistic. "But I have run into a bit of a snag."

"What about?"

He went on to describe the phone call he'd had with a staff member of Sean O'Brien's doctor, saying that the doctor could not talk about the patient's medical history because of HIPAA rules, which surprised him since the patient had died.

"That is actually correct," Janice said. "HIPAA rules restrict health information from being released for fifty years after death. Luckily MLIs don't have to confront that situation too often as most people don't know

ROBIN COOK

about it, even some medical personnel, and I certainly don't bring it up, particularly when I'm on a site visit. What were you trying to learn?"

"I'm not really sure what I was trying to learn," Ryan admitted. "I did speak briefly with Chloé Makris. She mentioned that Mr. O'Brien was somehow upset at the clinic that had diagnosed his cancer and that it had something to do with his doctor."

"That's curious. I wonder if that was part of his depression."

"That's what I had hoped to learn," Ryan said. "Anyway, that's not why I wanted to speak with you. I really wanted to talk about you having yet another case from last night that seems as if it should be added to my study. Although you labeled it as a suicide you did bring up the question about the bullet's trajectory being flatter than usual."

"Yes, for sure, and I was going to call you to bring the case to your attention. You are absolutely correct. I did consider it a suicide despite the position of the exit wound. But what stood out for me was that it was such a tragic affair. You'd think that after all the years I have been doing this, I'd get immune, but I'm not, and this case bothered me a lot to the point of having trouble going to sleep this morning."

"I'm sorry to hear," Ryan said. He was confused, knowing the number of suicides she had to deal with on a yearly basis, but he decided not to question her response. "Your report was very thorough as usual, but one thing in particular jumped out at me, which is the reason I wanted to call you."

"What was it that caught your attention?"

"At the end you said that you found it curious that there were no signs of a struggle or any disarray, which you had already told me that you don't ever find with a suicide. What am I missing here?"

"You are missing that this wasn't an isolated suicide," Janice explained. "It was a murder/suicide."

"Come again?" Ryan said with even more confusion.

"It wasn't an isolated suicide. It was, in my opinion and the NYPD's, a murder/suicide. Presumably Nathan Levi shot his wife prior to taking his life. Unfortunately, such a tragedy is not that uncommon. In fact, there are some six hundred such cases every year in the United States alone, and I've seen my share. In my experience, there are always telltale signs of an argument if not a literal fight, something like broken dishes strewn about the kitchen. Here there was nothing and the wife was shot in the back of the head, which is also not typical. In such cases, if it is a head wound it is usually temporal or face-on. Actually, in the cases I've done it's been a chest wound."

"Good grief," Ryan managed. He had to reorganize his thinking. "Were you the MLI for the wife as well as the husband?"

"Of course. We don't have the personnel to send out two MLIs on the same case, which essentially a murder/suicide is, even though it is two victims, nor is it necessary."

"What was the wife's name?"

"Marsha Levi," Janice said. "It sounds like you haven't seen my report on her."

"No, I haven't. I didn't even know about her. Can you send it to me?"

"Not until I get to the office this evening."

"Okay, that's fine. Don't worry. I'll find it here. Two last things: Who discovered the bodies and was that person your information source for both reports?"

"It was the wife's younger sister, Eva Hoffman, who lives less than a block away. She was a good source, as she knew both people well as they spent significant time together. She had been expecting a call from her sister last night, and when she didn't get it, she took it on herself to go over to the apartment, and she walked into a nightmare."

"Was there a history of a tumultuous relationship?"

"She described the couple as being feisty and argumentative with each other but absolutely not violent. At the same time she knew the husband had been disturbed of late and somewhat depressed with the stock market going down, but never in a million years did she expect him to go berserk."

"Do you have Ms. Hoffman's contact number?"

"I do. I have her business card. I'll text you her number as soon as we hang up. If you want to talk with her I'm sure she would be amenable, as she was angry as much as sad and therefore eager to talk. And she works from home, so she should be available."

"Thank you."

"Is there anything else you wanted to ask?"

Ryan tried to think, but his mind was in disarray. Then he remembered his meeting with Dr. Hernandez and hearing about the broken rib found at Cynthia Evers's autopsy. He asked Janice if she'd heard about it.

"No, I hadn't."

"When there is a surprise finding at the autopsy, is there an established way for the MLI on the case to find out about it?"

"There's no formal way, if that's what you're asking. It's up to the ME. But tell me this: Was it deemed a premortem or postmortem fracture?"

"Dr. Hernandez thought it was postmortem, as she found very little bleeding," Ryan said. He was impressed with how quickly Janice had picked up on the salient issue and asked.

"Well, there you go," Janice said. "I wouldn't expect to hear about something like that. That's not my bailiwick, nor would it be likely to change my thinking about the manner of death."

"So the broken rib doesn't awaken your thoughts about burking being involved?"

"No, not if it was postmortem."

"Okay. Thank you for calling me back," Ryan said.

"You're welcome, and if I can be of any more help, don't hesitate."

"I won't," he said as he disconnected the call. He then picked up the in-house phone and asked to be connected with Dr. Nala Washington's office. She picked up immediately.

After Ryan identified himself, he asked which medical examiner had been assigned Marsha Levi.

"Dr. Stapleton insisted on doing it," Nala said. "He did it at Detective Soldano's behest."

"Who is Detective Soldano?"

"He's a highly ranked NYPD detective who's a big fan of the OCME and who happens to be a personal friend of both Dr. Stapleton and our chief. He's in here at least once a month to observe autopsies, usually on criminal cases."

"Thanks, Dr. Washington."

"My pleasure."

Using his finger to disconnect the call while keeping the receiver to his ear, Ryan asked the operator to connect him to Dr. Stapleton's office. When the medical examiner picked up, Ryan wasn't surprised. He'd already learned that mid-to-late afternoon was the best time to catch the MEs in their offices. Ryan introduced himself and explained why he was calling.

"Of course you can come by and get a copy of Janice's report on Marsha Levi," Jack said. "My office is on the third floor."

"I know where it is," Ryan said. "Is now a convenient time?"

"Perfect," Jack responded. Although mildly curious as to why Ryan was interested in such a straightforward homicide and not the suicide, if that was the case, Jack was even more intrigued to meet this resident whom Laurie talked about the night before. The superficial similarities to the Aria Nichols debacle made Jack uneasy there could possibly be another unexpected outcome from allowing him to do any research on his own concerning the question of the manner of death.

CHAPTER 25

Friday, December 8, 3:25 pm

As seemed to be the norm with the MEs when they were in their offices, Ryan found Dr. Stapleton's door ajar with him at his microscope. To announce himself, he again knocked on the open door while saying hello.

"Come in, come in," Jack said welcomingly. He took a slide tray off his side chair and gestured for Ryan to sit alongside his L-shaped desk. "I'm glad to finally meet you."

"Thank you," Ryan said while taking the chair. As he did so, he regarded Dr. Stapleton, since he'd only seen the man from a distance. Whereas Dr. Blodgett and Dr. Fontworth had let themselves physically go to seed, in sharp contrast Dr. Stapleton looked particularly fit. He had his shirtsleeves rolled up, revealing muscular forearms, and he certainly had no paunch.

"Here's the MLI report on Marsha Levi," Jack said. He handed it to Ryan. "I printed it for you, so you can keep it."

"Thank you," Ryan said as he glanced at the single page. "Is this it? It seems so much shorter than the other reports that Janice had done."

"Janice is one of our best MLIs. Her reports adjust to the particular case she's handling. If the circumstances of the death are obvious, as with this case, she doesn't mince words. She knows exactly what should be included and what shouldn't, which makes our job as medical examiners that much easier. She doesn't bulk up her reports with a bunch of unassociated negatives."

"I can understand why that's helpful," Ryan responded as he began to speed-read the report. But he didn't get far. In the first paragraph he learned that Marsha Levi was thirty-four, meaning considerably younger than her forty-seven-year-old husband. He read that she worked as a highly paid journalist for a large corporation, namely Warner Bros. Discovery, so that even though her husband didn't fit into his study's commonalities, *she* did. Whether that had any meaning, he didn't know, but he made a mental note.

"I'm curious why you're interested in this case," Jack questioned.

"I'm more interested in the husband's case," Ryan said. "I'm doing a study looking into a group of suicides where there have been red flags questioning the manner of death."

"So I've heard. That's very industrious of you. Do you believe the husband's suicide falls into that category?"

"Janice raised the issue by noting the trajectory of the bullet was flat and not angled upward and the tongue was involved."

"Which Dr. McGovern found as well, but both he and Janice felt it was a self-inflicted wound after their concerted analysis. Do you disagree?"

"No, I don't disagree," Ryan said. "Certainly not. But I didn't know this was a murder/suicide case until I spoke with Janice a few minutes ago. Until that time, I was considering the husband's suicide as an isolated event. Anyway, I don't disagree with Janice and Dr. McGovern. Heavens, no. I'm new at this forensic game and both of them are experts."

"Good point."

Ryan wrestled with whether he should bring up Janice's mention of the lack of signs of a struggle or argument, which she associated with murder/suicides, but he suddenly had the urge to call Eva Hoffman, Marsha Levi's sister, who had provided Janice with the information about Nathan, but not so much about Marsha. A new idea had suddenly crystallized in Ryan's imagination. Despite being a forensic newbie, could there be an infinitesimally small possibility that the whole Levi murder/suicide was staged? Ryan didn't even know if that had ever happened in the past, but it could explain that Marsha was the target, and Nathan was collateral damage.

"Well, thank you for providing this," Ryan said, brandishing Janice's report and getting to his feet.

"You're welcome," Jack said. "But before you go, let me say something. Do you mind?" Jack motioned for Ryan to retake his seat.

Ryan hesitated, indecisive. He wanted to get back to the residents' room to at least google *staged murder/suicides* just to see if it had ever happened. He had no idea whether his idea had any merit whatsoever or was just his imagination running wild.

"Please," Jack said, while patting the empty seat with his palm.

Somewhat reluctantly, Ryan sat stiffly, obviously eager to leave.

"I know Dr. Montgomery has encouraged you to do this research. She also had encouraged another pathology resident by the name Aria Nichols to do some research a few years ago. I assume you are familiar with her untimely death."

"Very much so," Ryan said. He was now curious as to where this conversation was going, and relaxed to a degree. "I was a junior resident when she was killed."

"Then you know the whole sad story," Jack said. "My point is that Dr. Nichols took it upon herself during her research to leave the safety of the OCME to investigate outside the office and ended up confronting a very bad person, to say the least. I'm all for you researching these mildly strange and somewhat similar suicide cases by talking to the MLIs and MEs, but please promise that you will continue as you have started, meaning that you stay here on the premises."

"Does heading down to the high-rise count or is that off-limits, too?"

Jack laughed, which relieved the tension that had been building in his voice. "No, of course not. The split between this ancient morgue building and the Forensic Science Center is a pain in the ass. I can tell you that from my own experience. What I don't want you doing is going out investigating anything associated with these suicides, for any reason."

"Why would I do that?" Ryan asked.

"I don't know," Jack said, throwing his hands into the air. "Maybe you decide to make your own site visit or something like that. Anyway, don't do it. If you're tempted to investigate outside the office for whatever reason, call me, and we'll discuss it. I'm here every day practically from sunup to sundown and available through the switchboard on weekends. Okay?"

"I suppose," Ryan said. He wasn't thrilled. It seemed like he was being treated like a child, not a senior pathology resident.

"I'm not trying to talk down to you in any way," Jack explained, as if sensing Ryan's reaction. "I'm talking from personal experience. Did you know that I was purposely broadsided and almost killed while riding my bike a year ago by a psychotic nursing supervisor?"

"No, I hadn't heard that."

"Well, it's true, and all because I had taken it upon myself to do a bit of site investigation despite being warned not to do so by an experienced NYPD detective. It's a dangerous world out there, particularly when you are investigating bad people like I was and like Aria Nichols did. I just don't want you to do the same, as farfetched as that might sound."

"Okay," Ryan said. "I get it. I won't go out investigating, and if I'm tempted, I'll give you a call and discuss it with you."

"Perfect, that's all I ask," Jack said. He stood and so did Ryan. Jack thrust out his hand, and Ryan shook it. "Nice to meet you. And I do have to say that despite your negative feelings about your rotation with us, you are a lot more pleasant to talk with than Aria Nichols."

"I'll take that as a backhanded compliment," Ryan said with a smile. "I heard she was not the easiest person to get along with. I only had minimal contact with her."

"That's the understatement of the year," Jack said. "At the same time, she was smart and determined, and her loss was tragic. Despite her personality shortcomings, she would have made a mark in her pathology career. I'm sure of it."

CHAPTER 26

Friday, December 8, 3:50 pm

When Ryan got back to the residents' room, he found Sharon still dressed in scrubs, adding yet another autopsy to her list. It was depressing and made him feel paranoid that she was trying to show him up on purpose. Avoiding such thinking by making small talk, he asked: "So what did you and Dr. McGovern find with the flight attendant?"

"We didn't find much," Sharon admitted as she put away her autopsy log in her desk. "The only pathology was a large ovarian cyst."

"So you guys didn't find a cause of death?"

"Not yet, but Dr. McGovern thinks he knows. He's tasked the MLI to return to the scene at the hotel where the woman was staying and bring back any electrical devices, like hair dryers or curling irons. He seems certain the victim died of low-voltage electrocution. He told me such things still happen if people plug faulty appliances into outlets that are not GFCI."

Ryan had no idea what GFCI was, but at the moment he didn't care. "Question," he said, letting the word hang in the air.

"What?" she asked impatiently after waiting for a beat.

"When you told me about the autopsy on the suicide case this morning, why didn't you tell me it was a murder/suicide?" He had an accusatory edge to his voice.

"I thought you knew."

"How the hell would I know?"

"Everybody in the freaking OCME knew, even the maintenance people," Sharon said defensively. "It was the talk of the town. It was even on the cover of one of the tabloids this morning. Maybe if you didn't hide out in here and acted like a normal person, you would have known, like everyone else."

Ryan absorbed this mild diatribe, as he couldn't help but agree. He was hiding out for obvious reasons. With a nod of resignation, he turned on his monitor. He was eager to call Eva Hoffman, but first he wanted to google *staged murder/suicide* to see what he could find, as his mind switched back to his brainstorm about the entire Levi murder/suicide being a staged event, meaning the wife would have been the target.

After typing in *staged murder/suicide* he was disappointed since the Google search engine interpreted his request as if he was searching for a "staged suicide" whereas his interest was a "staged double murder," where a third party killed both people yet wanted the authorities to believe it was a murder/suicide. As Ryan struggled to find different ways to elicit the search he wanted, he became aware that Sharon had departed. He felt mildly guilty about having falsely accused her of hiding significant information and decided to apologize when he saw her on Monday.

After a significant interval of time trying to troubleshoot the search, Ryan gave up, recognizing that a staged murder/suicide was indeed a rare event if it had ever happened. The only potential reference he'd found was a trial of someone accused of such an event but found not guilty, meaning maybe it was a possibility, although highly unlikely.

Picking up his phone, he brought up Janice Jaeger's text with Eva Hoffman's number. As the call went through, he reminded himself that the woman was most likely still in a state of shock since she'd lost her sister and brother-in-law less than twenty-four hours ago. Unfortunately, he got her voicemail. Disappointed but undeterred, he left a message explaining he was a doctor calling from the medical examiner's office about the tragedy that had occurred the night before and asked for a call back.

Again feeling metaphorically becalmed in the middle of a storm, he put his phone down and looked at the notes he had scribbled that morning to try to decide what to do. Just when he was about to call Mia Parker again, his phone rang in his hand. It was Eva Hoffman.

Trying to be sensitive, Ryan apologized for disturbing her.

"You're not disturbing me," she said with a fiery tone. "The more I think about this disaster, the angrier and more disgusted I get. I was never a fan of Nathan. Never! But I certainly didn't think he was capable of doing something as dreadful and selfish as this. Never! I know my sister was intense and self-centered and probably difficult to live with as she had all these causes she was fired up about. She'd always been that way, but she certainly didn't deserve this. No way!"

"I'm sorry," Ryan said, and meant it. He knew as much as anyone how suicide in all its forms was destructive to everyone involved. "Depression is an underappreciated scourge," he added. He couldn't help but remember how he had struggled with it when he'd been confined to what were euphemistically called juvenile correctional institutes but were jails in reality. "Maybe Mr. Levi didn't even know how depressed he was."

"What are you talking about?"

"The medical legal investigator you spoke with last night said that you were aware Mr. Levi was depressed."

"I said he was distressed about the stock market's fluctuations."

"Didn't you also say he was depressed?"

"I don't know, maybe I did. But what I meant was he had carried on about the economy almost every day for the last year and a half. But if anybody was depressed, it was my sister."

"Oh? Was she a depressive type?"

"No, not at all. She was wired like me."

"What was she depressed about?"

"She'd had her yearly physical and ended up being diagnosed with cancer. The trouble was they couldn't tell her where it was in her body, just that it involved the GI tract. For her it was like having the sword of Damocles dangling over her head, and it weighed her down. Our father died of stomach cancer at a young age, and she was certain she had it, even though an X-ray had said she didn't. There'd been a few days that she couldn't even get out of bed."

"Do you know what company was involved with the testing? Was it Oncology Diagnostics?"

"That sounds familiar," Eva said. "It got so I couldn't even talk to her about it all, especially when she started getting paranoid and furious about the way the clinic was charging an arm and a leg looking for the cancer, which is stupid because she and Nathan could certainly afford it."

"Interesting," Ryan said, his mind in overdrive with the recognition he was stumbling onto something rather extraordinary. Three people out of eight—nine, if you now counted Marsha—associated with his research project, one-third or so, had been involved with the same diagnostics clinic. What were the chances of such a coincidence?

"Maybe it was her depression that drove Nathan berserk," Eva questioned. "Who's to know?"

"I suppose that's a possibility," Ryan said, but he was already thinking ahead, and wondering if any other of his subjects shared this unexpected cancer diagnosis connection. "Thank you so much for talking with me," he said. As soon as he could, and with a promise that he'd call back if he had any more questions, he ended the call. He then spent a few minutes adding Marsha Levi to his matrix and filling in what he'd learned, specifically a *yes* in the CADx column, along with the name *Oncology Diagnostics*. He also again noticed her demographics resembled the other people on his matrix, other than the outlier Nathan.

He then went back to his phone. Now that it was after four in the afternoon, he thought he'd try calling Robert Frank and Mia Parker again. Thinking there was a chance Mia might have gotten off work at three, he tried her first. He was rewarded when she picked up on the third ring.

Encouraged, Ryan went through his spiel. Out of the blue, he added that his role was to serve the living and not just the dead; it amused him that he was sounding like a fan of the OCME. At the conclusion to his brief monologue, he expressed his condolences about Norman Colbert's passing and hoped his calling her didn't add to her stress.

"Thank you for your concern," Mia said. "It's not been easy, but I'm a critical care nurse, and I deal with the threat and reality of death almost daily. It was more than two months ago that Norman took his life. I certainly miss him and wish I could have helped him more than I did, but I didn't see it coming. Be that as it may, how can I help you? I'm sorry I hadn't returned your call. It takes me some time to recover after one of my ICU shifts."

"No problem," he said. "I won't take much of your time. I'd just like to ask you a few questions. I've gone over the report the medical legal investigator did the night Mr. Colbert was found as well as speaking to her in person. Do you remember talking with her? Her name is Darlene Franklin."

"Yes, of course. That evening and night are burned into my memory."

"I can imagine," Ryan said as he again recalled his horrid experience discovering his father. The image was certainly burned into *his* memory. With a shake of his head, he sent the memory back into the recesses of his mind before continuing: "What I wanted to ask you about was your telling Darlene Franklin that Norman had been experiencing depression, but either you didn't elaborate or Ms. Franklin didn't record what you said."

"I did say that Norman had been experiencing depression, but I was hesitant to elaborate."

"Oh?" Ryan questioned. "Why was that?"

"As I've said, I am a critical care nurse and dealing with death is a fact of my life. My colleagues and I are reminded on a regular basis by the hospital counsel of HIPAA rules that restrict giving out medical information about patients even after death."

He inwardly groaned as he feared he was hitting a dead end with his inquiries, just as he'd been with Dr. Stein about Sean O'Brien. He tried to adjust. "You are correct," he said. "But it's also true that the OCME can get the information by obtaining a warrant. It's just a lengthy process."

"That's something I don't know anything about," Mia said. "I just know what my responsibilities are."

"How about if I just ask you some general questions rather than specifics. Are you okay with that?" Suddenly Ryan had an idea he could learn something significant by being a bit cagey. HIPAA was meant to guard against the dissemination of specific health information.

"I'm not sure what you mean."

"Let me ask you a general question about Mr. Colbert's depression that wouldn't reveal any personal details, like specific symptoms or treatments. Was it a reactive depression about some life event?"

Mia paused and Ryan waited. He felt confident his question was general enough, but he had no idea how Mia Parker would respond to it.

"Yes, I believe I can say it was a reactive depression," she said, finally breaking the silence.

As a medical student he'd had some minor experiences with psychiatry and he knew that reactive depression episodes, in contrast to major depressive disorders, were caused by stressful life experiences, primarily divorce, the passing of family members or friends, job loss, or serious health issues. As he already knew Mr. Colbert was single, that left three other major categories.

"Had Mr. Colbert suffered the deaths of any family or friends?"

"No."

"Had he been fired from AIG?"

"No," Mia said with a humorless chuckle. "My goodness! You are well informed. What makes you ask that?"

"I'm just eliminating possibilities," Ryan explained as his mind raced ahead. He knew what he wanted to ask but couldn't. He looked down at his matrix at the column he'd labeled CADx for cancer diagnosis, noticing a *yes* along with *Oncology Diagnostics* with three of his now nine cases. Then suddenly another question dawned on him that he thought he could get a response without Mia feeling she was revealing private personal health information. "Tell me this—did Mr. Colbert have any dealings with a clinic called Oncology Diagnostics?"

For a few beats there was silence. Just when Ryan was about to reword his question, she answered by saying: "He did, and he wasn't happy about it. That's all I can say."

He was stunned and suddenly eager to terminate the call. "Okay," he said. "Thank you so much for talking with me."

"I'm sorry I can't be more helpful and specific," Mia said.

"You've been very helpful," Ryan corrected. "And I respect your

attentiveness to HIPAA rules. I'm sorry to have bothered you by reminding you of what had to be a difficult and emotional event."

"You haven't bothered me," Mia said graciously.

He disconnected the call after goodbyes, and for a few minutes
stared over his monitor at the blank, painted concrete-block wall. He
was blown away by this startling commonality with four of his subjects.
After a few minutes of paralysis, he was able to pull himself together.
The first thing he did was to add to his matrix. He put a *yes* in Norman
Colbert's CADx column, along with *Oncology Diagnostics* to match what
was already listed for Lily Berg, Sean O'Brien, and Marsha Levi.

Ryan was now pretty certain Norman Colbert had been diagnosed
with cancer during his annual physical, and from having recently read
Dr. Washington's autopsy report, he knew no cancer had been found at
least on gross examination. With his background in medical statistics,
he knew that nearly fifty percent of the subjects in his study having such
an unexpected commonality most likely couldn't happen by chance
alone. He had no choice but to check to see if any of the remaining five
shared the same unique commonality, and if they did, find out what it
meant. He snapped up his phone and placed another call to Robert
Frank, the subway-commuting bank executive who'd not yet returned his
call. At the same time, he pawed through his notes to find and quickly
read all that he had jotted down about Cynthia Evers in his study diary.

As the call went through, Ryan murmured, "Come on, come on!"
while clenching his teeth in a futile attempt to make it happen. He was
experiencing a sense of urgency and excitement. To his relief, it was
answered after the fourth ring.

From the start of the conversation, Ryan tried to be sensitive to the
man's feelings. In the back of his mind, he could hear Janice Jaeger's
speculation that Robert Frank had been alienated by the police on the
night he'd discovered Cynthia Evers partially hanging from her shower

head, which had made him initially uncooperative. He couldn't imagine a more gruesome image for a lover to confront.

As Ryan went through his introduction, he apologized multiple times for having to bring up such a sensitive subject. The approach seemed to have a positive result. When he finished his brief monologue, Robert responded by apologizing for not getting back to him. "To be honest, I wasn't sure I wanted to be reminded of the whole awful episode."

"I totally understand," Ryan said with sincerity. "I'll try to make this short. I've gone over the details of Ms. Evers's case and there was something specific that I wanted to clarify. I read in the summary that prior to the unfortunate event, Ms. Evers had been depressed. What it didn't specify was whether this was an ongoing struggle with depression, which I also read she'd suffered as a teenager, or whether it was because of a recent event."

"It was definitely due to an event," Robert said without the least hesitation.

Ryan felt his pulse quicken. "Was it a personal health issue?"

"Yes. She'd been diagnosed with early cancer but not its location. All she was told was that her cancer involved the female reproductive system such that she had to undergo multiple tests to determine the source, but nothing seemed to be working out. As a confessed hypochondriac, it was all driving her to distraction, and she couldn't sleep or eat. Finally, I was able to get her to see her gyno to find out if she could help, and at first it did. Cynthia seemed to pull out of her depressive nosedive, and her emotions swung toward anger rather than depression concerning the costs involved. Her health insurance wasn't paying for some of the testing, particularly for a full-body scan she had to have. At least that's how it seemed to me, but she didn't tell me everything, and I'm not a doctor."

Ryan was again stunned but eager to learn more. "Was she by any chance being seen at a clinic called Oncology Diagnostics?"

"Yes, I believe that was the name."

The conversation went on for a few more minutes, but Ryan was eager to bring it to a close, and after appropriate goodbyes, he did just that. Putting his phone down, he added a *yes* and *Oncology Diagnostics* to his matrix for Cynthia Evers. That left only four subjects where the CADx column was empty: Stephen Gallagher, Sofia Ferrara, Daniela Alberich, and Nathan Levi. Realizing that Nathan being an outlier was almost certainly related to Marsha's similarities with the others on the list, and that he wasn't a part of whatever was going on here, he put a line through his name, bringing him back to eight subjects.

With building excitement and a touch of disbelief, Ryan made calls to Harold Gallagher, Nancy Beardsley, and Helen Ferrara to see if his last three names could be added to this unexpected commonality. Both Nancy Beardsley and Helen Ferrara answered. Only with Harold Gallagher was he forced to leave a voice message asking for a call back.

More important, Ryan learned from Ms. Beardsley and Mrs. Ferrara that both Daniela Alberich and Sofia Ferrara had been diagnosed with early asymptomatic cancer by Oncology Diagnostics and had been quite upset about it. When questioning why that hadn't been revealed earlier, both had claimed that they didn't believe it had anything to do with their suicides. Despite being upset at the diagnosis initially, both women did not think it had contributed to either suicide because days before both Daniela and Sofia had each been assured by their personal physicians that they were cancer free, meaning the Oncology Diagnostics results had apparently been false positives.

After the calls, Ryan had felt a certain amount of satisfaction adding a *yes* and *Oncology Diagnostics* to the proper places on his matrix. In the CADx column, only Stephen Gallagher's was blank. Knowing that Harold's relationship to his brother wasn't close, Ryan wasn't even sure if Harold would know if Stephen had had any dealings with Oncology

Diagnostics. But it didn't matter. The fact that seven out of eight of his subjects had been patients of Oncology Diagnostics cried out for an explanation. The chances of it happening by coincidence were statistically close to zero. If nothing else, Oncology Diagnostics had to be informed that a number of their patients, having been diagnosed with cancer, might be having serious difficulty coping mentally and, if so, were at risk of suicide.

CHAPTER 27

Friday, December 8, 4:20 pm

All at once Ryan felt an irresistible urge to understand all that he could about Oncology Diagnostics, especially the science behind its technology. To do this, he revisited their website to learn more. When he had the website up, he clicked on OncoDx, which was the cancer diagnostic test they offered. At the same time, he got a clean sheet of paper from one of his pads for note taking.

What Ryan learned was that Oncology Diagnostics did not do the OncoDx tests themselves, but rather sent patients' blood samples to a different company that had developed the test. What became clear to him was that Oncology Diagnostics' business model depended on providing cancer screening services to client corporations by offering OncoDx tests as a part of the corporations' required annual executive physical. Then, if the test turned out to be positive, it spearheaded the difficult process of locating the diagnosed cancer to a specific organ before referring the patient on to one of the major cancer centers for treatment.

Reading on, Ryan found out that the OncoDx test was based on the relatively new science and technology associated with extracellular vesicles. As a pathology resident, he knew that these extracellular vesicles were minuscule, membrane-enclosed structures that floated around in intercellular spaces and in the bloodstream, containing all manner of organic molecules from nucleic acids like DNA to proteins and lipids. He also knew that they were produced either by budding into the cell initially before being excreted and thereby called exosomes or by forming like a bud from the external portion of the cell membrane and called microvesicles.

He knew a reasonable amount about this new technology because when he first heard of it, he'd been intrigued on multiple levels. For him, the very existence of exosomes and microvesicles as a method of intracellular communication suggested an explanation for how multicellular organisms originally evolved. There had to be some form of communication so that separate cells could know what their neighbors were doing and thereby allow them ultimately to specialize into different functions, and extracellular vesicles provided this communication.

As Ryan continued to read, he learned that the OncoDx test was based on separating out from a blood sample a specific type of large microvesicles called oncosomes by ultracentrifugation. Once the oncosomes were isolated, they were counted in a defined space, and if the count exceeded a certain number, the contents of these large microvesicles were probed to find mutated DNA known to be from cancerous cells. Then, by further defining the cancerous DNA, the involved organ system but not the organ itself could be determined.

He outlined all this material for his study diary, so that he would have it at his fingertips in the future. Then he sat back and stared up at the ceiling with unseeing eyes as he integrated all this information into his mind. He was thoroughly impressed with this new technology and realized that it was a true breakthrough for preventive medicine. Suddenly here was an opportunity to diagnose cancer at the earliest stage possible when one or a few cells had made the transition from a normal cell with controlled replication to a cell that had been freed of all such restraints. Up until this breakthrough, cancer diagnosis depended on overt symptoms such as a palpable tumor or the interruption of a specific organ's function. The problem with that was it meant that there were already millions if not billions of cancer cells spreading their malignancy to different parts of the body, making treatment difficult if not impossible. The fact that this new screening test was able to diagnosis a malignancy so early explained why no one in his study group had been found to have cancer at autopsy or even by histology. With a microscopic amount of cancer involved in any organ, the chance of catching it, even with multiple biopsies, were negligible.

Suddenly Ryan tipped forward in his desk chair. A new thought had occurred to him. As wonderful an addition this new testing was for preventive medicine, it also had a downside. A positive OncoDx would create a whole new category of patients, which he labeled in his mind the walking sick. Being told that a cancer was smoldering someplace in your body would be devastating to most people, especially those individuals who tended to be hypochondriacal. He could surely attest to this reality by his researching suicides of at least seven and probably all eight individuals that had been diagnosed with cancer. The idea of harboring a growing, possibly fatal illness had apparently been too much for them to bear, and they had elected to take their fate into their own hands by killing themselves. He felt Oncology Diagnostics had to be warned of this reality, the sooner the better and before the upcoming weekend, and he wrote this in his study diary, underlining it several times for emphasis.

Returning to the Oncology Diagnostics website, he opened up the page labeled Management. There he read about the founders and owners, Dr. Jerome Pappas and Dr. Malik Williams. Both individuals happened to be physicians, which suggested to Ryan that they would not only be receptive to hearing that many of their patients had died by suicide but would also fully understand the importance of dealing with such an obvious mental health issue. He turned to the website's contact page to find the clinic's phone number.

Believing that the situation was an emergency of sorts and since it was late on a Friday afternoon, Ryan placed a call immediately. He felt that the sooner the clinic principals were made aware the better. As the call went through, he also decided it would be far more effective if he made the effort to travel up to the Upper East Side and deliver the news in person to one of the founding doctors. When his call was answered by a receptionist, Ryan identified himself as a physician from the OCME who needed to have an emergency meeting with either Dr. Pappas or Dr. Williams, whoever was available at that moment. Without a word the receptionist switched the call.

"Good afternoon," a woman's voice said, coming on the line. "This is Beverly Aronson, scheduling secretary. Who am I speaking with?"

He again identified himself, particularly emphasizing he was calling from the Office of the Chief Medical Examiner and then repeated his request. He then added with some urgency in his voice: "Might Dr. Pappas or Dr. Williams be available in the next hour or so? It is vitally important that I see either one or both as soon as possible."

"Hold the line," Beverly said.

She was gone for several minutes. When she came back she said, "Yes, Dr. Pappas will see you, but you need to come directly. We are located on Park Avenue between Eighty-Second and Eighty-Third Streets."

"I'll be there as soon as I can," Ryan said before disconnecting. He was convinced it was the correct thing to do under the circumstances and wrote as much in his study diary.

Grabbing his coat with the intention of heading downstairs and out into the street to catch a cab or call a rideshare, he hesitated. He suddenly remembered his promise to Dr. Stapleton that he would not make any site visits. *Is this a site visit?* he asked himself. *No* was his answer, as none of the suicides had taken place at the Oncology Diagnostics clinic nor was he going to confront any bad people. And yet . . . Ryan paused. The reality was that he was indeed heading out of the OCME, and it had to do with his study, so why not do what Dr. Stapleton had asked, and discuss the idea with him first? After all, it would only take a couple of minutes to go up to the third floor, and there was always the chance that Dr. Stapleton would not only see the need for immediate action, he might also believe someone higher up would be better suited to be the disturbing messenger, perhaps even him.

With that thought in mind, he hustled up to the third floor and walked to Dr. Stapleton's office. As he approached, he saw that the door was now closed, which wasn't an auspicious sign. Still, he knocked rather loudly.

"Dr. Stapleton just left," a voice sounded.

Ryan turned around. He could see into Dr. Mehta's office on the other side of the hallway. She was again sitting at her microscope and had obviously heard his vigorous knocking.

"He commutes on his bike and likes to try to get home before dark if at all possible," Dr. Mehta added.

"Wow, that's impressive," Ryan said. He now had an idea why the man appeared so fit in comparison with the other MEs. "How far away does he live?"

"Way up on the Upper West Side," Dr. Mehta said. "It's a haul, especially in traffic. None of us can quite understand it, especially after his accident a year ago, when he almost died."

With Dr. Stapleton unavailable, he debated getting Dr. Mehta's take on the situation since she was one of the MEs indirectly involved with his study, but then he nixed the idea. It would surely turn into a long explanation, and Ryan wanted to be sure to catch Dr. Pappas before he left for the weekend. On top of that, it wouldn't fulfill his promise to Dr. Stapleton. After excusing himself, he went back to the stairway and descended to the first floor.

But then, as he was passing the entrance to the administrative area, he had another idea. He could let Dr. Montgomery know what he had in mind vis-à-vis Oncology Diagnostics. It seemed like a perfect solution, since she knew exactly what he was researching, and since she was married to Dr. Stapleton, she could relay to him the information and thereby fulfill his promise of keeping Dr. Stapleton informed.

Ryan made a detour and walked up to Cheryl Stanford's desk. He and Sharon Hinkley had met the chief's personable secretary on the first day of their rotation when they had been welcomed by Dr. Montgomery. Before he could speak, Cheryl held up an index finger and pointed toward her earbuds.

With rising anxiety, as time was passing, Ryan stood in front of Cheryl as she repeated "yes" a number of times, then wrote a note before terminating the call.

"Sorry, Dr. Sullivan," she said. "What can I do for you?"

"I need to see Dr. Montgomery for two seconds," he said hurriedly. "It's extremely important." He held up two fingers to make his point that it would only be a short conversation.

"Sorry, but you've missed her," Cheryl responded. "She had to leave for an off-campus meeting and will be heading home from there. Can I schedule you for a few minutes first thing on Monday?"

Ryan vacillated. Obviously he was being foiled in his attempt to fulfill his promise, but would he want to talk with Dr. Montgomery anyway on Monday? Politically it seemed like an good move, as it would mean the chief would have already been informed of his progress so that he could say as much to Dr. McGovern later in the day when he checked on his progress as threatened.

"What does *first thing* mean?" Ryan asked. "How early?"

"I start her schedule at eight," Cheryl said. "You could be first."

"Put me down for eight, please," he said, deciding it was worth the effort of making sure he was on time for work.

"You got it," Cheryl said, as she typed Ryan's name into her computer.

Finally, outside and on his way, it was painfully obvious to Ryan that rush hour was in full swing with First Avenue chockablock with cars, yellow cabs, and buses all moving at not much more than walking speed. Since he lived in the neighborhood, he never particularly noticed the traffic because he walked to and from work, but he did now and to his dismay it added to his growing anxiety. Knowing that it would be nearly useless to try to hail a taxi and that a rideshare would undoubtedly take much too much time to get there, he walked northward. What he was counting on was cabs being almost always available at the hospital entrance a mere half a block north of the OCME. A few minutes later, as he hoped, he was in the back seat of a yellow taxi creeping uptown.

Because of the gridlock, it took longer than Ryan had expected to get to 968 Park Avenue, and he was glad he'd called the clinic to set up a meeting rather than arriving unannounced. By the time he entered Oncology Diagnostics, it was almost 5:30 and apparently the clinic was about to close.

He was impressed with the décor. The ambience was decidedly upscale and appeared newly constructed. In the empty waiting area, there were framed period oil paintings and a high-gloss hardwood floor with a lush, central oriental carpet. To the right was a chest-high counter supporting sliding glass partitions fencing off a brightly lit secretarial area. As Ryan approached, a fashionable young woman slid open the glass pane.

"May I help you?" she said with a welcoming smile.

"I hope so," he said as he approached the countertop. "I'm Dr. Sullivan, here to see Dr. Pappas. I spoke with Beverly Aronson."

"Yes, of course," the secretary said. "I'll let Beverly know you're here." She then slid the glass partition closed.

Before Ryan had time to sit in one of the expensive-looking chairs, a serious-looking, well-dressed, middle-aged woman with an old-fashioned hairstyle frozen in place by hairspray suddenly appeared through a paneled, red mahogany door.

"Dr. Sullivan?" she questioned.

"Yes. I'm here to see Dr. Pappas."

"Of course. We've been expecting you. If you'd follow me, please." She gestured with a short wave of her hand as she walked back through the doorway.

Ryan dutifully followed. On the other side of the door, the environment changed from over-the-top warm sumptuousness to white, aseptic institutional. They passed a number of closed doors fitted with medical chart racks indicating examination rooms. At the end of the hall the woman opened a door, stepped to the side, and gestured for him to enter.

The transition was abruptly back to being plush, with lots of dark wood and another oriental-carpeted floor. As he entered, Ryan heard the door close behind him. Sitting behind a massive desk was a stocky, square-shaped man whose facial features looked as if they had been poked into puffy pale skin with the consistency of unbaked dough. His eyes were red and watery behind his glasses. His expression was a tight, tense smile. He was dressed in a starched, long white doctor's coat with a white dress shirt and blue tie. His hair was moderately long, very dark like his pupils, parted in the middle of his head, and motionless like Ms. Aronson's.

As Ryan approached, the man got to his feet and came around from behind his desk with his hand outstretched. "Welcome!" he said as he shook Ryan's hand. He gestured toward his low black leather couch. "Please!"

"Thank you," Ryan said. He was encouraged by his reception, although the smile seemed strained and fleeting, and the man's palm was rather moist. As Ryan sat down, Jerome stepped over to a paneled wall and pressed opened one of the cabinets. Inside Ryan could make out a wet bar.

"It's the end of the day, and I allow myself a finger of scotch," he announced. "Can I offer you the same?"

"No, thank you," Ryan responded. It might have been the last thing that he wanted at that moment. He watched as Jerome poured himself what looked to Ryan more like two fingers of scotch. The man then came over and took a wooden armchair next to the couch, such that he was sitting significantly higher than Ryan, making Ryan question if it was on purpose.

"Okay," Jerome said, ostensibly making himself comfortable. He smiled again, but again it didn't last. "So, what can I do for you today? You're the first official visitor we've ever had from the Office of the Chief Medical Examiner."

"Thank you for seeing me," Ryan began. Then he hesitated. He hadn't given any specific thought to exactly how he was going to tell these people what they needed to know, but now that he was about to begin, he sensed he had to provide some element of background to give himself credence. "First of all, I am not a medical examiner. I'm an NYU anatomical pathology resident currently doing a month's rotation

in forensic pathology at the OCME. In that capacity, I have been studying what started out as six cases but now has ballooned to eight. Briefly:
these cases all involve suicides that had in one way or the other at least
raised the question of potential homicides. In all cases so far they have
been confirmed to be suicides. My study was an attempt to find commonalities to try to answer the question of why so many similar cases
were occurring in a short six-month period. Interestingly enough, I was
having some success. This afternoon, though, I discovered a particularly
unexpected commonality. It seems that at least seven of the eight were
Oncology Diagnostics patients. All of them had positive results from the
cancer screen test you provide and were in the stressful process of locating the origin of their cancers."

Jerome, who had been intently staring at Ryan up until that moment,
tossed back his scotch in one gulp and then, with a shaky hand, noisily
placed his empty glass on a side table. He seemed stunned by this information. "Do you happen to have the names of these patients?" he asked
hesitantly.

"I do," Ryan said. He produced a handwritten list and handed it to
Jerome. Ryan had prepared it, hoping he'd be asked for it. He was interested to get confirmation that they all were Oncology Diagnostics
patients.

Jerome took the page and glanced at it before putting it next to his
glass, as if he preferred not to hold it. "I recognize many of these names.
The others I can easily have checked. God! It is such a tragedy that
these patients have taken their own lives after all the effort we've been
expending to preserve their health. What a terrible waste of promising
lives."

"I was eager to share this information as soon as possible in case you
might want to reach out to your current patients with positive test results and highlight this risk and, most important, encourage them to

seek appropriate mental health intervention if indicated. I assume you're aware that a cancer diagnosis significantly raises the incidence of suicide."

"Oh, absolutely," Jerome said before suddenly snatching up his empty glass and getting to his feet. He headed back to the bar. "Such awful news necessitates another scotch," he called over his shoulder as he poured himself a good inch with a shaky hand. "Are you sure I can't tempt you to join me?"

"No, thank you," Ryan said.

After Jerome returned to his seat and tossed back his second scotch he asked, "Have you been working on this study with anyone else, perhaps another resident?"

"No, I came up with the idea on my own. I was just trying to be resourceful and use my time to my advantage."

"Is your study being overseen by one of the medical examiners?" Jerome asked.

"No, not really or not yet," Ryan said. "The medical examiner in charge of all teaching efforts at the OCME just gave me the list of the first six victims that had been put together by several of the medical legal investigators. I don't believe he intended to do anything with it, and he didn't direct me at all. I'm scheduled to present to him what progress I have on Monday. All six of the original cases had been handled by different medical examiners, so I collated all the autopsy reports and the reports of the medical legal investigators. More important, I got to talk with the victims' family members or friends, whoever had initially discovered the bodies, identified them, and provided background information. It was they who ultimately revealed this commonality."

"You seem like a resourceful young man," Jerome said with a nod. "Congratulations." He then rapidly got to his feet. "I want to thank you for making the effort to come see me this afternoon. I'm sorry to cut this short, but I want to get together with my partner on this disturbing information so we can put together a warning and get it disseminated. This is a true emergency. We had no idea."

It took Ryan a bit of extra effort to get up from the deep couch. "Thank you for listening. I appreciate you seeing me under such short notice and I'm sorry to be the bearer of bad news."

After a final handshake, Jerome opened the door. "I trust you can find your way out." He pointed down the hall with a shaky hand. "The door at the end leads into our waiting room."

"No problem," Ryan said, nodding to the doctor as he passed.

As he walked down the glaringly white, sterile hallway, he felt good about having made this visit, since it had the desired effect of motivating Oncology Diagnostics to act quickly and appropriately. Ryan had no idea how many patients the clinic handled, but from the glitzy office and its location on Park Avenue, it had to be a significant number just to pay the overhead. Still, having at least seven take their lives, the problem needed to be addressed, no matter what the percentage of the total patient population of the clinic the seven cases represented.

Once out on the street, Ryan took out his phone and called for an Uber to pick him up. Although it was only a bit after 5:45, it was already dark. As the minutes clicked by while he waited for his ride, he found himself debating whether to go back to the OCME as he'd arranged. His plan was to retrieve his matrix and study notes, so he could work on the project over the weekend if he was so inclined. Yet the more he thought about the idea, the more he felt he wanted to just forget about the OCME for a couple of days. After all, he'd certainly made enough progress to satisfy Dr. McGovern. Ultimately he decided to just to head home. To that end, he went back on his phone and changed his upcoming destination.

As he stood there watching for a white Toyota, he found himself indulging in a bit of wishful thinking that when he got home, he'd find Isabella in his apartment, like she'd been last night. But the happy thought lasted only for a moment, knowing the chances of it happening were essentially zero. This new realization made him feel uncharacteristically lonely, which took him by surprise.

Normally Ryan loved being alone and away from the world in the safety of his apartment. It clearly was Isabella and her unique personality that was causing this emotional dissonance, especially his knowing she was otherwise undoubtedly socially engaged both that night and Saturday. Wanting to spend time with someone was new for him and a little scary because it made him question if she felt similarly, and if she did, whether it would last once she learned the whole history of his disastrous childhood. Unfortunately, the story of his upbringing was as much a part of who he was just as much as his being a socially acceptable doctor.

Fifteen minutes later, as he was climbing into the back of the Uber, Ryan experienced another mood flip-flop. He was now fondly anticipating getting back to his apartment and enjoying the solitude and familiar surroundings. He was glad his study materials were where they were. After such a busy, challenging, and fruitful day, he looked forward to doing nothing more than some mindless gaming, YouTube surfing, and TV watching. Sunday would come soon enough.

CHAPTER 28

Friday, December 8, 5:35 pm

Tossing back yet another scotch, Jerome glanced down at the patient list the pathology resident had provided, which he'd set down on the bar counter when he'd helped himself to yet another shot of whiskey. When he'd told Ryan Sullivan he recognized some of the patients, he was lying. He recognized all of them, as they were about three-quarters of the patients who had raised an alarm about their OncoDx being a false positive and had to be tasked to Action Security to handle.

"Good god!" Jerome complained out loud as he took a deep breath, trying to calm himself. He wanted to throw his now-empty scotch glass against the opposite wall in frustration, but he held himself in check. Dr. Sullivan's visit coming out of the blue was more than a troublesome shock; it was a disaster in the making that had his blood pressure skyrocketing. There was no doubt it needed to be handled immediately.

Each time one of these episodes that had necessitated Action Security's intervention had reared its ugly head, he'd questioned whether the risks they were taking were worth it, despite Malik's and Chuck Barton's reassurances all was hunky-dory. At the same time, he recognized the extent of the disaster that awaited for his and Malik's lifestyles if Full Body Scan was allowed to go into default, so it was a toss-up of which was worse. He'd been a worrywart as far back as grammar school. What he really wished was that he could somehow become more like Malik, whose personality seemed capable of taking everything in stride.

Once Jerome could feel the warmth of the third scotch spread through his body and his anxiety lessen a degree so that his pulse wasn't pounding in his temples, he set off for Malik's office, taking with him the list of patients. The location was close, just on the other side of Beverly Aronson's intervening office space, but as far as décor was concerned, it was as if it were on the other side of the moon. In sharp contrast to his preference for old-style dark wood and rich fabrics, Malik favored white, minimalist modern. Even the man's desk chair looked more like a torture device than an inviting place to sit.

As keyed up as Jerome was, he didn't stop to chat with Beverly, whom he breezed past with a mere half-hearted wave, so she wouldn't be alarmed. Reaching Malik's door, he knocked but didn't wait for an answer.

As per usual, Malik was on his phone. Accustomed to his partner's idiosyncrasies, he responded by merely holding up his right index finger to communicate to Jerome that he'd be with him in a moment and continued talking. He had earbuds in and was pushed back from his desk to cross his long legs. Like Jerome, he was dressed in a white shirt, but his collar was open and his tie loosened. The one way the partners were alike was that they shared a preference for traditional doctors' style of dress with long white coats despite their contact with patients being minimal, as both concentrated on their business interests.

Jerome wasn't content to wait. Instead, he marched right up to Malik's desk and slapped the list he'd gotten from Ryan Sullivan directly on top of the spreadsheet Malik had in front of him, flattened it out with his palm, and ordered, "Take a gander at this!"

Malik glanced at the list of names but continued his conversation about a tax issue. He moved the list to the side and carried on with a relatively long monologue before going silent to listen and even make a few notes on a pad to the right of the spreadsheet.

Recognizing that his partner was talking to someone at their accountant's office and wasn't about to cut it short, Jerome threw up his hands in frustration and began angrily pacing in front of Malik's desk. Every second that passed increased his anxiety, making him wish he'd brought his scotch bottle. Since he knew Malik was a teetotaler, he didn't try to look for any alcohol in the blank white cabinetry that filled one entire wall.

After what seemed like eternity, Malik concluded his conversation and said goodbye. He then removed his earbuds and looked up at his partner. "Okay, what now?"

"You're not going to believe this," Jerome spewed. He returned to Malik's desk, reached over, grabbed the list of patients, and then repositioned it under Malik's nose. "See these names?" he questioned, almost shouting.

Malik looked back at the paper. "I see them. Calm down. It looks to me like some of the patients we had Action Security deal with. Am I correct?"

"Yes, you are correct," Jerome said. In the face of Malik's persistent calm composure, Jerome's anxiety began to abate. He closed his eyes for a moment and took a deep breath. "You are right, but this list didn't come from Action Security. Oh, no! We got this list a few minutes ago from a resident at NYU who is spending a month at the medical examiner's office. That's where they autopsy people to find out how they died. Tell me truthfully: Doesn't that make your blood run cold?"

"No, not yet," Malik said calmly. "I need more information. Why don't you sit down, and we'll talk about the situation."

Jerome looked around at the selection of seating, all of which was as hard as nails. "No, thank you," he said after considering the options. "I'll stand, unless we go back to my office."

"Whatever you'd prefer," Malik said in his usual consolatory tone.

Using a lot of hand gestures to help give vent to his doomsday terror, Jerome rapidly related Sullivan's visit word for word and in the process described the pathology resident as a smart, resourceful, and particularly dangerous threat to their whole operation.

"Okay, okay," Malik said when Jerome began to repeat himself. "I get it, now let me ask a few questions."

"All right," Jerome said. He wiped his brow, as he'd begun to perspire. "Ask away."

"Let me get this straight. You said that this young doctor was doing this study on his own, meaning he wasn't sharing his revelations with anyone, including his discovery that his list of subjects were all patients of ours. Right?"

"That's my understanding. Yes."

"And, as I recall, you said he was scheduled to share what he'd learned with his adviser on Monday. Is that also correct?"

"It is."

"Well, it seems to me that rather than panicking or despairing, we should be thankful because it's not really our problem. Put it this way: No dam has been breached such that we are going to be washed away like the Johnstown Flood. The dam has just sprung a little leak that needs to be plugged."

Jerome stared back at his partner as his soothing style of speech and his words penetrated his brain, and he felt a kind of calm come over him. It was almost akin to having yet another scotch.

Malik held up the list. "We should try to think of how to appropriately acknowledge this resident who brought us this lineup. He's actually done us a great favor by coming to us straightaway."

"I see your point," Jerome said.

"Do you want to call Chuck Barton or do you want me to?"

"I'll do it," Jerome said with finality.

"The sooner the better," Malik added.

"I couldn't agree more," Jerome said.

CHAPTER 29

Isabella disconnected the call as soon as she heard Ryan's voicemail message yet again. It was the fifth time she'd tried to call him that morning after first trying a number of texts, and as the hours had passed, she'd gone through a wide range of emotions. As enthusiastic as he had seemed about getting together and having breakfast and seeing the Rockefeller Center Christmas tree, she'd assumed she'd hear from him on the early side. She'd even set her alarm and awakened at eight to get ready, significantly earlier than she would normally have, as she'd gotten home in the wee hours after going out clubbing. But by nine o'clock, she'd become impatient that he'd not yet contacted her, and with mild irritation decided to call him.

With her first voice message, she forced herself to be cheerful despite her irritation, saying she was hungry and looking forward to seeing him and that he should call her back ASAP. When a half hour had ticked by and he hadn't called, Isabella's impatience metamorphosed into more serious annoyance. Although she'd used the time to her advantage by doing a bit of apartment cleaning, she felt she was wasting time. Besides, she was getting hungrier.

With mounting emotion, she called a second time and again had to leave a voice message. This time she let her growing irritation reveal itself. She wasn't nasty by any stretch of the imagination, just to the point. She said she'd been ready for more than an hour and was now starving and he needed to call her.

About fifteen minutes after her second call, attempting to give Ryan the benefit of doubt, she wondered if he had his ringer off. To that end went back to texting. But even that was to no avail. She didn't get a call nor a return text, and her text even remained unread.

By nearly ten o'clock Isabella's irritation turned to anger. She didn't schedule a lot of social plans, generally preferring to let things evolve, but when she did, she expected them to happen. To her, this situation was a slap in the face. But it was also confusing, as it seemed so contrary to Ryan's generosity with his apartment and his computer.

Luckily she had ripe Anjou pears and bananas in the refrigerator, which quickly satisfied her hunger. She also had some work-related projects to review, which tempered her anger. As the morning passed and her indignation abated, she came to believe there had to be an explanation forthcoming. After all, maybe there'd been an emergency at the medical examiner's office.

Although earnestly engrossed in what she was doing, she called Ryan's number two more times over a period of an hour, and each time she became more curious than irritated. She even found herself again wondering if there were ever situations where an autopsy was done as an emergency. She couldn't imagine that could be the case since the patient was already dead, but what did she know?

By the time Isabella made her fifth call her emotional state had again changed. Although it had gone from indignation to irritation to anger and, finally, curiosity, it was now more in the category of concern. And along with this new mindset came the question of what to do.

After her final attempt to call Ryan, she put her phone down on her table, where she had several advertising layouts spread, and stared out her window at the south-facing, sun-drenched buildings lining East 22nd Street. At least the weather was cheerfully pleasant, especially for early December, which encouraged her to go outside for a walk and maybe grab a Sunday paper and a croissant. And while that thought occurred to her, it also reminded her that Ryan's apartment was a mere three blocks to the north.

Breaking off from staring out the window, Isabella glanced down at the key to Ryan's apartment. It had remained in the center of her dining–work table where she had put it when she'd returned from spending Thursday evening using his computer. In her current state of mind, the key's presence beckoned her to head over to his place to make sure he was all right. The more she thought about the situation, the more she'd come to see just how out of character this was. If she could at least determine he wasn't there, it would suggest his lack of communication was work-related and not a personal rebuke.

With sudden motivation to at least do something, she grabbed the key, put on some shoes, and pulled on a winter coat. As she emerged from her building, she realized she could have worn a much lighter jacket, as the temperature felt balmy, especially in the sun.

Since New York City streets were a grid, she had two choices for a route. She ended up taking the slightly longer way since it kept her in the sun.

In just a little more than five minutes she was on Ryan's street. From a position directly across from his building, she could see his windows on the third floor. For two or three minutes she watched to see if she could detect any movement. She couldn't. For a lingering moment she questioned the appropriateness of what she had in mind. What if he was home but was there with another woman? If that were the case, she'd feel totally stupid.

"Oh, come on!" she chided herself at her insecurities. With renewed resolve, she crossed the street, located his buzzer, and gave it a good, solid push. She waited. Nothing happened. She tried again, this time holding the button in for at least ten seconds. Still no response. Just as she was about to try for a third time, the entrance door was yanked open, catching her by surprise.

"Oh! Sorry," a woman about her age said as she emerged, practically bumping into Isabella.

"No problem," Isabella said as she quickly recovered.

The woman nodded, skirted around Isabella, and started up the street.

"Excuse me!" Isabella called out, causing the woman to stop and turn around. "I hope you don't mind me asking, but are you a resident of this building?"

"I am," the woman responded.

"Do you know Dr. Ryan Sullivan, by any chance?"

"I believe so, if it's the guy who lives on the third floor. I think he said his name was Ryan."

"He does live on the third floor. Have you seen him today?"

"I haven't," the woman said. "But this is the first I've been out of my apartment today."

"Thank you," Isabella said. Turning back to the building, she got out Ryan's apartment key that opened the outer door as well as his apartment door. Once inside, she used the open stairway since it was only two flights and the tiny elevator was unpleasant, if not scary.

A few minutes later, she was outside Ryan's door, where she again paused to ramp up her courage in case he was home and either purposely ignoring her or, worse yet, with someone else. She hadn't known him long enough to be able to guess what the chances were between those two possibilities but long enough to be fairly convinced he had to have been called out on some kind of an OCME or hospital emergency. In her mind it just stood to reason. He'd been so generous with his computer and his apartment that she doubted he could be mean-spirited.

Building up her courage, Isabella finally got herself to knock. First she did it rather quietly. When there was no response, she did it again, but this time using the base of her fist with enough oomph to be heard throughout the apartment. She waited. To attest to the strength of her knocking, a man in a T-shirt stuck his head out one of the other apartment doors.

"All okay out here?" the man inquired.

"Yes, everything is fine," she said. "I'm just looking for Ryan. Have you seen him today?"

"I haven't," the man said simply, and closed his door.

Isabella turned back to Ryan's door. After yet another moment of indecision, she took out his key and unlocked the door. She then pushed it open but stayed in the hallway. "Hello, hello!" she called out. "Ryan?" When there was no response, she stepped over the threshold, leaving the door ajar behind her.

The apartment appeared just as she remembered from Thursday night, including several large pathology books open on the coffee table. His computer was still on the table where she had been using it. From where she was standing, she could see into the kitchen that was separated from the main room by a countertop eating area. It was spic-and-span and devoid of clutter, unlike her own. Some dishes stood in a kitchen dish rack.

"Ryan! Are you here?" she called out, loud enough to be heard even in the bedroom reached by a moderately long hallway. Along the hallway was a bathroom door on one side and a closet on the other. Remaining motionless and even momentarily holding her breath, Isabella listened for a response. Nothing. Although she called out yet again, she was now convinced Ryan was not at home, which is what she expected. But just to be certain, she started toward the hall to take a peek into the bedroom, mostly to see if the bed appeared to have been slept in. The moment she entered the hall, she picked up a whiff of an unpleasant odor. As she was coming abreast of the bathroom with a half open door, the odor intensified, and with some hesitation, she reached out and pushed the door more widely open.

Isabella's scream, issuing from deep within her chest, could have broken glass. To her horror, she'd found him. He was partially hanging by an extension cord noose attached to the shower head with his knees buckled. Worst of all, his congested face was horribly contorted with a protruding tongue and ghastly bulging eyes.

With her hand clasped against her mouth to stifle yet another scream, she turned and stumbled back into the main room. She struggled to get her phone out of her pocket, but once she had it in her hand, she dialed 911.

As the call went through, Isabella sank down onto her knees as if she could no longer support herself. This was so utterly tragic. She had only begun getting to know Ryan, but she felt strangely at fault. He'd suggested they get together Friday or Saturday night. Why had she refused? She didn't know.

CHAPTER 30

Sunday, December 10, 2:45 pm

U p until Laurie's phone vibrated with an incoming call, it had been a near perfect day. She and Jack had gotten up earlier than they would have liked for a Sunday morning because their circadian clocks were set from having to wake up so early Monday through Friday. They had been up an hour before the children woke up, but they had waited to eat so they could all have breakfast together, including Caitlin and Dorothy. As was their habit, it was a group effort making pancakes and eating them with the special treat of real maple syrup. It was JJ's favorite.

After breakfast, Jack and JJ had headed over to the park with their lacrosse sticks for an hour while Laurie and Dorothy kept Emma busy with material the behavioral therapist had provided. By late morning the family, minus Dorothy and Caitlin, set out for the American Museum of Natural History, which both children adored. JJ was in love with the Hall of Saurischian Dinosaurs, with its imposing tyrannosaurus skeleton, whereas Emma showed a surprising interest in the dioramas in the

Hall of African Mammals, her favorite being the mountain gorilla display. Although Emma wasn't vocal about what she was seeing, she'd always remain in front of the exhibit for a long period of time, just as she had been doing that morning. Laurie wished she could see into her daughter's mind to understand what was going on in there. It was Laurie's habit to patiently stay with her while JJ and Jack moved on to other exhibits. Because of the amount of time Laurie had stood riveted to that spot over multiple museum visits, she was aware that the diorama's locale was near the Volcanoes National Park in Rwanda as evidenced by two immense volcanoes painted in the background. In the foreground were three enormous adults and one youthful mountain gorilla all seemingly interacting with one another as if alive.

Not wishing to disturb Emma's concentration or bother any of the other museum visitors, Laurie guiltily glanced around the relatively crowded hall as she pulled out her vibrating phone to see who was calling. She thought it might be Jack saying he and JJ were heading off someplace else in the museum, which could be quickly and discreetly handled. When she saw it was from the OCME, she wasn't happy. There weren't too many emergencies that couldn't wait until Monday morning, so if it was the on-call medical examiner, there might be something serious brewing.

As Laurie feared, it was Dr. Nala Washington, who apologized for calling.

"That's quite all right," Laurie said. She spoke quietly and covered her mouth with her hand as she was acutely embarrassed to be using her phone. "I'm in the Natural History museum. Can I call you back in a few minutes?"

"Of course," Nala said. "I'm in my office."

Laurie pocketed her phone and now looked around the room for Jack. A mini-herd of eight sizable stuffed African elephants in the center of the hall plus all the milling people made it difficult. When she didn't see him, she reluctantly used her phone to call him.

"Uh-oh," Jack said when he answered, knowing her reluctance to use her phone. "What's up?"

Again, speaking quietly and quickly, Laurie told him about the call from Dr. Washington and that she needed to return the call. "Can you come back to the gorilla diorama so I can go into the hallway to make the call?"

"Gotcha," Jack said and disconnected.

After handing off the kids to Jack, Laurie left the exhibition hall and found an area around the corner at the head of a wide but little-used staircase. Since there were several other people making phone calls, she felt comfortable making hers. A moment later she was back on the line with the on-call medical examiner.

"I hope you are sitting down, Laurie," Nala said without preamble.

Laurie felt her pulse tick up. "What's going on?" she asked with mild sense of umbrage. In some respects, it was hard for her to adjust to the younger generation's innate familiarity. When Laurie had joined the OCME more than twenty years previously, she would never have had the inclination to be so familiar with the then chief, Dr. Bingham.

"About an hour ago, I got a call from one of the medical legal investigators who was out on a site visit for a suicide case, Cheryl Myers. She'd just confirmed the identity of the deceased and was shocked. She called me at home, and I was shocked, too, so I immediately came in to make certain the identification was correct, even though Cheryl Myers is one of our most experienced MLIs."

"Who is it?" Laurie demanded with mounting concern.

"It's one of the NYU pathology residents currently rotating here," Nala said. "His name is Ryan Sullivan."

Laurie leaned up against a wall for support. She was stunned. *It can't be true, no way!* her mind was silently yelling at her. *Not again! It's impossible.*

She cleared her throat, trying to rein in her thoughts and emotions. "So there is no question about the identification?" Laurie asked hesitantly in the vain hope there might be some grisly mistake.

"No question whatsoever," Nala said. "I thought the same thing. But it's true. I just spoke with Ryan on Friday. He was asking me questions about one of my past suicide cases, Norman Colbert. He was doing a study of a series of suicides where there had been a question raised about the manner of death."

"I know," Laurie blurted. "I encouraged him to do the study. It stemmed from a suicide I posted with him on Thursday."

"What do you want me to do?" Nala asked. "Cheryl has yet to finish her report but promises to do so before she leaves. The body has already been brought here. It's downstairs in the cooler."

Laurie's mind was going a mile a minute and, moving beyond the immediate tragedy of a promising life lost, wondering what the overall repercussions were going to be. "Has a formal identification been done?" Laurie asked, more to give her time to think. This was a major disaster. It was the second death of an NYU pathology resident while rotating through the OCME under her watch as the chief, which is two more than anyone in their right mind might expect. And closer to home, how was she going to deal with her own sense of responsibility? She had in some ways forced him to do an autopsy on a suicide case that'd sparked identification for him and that he was demonstrably hesitant to do. On top of that, she had encouraged him to investigate other similar suicide cases, essentially immersing him in suicide details on a full-time basis. She shuddered to think in retrospect how insensitive she'd been. Once she had learned how emotional a topic suicide was for him, she should have nixed the idea.

"Yes, the identification process has been completed," Nala responded.

"Who made it?" Laurie asked. From her meeting at the NYU Pathology Department she knew he had no immediate family except an adoptive father, Robert Matson, of the renowned Matson family. How close Matson was to Ryan Sullivan, she had no idea.

"It was a girlfriend," Nala said. "She was the one who discovered the body. And as far as I know, she is still down in ID speaking with one of the clerks."

"Do you know if a Robert Matson has been informed of his death?" Laurie asked. As the adoptee of a landed and wealthy scion, Laurie wondered what the political fallout of Ryan's suicide might entail.

"I have no idea," Nala said. "Who is that?"

"If you don't know, it would take too long to explain."

"What would you like me to do, Dr. Montgomery?" Nala repeated. "Normally, a weekend death like this would be scheduled to be posted tomorrow."

"Don't do anything," Laurie said. "At the moment I'm out with my children. I'll take them home and then come in."

"That'll be a relief," Nala said. "What should I do if any journalists show up? This might be fodder for the tabloids."

"Ignore them," Laurie said. "Or say that I am on my way into the office, and they can speak with me."

"Got it," Nala said. "Do you want me to wait here for you?"

"It's not necessary," she said.

After disconnecting the call, Laurie looked around, but not really seeing anything. Silently but with profound anguish, she kept repeating over and over that this couldn't be happening. *Not again!*

A moment later, as if waking from a nightmare, Laurie pocketed her phone and half walked, half ran back the way she'd come. One thing was clear: She had to get to the OCME.

CHAPTER 31

Returning into the Hall of African Mammals, Laurie found her family in the throng of people ogling the lions diorama, another crowd favorite. The scene highlighted a pride of lions resting in the grass of an expansive central African plain.

"Okay, gang," Laurie said, trying to sound normal but with an edge to her voice. "I'm afraid we must leave. Unfortunately, Mommy has to go to work."

"Awwww," JJ complained. "We haven't been to see the dinosaurs."

"I know it's disappointing," she said as she took Emma's hand. "But we'll make a point to come back next weekend."

"What's up at the office?" Jack asked. "Maybe I should stay here with the kids while you do whatever you have to do."

"I'll need you to come with me," Laurie said, already moving toward the exit. She didn't elaborate, but he clearly got the message. Something out of the ordinary was afoot with her sounding clearly more stressed than usual.

It wasn't until they were in an Uber heading north on Central Park West that Jack again asked what was going on. He was in the front seat, with Laurie in the back with both children.

"I'd prefer to tell you when we're alone," she responded. She was busy trying to console Emma, who had trouble with abrupt changes in the schedule. Even JJ wasn't a happy camper and was still complaining that they'd not gone to see the dinosaurs, and he demanded that the next time they visited the Natural History museum, he wanted to go to the dinosaur halls first. To appease him, Laurie agreed.

Both Dorothy and Caitlin were surprised to see them return so soon and were good sports about taking over with the children when they heard that Laurie had an emergency at work and that Jack was going to accompany her. Caitlin took over with Emma while Dorothy watched JJ play computer games, something he wasn't normally allowed to do during weekend afternoons unless the weather was bad and all his homework was done.

While Jack and Laurie were by themselves, quickly changing into more suitable clothes, he again asked what was happening.

She stopped what she was doing and hesitated before speaking: "I know I'm being opaque, but to be honest I'm still trying to wrap my head around what I've learned. I know it's asking a lot, but can we wait until we're on our way?"

"Of course," Jack said. He was hugely curious, but not at Laurie's emotional expense. His concern for her mounted. He tried to guess what could be upsetting her to such an extent but was at a loss.

Fifteen minutes later they were back in a rideshare, heading south on Central Park West. Despite the tension inside the car due to Laurie's obvious distress, the scene outside was serene with soft winter sunlight illuminating the Central Park woodland, now devoid of its leaves.

"I can tell you're stressed," Jack said finally, breaking the silence. "I've tried to be patient and supportive, but it's difficult not knowing what's happening and what has you so upset. Can you tell me now?"

"Yes, of course," she said. "I'm sorry, I'm still trying to process it all. Nala Washington, who's on call for the weekend, phoned me to tell me that Dr. Sullivan died by suicide sometime last night and was now at the OCME as a patient."

"Good God!" he murmured. "That's unbelievable."

"Tell me about it," Laurie exclaimed with a shake of her head.

Jack returned to staring out the car window at the tranquility of the park, which was in stark contrast with the disturbingly tragic and sad news he'd just heard. He turned and looked over at Laurie, who was staring at him with a pleading expression.

"That's tragic on so many levels," Jack said. "I hardly know what to say. How do you feel?"

"Awful," she responded. "And responsible."

"I can understand the awful part," he said, "I feel awful, too. I just spoke with the man Friday afternoon, warning him not to do any outside investigation for his study. I told him it can be dangerous, particularly if any of the cases he was researching were actually homicides. I was trying to warn him like Lou tried to warn me in the past and you, too, for that matter. It never even occurred to me that his threat was internal. With that said, I don't understand why you feel responsible. If he took his life, he's responsible, and you told me he had a family history of suicide, as well as his own suicide attempt, which puts him in a high-risk category."

"Yes, he took his life, but the fact of the matter is that I helped put him in harm's way."

"How do you mean?"

"I more or less forced him to do an autopsy on a suicide victim. At the time, I wasn't aware of how much suicide had played a role in his life, but his hesitation was real and obvious. I should have erred on the safe side when I sensed he was making an identification with the patient. The problem was that I was so looking forward to doing a case with him to try to encourage his interest in forensics that I wasn't as sensitive as I should have been."

"I'm sorry you feel responsible, but I assure you, from an outsider's viewpoint, I don't think you are being fair to yourself."

"Possibly, but there's more," Laurie said. "I also encouraged him to do the study he was doing, which put the issue of suicide front and center in his mind. On top of that he asked to be relieved of his autopsy responsibilities so he could concentrate on the study. In retrospect, my agreeing was probably the worst possible thing I could have done because he wasn't thinking about anything but suicide cases." Laurie threw up her hands in frustration with herself.

"I can understand everything you're saying, but if it helps, my intuition is telling me that something else happened in Ryan Sullivan's life that keyed up this awful event, maybe in his private life. I would like to ask you to hold off beating up on yourself until we know more. Who's the MLI on the case? Did Dr. Washington happen to say?"

"She did. It's Cheryl Myers, and she has yet to finish her report."

"That's a positive," Jack said. "Cheryl is as experienced and possibly as good as Janice. If there are important details that will shed light on Dr. Sullivan's motivations, she's liable to find them. Who discovered the body?"

"A girlfriend," Laurie said.

"A girlfriend?" Jack questioned. "Hmm. That might be significant. I wonder if she and Dr. Sullivan were getting along okay or if there had been some significant bumps in the road."

"Maybe," she said, but by the sound of her voice, he sensed that she was holding on to her feelings of responsibility.

CHAPTER 32

At Laurie's direction, the Lyft driver crossed First Avenue at 30th Street instead of turning left as his GPS dictated. She wanted to enter the OCME through the freight entrance where bodies arrived and departed, not through the main entrance on First Avenue. It would give her an opportunity to view Ryan Sullivan's body in the walk-in cooler next to the autopsy room before doing anything else. Despite a proper identification having already taken place, she wanted to be certain it was he.

Jack and Laurie used the steps up to the loading dock, passed the security office, and walked down the corridor where Jack normally locked his bike.

Jack stepped ahead, pulled open the walk-in cooler door, and held it open for her to enter. Inside there was a profusion of bodies on gurneys, all covered with sheets. Guessing that Ryan Sullivan's body would have been one of the latest to be brought in, Laurie started briefly lifting sheets covering the faces of those closest to the door. The third one she exposed was Ryan Sullivan.

Despite her being accustomed to such visuals over many years of being a medical examiner, Laurie sucked in a lungful of air at seeing the familiar young man as a corpse. A brown electrical extension cord was still obliquely cinched high up around his neck. His bloodshot eyes were wide open with a few small petechiae, and his tongue protruded slightly. His face also showed a mild amount of congestion and appeared to be mildly cyanotic.

As she continued holding the sheet aloft, momentarily transfixed by the face, Jack stepped alongside the gurney. He reached down and pulled up the side of the sheet to expose the victim's right arm and hand. Lifting the hand, he externally rotated it so that he could look at the wrist's volar surface. "You were certainly correct when you told me he'd slashed his wrist as a teenager. Look at these scars!"

Laurie glanced at Ryan's wrist. She nodded. "I wish I had noticed that Thursday morning before the autopsy," she said, breaking her silence.

As Jack replaced the victim's arm and pulled the sheet back down, she did the same to re-cover the face.

"Would you have really done anything differently if you had seen the scars?" Jack asked.

"It's hard to say. I'm not sure."

"Well, what do you intend to do now that we are here?"

"First let's get out of this cooler."

"Fine by me," Jack said.

Once outside in the hall, they stood facing each other. "We could just go home and confront this situation tomorrow," Jack said after a moment of silence. Laurie seemed a bit overwhelmed by the circumstances and the potential ramifications.

"No, we need to deal with this today. In fact, I think it would be best to do the autopsy immediately, so we'll have all the information available in case there are any surprises. I can't imagine what tomorrow is going to bring, especially if the tabloids get ahold of this disaster, which they probably will. I'll certainly be hearing from the NYU Pathology Department, the NYU Medical Center Board of Directors, and maybe even the mayor. This could even affect our appropriation fight with the city council and our budget."

"Whoa!" Jack advised. "You're letting your imagination run away with itself. You might feel responsible for this suicide, but I seriously doubt anyone else will. Do I need to remind you that Ryan, sadly, killed himself?"

"I wish I could share your confidence about casting blame, but if there is one thing I have learned about being chief medical examiner, it's that the role is ninety-percent-plus political, and this is shockingly enough the second death of a pathology resident here in a couple of years, which is politically intolerable. I believe the only way we have a chance to control the fallout is to get as much information as soon as we can. I wonder if Cheryl Myers has finished the report yet."

"I can find that out," Jack suggested.

"Great! And then put your energies into getting the autopsy done ASAP. We can do the case together."

"Oh, that sounds like fun," Jack said sarcastically. "I did the autopsy on Aria Nichols right after working with her. I'm not excited about a repeat experience. Why don't we let Dr. Washington have the pleasure?"

"No, I'm not going to put that kind of a burden on her. It's her first year here, and this is going to be a politically charged case. We'll do it together. But first go ahead and find out if Cheryl's report is finished. Although I'm eager to get the autopsy done, I don't want to put the cart in front of the horse, so we need that report. I like all the information possible before the autopsy."

"Yeah, I know," Jack said. "Okay, I'll check with Cheryl and see where she is on the report. I'll also see if I can entice Vinnie to come in on his day off because I don't know which mortuary techs are on duty this weekend. What are you going to be doing?"

"Nala said that the girlfriend who discovered Ryan's suicide was still here in ID. If she is, I'd like to talk with her, hopefully to get a bit of perspective on his private life. Maybe I'll find something out that'll make me feel less responsible for this tragedy."

With those plans in mind, they used the back elevator, with Laurie getting off on the first floor while Jack stayed aboard on his way up to the third. Quickening her step, Laurie passed the Sudden Infant Death office and walked directly into the ID area. The identification function was a critical part of the OCME responsibility, as proper identification was the first step in any death investigation. Usually it was not problematic, but occasionally that was not the case in a city the size of New York. At any given time, there were always a number of bodies down in the walk-in cooler that had yet to be identified. Those who were never identified were eventually buried on Hart Island out in Long Island Sound.

Since death never stopped in New York City, the identification clerks were busy 24/7. Laurie stuck her head into the first open office door that she came to, interrupting one of the clerks who was interviewing a family. Shocked at seeing the chief, particularly on a Sunday, the clerk excused herself from the family and stepped out of her office.

"I'm sorry to interrupt you," Laurie said. "I need to know who has been assigned the Ryan Sullivan case."

"That's Marjorie Cantor," the clerk said nervously, pointing across the hall. "She's right over there."

"Okay, good," Laurie said. "Thank you." She then strode across the room, leaving the surprised ID clerk behind. At Marjorie's office, Laurie knocked on the open door to announce herself and stepped inside. Marjorie Cantor, who was alone at the moment, was a winsome, older woman who looked like a picture-perfect grandmother. Laurie was reasonably acquainted with her, as she was one of the more senior members of the ID team and helped with recruitment for the department. She stood up as Laurie entered.

"I assume you are here about Dr. Sullivan," Marjorie said. "Such a sad shock."

"It's hard to think of something worse," Laurie agreed. "Is the woman who found the body and provided the identification still here?"

"She is," Marjorie said. "The poor woman is distraught, to say the least. She heard that we had been trying to reach Dr. Sullivan's adoptive father, which we finally did, and she wanted to stay to meet him and express her condolences. She's waiting out in the main lobby, as far as I know."

"What's her name?"

"Isabella Lopez."

"And Robert Matson is coming here, even though you already have proper identification?"

"Yes," Marjorie said. "I told him it wasn't necessary, but he was adamant he wanted to come in anyway."

"I hope he's not expecting to view the remains," Laurie said. The image of Ryan Sullivan with the noose still around his neck would be too much for any relative to see, yet by established protocol it was not to be removed until the autopsy was begun.

"I have no idea what his intentions are," Marjorie said.

"Well, I'll be here if he'd like to see me," Laurie offered, even though she expected to be in the autopsy room imminently. It seemed to her that it would be appropriate for her to make an effort to meet with him, since the Matson family was politically connected.

Leaving the ID area, Laurie headed out into the main lobby. She hesitated at the threshold and surveyed the crowd made up of individuals or families waiting to identify the deceased. Due to Saturday night's invariable mayhem, Sundays were always busy. Like the rest of the building, the lobby had long since passed its prime. Furnished with mismatched couches and chairs, it was often the scene of grief and raw emotion. As Laurie's eyes swept the room, they centered on a lone figure of a young, fashionable, and comely brown-skinned woman who Laurie imagined fit the name *Isabella Lopez*.

"Ms. Lopez?" Laurie inquired as she neared. Initially the woman did not move or even blink. When she did, she merely raised her eyes to engage Laurie's. "I'm sorry to intrude, but are you Isabella Lopez?" Laurie added.

Isabella nodded and finally spoke. "Yes, I am," she said simply.

"I'm Dr. Montgomery, the chief medical examiner. I understand you have been very helpful in identifying Dr. Sullivan and supplying other information for us. I want to thank you for that, and express my sorrow for your loss. It is our loss as well, as Dr. Sullivan was part of our team, even if temporarily."

"I'm glad I could help," Isabella said. Her voice was flat, sounding as if she were exhausted.

"I understand you're waiting to talk with Dr. Sullivan's adoptive father," Laurie continued, "but I was wondering if you would be willing to speak with me briefly as well."

"I suppose."

"Thank you. If you'll follow me, my office is close by and will afford some privacy."

"Yes, of course."

Laurie led the way to the north end of the room, where a locked door led into the OCME's interior. A beefy, uniformed security member recognized Laurie and unlocked the door. Laurie nodded a thank-you as she passed through, Isabella in tow.

In the administration area, Laurie led the way around Mrs. Stanford's desk and opened the door to her office. Inside she switched on the overhead lights, significantly brightening the cheerfully decorated room. The high windows along the north wall let in some daylight, but due to the neighboring hospital high-rise building, it was rather meager.

"Please," Laurie said, gesturing toward the colorfully upholstered couch. Isabella sat at one end and Laurie at the other.

"I'm sure this whole experience has been a burden for you," Laurie said to begin.

"The worst," Isabella agreed.

"I know you have spoken with our medical legal investigator Cheryl Myers, and I have yet to read her report, so I apologize if I ask similar questions."

"That's okay," Isabella said.

"Have you known Dr. Sullivan for a long time?"

"No, just a few months. We were just getting to know each other, to be honest."

"Again, I'm sorry if I am asking the same questions, but did you feel that Dr. Sullivan was depressed, particularly of late?"

"No, I didn't. He was distressed, but I wouldn't have characterized it as depressed." Isabella remembered that was the same distinction Ryan had made Thursday night on his first call about one of the patients in his study.

"Had you spent time with him recently?"

"Yes. Thursday night I was with him at his apartment. I'm a graphic designer for an advertising company, and he let me use his computer, which is better than mine for the kind of work I do. I was there working with him up until almost eleven o'clock, when he said he had to come back here to interview some of the night shift investigators."

"What was he doing while you were working on his computer?"

"He was making calls, working on his research project."

"Was making these calls upsetting him?"

"No, just the opposite. If anything, he was energized by what he was learning. I got the impression the calls were productive."

"But you just said a moment ago he was distressed. Can you tell me more about him feeling distressed and energized at the same time?"

"He was overall distressed by having to spend time here. I imagine you don't want to hear that, but he truly hated being here and doing autopsies, which I can certainly understand. But he was energized about his research because he said it was keeping him from doing autopsies, especially since he was making significant progress. He even showed me a matrix he was making on a standard sheet of paper and a notepad diary he was keeping about the suicides he was investigating. He was proud of what he was accomplishing by finding unexpected commonalities."

"So, he had this matrix and diary at his apartment?"

"Yes."

Laurie hesitated, making a mental note to ask Cheryl Myers about a matrix and a diary, and if she had come across them at Ryan's apartment. She would like to look at them to see exactly what this progress entailed, even though she doubted it would help her deal with the heavy sense of responsibility she felt. Then, as if Isabella echoed Laurie's emotions, she suddenly said: "I feel awful about what has happened. I'm afraid I might have contributed to Ryan's suicide." Along with the surprising comment came a few tears, which the young woman wiped away with a finger.

"I'm sorry to hear that," Laurie said with intimate understanding. "What makes you feel that way?"

"He had confided in me that his father had died by suicide," Isabella said. "And I've read that people who have dealt with suicide are more apt to struggle with suicidal thoughts."

"That's true, but how does that apply to you?"

"As I said, I haven't known Ryan very long, just a few months, and it has only been recently that we've really talked and become intimate. Even in that short time, I could sense that he was a lonely sort of person and maybe moving a bit faster than I was with our relationship. This weekend he wanted us to get together Friday night or Saturday night or even both, but I wanted to slow things down and only agreed to see him this morning for breakfast. I could tell he was disappointed."

"Disappointed enough to be depressed?" Laurie questioned.

"I don't know. How do you tell? It just makes me feel that if I had agreed to see him on one of those nights, he'd be alive now."

Laurie felt an almost irresistible urge to give this grieving woman a hug to reassure her that she was not to blame for Ryan Sullivan's death. Yet she held back, realizing that her similar feelings of responsibility were not soothed by mere words, as Jack had tried.

"We do the best we can with those we care for," Laurie said. "Life can be cruel."

"Dr. Montgomery!" a voice called, along with a knock on her open office door.

Laurie looked up to see Marjorie Cantor standing with a tall, tan man dressed in a suit with flowing white hair and an unmistakable aristocratic aura. "I'll be with you in a moment," Laurie responded, as she stood. Isabella followed suit.

Then Laurie defied herself and gave Isabella a hug and whispered in her ear that she was absolutely certain that Isabella bore no responsibility for Ryan's death.

"Come in!" Laurie then called out to Marjorie.

After Marjorie introduced Dr. Robert Matson to both Laurie and Isabella, Isabella spoke up: "Dr. Matson, I've only known your son for a short time, but I will miss him and his generosity. I'm so sorry for your loss. I just wanted to tell you that."

"Thank you," Robert said, taken aback and mildly flustered. Pulling himself together, he looked at Laurie and asked to speak with her privately.

Laurie agreed and asked Marjorie to escort Isabella out and to give her Laurie's direct contact information. Laurie then gave Isabella a final hug and encouraged her to call if she had any questions whatsoever. The two women then left, Marjorie closing the office door behind them.

"Would you like to sit down?" Laurie said to Robert, gesturing toward the couch.

"I'd prefer to stand, thank you," Robert said with an angry edge to his voice.

"What can I do for you?" Laurie asked, sensing the conversation was not going to go well.

"On my way here, I learned something shocking," Robert said. "I learned that my son's death, while working here under your watch, wasn't the first such death, but the second. As a physician myself, I find that is an intolerable record, and it adds anger to my grief."

"I'm so very sorry for your loss," Laurie said. "I can assure you that we find it equivalently shocking."

"I should hope so. And I thought it best to warn you that I intend to have this situation and history addressed from the highest circles. This is a travesty."

"We're here to help in any way we can," Laurie said as diplomatically as she could.

Without saying another word, Robert turned on his heels and strode from the room. For a moment, Laurie stared at the open doorway. Her only thought to possibly prepare for whatever Robert was contemplating was to try to put in a call to Dr. Camille Duchamp to give her fair warning of Dr. Sullivan's suicide before she heard from anyone else. At least the woman was already aware of Dr. Sullivan's reaction to the autopsy he'd done with Laurie and his history with suicide. On top of that was a rather unique organizational issue. Although Dr. Duchamp was the chief of NYU Pathology, and the Department of Forensics was under the NYU umbrella, her position as chief of forensics had nothing to do with Dr. Duchamp. By law, Laurie was chosen by the mayor and served at his pleasure.

Going behind her desk, Laurie sat down. She picked up the phone, dialed the autopsy room first to see if anyone would answer and second to find out how preparations were going. She was moderately surprised when the phone was picked up on the first ring by Jack.

"What's happening?" she asked.

"Things are progressing," Jack said. "After a bit of a harangue and some unprintable expressions, Vinnie's on his way in, so we won't have to deal with an inexperienced mortuary tech. He should be here any minute. I ordered an Uber for him, so you and I can get this done and get back home."

"I hope none of the on-duty techs will have their feelings hurt with him coming in."

Jack laughed. "I doubt that very much. There's plenty of work to go around."

"How about the MLI report. Has it been done?"

"Oh, yeah. All is ready for when Vinnie gets here."

"Excellent," Laurie said. "Did you go over it?"

"I was skimming it when you called."

"Any surprises?"

"Nope. Seems like a straightforward suicide, according to Cheryl."

"Is there anything in the report about finding in his apartment any work that Dr. Sullivan had been doing vis-à-vis the group of suicides he was researching?"

"Not that I recall, but that's not the kind of detail I'd be apt to hone in on, so I can't be a hundred percent certain."

"I spoke with the girlfriend, who discovered the body," she said. "She had just spent Thursday evening with him. When I asked her if he seemed depressed, she said he seemed energized about his research project. She mentioned a matrix and a study diary that he'd shown her and was excited about."

"Well, I happen to know from personal experience that depression can come on suddenly like a ton of bricks."

"True," Laurie responded, but she wasn't convinced. In this circumstance, being energized and depressed didn't go together as far as she was concerned. "I'll see if I can get in touch with Cheryl. I'd like to see this work-related material if possible. After I make the call, I'll come down. Hopefully Vinnie will have arrived, and we can get started."

"I'm all for that," Jack said. "The sooner we start, the sooner we'll be done and can be homeward bound."

The moment she disconnected from Jack, she called the switchboard and asked the operator to get in touch with Cheryl Myers. Hanging up the phone, she happened to glance at the Monday schedule that her secretary customarily left on her desk on Friday nights. What caught her attention was her first meeting, at 8:00, was supposed to be with Dr. Ryan Sullivan! A note explained that Dr. Sullivan had stopped by Friday late afternoon and had been very insistent and anxious to see her.

Laurie raised her eyes and stared across her office. It seemed that fate was conspiring to magnify any guilt or sense of responsibility she might be feeling about this tragedy. If she hadn't left early on Friday for the ultimately unsuccessful meeting with the Hunter College dean, she could have met Ryan and possibly averted disaster. As she continued to stare across the room, she tried to think of what possibly could have made him anxious. With a shake of her head, Laurie reconciled herself to the reality that she probably would never know answers to either question.

The sound of her phone ringing brought her back to the present. As she expected, Cheryl Myers was calling. Laurie got right to the point: "Dr. Stapleton and I will be doing the autopsy on Ryan Sullivan momentarily. First let me admit up front, I have yet to read your report, but Dr. Stapleton has. I asked him if there was any mention of work the victim had done related to his study about that list of suicides with red flags that your MLI colleague had put together. You know the list I'm talking about?"

"I do."

"Dr. Sullivan had been researching those cases," Laurie said. "And according to the girlfriend, he'd made a handwritten matrix and diary."

"I didn't find anything like that," Cheryl said. "Nor were there any recent entries in any Word documents on his computer. I was able to access his computer because the password was on a sticky note on the table."

"That's probably because the girlfriend had been using it of late."

"She mentioned that."

"Did you find her helpful in general?"

"Very helpful," Cheryl said. "I think she felt responsible and guilt-ridden."

"I got the same impression," Laurie said. She resisted the temptation to admit she shared the same feeling. "As I said, I have yet to read your report, but as long as I have you on the line, was there anything about this case that caught your attention?"

"Strange that you should ask because there was something. Knowing this was going to be a very important case, for obvious reasons, I wanted to be thorough. I checked everything at the scene. I checked the refrigerator for anything out of the ordinary to give me an idea of Ryan's mindset, and I checked the medicine cabinet for unexpected medications. I even went through the trash.

"As you know, if this was a suspicious suicide and possibly staged, there would have been signs of disarray from a struggle or evidence of a cleanup. Well, there was nothing. In fact, and this is going to sound strange, it went so far in the opposite direction that it caught my attention. Dr. Sullivan was meticulous. Except for a couple of open pathology books on the coffee table, everything was in its place. His clothes were folded in the bureau, his dirty clothes were in a hamper in the bathroom, and even the spice rack was carefully arranged with all the labels pointing outward."

"So what are you saying?"

"I don't know what I'm saying," Cheryl admitted. "Which is why I didn't include any of this in my report. I suppose I'm saying the apartment was obsessive-compulsively immaculate. On top of that, there was significant fresh food in the refrigerator. He'd also made himself some dinner and washed the dishes afterward. That's an awful lot of activity."

"Let me guess what you are implying," Laurie interjected. "It bothered you that there wasn't any sign of depression, which is almost invariable with a suicide."

"I guess I am," Cheryl admitted. "But it wasn't enough for me to put in the report nor enough for me not to deem it a suicide."

"I can appreciate all this," Laurie said. "I'm glad you've told me, and I will mention it to Dr. Stapleton, so we will keep it in mind when we do the post."

"Thank you," Cheryl said. "I'm glad I've had a chance to mention it."

After the conversation with Cheryl, Laurie sat at her desk, wondering about the matrix and study diary that Isabella said Ryan Sullivan had shown her. Why didn't Cheryl find it, especially investigating the apartment as carefully as she apparently had? The main reason Laurie thought particularly about the matrix was because his making one reminded her of doing the same years ago. She had used the technique to help solve two of her most interesting cases when she'd been a new medical examiner.

"Those were the days," Laurie said quietly to herself. Such fond memories reminded her how much more she preferred practicing forensic pathology than dealing with the political burdens of being the chief.

CHAPTER 33

Sunday, December 10, 4:55 pm

W hy me?" Laurie questioned.

"Because I get to do autopsies most every day, and you don't," Jack said. "You do the case and I'll assist." They were standing in the autopsy room in front of the required and normal X-ray of Ryan that Vinnie had put up on the view box. Both doctors were dressed in full autopsy gear including face shields. Behind them Ryan's now naked corpse was stretched out on table #8. The only other person in the room was Vinnie Amendola, who was still in the process of laying out the required instruments, specimen bottles, and other paraphernalia required to do the autopsy.

Laurie and Jack had already completed an exhaustive external examination, at which time they had removed the electrical cord noose and carefully photographed the mildly oblique-shaped ligature mark consistent with a partial hanging. They had also carefully photographed his bilateral wrist scarring as well as a smattering of petechiae on Ryan's sclera bilaterally. Now, as they returned to the body, Jack asked Laurie if the corpse looked at all cyanotic to her. Her response was equivocal, and Jack had agreed, saying he couldn't decide, either.

"I've never autopsied someone I knew," Laurie said. "I'm not sure how I feel about it."

"I know how I feel about it," Jack said. "I had to do Aria Nichols. And as if that wasn't bad enough, last year I did Dr. Sue Passero. From both those unpleasant experiences, I can safely say, I don't like it."

"It's about the last thing in the world I would like to be doing," Laurie said, "but it's got to be done. I truly don't know what the fallout is going to be over this new disaster, and don't want to be caught off guard by anything. I keep thinking about what Cheryl Myers told me about Ryan's apartment being almost too orderly."

Jack laughed hollowly. "Yes, I've been thinking about that, too. It makes me wonder if Dr. Sullivan is trying to tease us posthumously."

Laurie turned to Jack. "What do you mean?"

"He'd been studying cases of suicides that could be staged homicides, so he's been learning about all the subtleties of making the distinction. Maybe he's trying to play with us by creating a staged staged-suicide, meaning he staged it to look like it had been staged."

"I don't find that funny in the slightest," she snapped.

"As a medical examiner, I have a morbid sense of humor."

"So, I've noticed," Laurie said. "Come on. Let's get this over with, wise guy."

"Hand the beautiful lady the scalpel, please," Jack said to Vinnie. "She's the prosector on this case."

"My pleasure," Vinnie said, extending the instrument. "It will be a relief assisting someone who knows what the hell they're doing."

"All right, boys," Laurie said as she took the blade. "Let's keep the sarcasm to a minimum for my benefit."

She didn't waste any time. Using her left hand to produce contravening pressure, she made the typical Y-shaped incision, taking a slight detour around the umbilicus. After some rapid undermining of the skin, the body lay open like a book to expose the sternum and rib cage above and the omentum covering the abdominal organs below.

Although there had been some conversation during the external examination, during the internal part of the autopsy there was little, and Laurie worked quickly with practiced hands. Soon most of the internal organs were in view, including the lungs, heart, and coils of intestines.

Next, Laurie dealt with the thoracic organs, and after obtaining a sizable blood sample for Toxicology from the heart with a syringe, she removed both the heart and the lungs, verifying that all were normal for a healthy, nonsmoking, thirty-year-old male, although there was a small number of emphysematous bullae on the right lung's surface.

"What do you make of these bullae?" she asked.

"Not much," Jack said. "Too few for any significance. Hell, he could have gotten them from having a coughing fit a few days ago."

Laurie nodded, then turned her attention to the abdominal cavity. Meticulously she went through all the contained organ systems and determined all was normal. Although she palpated the entire intestine when she removed it, she allowed Vinnie to take it over to one of the sinks to open it and run it, meaning visually check the full length of its interior.

"Boringly normal autopsy," Jack commented when she finished with the main part of it.

"So far," she agreed.

"It's amazing how the human mind works," Jack added. "Now that we're into the procedure, it doesn't bother me so much that I knew him."

"Speak for yourself," Laurie said, although she knew what he meant. Concentrating on the process made it easier. "Now is the more technically difficult part with the neck dissection. I've always struggled with it."

"So you say, but it's never been apparent." Jack and Laurie had done many autopsies together over the years.

"You are being too kind."

She asked Vinnie to provide a new blade for the scalpel, and when she had it, she began. As Jack and Vinnie watched, she exposed the sternocleidomastoid muscles bilaterally. Almost immediately it was apparent there had been some hemorrhaging.

"Uh-oh," Jack said, looking down at Laurie's handiwork. "Seeing hemorrhage like that, especially taking into account the possible cyanosis, maybe we have to at least consider strangulation."

"Why is that?" Vinnie asked. He had become quite proficient in forensics over the years and was always eager to learn more. It was one of the reasons Jack preferred working with him.

"If a suicide-by-hanging is staged," Jack began, "meaning the victim was strangled first, there are subtle differences found at autopsy. One is that there tends to be more bruising of the muscles of the neck, but it's not a hard-and-fast rule. This just might be because the electric cord is a bit more cutting than a rope."

"Let's see what the hyoid bone looks like," Laurie said, as she continued her dissection.

A few minutes later the hyoid bone came into view, and it was fractured. "Well," she said. "A hyoid bone fracture points more toward a hanging and not strangulation, as it is more common in hanging. Let's move on and see what the carotid arteries show." A few moments later, all could see that there was visual damage both externally and internally.

"That's a relief," Jack said with a bit of levity. "That's two to one hanging over strangulation. And that gets added to the oblique ligature mark. With strangulation, the ligature mark is always more horizontal."

"There's usually scratch marks on the neck with cases of strangulation," Laurie said, trying to bolster her decision. "And there are none here."

"Right you are," Jack said. "We've noted a few questionable findings raising the issue of strangulation, but overall, like Cheryl Myers, I'm convinced we're dealing with a suicide by hanging, especially with the overt evidence the patient had attempted suicide before."

"I agree the preponderance of evidence points in that direction," Laurie said. "At the same time, I must admit I find it troubling that there is a question at all, as it adds a layer of confusion that's unsettling, coming as it does on top of my guilty conscience."

"I can understand why you feel so bad," Jack said. "What do you want to do to make yourself feel better?"

She shook her head. "It's late Sunday. I don't think there is much I *can* do. I could try to call Dr. Duchamp to give her a heads-up, but what would that accomplish, other than ruining her evening? I'm afraid I will just have to wait to see what tomorrow brings. Just before I came down here, Robert Matson came in to see me and essentially threatened me."

"Robert Matson of the New York Matson family?"

"Yes, the real Robert Matson. Ryan's adoptive father."

"That's not appropriate. How and why did he threaten you?"

"The 'why' was out of grief for his son's suicide," Laurie said. "The 'how' is less clear. He was aware that his son's death marks the second pathology resident to have died while rotating under my watch. He said he was going to have the 'issue,' as he called it, addressed from 'the highest circles.'"

"What on earth does that mean?"

"I have no idea. Maybe I'll find out tomorrow morning. If I had to guess, he'll contact the NYU Pathology Department, maybe with the idea of getting me terminated."

"But they can't do that. You serve at the pleasure of the mayor."

"True, but they could probably strip me of my professorial title."

"I suppose, but what would the fallout be of that? You're paid by the city, not NYU."

"Who's to know what the consequences might be? Meanwhile, I have an equivalent problem trying to figure out how to deal with my sense of responsibility and guilt."

"Hey, you guys!" Vinnie called out in frustration. He'd been standing at the head of the table irritably shifting his weight back and forth. "How about we cut the chatter and get this case done, so I can go back to watching Sunday NFL football."

"Good idea," Jack said as he picked up the scalpel to rotate a scalp flap. "Do you have the bone saw?"

Vinnie picked the instrument up and brandished it.

Laurie and Jack exchanged a knowing glance. They, too, wanted the case to be over, particularly Laurie. Suddenly all she could think about were the children and whether she could rescue the day for their sake.

CHAPTER 34

Thank you for the ride," Laurie said as she alighted from the
OCME vehicle. To her chagrin, Jack had taken his new bike,
leaving her to commute by herself. The driver, who was a new
hire, had introduced himself when Laurie had gotten into the van
outside their house, but as agitated as she was, the name had slipped
her mind.

It had not been a good night. After doing the autopsy on Ryan Sullivan, she and Jack had gone home to salvage what they could from what
should have been a sacrosanct family day. To give the kids credit, they
had recovered for the most part after their disruptive exit from the
American Museum of Natural History and were acting normally. It was
Laurie who had trouble. She hadn't been able to stop thinking about the
tragedy of Ryan Sullivan's death, her sense of personal responsibility,
and what the consequences were in store for the OCME. The worst
time was hours later when she'd gotten into bed and couldn't turn off
her mind. The fact that Jack was able to do so, and had immediately

fallen asleep, made the situation harder to bear. Finally, after tossing and turning for more than an hour, she'd gotten up and gone down to the kitchen to make a cup of herbal tea.

Sitting in the dark sipping her tea, she came to what she considered a reasonable conclusion. There was no way in the short term she would be able to do justice to the burden of being the chief medical examiner, particularly with the hugely important negotiations that had just started with Hunter College about space and location for the new OCME Forensic Center. Two years earlier, when Laurie had her breast surgery, she'd turned over the chief's responsibilities to the deputy chief, Dr. George Fontworth, who'd aptly filled in for her temporarily, and he could do it again.

Wondering why she hadn't thought of this solution earlier, she snapped up her phone. Despite a mild concern she might be disturbing George's sleep if he kept his phone on, she decided to text him on the spot. She typed a curt message asking him to come in early if possible in the morning, preferably between 7:00 and 7:30, to meet with her.

The moment she had clicked the send icon, she felt better. The idea that she at least was doing something was the antidote she needed. Fifteen minutes later, when she had climbed back into bed, she'd rapidly fallen asleep.

Now Laurie stepped into her inner sanctum, where she hung up her coat in her closet, wondering if George had gotten her text. Even though she'd not heard back from him, her hope was that he had received it because the sooner she could temporarily turn over the reins as chief, the better she was going to feel. Doing so would allow her the time and mental space to face whatever fallout was going to accrue from Ryan Sullivan's suicide as well as afford her the opportunity to deal with her feelings of responsibility and guilt.

Taking her seat behind her desk, she picked up the day's schedule, so that she would be prepared to clue in George to what kind of day he would be facing by adding her schedule to his. Unfortunately, she had forgotten that Ryan Sullivan's name was on the top of the list. Its mere presence reawakened Laurie's distress, wondering again if the whole mess could have been avoided had she been in the office when he'd come to see her on Friday. After putting the schedule down and rubbing her eyes, she tried to regain her composure. Luckily she had help.

"Good morning," George Fontworth said cheerfully as he came into her office.

Laurie looked up, happy and relieved to see him. George'd been the deputy chief for four years, and although initially she'd had reservations about his appointment by the select committee due to his lackluster performance as a medical examiner, he'd proven himself to be a superb addition to the administration team. And he had thrived in the role, even sharpening his appearance.

He removed his coat, draped it over the back of the chair facing her expansive partner's desk, and sat down. "What's up?"

"I'm happy to see you," Laurie began. "I wasn't sure you got my text."

"Sorry, I should have texted you back. I didn't see it until this morning, but then wanted to hustle to get here ASAP. I saw that you'd sent it at one-thirty. Is something amiss?"

"Yes. There was a major disaster over the weekend."

"What happened?" George asked, drawing his brow together in concern.

Laurie told the whole story of Ryan's suicide, including what she and Jack had found at the autopsy and what Cheryl Myers had found during her investigation.

"So, it's going to be signed out as a suicide even with a few red flags?"

"Yes, it is."

"Whoa, that's a major irony!" George said. "Dr. Sullivan came to me on Friday asking about one of my cases, Sofia Ferrara, explaining he was looking into that list of mildly questionable suicides. Then he goes ahead and adds himself to the same list."

"That's a unique way to look at it."

"Is there something you want me to do?"

"Yes, there is," Laurie said. "I want to turn over the reins as chief to you for however long it takes me to deal with this unprecedented situation, hopefully just a day or two, similar to when I had my surgery. To be honest, I have absolutely no idea what the fallout is going to be, or what it's going to require time-wise. I have yet to inform the Pathology Department about the death of yet another of their residents."

"I'll help any way I can," George said with true sincerity.

"Thank you. It will be an enormous relief for me. The only real issue that can't be put off is another meeting today at eleven-thirty at Hunter College with the dean of Nursing and Health Professionals about space and location for our facility in the new center. Honestly, it will probably help our position to get a new voice involved besides mine. We need adequate space, as you know, and we want the location to be along Twenty-Sixth Street, so we can physically connect to our high-rise building if at all possible."

"Obviously," he said. "I'm happy to go."

"Here's my schedule for today," Laurie said, handing it across the desk to George. "Look it over and check with your schedule and secretary. Anything you can't or don't want to do besides the Hunter College meeting, which is a command performance, just have Edna or Cheryl reschedule for next week."

"Okay," George said. He stood up. "I'll let the on-call ME and the switchboard know that I'm temporarily serving as chief and why. That combination will guarantee it will get into the office grapevine, and everyone will know in no time."

Laurie smiled. The OCME grapevine was almost as efficient as a PA system.

As soon as George departed, Laurie girded herself for her call to the NYU Pathology Department. Her hope was to get Dr. Camille Duchamp and personally inform her about Ryan Sullivan with the hope she'd not already gotten word of the tragedy from some other source. But instead of getting the department, which she dialed directly, she got the main NYU hospital switchboard. When she asked to be connected to the Pathology Department, she was informed the department didn't open until 8:00.

With nothing else for her to do at the moment, she got up and headed down to the ID room and the communal coffeepot. After getting less than five hours of sleep, she was in dire need of a pick-me-up.

CHAPTER 35

Cheryl Stanford arrived and when she poked her head into Laurie's office to say hello, Laurie waved for her to come in and take a seat. Laurie told her the whole sad story about Ryan Sullivan.

"Oh, goodness gracious," Cheryl said at the conclusion. "That poor dear man. Did you see he was scheduled to see you this morning?"

"I did," Laurie said, feeling another surge of guilt.

"It's too bad you weren't here," Cheryl said. "He was anxious to see you."

"So you said in your note. Did he give any hint as to what was on his mind?"

"He didn't," Cheryl said.

"It's such a tragedy," Laurie said, wanting to change the subject from Ryan's mindset. "And I'm not sure what the consequences will be. To give me the freedom to deal with whatever happens, I've asked George to take over my role for a few days, so please work with Edna to juggle our schedules. I'll know more as the day progresses."

"Of course," Cheryl said. "There's a lot that can be put off until later in the week or next week."

"I'll appreciate whatever you can do," Laurie said. "But before you do anything, check with George. I know he's comfortable going to the meeting this morning with the Hunter College dean. Meanwhile, I have to inform the NYU Pathology Department, which I'm not looking forward to doing. Can you get Dr. Camille Duchamp on the line?"

"Of course," Cheryl said. She left the room, closing the door behind her.

As Laurie waited, she rehearsed several permutations of how she was going present the awful news, but there was no way to soften the reality. A moment later, Cheryl was on the intercom saying that Dr. Duchamp was on line one.

After taking a deep breath for fortitude, she picked up the phone. Following a brief greeting, Laurie asked straightaway if Camille had heard the terrible news.

"I don't think so," Camille responded. "What terrible news?"

For the third time that morning Laurie told Ryan Sullivan's sad story. Although she mentioned that the autopsy had already been done yesterday, she didn't go into any details about the slight questioning of the manner of death. When she was finished, she paused and let the silence hang in the air. She braced herself.

"Oh, the poor man," Camille said with true sympathy. "Such a tragedy, especially for someone who had to face so many adversities in his youth and showed such promise. I'm devastated. And I can't imagine how it made you feel as the chief."

"It was a shock, for sure." Laurie was touched and relieved by Camille's obvious and sincere compassion.

"Having to deal with the death of another resident is asking a lot of you," Camille added. "Especially since we failed to share with you the troubled histories of either one."

"I appreciate your empathy. To be honest, I was afraid you might feel the opposite since both happened under my watch."

"Heavens, no. The first was murdered by my predecessor, and Dr. Sullivan had an unfortunate history of suicide. Did your investigator uncover any specific cause for him to take his life?"

"No, and that is a part of the mystery that needs explanation. Without it, to be honest, I feel rather responsible. As I mentioned Thursday, I insisted that he autopsy a suicide victim that he identified with and then encouraged him to study a series of suicide cases, meaning for the last few days he's been immersed in suicide issues, all thanks to me."

"I can't believe a pathology resident would be so fragile, nor do I believe that you had anything to do with his suicide."

At that moment, her door opened and Cheryl stuck her head inside. Laurie frowned, as Cheryl had never done such a thing in the past especially under the current circumstances. "So sorry to interrupt," Cheryl whispered but with sufficient volume for Laurie to hear. "The mayor's office is on line two and demanding to speak with you immediately and I mean stat!" The next second, she was gone and the door closed.

"Uh-oh, Dr. Duchamp," Laurie said. "I'm getting an urgent call from the mayor's office."

"Oh, dear," Camille said. "Take it, and we can talk later." She disconnected.

With some trepidation, Laurie switched lines and introduced herself.

"I'm His Honor's chief of staff," a female voice snapped. "He's ordering you to come to his office immediately. Is that understood?"

"I suppose," Laurie said, startled by the command.

"Good. We'll see you shortly."

A moment later, Laurie was holding a dead line. She slowly hung up the receiver. *Good grief,* she thought. *Am I going to be fired?*

CHAPTER 36

Monday, December 11, 11:15 am

For at least the tenth time, Laurie looked at her phone to check how long she had been sitting outside the mayor's office. She'd seen dozens of people arrive, disappear within, presumably to meet the mayor, and then leave while she cooled her heels waiting to be seen. To her it was an obvious snub, and she got progressively irritated. If she was going to be fired, so be it, and she was angry enough not to know if it would be a blow or relief. She even entertained the idea of just getting up and walking out, come what may.

Although Laurie had met the new mayor on several occasions at the OCME—the last time had been in June of 2022 when the new OCME DNA Gun Crimes Unit had been announced—she'd never been in his downtown office and was taken by the classic Greek Revival splendor with marble fireplaces and chandeliers, which seemed even grander when compared with the humdrum, decaying, and drab OCME.

"Okay, Dr. Montgomery," the secretary called out. It was she and her desk that guarded the mayor's inner sanctum like a medieval portcullis, "The mayor can see you now."

Laurie heaved herself to her feet, stretched her back and shoulders, then walked around the secretary's desk and headed into the inner office. Within, the Greek Revival was even more impressive, with a soaring ceiling, fluted pilasters, lacquered wooden walls, luxuriously ornate velvet drapes, decorative crown moldings, and life-sized framed portraits of stern forebearers.

The mayor, in his usual sartorial splendor of a fitted crisp white dress shirt and a carefully knotted bloodred silk tie, was seated behind an expansive mahogany desk rimmed with hand-carved fluting. His dark blue suit jacket had been carefully draped over the back of his leather-tufted desk chair. He didn't look up as Laurie entered but used the pen in his hand to gesture toward one of the two straight-back chairs facing the desk. He was obviously in the middle of signing a moderately sized stack of documents.

Laurie took the seat and used the opportunity to appreciate the ornate surroundings more fully, comparing them to the cheerful, bright, down-home, whimsical décor of her office. Behind the mayor were two flagpoles with an American flag on one side and a New York State flag on the other. Off to the side she was surprised to see an exercise bike.

"Okay," the mayor said finally as he pushed the stack of signed documents to the side. He looked up at her as she turned her attention to him. "Thank you for coming in," he said. Laurie didn't respond. "As a former police officer," he continued, "I absolutely recognize the important role you and your OCME team play in our fine city, and I am completely sympathetic to your need for a new autopsy theater, but I find it particularly disturbing to have learned early this morning from a major supporter of mine that two promising pathology residents have passed away under your leadership. The significant political connection of this latest death promises to make my job that much more difficult. I need some explanation, so I can put out this fire before it gets out of control."

She was momentarily nonplussed by the direction of the mayor's comments. The longer she had been kept waiting, the surer she'd become she was about to be summarily fired. Now it seemed that the mayor was struggling with his own issues, as it seemed obvious that Robert Matson had called and lodged a complaint about her early that morning.

"What's the matter? Cat got your tongue?"

"I'm . . ." Laurie stumbled over her words. "I'm surprised. I expected to be fired."

"Fired?" the mayor questioned, seemingly shocked. "We need you and your team doing what you do, just not killing off pathology residents, particularly those related to politically connected families."

"I assume you got your information from Dr. Robert Matson," Laurie said.

"I did indeed. And he told me that he was the adoptive father and crushed by his boy's death, saying that the promising young man had been driven to suicide while serving at the OCME."

"Allow me to give you a little background," she said, encouraged by this switch of circumstances. "There have been two resident deaths while doing their required month's rotation with us. The first was a woman with unique social issues who was murdered by the then-chief of the NYU Pathology Department. This second death, which has already been investigated by our Medical Legal Investigator Department and autopsied by me, was the suicide of a man who had attempted to take his life as a teenager and whose older brother and father had died by suicide, a history which put him in a high-risk category. We didn't know the history until Thursday, when I took it upon myself to talk directly to the new Pathology chief, because the resident had not been performing up to our standards."

"Well, that does put a different spin on things," the mayor admitted.

"At the same time, I want to say that I do feel a certain responsibility, particularly regarding this second death. To that end, I did talk to the new Pathology Department chief this morning, who tried to assure me that she felt differently. More important, we have agreed to have more interdepartmental communication regarding pathology residents with unique mindsets. Hopefully, nothing like these two tragedies will happen in the future."

"I hope so, too," the mayor said. "Meanwhile, I will get back in touch with Dr. Matson and assure him that you have been adequately chastised."

"Is that it?" Laurie questioned.

"One other question: Are you happy with the Kips Bay Health Science Center for your new autopsy suite? I've been meaning to ask you that for a month."

"We're thrilled," she said as she stood up. "Particularly because it will be right next to our Forensic Science Center. Thank you for your support for the project."

"It's going to be one of the key accomplishments of my administration. Now let's both of us get back to work."

As Laurie left the inner office, she felt motivated to smile graciously at the irritating mayor's secretary as it seemed that at least a part of the burden of Ryan's suicide had been lifted off her shoulders. Now that she'd dealt with both Dr. Duchamp and the mayor, she could concentrate on hopefully coming to terms with her own feelings of personal responsibility.

CHAPTER 37

Monday, December 11, 12:30 pm

For the first time in the six years Laurie had been chief medical examiner, she entered the old OCME building without the nagging concern that she might be facing a new, unexpected fiasco involving any one of the six hundred employees or any one of the nearly two hundred deaths per day in the city. Whatever might have happened while she'd been at City Hall, she was confident George Fontworth could have handled it with the help of the two capable administrative secretaries.

Coming into her outer office, she saw that Cheryl and Edna were both on phone calls. She stopped at Cheryl's desk and silently mouthed: *Everything okay?*

In response, Cheryl flashed a quick thumbs-up before scribbling a note to say that Dr. Fontworth was still at Hunter College. She did this without interrupting the conversation she was having.

With a renewed sense of relief, Laurie went into her office and closed the door. For a moment she stood just inside, marveling how different the décor was from the mayor's elegant surroundings. With a shrug of indifference, she took off her coat, hung it up, and then sat down at her desk.

With considerably less weight on her shoulders from her conversations with Dr. Duchamp and the mayor, she could now concentrate on dealing with her painful and nagging guilt. What she needed to discover was some ostensible and understandable cause of why Ryan could have been pushed over the edge above and beyond her role of insisting on him autopsying a suicide victim. She couldn't imagine that it had been Isabella Lopez's refusal to see him Friday or Saturday night like the young woman feared, especially since she had agreed to a Sunday-morning rendezvous.

While Isabella was on her mind, Laurie remembered her mentioning that Ryan had shown her his matrix and a study diary that had been a source of pride for him, and something he was energized about. Could the loss or inadvertent destruction of his material have been enough to cause Ryan to lose control of his emotions? It seemed far-fetched, yet where were the matrix and diary? Laurie remembered Cheryl saying she'd done a particularly conscientious search of the man's apartment, even going through the trash, and had not seen anything that might be called a matrix or a diary.

Laurie decided to head up to the residents' room and check the desk he'd been assigned to see if the papers were there. It would also give her a chance to ask Ryan's fellow resident, Sharon Hinkley, whether she knew anything about such documents, and also if she had been aware of Ryan being depressed. From having talked with Chet about the two residents, she knew they were not at all socially close and had completely disparate attitudes about their rotation. Despite all that, it was worth asking the woman for her thoughts.

To avoid having to interact with the secretaries, Laurie exited her office through the connecting door that led into the conference room. From there, she used the stairs to get up to the second floor. Walking through the lunchroom, which was crowded at that hour, Laurie acknowledged greetings from most of the people but didn't stop before entering the residents' room, where she'd not been for years. Just inside, she hesitated. She was probably more conscious than anybody of the sad shape of the entire building except for a couple of the MEs' offices and the toxicology laboratory, which had been renovated. Yet she wasn't prepared for how bad the room appeared and how depressing it was with no windows and beat-up, aged metal office furniture. The sight of the room was another stark reminder of the need for a new forensic medical establishment.

Unfortunately, Dr. Hinkley was not to be seen, and Laurie assumed she was in the autopsy theater, where Chet had said she was enjoying herself immensely. Looking at the two desks in the room, it was easy for Laurie to tell which was Sharon's and which was Ryan's after Cheryl Myer's description of Ryan's apartment. One desk was littered with reprinted articles, several coffee cups, a few journals, and a couple of forensic books. The other had just a lonely monitor and keyboard.

Laurie made a beeline to the desk that looked unused and began opening the drawers, most of which were empty. But then she was rewarded when she opened the center drawer. There, front and center, was what appeared to be a matrix on top of a notepad. Lifting both, Laurie closed the drawer with her hip, while briefly checking out the matrix. On the horizontal rows were patients' names, including Sean O'Brien's, while on the vertical columns were ten categories such as age and profession, et cetera. Next she thumbed through the notepad and was rewarded to see that it was chock full of easily readable mixture of joined and unjoined script.

Laurie then checked the drawers on the right side of the desk to make sure there wasn't anything else of interest. In the top drawer, there were a few lonely pens and pencils, a clear plastic ruler, and several unused notepads. The other two drawers were empty. Laurie took the matrix sheet and the notepad and exited the depressing room.

Although she was particularly eager to get back to her office to study the material she had found in hopes that it might shed some light on Ryan Sullivan's mindset, as she passed through the lunchroom again she felt obligated to stop at a number of the tables for brief chats. As the chief, she felt it was socially appropriate for her to engage all employees. It was a way to recognize their input, which enabled the OCME to carry out its mission.

Fifteen minutes later, Laurie again used the back entrance to her office and settled at her desk. It was a rare and welcome feeling to know that unless the sky was about to fall, she wouldn't be disturbed. Putting the notepad to the side, she placed Ryan's matrix in front of her. Once again, the idea that Ryan had resorted to a matrix format to research a series of possibly related deaths reminded Laurie of having used the same organizational trick on two occasions. The first had been within months of her being hired when she had been faced with a strange series of staged cocaine overdoses; the second was about ten years later when she'd encountered a run of mysterious postsurgical deaths. On both occasions, the matrix had proved invaluable for ultimately solving the mysteries.

Laurie looked at Ryan's matrix carefully. The first column noted the similarity in ages of all eight people. As her eyes went down the list of names, Laurie saw that the last name that Ryan had added was Marsha Levi. This was an immediate surprise to her, because she distinctly remembered Jack telling her after doing the woman's autopsy that she had been murdered by her husband as part of a murder/suicide case. In fact, her husband's name was on the line above hers, but had been crossed out.

For a few a few beats, Laurie stared across her office, trying to imagine why Ryan had added a murder victim to his list of questionable suicides. Looking back at the matrix, Laurie's curiosity was raised when she noticed that Marsha Levi was also the only person on the list who was married, whereas everyone else was single. It didn't make any sense unless . . . Laurie again raised her eyes to stare ahead. Since the list was of possible staged suicides, perhaps Ryan had somehow decided that the Levi case was a staged murder/suicide. Laurie had only heard of one such case in the forensic literature, which had been recently litigated with a finding of not guilty for the person charged with the crime.

Despite hoping to uncover Ryan's thoughts about the Levi case by carefully reading his study diary, which she assumed would include some of Ryan's personal musings as well as the results of all the interviews he'd apparently had with various MLIs and MEs, Laurie still went back for the time being to the matrix. It was then that her attention was drawn to the next to last column, labeled CaDx. At first she was confused by exactly what CaDx stood for, but when she saw that Sean O'Brien had a *positive* along with *Oncology Diagnostics*, she gathered that CaDx was short for "Cancer Diagnosis."

Laurie then noticed that seven out of the eight names on the matrix had *positive* or *false positive*, and *Oncology Diagnostics* in the CaDx column. Everyone except for Stephen Gallagher, where the space was blank. Laurie was taken aback as this was indeed a remarkably strange commonality, certainly stranger than the similar ages, marital statuses, types of employment, and living styles.

With renewed intrigue, Laurie put the matrix page aside and began looking at the study diary. Settling back into her desk chair, she started from the beginning. At first she was disappointed because there was less of Ryan's musings than she had hoped. What she was reading was mostly synopses of his conversations with all the MLIs and MEs as well as his recaps of their original reports. But as she read on, she came to more and more sections where he recorded his thoughts about what he was uncovering.

Laurie became particularly interested in Ryan's ruminations when he posed the question of whether the medical examiners or the medical legal investigators were more capable of determining the manner of death. Laurie had to smile because despite her biases she had to admit he had a point and that perhaps she should encourage Chet to open a dialogue about the issue at one of their all-borough conferences and invite Bart Arnold to attend. Perhaps in difficult cases, a consensus should be sought before the final decision was made about the manner of death.

With increasing interest, Laurie continued reading. She couldn't help but agree when Ryan expressed the belief that Oncology Diagnostics needed to be informed that some of its patients were having serious mental issues and killing themselves, although she couldn't imagine they didn't know. After all, it was general knowledge in the medical profession that having cancer increased the risk of suicide.

The next part of the study diary truly captured Laurie's attention. In a very effective style, Ryan summarized the science and the technology of early cancer detection using extracellular vesicles of a specific variety aptly called oncosomes. What Laurie found particularly compelling was Ryan's speculation that extracellular vesicles had played a key role in the evolution of life from unicellular organisms to multicellular organisms by providing a method of intracellular communication.

All at once, Laurie stopped reading and stared at a particular sentence. In it, Ryan stated: *Oncology Diagnostics has to be warned of this reality immediately.* She knew that "this reality" referred to the suicides, but it was the word *immediately* that truly captured her attention. She knew that he had written the sentence on Friday, as the date was at the top of the page, and the wording begged the question of whether Ryan had contacted Oncology Diagnostics before he'd died. What if he had— or better still, had visited the clinic—and by doing so, learned something that had keyed off a major depressive reaction? Laurie sighed. On the surface it seemed an unlikely speculation, but then she remembered Ryan's mother had died of cancer when he was a mere eight years old. Maybe it wasn't so far-fetched.

Laurie shrugged, let out the breath she didn't realize she'd been holding, and turned the page. In the next and last paragraph, Ryan answered her question. He wrote that he had indeed called Oncology Diagnostics and had spoken with a receptionist and that one of the principals of the clinic, Dr. Jerome Pappas, had agreed to meet with him if he could come directly. So not only did Ryan call the clinic, but he visited. Now the question was what could have transpired at that meeting to possibly put Ryan Sullivan in a mental tailspin.

Laurie googled Oncology Diagnostics to get their contact information. As soon as she got the number, she started punching it into her phone, but she never finished. All at once, she changed her mind. Instead of merely calling, she decided she would rather visit in person, unannounced but officially as the chief medical examiner of New York City. She wanted to see Dr. Pappas's reaction firsthand to the news of Ryan's suicide and its possible connection to his visit, rather than attempting to interpret it over the phone. If something untoward or grossly out of the ordinary had happened, perhaps Dr. Pappas might not be as forthright as Laurie would hope.

Laurie checked the time. It was nearly 1:30, meaning she'd most likely arrive at Oncology Diagnostics around 2:00, which seemed perfect. Laurie got out her coat, and as she did so, she wondered if Ryan's planned visit to Oncology Diagnostics was the reason he'd been eager to see her late Friday afternoon. Of course, in retrospect there was no way to know, but the thought alone made Laurie again wish she'd not left early that afternoon.

She exited the normal way, stopping at Cheryl's desk to tell her that she'd be back in a couple of hours. She didn't bother to say where she was going, just that she was still dealing with the fallout from the Ryan Sullivan death.

CHAPTER 38

The moment Laurie climbed out of the transport vehicle on the Upper East Side, she sensed she was going to be duly impressed with Oncology Diagnostics. Even the immediate neighborhood was clearly upscale, which she imagined the clinic would undoubtedly reflect. After telling the driver that he could inform the transport team supervisor that she would not be needing a return trip since she'd be taking a rideshare back to the OCME, she sent him off. She didn't want to be an added burden for the transport team as shift change at three p.m. was always problematic.

Turning to face the clinic's entrance, she got out her wallet with its medical examiner badge. She couldn't remember the last time she'd used the badge, but on her current mission, she thought it would stand her in good stead. It looked seriously official with a gold American eagle surrounded by four silver stars on the top and the word CHIEF spelled out in bold, black letters against a gold background along the bottom. There was no doubt that it had a significant wow factor.

After taking a fortifying breath, Laurie started toward the door.

It had not been a good day for Dr. Jerome Pappas. He'd expected to have heard something in the press about Ryan Sullivan, corroborating his supposed suicide, but there had been nothing. Jerome had even asked Beverly Aronson to pick up a *New York Post* and a *Daily News*, both of which luxuriated in such sordid stories. Jerome could remember two years earlier when both tabloids had taken great interest in the murder of another pathology resident, so he imagined they'd be all over this new story. He'd even kept the TV on NY1 on all morning while he worked in hopes of hearing something.

In an attempt to unwind over the weekend, Jerome had gone out to his home in the Hamptons, which was always tranquil in the off-season. At first, things had gone well. Late Saturday night, on schedule, he received a call from Chuck Barton informing him that the mission involving Ryan Sullivan had gone down flawlessly, so he could relax. And Jerome did relax, but only for that night. Beginning on Sunday, he expected some kind of confirmation that the resident's death was deemed a suicide, but he'd heard nothing in the normally gossipy New York media. And now it was already the middle of the afternoon on Monday, and there had been naught.

Jerome pushed away the depressing Full Body Scan spreadsheets he had in front of him and stood up. He decided he'd earned another sip from the bottle of Macallan twenty-five-year-old scotch he'd purchased over the weekend. But he never got all the way to the bar. Instead, his intercom buzzed, forcing him to retreat back to his desk.

"Yes!" he said irritably after pushing the on button. He noticed the call wasn't coming from Beverly but rather the clinic's reception desk, whose personnel were specifically instructed not to bother either Jerome or Malik.

"Sorry to bother you, Dr. Pappas," a pleasant but nervous female voice said. "But the chief medical examiner of New York City is here, demanding to see you immediately. I was shown a badge."

Jerome's already fibrillating heart seemed to do a flip-flop of sorts, requiring him to momentarily support himself by placing both hands palms-down on his desk. Luckily the event was transitory, and he recovered and found his voice.

"Call Beverly and have her show the medical examiner to my office," Jerome managed with a slightly squeaky voice. With renewed urgency, he made a beeline to the bar. He poured himself a finger of his normal scotch, not the expensive stuff, and tossed it down. He then closed his eyes. Luckily the fiery fluid had an almost immediate calming effect, giving him the fortitude to collect himself. As unique as it was to be visited by the chief medical examiner, it wasn't Armageddon by any stretch of the imagination. Obviously it was to be a discussion and nothing more. Otherwise it would have been law enforcement in some form or fashion. Even though Malik seemingly didn't share his concerns, Jerome knew they were existing as if stranded on the sheer face of El Capitan, holding on by their fingertips.

Jerome's next thought was whether he should alert Malik and have him sit in on this extraordinary meeting, but he didn't get to entertain the idea for long, as there was a knock on his door.

"Come in," he called out with the same squeaky voice. Hurriedly he closed the cabinet door to shield the bar.

Beverly stepped into the room and gestured for the visitor behind her to do the same. Although Jerome didn't believe he had any preconceived notion what to expect, he was taken aback that the visitor was a woman. As old school as he was, he'd expected a man, and not only was the chief a woman, she was a woman who also appeared much younger than he might have expected. He also noticed that her auburn hair had a natural bounce as Beverly took her coat in sharp contrast to Beverly's hair-sprayed, motionless helmet.

"Thank you for seeing me on such short notice," Laurie said once free of her coat. She then approached Jerome with an extended hand, eyeing him as she did so.

Jerome shook the proffered hand. In contrast to his, hers was dry and her grip forceful.

"Please," Jerome said, while pointing toward the chair Beverly was in the process of moving closer to the front of Jerome's desk.

"Thank you," Laurie said as she sat down. Her eyes quickly swept the room before settling back on Jerome.

"I will leave you two," Beverly announced before withdrawing.

Jerome stepped behind his desk and sat down. Placing his elbows on his desk, he tented his hands, pressing his fingertips together to minimize any tremor.

"Can I offer you any refreshment? Water, coffee, tea?" Jerome asked.

"Thank you, no," Laurie said. She had continued to regard the entrepreneurial physician in front of her. From the moment she'd entered the room, she had the impression he was nervous and on edge a bit more than she had expected.

"Something stronger, then?"

"Heavens, no," she responded with surprise.

"It seems that my receptionist was taken aback by seeing your badge," Jerome said in an attempt to lighten the atmosphere. "May I see it? I've never seen a medical examiner badge. I didn't even know there was such a thing."

"Of course," Laurie said. She extended the badge toward Jerome, who took it and examined it carefully.

"Very impressive indeed," Jerome commented with a forced smile. "It looks like a law enforcement badge."

"Yes, it does," she agreed. "We work closely with law enforcement."

"Ah, yes. You do indeed," Jerome said. He was recovering from the shock of Laurie's visit but still tense. "What can I do for you on this unseasonably warm, bright December day?"

"Yesterday we experienced a devastating shock," Laurie began, watching the doctor carefully. Her arrival had had the effect she'd intended, and she had given him the time and space to calm down a bit, but now she was ready to do what she came to do. "A senior NYC pathology resident named Dr. Ryan Sullivan, who has been rotating through the Office of the Chief Medical Examiner, died by suicide sometime Saturday evening. As a physician, you know what *rotating* means . . ."

She paused, forcing Jerome to respond.

"Of course," Jerome said. "Every residency is composed of a series of rotations to expose the resident the full range of whatever specialty they're studying."

"Exactly," Laurie said, but then paused again for the same reason. She watched as Jerome now began to nervously rub his hands as he stared back at her, waiting for her to continue. Following a vaguely thought-out plan, she wanted to give the man plenty of opportunity to voluntarily mention Ryan's visit on Friday and reveal what had been discussed, which she was reasonably certain he would do unless there was something he didn't want her to know about. It was her version of a spontaneous cat and mouse game.

"Well," Jerome voiced finally, switching back to tenting his now-trembling fingers. "It is such a tragedy, especially considering all the time and effort it took him to get where he was. But I'm confused. Why did you come all the way here to tell me this bit of bad news?"

"Because I was hoping you might be able to tell me why he took his life."

"How should I know?" Jerome questioned with sudden irritation.

The tension he was feeling suddenly became acute, and he momentarily lost control. Under the circumstances a surprise visit by the chief medical examiner, of all people, was an enormous stress. What he needed was another "hit" of scotch and debated just standing up and getting it.

"Because Dr. Sullivan came here late Friday afternoon and met with you," Laurie said with equal ardor. "Exactly what transpired here and what was your conversation about such that this man would be thrown into a mental downturn serious enough for him to take his life?"

For several beats the two stared at each other. Laurie had no idea what to expect, although the man's obvious nervousness and his lack of forthrightness suggested he was keeping something important from her. Whereas Jerome's reaction was the opposite. He felt an almost instantaneous sense of relief with the sudden understanding that Laurie was "fishing" and that all she knew was Ryan Sullivan had been to Oncology Diagnostics. It was Jerome who broke the silence.

"Dr. Sullivan came here from your organization with important and serious information, along with a recommendation. He informed us that a few of our hundreds upon hundreds of patients who had been diagnosed to have an early, asymptomatic cancer had been struggling to cope mentally and had killed themselves. He even provided me with a list of eight such patients, most of whose names I recognized. They were all undergoing the difficult process of various diagnostic tests in an attempt to locate their asymptomatic cancers. His recommendation was simple and timely, namely to encourage us to alert our patient base about this suicide risk and encourage everyone with such self-destructive thoughts to seek mental health support. To that end, I'm happy to report that we took Dr. Sullivan's recommendation to heart and had our communications people accomplish it over the weekend."

"Why didn't you tell me that as soon as I told you about his suicide?" Laurie questioned. Her tone had changed dramatically, as she realized that she'd been putting too much weight on Ryan's visit to Oncology Diagnostics to explain his suicide, meaning she was back to square one regarding her sense of responsibility.

"Simply because I was totally discombobulated about your sudden, unexpected visit," Jerome said. "Until Friday when Dr. Sullivan visited, we'd never had anything to do with the medical examiner's office. We don't deal with death, since our concern is the early diagnosis of cancer, but not its treatment. Accordingly, to have the chief medical examiner show up out of the blue was shocking. I think I handled myself rather well."

"I suppose that makes sense," Laurie reluctantly agreed.

"Let me ask you a question," Jerome said, gathering courage. "Why did you come yourself instead of sending any member of your extensive team? I would imagine running such a large organization must keep you extremely busy."

"Because I feel personally involved," Laurie admitted. "Dr. Sullivan is the second resident to die under my watch. Unfortunately, I had encouraged him to look into the series of suicides that he was studying. In retrospect that was a bad decision on my part, since suicide had played a major role in his life. I was hoping by my coming here and talking to you, I might find an explanation of why he killed himself. My sense, from what you have told me, is that when he left here Friday, he wasn't acting depressed or distressed in any fashion."

"Correct," Jerome said. "On the contrary, he was acting pleased, especially when I sincerely thanked him for his visit and told him that we would immediately follow his recommendation."

After a short pause, he continued, "Let me ask you another question: Are you saying you've taken on attempting to find out Dr. Sullivan's mindset as a kind of personal crusade, perhaps as a way to assuage guilt?"

"I suppose that is one way to put it," Laurie said. She gave Jerome a crooked smile and then got to her feet. Jerome followed suit.

"I guess I will have to keep digging to have any chance of dealing with my guilt," she said. "He did leave behind copious notes on the study he was doing of what has turned out to be all Oncology Diagnostics patients. I've read through all this material rapidly, but I need to go over it more carefully to see if I can find what sent him into a mental tailspin. Obviously, something significant happened between his visit here and Saturday night to bring on a fatal depressive reaction."

"Good luck," Jerome said. Eager to bring the meeting to a close, he used his intercom to ask Beverly to bring Laurie's coat. He then stood up and came around his desk with the intention of escorting Laurie to the door.

"There is one more question I'd like to ask," Laurie said as she got to her feet. "Dr. Sullivan had made a kind of matrix to record the demographics of the patients he was studying to uncover commonalities. One of the columns was for Cancer Diagnosis, under which he listed all patients being either positive or false positive. Why would he list false positive? My understanding from the literature is that the OncoDx is very accurate. But does Oncology Diagnostics experience a lot of false positives with the OncoDx test? It seems doubly tragic if patients resorted to suicide over a false positive cancer test."

Jerome froze in place. This was the last question he wanted to be asked, and her having done so totally undermined the confidence he'd begun to feel that her visit wasn't the disaster he originally feared. In fact it was worse. Reporting selected patients' OncoDx were positive even though they were in reality negative was at the core of the method he and Malik had come up with in their desperate attempt to avoid bankruptcy with Full Body Scan. All Ryan Sullivan's cases were staged suicides of people who'd discovered their tests had been false positives.

"Well, um, no," Jerome finally managed, stumbling over his words. He then cleared his throat and repeated, "No, there's no problem with false positives with the OncoDx test."

Laurie nodded. "That was my understanding. Well, that puts the burden back on my shoulders. I'll have to go back and look into this issue about false positives and see if Ryan explains in his study diary what he meant when he added it to his matrix."

At that moment Jerome was saved by Beverly's arrival with Laurie's coat. As she helped the medical examiner into it, Jerome smiled to cover the panic he was experiencing. He even thanked Laurie for coming and apologized for not being more of a help with her crusade. He then closed the door after the two had left and leaned against it for support while he waited for his pulse to slow. Laurie's comment that she was going to make a point of looking into the issue involving false positive OncoDx tests was a worst-case scenario, which demanded immediate attention.

Pushing off from the door as soon as he felt capable, Jerome hustled over to the cabinet hiding the bar. After yanking the door open, he poured himself two fingers of his everyday scotch with a shaky hand and tossed it down. In his agitated state, even that had minimal effect.

Dashing back to his office door, he opened it carefully, glancing down the long corridor to make certain Laurie and Beverly were no longer in view. When he saw they weren't, he closed that door, then used the connecting door to get to Malik's office, racing past Beverly's empty desk.

As per usual, Malik was on his phone, which was how he spent most of his workday, but on this occasion Jerome didn't wait. After bursting in, he rushed over to Malik's desk and disconnected the call.

"What the hell?" Malik questioned.

"Shut up and listen," Jerome commanded. "You are not going to believe who was just in my office."

"Do I really have to try to guess?"

"The goddamn chief medical examiner of New York City," Jerome bellowed. "She waltzed into our reception area flashing her badge, demanding to see me."

"What on earth for?" Malik asked with furrowed eyebrows. For the first time in their long association, his reaction to a Jerome outburst was immediate concern.

"She came because of Ryan Sullivan's death. She found out he'd been here Friday."

"Okay," Malik said trying to calm himself and Jerome. "Tell me what happened. What did she say? Why did she, of all people, come here?"

Almost word for word, Jerome described Laurie's visit. He even included his reaction that had gone from nervous concern to relative calm and back to panic when she said she was going to look into the issue of false positive OncoDx tests.

"Okay, okay," Malik said, raising his hand, waving for Jerome to calm down, as Jerome had worked himself up to a near frenzy. "Let's concentrate on the positive. She explained that the reason she'd come here to see us in person was because she was on a kind of personal crusade to console herself, suggesting she'd not been sharing any of this with her underlings."

"Yes, that's what she said and what she implied," Jerome said. He was back to nervously pacing in front of Malik's desk. His normally pale face had reddened considerably.

"Can you stop parading back and forth in front of me so I can think?"

"No, I can't. We're on the edge of a precipice here."

"Good god!" Malik voiced under his breath. He shut his eyes, rehashing all that Jerome had told him. The one positive was that the situation was similar to the Ryan Sullivan problem, meaning there was an opportunity to contain the damage, provided it was addressed quickly.

With the chief medical examiner, *quickly* meant that afternoon. Was that possible? Malik didn't know, but he thought it was worth finding out.

"Okay," Malik said with sudden resolve. "Here's what we are going to do. We're going to call Chuck and see if Action Security can deal with this on a super emergency basis."

Jerome stopped his pacing and stared down at Malik. "Do you think that is even possible?"

"We won't know until we ask," Malik said. He got out a burner phone and placed the call. He put the phone on speaker and set it on his desk as the electronic ringing began.

Jerome stepped up to the desk and leaned over the phone, resting his upper body on his knuckles. Both he and Malik silently counted the rings. The phone was answered on the third.

"What's up?" Chuck asked with no preamble.

"We have a serious, acute emergency," Malik said without identifying himself.

"Ten-four," Chuck said, which was a predetermined response that meant that he would be calling back immediately on a secure line.

Malik disconnected the mobile phone and sat back. Jerome straightened up and returned to his nervous pacing. But he didn't have to pace long. The burner phone rang in less than a minute.

Again using the speakerphone, Malik briefly explained that they were facing a super emergency associated with a fallout from the Saturday-night mission. He then introduced Jerome, so that Jerome rehashed the exchange he'd had with Dr. Laurie Montgomery.

"So, there you have it," Malik said when Jerome was finished. "I think it's clear why this situation is an emergency."

"No doubt," Chuck said. "This is a brushfire that must be extinguished straightaway to avoid a forest fire."

"It's our feeling as well, with the idea the window of opportunity is narrow, like, this afternoon," Malik said. "Is that possible?"

"It's possible, but it will require bringing together lots of resources and will be expensive."

Malik looked up at Jerome, who was standing over him. Jerome nodded assent, as there was no choice. "We're fine with that," Malik said. "Can you give us an estimate on the possibility of success?"

"I'd say very good, with the right personnel," Chuck said. "In favor of a successful resolution, Dr. Laurie Montgomery, as the chief medical examiner, is a public personality, meaning that with our resources we can learn an enormous amount about her, her lifestyle, and her habits in a short amount of time. That will give us the opportunity to come up with a surefire plan. The critical issue is that you must give me the green light ASAP. There's not a moment to waste."

Malik again glanced up at Jerome, who again nodded in assent, this time with demonstrable relief. "It's a go!" he said before disconnecting the call.

CHAPTER 39

Monday, December 11, 3:15 pm

During her ride back from her unproductive visit to Oncology Diagnostics, Laurie began to come to terms with never finding out what had pushed Ryan Sullivan over the edge. Ultimately, she thought, she would need to just accept some degree of responsibility.

As she came into the administration area, she could tell that Cheryl and Edna had been having a friendly conversation across the room, which they were wont to do when there was a lull in their duties.

"All okay?" Laurie asked Cheryl just to be sure.

"Everything is fine," Cheryl said. "Just a bunch of routine stuff." She held up a list.

"What about George? Is he doing okay?"

"He's fine," Edna butted in, calling out from her side of the room. "I just spoke with him. He's on his way back from Hunter College. The meeting with the dean had been put off until after lunch."

Laurie nodded. She was interested in finding out what he had learned and if he was more optimistic than she had been after her last meeting with the college dean. "Have him pop into my office when he has a chance."

Edna nodded and waved to say she'd gotten the message.

Turning her attention back to Cheryl, Laurie asked her to get Dr. McGovern to come by to see her for a quick chat. She then went into her office and closed the door. After depositing her coat in her closet, she sat down at her desk. Her plan was to go back over Ryan's matrix and diary with significantly more care than she'd expended on her first go-round, trying to figure out the false positive issue and why he included it with several exclamation points as if it had some particular significance. But first she wanted to check in with Jack. She'd not talked with him all day. She used her mobile to call his. He answered on the first ring as if expecting her call. As it turned out he just happened to be holding his phone in his hand.

"You just caught me," Jack said. She could tell he was in the stairwell with the echo of footfalls on the metal stairs.

"Where are you headed?"

"Autopsy room. I'm about to do a late case with Lou. He's on his way here as we speak."

"What kind of case?" she asked. Late-afternoon cases were usually put off until the morning unless there was an extenuating circumstance.

"A police officer was found dead in his patrol car a few hours ago," Jack explained with slightly more audible breath sounds. "He'd been shot. The immediate question is whether it was a self-inflicted wound, which Lou believes it was. Lou just wants to be sure and wants to know ASAP to contain any potential overreaction by his fellow officers."

"I've been having a busy day, as you can imagine," Laurie said. "I've even temporarily turned over the reins to George to clear my schedule."

"So I heard," Jack said. "I've been meaning to check in with you, but I've been busy, too. This will be my fourth autopsy."

"Good for you," she said. She knew he was happiest when busy. "How has your hip held up? Any pain with that much standing?"

"Not a twinge," Jack said.

"Marvelous. Any particularly interesting cases?" Laurie often found herself jealous of Jack's daily immersion in forensics.

"Unfortunately, no challenges," Jack said. "What about you? How has it been dealing with Ryan Sullivan's death?"

"It's been troublesome. Well, that's not entirely accurate. Other than my continuing struggle with my feelings of guilt, it's gone better than I expected, even though I was obligated by the mayor to give a command performance at his office in person."

"Good grief! How did that go?"

"As I said, it went better than I expected, especially after I'd been forced to wait interminably, making me think I was going to be fired on the spot. I also spoke with the new chief of NYU Pathology Department. In many ways, that was an equivalent surprise. Instead of being upset and accusatory, which I feared she might be, she was remarkably sympathetic."

"I'm not surprised," Jack said. Then she heard him yell in the background: "I'll be in there in a second, Vinnie. Go ahead and get set up!" Coming back on the line, he said: "Sorry."

"No problem," Laurie said. She thought briefly about telling him about her visit to Oncology Diagnostics but decided to put it off until that evening as it might take too long, and he was obviously preoccupied.

"As soon as I finish down here with Lou, I'm going to hop on my bike and head home," Jack said. "I got several calls from both Warren and Flash. There's going to be a big b-ball turnout tonight to take advantage of the weather. We're going to have quite a mob, so I'd like to get out there as early as possible to get in the first game. Did you know it's almost sixty degrees?"

"I was just outside," Laurie said. Although she wasn't happy with him riding his bike or playing basketball, she'd come to accept the inevitable and didn't say anything negative. Instead, she added: "It's surprisingly balmy for December, and it's nice you'll be able to take advantage of it."

"I couldn't agree more," Jack said. "Listen, I gotta go. I'll see you later tonight."

Putting her phone down, she turned her attention back to Ryan's material, but she only managed to get it reorganized when there was a knock on her door. After she called out to come in, Chet appeared. As was typical, he headed directly to the couch and sat down. He, Jack, and Laurie had all started at the OCME around the same time and had a natural familiarity with each other despite Laurie being the chief.

"Thanks for coming by," Laurie said. "I wanted to ask you about Ryan Sullivan. When did you find out about his suicide?"

"The moment I got here this morning," Chet said. "What a disaster. I sensed he was going to be a problem from his first day, but I never expected this."

"Nor I," Laurie said. "And I have to admit I'm feeling some responsibility for forcing him do the autopsy on Sean O'Brien and then encouraging him to study the group of suicides. I'm afraid I contributed."

"Hey, if anybody should feel responsible, it's me," Chet said with evident emotion. "I was the one who assigned him the case, not you. But I don't feel responsible. His attitude was problematic from the get-go."

"I wish I felt the same," she said. "But I don't. For me to feel better, I need to find out whether something happened to him or if he learned something terribly upsetting after he left here on Friday. Something that I can hang my hat on. Do you have any ideas whatsoever?"

"I don't," Chet said with a shake of his head. "Not a clue."

"What about Dr. Hinkley? Do you think she might have some idea? I'm thinking of talking with her."

"Save your breath," Chet said. "She's as confused about his behavior as I am. She and Ryan couldn't have been more different. She's a delight to work with and has taken a strong liking to forensics."

"So, I've heard," Laurie said. "Have you talked with her about Dr. Sullivan's death?"

"Of course," Chet said. "Everybody's talking about it. She's as mystified as everyone else. She said she'd talked with the other residents, and nobody can believe it."

"Okay, thanks," Laurie said.

Chet got to his feet. "Neither of us was responsible for this tragedy," Chet said. "Give yourself a break. We need you as our chief. George is a good man, better than I thought he'd be as deputy chief. But he is not you, and this is a critical time, particularly with the growing need for a new forensic medical center. I know it's not my role to say this, but I will anyway: Buck up, Laurie!" He started for the door.

"Thanks, Chet," she called out.

"You're welcome," Chet said over his shoulder and then was gone.

For a few minutes Laurie stared down at Ryan's papers while recognizing that Chet was most likely correct. Although she was eager to go back over Ryan's matrix and diary and investigate the false positive issue, she did have more immediate and overarching responsibilities. With a sudden sense of recommitment to being chief medical examiner, she decided that as soon as George returned from Hunter College and she'd debriefed him about what he'd learned, she would officially take back the reins of the OCME.

She got out her larger of two briefcases and put in Ryan's matrix and diary. The benefit of rereading it at home was that she could get Jack's opinion. And then, thinking of Jack, she picked up her phone and texted him that she might be home a bit later than usual and warned him not to overdo it at basketball. At that point, she heard George's voice out in the reception area, followed by a knock on her door.

"Come in, George!" she called out while closing her briefcase and pushing it aside.

CHAPTER 40

Monday, December 11, 4:45 pm

With an index finger shaking from pure excitement, Hank Roberts pressed the buzzer outside of Action Security's door in the Bloomberg Building on Lexington Avenue. He was keyed up from getting another call from Chuck, whose code language had been particularly enticing. Although he'd again used the phrase "the weather looks good," meaning a mission was in the offing, he'd added an enticing "very" in front of the phrase "immediate future," meaning there was extreme urgency involved.

Just like on Hank's previous visits to the office, Chuck opened the door. As he welcomed Hank, Hank sensed that even he was excited, which fanned his own anticipation. Having had missions on Wednesday, Thursday, and Saturday, the idea of yet another mission seemed too good to be true. In addition to the significant extra money such activity afforded, the nonstop action had reduced Hank's PTSD symptoms to near zero, currently merely involving mild, unsettling dreams.

As they entered Chuck's office, Hank noticed there was no one else there, which hadn't been the case on the previous two meetings. "Am I back to being solo?" Hank questioned as he took a seat.

"Oh, no," Chuck said. "This one is going to be even more challenging than the last, so you and David will be teamed up again. He should be here at any moment. Can I get you anything to drink? Coffee?"

"I'm fine," Hank said, wondering what was going to be involved in the mission. The job involving the Levi couple had been one of the more difficult ones, and Hank felt lucky it had been pulled off as well as it had. As tense as he was, he jumped when a sudden loud chiming reverberated around the room.

"Oh, good," Chuck commented. "That must be David."

To pass the time while Chuck went to welcome David, Hank glanced up at the framed photos on the wall behind Chuck's desk, thinking that maybe he should dig out some of his Navy photos and have them framed. There was no doubt he felt a nostalgia for his time in the service now that his PTSD was under control. But he didn't have long to wait before both men appeared. As David sat down, he and Hank acknowledged each other with a half-hearted salute. Turning their attention to Chuck, they both watched as he went behind his desk and took his seat.

"Okay, listen up," Chuck ordered, his tone changing dramatically. "About two hours ago, we got a Code 3 call from Oncology Diagnostics. It seems that there is a potential fallout from Saturday's mission that has to be dealt with immediately."

"What kind of fallout?" Hank demanded. In his mind the mission had gone flawlessly, and he felt defensive about any suggestion otherwise.

"The client claims Saturday night's target kept a diary of work he was doing studying the suicides of your first six missions with the idea they might be homicides staged to look like suicides. And while engaged in this study, the target was not only able to relate them all to Oncology

Diagnostics, he knew about what the client calls false positives, the significance of which I don't understand so don't ask me. Most importantly, the client told me the bearer of all this shocking news was the chief medical examiner of New York City, who made a surprise visit to his clinic."

Hank's face reddened. "How could he possibly have thought the deaths were homicides," he managed, "when I followed to the letter absolutely all the suggestions and recommendations of your research people to make them appear to be suicides?"

"I have no idea," Chuck said. "And it's not the current problem. We can deal with that question later. The critical issue is this chief medical examiner. On the positive side, the client thinks she is acting entirely on her own as a kind of personal crusade, which gives us a window of opportunity to deal with her before she involves other people."

"That's not going to be easy," David said, speaking up for the first time. "She's in the public eye. She might even have a security detail."

"First off she has no security detail," Chuck said. "As for being in the public eye, that's true, but in some ways that's been a benefit. At least so far."

"How so?" Hank asked.

"Because there is an enormous amount of information readily available about her," Chuck said. "Immediately after the panicked call from our clients, I put both our entire cyber and operations teams on the project, and it is amazing what they have produced." Chuck picked up several thick memoranda and handed one each to Hank and David. Both took them, gauging their weight, as each was seemingly novella length. On the cover was only the name DR. LAURIE MONTGOMERY.

Nearly in lockstep, Hank and David turned the cover page. Even the summary was extensive.

"You'll have adequate time at some point to read the entire report if you are so inclined," Chuck said. "Meanwhile, let me tell you what I and our operations team have decided, with the idea that speed is important. Since she is married and lives in a multistory, multi-unit town house with her husband, two children, nanny, and mother, any type of home invasion is out of the question. Since there is reasonable but not great security at the Office of the Chief Medical Examiner, that location has been ruled out. That leaves only her commute from work to her home on West 106th Street."

"So, is this to be a straight-out homicide?" David asked.

"No," Chuck said with conviction. "It's going to be a kidnapping. The team consensus is that an abduction is the only alternative that is certain to work, and there is only one place it can occur. She has to be snatched when exiting her medical examiner transport vehicle in front of her house and before she has time to mount her ten-step stoop. Or at the very least you get to her before she is able to open the front door to her building and disappear inside.

"How this is going to work is you two will be in the back of an idling van with a talented driver when her ride pulls up in front of her house. The second she exits her vehicle, you'll do the same. Between the two of you, I'm certain you will be able to lift her off her feet, contain her, carry her to the van, and be off. It will only take seconds. To aid you, I was told by the client that she is a svelte woman, probably around 110 pounds."

"Where will we take her?" David asked with knitted brows.

"Don't worry," Chuck said. "It's all planned. The driver knows exactly where to rendezvous with a separate van, where an exchange will occur from a white van to a black one. This second van will take her up to a deserted farmhouse in the Catskills that Action Security owns through an offshore trust. There, Laurie Montgomery will just disappear. Story over. Any questions?"

"I have so many I don't know where to begin," Hank said. He didn't like that they wouldn't have time to practice the snatch. When he'd been on active duty, the need for practicing over and over before a mission had been drilled into his brain.

"I know what you're thinking," Chuck said. "But there's no time. Time is the critical factor. To compensate for any anxieties caused by lack of time for normal preparation, the pay will be three times the usual."

"What if there are pedestrians on her street?" David asked.

"There may be," Chuck said. "But it will not matter. You two will be in all-black outfits with ski masks. Any people who might be in the vicinity will be stunned and paralyzed. Worst case they might shout something, but by then you'll be in the van and on your way. I forgot to mention that in the van with you will be a medic with a ketamine injection to render the mark unconscious."

Hank looked at David. "What do you think? Are you in?"

"I like the three times fee situation," David said. "As for the operation, it should work. I like the simplicity. My motto is: the simpler the better."

"One thing I haven't said," Chuck added. "I've already gotten confirmation that the van is in a perfect position almost directly in front of the mark's brownstone, meaning you will only be carrying the mark a dozen or so feet."

"All right," Hank said. "I'm in." He then felt a welcome jolt of adrenaline by just agreeing.

"Me, too," David said.

"Great!" Chuck said. "There's one other issue. What we are hoping is that Laurie Montgomery will be carrying some kind of briefcase or shoulder bag. If she is, we want that, too. We are hoping that she has with her a so-called diary that the previous mark made. We will need you to confirm if anything like that is obtained as soon as possible. If it's not with her, in a totally separate operation, we are planning an assault of sorts at the OCME to obtain it. It needs to be destroyed."

Both Hank and David nodded. At the moment they weren't worried about a briefcase. Their minds were completely absorbed in running through all the possible permutations of what might go wrong on a rushed, unrehearsed, abduction mission.

CHAPTER 41

By twenty after six in the evening Laurie signed the last letter in the stack that Cheryl printed out before leaving for the day, and now Laurie was completely caught up with Monday's outgoing correspondence. An hour or so earlier, she had taken the time to call home and speak with Caitlin, telling her she'd be a bit late and encouraging her to go ahead and feed the kids. At the time Laurie estimated she'd be home around 7:00, and now that she had finished everything she'd set out to do, she could tell her estimate was going to be on the mark. During evening rush-hour traffic, the commute took at least a half hour.

Using the house phone, she dialed the Transport Department to check if a vehicle was available. She was happy to learn that there was, and she arranged to be picked up in front of the building in five minutes.

With a ride scheduled, Laurie hustled to get herself ready. First, opening her briefcase and pushing aside Ryan Sullivan's material, she added a small stack of unread incoming mail, several hefty budget analyses, and the as of yet unread summary of George's meeting at Hunter College, which she'd gotten only fifteen minutes earlier when he left for the day. She then got her coat from the closet, took one last glance around her desk to make sure she'd not forgotten anything, and turned out the lights. As she passed through the door into the building's main lobby, she said good night to the security guard. Once outside she found that she was a bit early, forcing her to impatiently wait for her vehicle to appear. She was looking forward to getting home. It had been an unusually stressful day.

———————

Jack was in seventh heaven. The weather couldn't have been better as it was still in the mid-fifties, which seemed extraordinary for December in New York two hours after sunset. He'd gotten out onto the neighborhood basketball court early enough after a quick bike ride home to be among the first ten players, which meant by street rules that he would play in the first game. Even more auspicious was that Warren, Flash, Spit, and Dunk had arrived simultaneously with him, and since they knew each other well, they played together. Since Warren and Flash were by far the best players and Spit, Dunk, and Jack were not bad, either, the team did well. As always, the winning team stayed on court to take on the next five players, so that Jack's team had been playing nonstop, making the other twenty-some-odd players alternately have to cool their heels, waiting to get back into a game.

Conveniently the neighborhood basketball court was in the rear of a small park directly across from Jack and Laurie's brownstone such that from the front windows of their apartment and even from their stoop, the court was visible. On those days when Jack was on the fence about whether he wanted to play, he could see from home what kind of game was going on, whether half-court or full-court and how many players were involved, both of which often contributed to his decision.

"Are you going to run again?" Warren yelled to Jack, who had gone over to grab his water bottle courtside for a drink. They had just won their third game in a row and were dominating the playing time.

"You'd better believe it," Jack yelled back. There was no way he was going to turn down such an opportunity, as it was a rare circumstance, especially since they might not see weather like this again until springtime. He also knew that Laurie was not yet home from work because he'd been keeping an eye out. Once Laurie got home, he'd feel significantly more guilty that he was spending as much time as he was out on the court. Putting his water bottle down, he got out his watch from his sweatpants pocket and winced: It was already 6:30.

––––––––

Hank Roberts intertwined his fingers, pointed his palms away from himself, and stretched his arms out as far as they would go. He was feeling cramped and anxious. He and David had been slouching uncomfortably in the flat storage part of a white van parked on 106th Street waiting for Laurie Montgomery to arrive home. Sitting up front in the passenger seat was the EMT whom Hank and David ignored as merely ancillary help. As special forces operatives, Hank and David were totally concentrating on the upcoming mission to the exclusion of all other thoughts. There was also a driver in the vehicle's driver seat, keeping the engine at a slow idle with the AC at a low fan setting to keep the interior temperature reasonable. The group had been in position for almost an hour, causing both Hank's and David's patience to wear thin. There was no talk except for an acknowledgment when they relieved each other from staring out one of the two windows situated high on the back doors. The view was of Laurie Montgomery's house all the way back to the traffic light on Central Park West.

A half hour ago, the car parked in front of the van left, which gave the driver an opportunity to pull ahead, so that the van was now occupying two spots. This was advantageous, in that it would give Hank and David more room getting the mark into the van, as well as making it easier for the driver to rapidly pull away.

"Okay, your turn," David said as he backed away from staring out the window and retreated into the darkness of the van's interior.

Without comment, Hank moved ahead and looked out. Laurie Montgomery's stoop was to his right, a mere thirty feet away. At a distance of about fifty feet was a streetlight that cast light around the entire area. When they had first arrived on scene, they'd thought about taking the light out, but decided against it, thinking it would help them make an identification of Laurie, which they were going to do from having committed to memory several photos that had been in the memorandum Action Security had created. They also had become less concerned about the streetlight when they came to realize how little pedestrian traffic was in the area. The only exception was a playground with a lighted, active basketball court with a large group of engaged players. But the playground was on the opposite side of the street, and the basketball court was set back considerably behind swings, a large sandbox, and a group of benches all of which were unoccupied.

As Hank stared at the stoop he went over the snatch procedure that he and David had agreed on. Immediately after Laurie alighted from her vehicle and her identity was confirmed, he and David were going to leap from the van with David in the lead and Hank close behind. The plan was for David to nab her well before she got to her stoop, pin her arms against her body, and lift her off the ground all in one motion. Hank's job was to throw a black hood over her head and forcibly compress it against her face to stifle any screaming. They would then rush back to the van, dive in all together, and let the medic do his thing while the driver pulled out and headed for the rendezvous point.

Hank nodded to himself in the darkness, believing it all should work. His only reservation about the whole plan was that they hadn't thought to set up a lookout at the OCME to give them warning when she was on her way. As he thought about this procedural mistake, the fear went through his mind that she might not come home for hours or, worse yet, she might arrive just when the basketball game was over, flooding the area with men on their way to their respective apartments. But while that disturbing thought went through his mind, he saw what appeared to be a small, SUV-sized van make the turn from Central Park West onto West 106th Street. Thanks to the streetlights at the intersection, he glimpsed writing on the van's side that matched the OCME transport vehicles pictured in the Laurie Montgomery memorandum.

"Heads-up," he said excitedly over his shoulder. "We're looking good."

In response, David scrambled forward in the van's dim interior. He looked out the rear window on his side. The vehicle in question was rapidly nearing. "That's it!" David exclaimed.

Both men adjusted their black balaclavas to cover their faces. Then Hank snapped up the black hood from the floor. Both tensed their muscles. According to their plan, David was going to rotate the release handle of the van's rear doors but not push the doors open immediately. Instead, he was to wait until Laurie alighted from the vehicle to avoid alerting her for fear she might remain in it and possibly drive off.

The vehicle pulled to a stop on the opposite side of the street from Laurie's house. The traffic on West 106th Street ran in both directions, unlike most crosstown streets in the area, which were one-way. A moment later the rear passenger door opened, and a female figure got out, her face suddenly illuminated from the overhead streetlight.

"It's her!" Hank blurted.

"Roger that!" David agreed as he waited another few beats for the van to begin to pull away while Laurie started across the street. "Go, go!" he barked as he threw open the van's rear doors.

In the next instant, the two special forces–trained operatives leaped out of the van just as Laurie was already nearing the sidewalk on the same side of the street. What surprised both men was how unexpectedly fast she was moving.

———————

As it was now significantly after 7:00 and much later than Laurie would have liked since she had not seen the children all day, she was excited to get home and had literally run across the street despite lugging her hefty briefcase. As weighty as it was containing the two sizable budget documents, it hardly swung as she leaped up onto the sidewalk. A moment later, gritting her teeth against the briefcase's drag but taking advantage of her momentum, she started up her steps heading up to the front door.

Whether it was a unique sound or catching some movement out of the corner of her eye, Laurie didn't know, but as she climbed something caught her attention, causing her to glance to her right. To her shock and consternation, she saw two sinister-looking, black-suited figures with ski masks coming toward her at a run with one in front of the other. Reacting to this threat as she gained the broad top step, she whirled around just as the two figures reached her level.

Reacting more by survival instinct than conscious thought, Laurie held on to her briefcase as she turned, and it swung in a great arc to smash into the lower abdomen and genital area of the man in front. The speed and the weight of the briefcase combined to create enough momentum to stop the leading figure momentarily in his tracks, forcing the second figure to collide into his backside.

Immediately on the briefcase's contact with her attacker, Laurie let go of it, causing both figures to stagger back against its heft. Rapidly recovering their balance and batting away the briefcase's contents, which had spilled out in a barrage of papers, they regrouped and again started forward. But in the interim, Laurie had enough presence of mind as well as the time to bellow *Help!* repeatedly at the top of her lungs. She also leaned back against her front door to raise her foot, which she used to kick at the leading man several times before he grabbed her leg and upended her.

———————

Jack heard Laurie's very first scream for help and stopped in his tracks. He intimately knew his wife's voice. But it wasn't only Jack who had come to a sudden standstill. All the players and all those waiting to play had simultaneously come to a halt from whatever they were doing upon hearing the screaming, especially as it had continued unabated.

As everyone on the playground were locals in a city built on a strong sense and allegiance to neighborhoods, they were sensitized to hearing such a cry for help, and no one hesitated. Although Jack was the first to spring to action, setting out at a full-speed dash toward his house where he could clearly see a struggle happening on the stoop, the entire basketball court crowd exploded in pursuit, all eager to help whoever was in need.

Although Jack was running at full tilt, he was quickly passed by several younger, lither players of both sexes. In the seconds it took for the throng of people to reach Jack and Laurie's stoop, Laurie's attackers had only managed to get her down the ten stairs and halfway to an idling van, and they had only been able to do that by Hank holding her legs and David struggling with her upper body. Laurie had been able to resist her head being covered, a goal they had abandoned in their haste.

What ensued was a momentary, tense standoff as the basketball crowd swarmed around and then completely engulfed the struggling threesome with Jack at the forefront. The open doors of the van were a mere ten feet away but not reachable by the two men dressed like ninjas. Seeing all the people who'd come to her rescue, Laurie stopped screaming.

After a short silence Jack said as an order not a request: "Put her down!"

Hank and David exchanged a nervous glance followed by an acquiescing nod. Without saying a word, Hank placed Laurie's feet onto the ground, while David pushed her torso upright. Once free, Laurie bolted for Jack, who enveloped her in a hug. Two of the younger, more headstrong male basketball players, stepped into the circle that had formed around the two special forces veterans, and one of them reached out to give Hank a deserved shove as a kind of challenge and an expression of disdain. Hank reacted instantly with a rapid martial art takedown to the shock of everyone at the speed involved. The youth wasn't seriously hurt and immediately scrambled to his feet.

"That's it!" Jack called out. He raised his hands palms out to placate the group. He could instantly tell that these two men were highly trained professionals who probably were armed, and he didn't want anyone injured now that Laurie was safe. As a medical examiner who'd handled mass casualty events, he'd seen what men like these were capable of. "Let them go!" Jack shouted. "It's not worth anyone getting hurt. Let them go!"

Without a word from the crowd, an open pathway miraculously appeared, leading to the open doors of the idling van. Everyone knew instinctively that the goal of these two men had been to abduct Laurie, and they had been thwarted.

Wary and tense, Hank and David slowly moved toward the van. David climbed in, and Hank followed, closing the doors as he did so. A moment later, the van lurched forward, pulling out of the parking place, but it didn't get far. To the crowd's surprise, a raised F-150 truck with monster wheels came barreling along 106th Street and smashed into the white van. Everyone cheered when Spit climbed from the cab. When the entire basketball throng had run toward Laurie, he'd run to get his truck and while doing so had called the police.

As four men quickly exited the disabled van, everyone heard the familiar sound of police sirens becoming progressively louder and coming in their direction. When the strangers heard the approaching sirens, they all took off running toward Central Park a block away. Although a few of the basketball players threatened to give chase, Jack again called out to leave them be. "Let the police deal with them!" he yelled. "They'll be here momentarily."

Laurie let go of her grip around Jack. "Good lord," she managed, while rearranging her coat and dress, which had ridden up on her torso. "That was a shock. What a nightmare."

"Are you okay?" Jack asked solicitously as he looked her up and down.

"I think so," Laurie said. She took a deep breath and ran a shaky hand nervously through her hair.

"What the hell was all this about?"

"I haven't the slightest idea."

"Did something strange happen to you today to cause this? Those men were trying to kidnap you."

"Lots of strange things happened to me today, like being called on the carpet by the mayor, but nothing to explain something like this. But—wait!"

"What?"

"I did do something very out of the ordinary this afternoon," Laurie admitted. "I made an impulsive visit to an oncology clinic on the Upper East Side where I learned that Ryan Sullivan had gone late Friday afternoon. I learned that from reading his study diary. My thought, and maybe my hope, was that they could have said something to him that put him in emotional turmoil. That wasn't the case, but still . . ."

"Still what?" Jack asked as Laurie paused.

At that moment the police sirens reached a crescendo and then fell off as a couple of cruisers turned onto 106th Street from Central Park West and came to an abrupt halt abreast of the crowd. The vehicles were immediately surrounded by an excited group of basketball players who were madly pointing east toward the park, with everyone yelling at once about the fleeing perpetrators. A smaller number of players who had rescued Laurie's briefcase were now racing around and gathering up all the loose papers.

Amidst all the mounting pandemonium, Jack's emotions and sense of relief took over, and instead of continuing his conversation with Laurie in an attempt to understand what had just happened, he enveloped her in a warm, extended embrace. He then leaned back but continued holding on to her as if he was afraid to let her go. He could feel she was still trembling from the ordeal. "I'm so thankful you're safe," he managed to say. "God! What a terrifying episode. Let's go inside and call Lou and get him involved. He'll be able to figure this out, and more important, he'll get you some official police protection until he does."

Laurie nodded. "Okay, but first let me say that I'll forever be indebted to you and your basketball buddies, and I promise never again to complain about your playing. Had you all not been out there this evening, I don't want to think about where I might be now."

Jack looked at his wife. He didn't know if she was being serious about his basketball playing, which he knew she scorned, but he didn't care. All he knew was that she was the most important person in his life and that she was safe and well.

Thursday, February 15, 4:10 pm

Lieutenant Commander Detective Lou Soldano pulled his year-old, unmarked black Chevy Malibu between two OCME sprinter vans outside the morgue's receiving dock and parked. After tossing his NYPD placard onto the dashboard, he climbed out of the car. Contrary to his usual habit of just showing up on his visits to the medical forensics building, he'd called ahead to make sure that the chief would be available and been assured she would be at 4:15.

The reason Lou was eager to see her was because there had been a number of indictments filed that morning, which he was certain she'd find particularly compelling and, more important, assuaging. After several months of concentrated investigative work that Lou had spearheaded, interesting details had emerged about Dr. Ryan Sullivan's accomplishments and death. Early on Lou had been made aware of Laurie's struggles with feelings of culpability about his passing, and he was confident that what he was going to tell her would be a relief.

Lou popped into the tiny security office adjacent to the loading dock and left his car keys in case his Malibu had to be moved. It was a gesture that he knew was appreciated. One never knew in a city the size of New York when there might be a rush of bodies arriving.

Walking into the administration area, Lou was greeted by Laurie's secretary with a smile, a thumbs-up, and then a gesture toward Laurie's inner office door. Lou knew the gesture meant that Laurie was in her office, available, and expecting his arrival. Following a knock, Lou walked in and was pleasantly surprised. Not only was he going to get to see Laurie, but also Jack, who was sprawled out on her sofa.

"Well, well!" Lou exclaimed. "This is my lucky day. Double trouble." They had all been close friends long enough to feel comfortable ribbing each other. It was mostly Jack's influence from his love of playful sarcasm.

"When Cheryl mentioned you were coming over with some news related to the Ryan Sullivan disaster, I knew Jack would rather hear it directly rather than secondhand. Besides, we have some startling and exciting news for you."

"Oh?" Lou questioned as he took one of the seats facing Laurie's desk while Jack pushed himself up into a sitting position on the couch. "What kind of news?" Lou added. He was immediately intrigued and, as a detective, hated secrets.

"You first," Laurie said. "Come on! You are being uncharacteristically mysterious, and you called this meeting, not us."

Lou laughed. "You're right, and I suppose I have been a bit mysterious. But it's all been because I've been so eager to share with you what's happened. This morning there was a slew of indictments filed. A major breakthrough occurred yesterday when Hank Roberts, a retired Navy SEAL, who was one of the men who tried to abduct you, broke down under interrogation and plea bargained. His testimony has opened the whole case big-time. What we learned straight off was that all those suicide cases your deceased resident, Ryan Sullivan, was investigating were all homicides staged as suicides, including his own. That poor fellow didn't kill himself. He was murdered like the rest of them."

"How did this Hank Roberts know?" Laurie questioned. Inwardly she shuddered as Lou's comments brought back the ordeal of Ryan's passing and her attempted kidnapping with disturbing clarity. For the ensuing investigation that the events engendered, she'd had to surrender all of Ryan's materials and had never had a chance to go over them again. For the last two months, she'd been in the dark as to what the investigation was revealing.

"He knew because he was the one who killed them all," Lou said with an angry tone. "He was carrying the homicides out at the behest of his employer, Action Security, which was acting on behalf of *their* client, Oncology Diagnostics. And to complicate the gruesome story further, he was justifying what he labeled *missions* as a kind of immersion therapy for the extreme post-traumatic stress disorder he'd been suffering since his discharge from the Navy."

"Wait, hold on!" Laurie said. She rested her head in her hands with her elbows on the desk. It was too much startling information all at once. "Why would Oncology Diagnostics want their patients murdered?"

"To avoid exposure of what Oncology Diagnostics was doing behind the scenes," Lou said with equal irritation. "The two company principles, Jerome Pappas and Malik Williams, are also the founders and owners of another healthcare company called Full Body Scan. They started this company a decade ago back when the demand for such scans rose dramatically as a cancer screening methodology irrespective of its efficacy, which I've been told was questionable from the start and the reason why it wasn't covered by health-insurance plans and still isn't. But you as physicians understand all that health-insurance malarky better than I. To stay ahead of the demand, Pappas and Williams personally guaranteed ginormous loans to enable them to invest heavily in new expensive X-ray scanners only to have the demand suddenly disappear when much more accurate cancer screening technologies emerged over the last few years using simple blood testing."

"Wait a second," Laurie demanded. "You are giving me information overload. More important, it isn't explaining why Oncology Diagnostics would want to murder their patients."

"I'm coming to that," Lou said. "The only way that Pappas and Williams could save Full Body Scan and avoid the disaster of personal bankruptcy was to increase demand for Full Body Scan's services. What they came up with was founding Oncology Diagnostics to offer to receptive corporate clients cancer screening services, including the newest blood testing technology in hopes of finding a whole bunch of new patients for Full Body Scan. Unfortunately, that didn't produce enough patients because there weren't enough people being diagnosed with early cancer. Undeterred, they then came up with the idea to record tests as positive from a large select group of people even when the results were negative."

"A false positive!" Laurie said with sudden understanding. It was that exact issue she had been interested in exploring on her planned careful reread of Ryan's study diary.

"Yes, a false positive," Lou said. "And they did this on hundreds of cases, creating a sizable demand for Full Body Scan. When someone is diagnosed with an asymptomatic cancer by the new blood test, the trick is then to find the cancer's location and full body scanning can be more or less justified."

"Reporting false positives is reprehensible enough," Jack said, "but it still doesn't explain why they would commit murder on top of it."

"Here's where some people much smarter than I had to be brought in to lend a hand," Lou said. "What they discovered going through this large group of false positive patients was that there were a few who had their private physicians repeat the test, and when it came back negative, contradicting Oncology Diagnostics' results, they held Oncology Diagnostics to account, either demanding any money they had spent, since a lot of this new cancer screening is not covered by health insurance or accusing them of fraud and malpractice. Anyway, it was some of these few patients out of hundreds that Oncology Diagnostics felt they had to get rid of. They did so by searching out Action Security, who performed the service for a price."

"What some people will do for money," Laurie lamented. "So, does this mean there are murder indictments against Jerome Pappas and Malik Williams?"

"Absolutely," Lou said with a sense of pride. "Murder as well as attempted kidnapping in their rush to deal with the threat you presented, Laurie. And these charges are not restricted to the two doctors but include a number of the people at Action Security who were aware of what was going on. The Justice Department has closed it down, as well as both Oncology Diagnostics and Full Body Scan."

"Good lord!" Laurie voiced. For her the whole lurid story was yet another example of why medicine and capitalism made such poor bedfellows. Jerome Pappas and Malik Williams had turned a truly epochal biomedical breakthrough of early diagnosis of cancer using blood analysis into something obscene for their own monetary benefit by attempting to support a technology that the medical scientific community had never embraced.

"One of the reasons I was so eager to bring this news to you is to dispel any lingering feelings of responsibility for Ryan Sullivan's death that you might still have."

"It has, but it also underlines just how tragic his death was," Laurie said wistfully. "In retrospect the man was a true hero. It was he and no one else who recognized the commonalities in a group of questionable suicides, and he deserves full credit for having done so. Shutting down these vile organizations will save a lot of lives."

"Amen," Lou said. "Without a doubt. If it hadn't been for Ryan Sullivan and, ironically enough, his distaste for the autopsy procedure, Oncology Diagnostics and Action Security would still be carrying on with their mayhem for God knows how long. But enough of this macabre narrative for the time being. Let's have the startling and exciting news you guys are withholding. Let me guess—another bambino?"

"Heaven forbid," Jack responded with a chuckle. "No, it's something way more unexpected. But I'm going to let Laurie tell you, because it's her decision."

"You're going to be surprised," Laurie said, further teasing Lou, as both she and Jack were aware how much he hated secrets.

"Come on!" Lou pleaded. "You're torturing me. Out with it!"

"I've decided to turn in my resignation as chief to the mayor," Laurie said with obvious conviction and determination.

"What?" Lou questioned with alarm. "You're pulling my leg. At least I hope you're pulling my leg. The OCME has never run as smoothly as it has for the last five years! Say it's not so."

"But it is so," Laurie said. "At first the motivation to step down was the attempted kidnapping, thinking as a mother I couldn't take that kind of risk for my children. But even when it became apparent the attempted kidnapping had nothing to do with my being the chief medical examiner, I came to accept that my true professional interest happens to be the application of forensics, meaning being a medical examiner, and not the nonstop politics of running a huge forensics organization."

"I'm shocked," Lou said. "Are you sure about this?"

"Very sure! Although we women have been fighting for positions of authority, I feel that I have made my mark in that arena, and now I want to go back to doing what I love, namely medical forensics. I'm tired of Jack having all the fun and me having to spend all my time and energy struggling with the city council over the budget or arguing with the dean of Hunter College about adequate space for our new medical forensics home base."

Lou looked over at Jack for help. He knew how utterly important the medical examiner's office was to law enforcement, and now that it was working so smoothly, he didn't want change.

Jack shrugged. "It's her call," he said. "And frankly I'm going to love having her back as a true partner even though it will mean I will now have to compete for the most intellectually interesting cases."

"All right," Lou said with resignation, turning his attention back to Laurie. "Promise me this: You won't step down until someone is found by a search committee about whom you feel totally confident."

"It's a promise," Laurie said happily.